THE
SHADOW
CHILD

THE
SHADOW
CHILD

Rachel Hancox

CENTURY

1 3 5 7 9 10 8 6 4 2

Century
20 Vauxhall Bridge Road
London SW1V 2SA

Century is part of the Penguin Random House group of companies
whose addresses can be found at global.penguinrandomhouse.com

Penguin
Random House
UK

First published in the United Kingdom
by Century in 2022

www.penguin.co.uk

A CIP catalogue record for this book is available from
the British Library.

ISBN 9781529136043 (hardback)
ISBN 9781529136050 (trade paperback)

Typeset in 12/16.85 pt Sabon LT Std
by Integra Software Services Pvt. Ltd, Pondicherry

Printed and bound in Great Britain by Clays Ltd, Elcograf S.p.A.

The authorised representative in the EEA is Penguin Random House Ireland,
Morrison Chambers, 32 Nassau Street, Dublin D02 YH68.

Penguin Random House is committed to a sustainable future for
our business, our readers and our planet. This book is made from
Forest Stewardship Council® certified paper.

MIX
Paper from
responsible sources
FSC® C018179
FSC
www.fsc.org

For CWC and BSC, the best of parents

THE
SHADOW
CHILD

Self-Portrait with Shadow

Emma is sitting at the kitchen table, paper and crayons scattered around her. She's just turned four, and she's done a lot of drawing recently: her pencil grip, they were told at her last health check, is well advanced for her age. And her imagination, Cath thinks. Her pictures tell stories, and if you catch her at the right moment she'll share them with you, spilling them out in a tumble of sentences that Cath finds utterly irresistible.

'Are you busy, Em?' she asks, as she comes into the kitchen. 'Busy drawing?'

'Yes,' Emma says. Nothing more for a moment or two: her hand hovers over the selection of coloured pencils, pouncing eventually on the pink one. 'I'm drawing me.'

Her favourite subject, Cath thinks. Emma's self-portraits have evolved, recently, from round faces with four sticks coming out of them: they have acquired bodies, and clumped hands like bunches of grapes. This one has eyes, mouth, ears and hair.

'Lovely,' she says. 'How pretty you look.'

Emma halts for a moment, looking down at herself.

'I've got a blue stripey dress on,' she announces. She reaches for a blue pencil and draws three fat lines down the square body, then sits back, satisfied.

It's curious, Cath thinks, the relationship between representation and reality. The dress Emma's wearing is pale blue, with stripes much narrower than those fat pencil streaks, but even so, she recognises the picture as an image of her, and of the dress. It's fascinating, watching all this emerge.

'Have you got a shadow, Mummy?' Emma asks suddenly.

'Yes, of course,' Cath says. 'Everyone has a shadow.'

'Have you brought it inside? 'Cos Mary says you only have a shadow outside, not inside.'

'Well.' Cath considers. Contradicting Mary, doyenne of the nursery class, is risky. 'Your shadow is strongest when the sun's shining. But if there's a bright light inside, you can have a shadow there too.'

Emma puts down her pencil and looks at her mother, a quaintly adult expression on her face. 'So what is a shadow, azzackly?' she asks. 'How does the sun make it?'

'You make it,' Cath says. 'You make it by blocking out the sun. Your shadow is the place which the sun can't get to because you're in the way.'

'Why do you stop the sun shining on your shadow?' Emma asks. 'That's not very nice of you.'

Cath smiles. 'You can't help it, darling. You do it just by being there. The light can't get through you, you see.' She pauses, looking at her daughter's frowning face. 'You can only see your shadow when you're there to block the light, so it doesn't mind.' That's rather a flight of fancy, she thinks, but a harmless one.

Emma considers this. 'Your shadow always lies down,' she says. 'Does it lie down 'cos it's got no sun?'

'Well – actually it doesn't always lie down,' Cath says. 'Only when the ground's flat. If you stand near a wall, your shadow stands up.'

Emma dismisses this. 'I stand up, and my shadow lies down,' she says, 'shadows nyooshally lie down,' and she picks up a black crayon and starts drawing another version of herself, lying on its side beside the pink version in the blue dress.

Cath watches her fingers, her sweet chubby fingers, meticulously copying the outline of her dress, and then filling it in – a surprise – with blue stripes.

'This is me, and this is my shadow,' Emma announces when she's finished. 'My shadow's called Rose, and she's got a blue stripey dress on too.'

PART 1

JANUARY

Cath

The house is tiny, but impossibly pretty and impeccably presented. It's on the end of the terrace, with two bedrooms and the original Victorian road sign – 'St John's Street' – still attached to the façade. The agent smiles as she opens the door, knowing she has a treasure to show them.

'It's been completely renovated,' she says. 'New boiler, new roof, new wiring.'

Cath is hardly listening, her eyes straying from the sash windows to the little fireplace with its tiled surround. To the right, beyond a wooden staircase, the kitchen gleams. She feels a rush of pleasure.

'We've had a lot of interest,' the agent is saying now. 'A lot.' She pauses. 'Do you know the area?'

'We live between here and Fulford,' Jim says.

'Oh, not far, then.' The agent smiles again, a little less certainly. 'Downsizing?'

'No,' says Cath, 'we're ...' She hesitates. Now they're here, she doesn't like to think of this as a commercial transaction. Her mind is filling with the past, not the future. She turns to her husband. 'Imagine, Jim, we could have started out in a house like this.'

'Davies Lane wasn't so different,' he says.

Cath shakes her head. The house in Leytonstone, with its crumbling plaster and threadbare carpets, felt like a palace at the time, but what a difference it would have made if they'd ripped off the flock wallpaper, polished the floorboards. All that putting up, making do. That's what they've always done, isn't it? But she wonders now whether a pretty, white-walled house like this one might have set them on a different course.

Whether they might, perhaps, have steered more safely around the dangers they had no idea, back then, that life had in store for them.

When Emma was little, Jim used to tell her the story of his and Cath's first meeting. Wrapped in a towel after her bath, she'd snuggle against him, warm and sweet-scented, and say, 'Tell me about in the beginning, Daddy. Tell me again.'

'I was covering the Lord Mayor's Show,' Jim would say. He had a special voice for this story: his *Jackanory* voice, Cath called it. 'I was taking photos of the parade, and I saw a face peeping out from one of the floats – the prettiest face I'd ever seen, with dark, dark eyes.'

By the time she was five, Emma knew the story by heart.

'Queen Anne Boleyn,' she'd say. 'She was dressed as Queen Anne Boleyn, wasn't she, Daddy?'

'She was. In green velvet and a jewelled headdress, with pearls around her neck.'

Cath's school had been chosen to take part in the parade because it had some link to the livery company whose Master was Lord Mayor that year, and Cath, the newest recruit to the teaching staff, had been nominated to play Anne Boleyn to the Head's Henry VIII. She hardly remembers the parade now; it's been eclipsed by constant retelling.

'I was leaning out of a window,' Jim would say, 'and when I saw your mummy I nearly fell right through it. I sprinted downstairs and followed her float all the way through the streets of London. And when they reached the end of the route, there I was.'

'There you were.' Emma would smile, a sleek, satisfied smile. 'And there she was.'

'She was even more beautiful close up,' Jim would say, 'but I was a mess. I'd started out a mess, and two hours jogging through the streets hadn't improved things.' He'd pull a face then, miming sweat and dishevelment. 'Luckily I had my biggest camera round my neck, and I told her I wanted to take some photos for my piece.'

Cath had always hated having her photograph taken – an irony, for someone who was about to find herself marrying a photographer – but she'd been flattered. She hadn't met many men like Jim. Hadn't met many men at all, in fact: she'd been to a girls' school, then a teacher training college filled with women, and the only men on the staff at the primary school in Redbridge where she'd landed her first job were the Head and the caretaker. At twenty-two, she'd been about as sheltered as it was possible for a London-born-and-bred girl to be.

So she'd said yes, to the photographs and to the drink he'd suggested in almost the same breath. A little pub in the back streets of the City, where she'd peered through the gloom at this man in a grubby T-shirt and scuffed jeans and felt as though she'd slipped into another world, almost as strange to her as it would have been to Anne Boleyn. They'd walked up Cheapside, past St Mary-le-Bow and Bread Street and Gutter Lane, and seen the dome of St Paul's emerging from behind the plate-glass planes of merchant banks and the November sun sinking in audacious technicolour, pink and purple and orange.

The Lord Mayor's Show was a commission for a news magazine that folded the following year and never published Jim's photos – nor, indeed, paid him for them. 'Lucky I got a different reward for that day's work,' he'd say to Emma, tucking her up in bed and resisting her pleas for the next bit of the story, the bit she appeared in. But he was working mainly for the *New Musical Express* back then, and he'd talked casually, dazzlingly, to Cath about his work – about guitarists and labels and recording studios – while she cast about for a single interesting anecdote from the staff room. Mr Copperfield, the caretaker, played in a ceilidh band, but she knew as soon as she mentioned it that it was the wrong sort of band, the

wrong world for Jim Polkinghorne. He'd smiled, though,
amused by her embarrassment, and said, 'I love all that –
folk music,' and at that moment Cath had known she
couldn't help herself. She was going to fall in love with
Jim whether she liked it or not.

As they climb the stairs of the tiny house, that day floats
through Cath's mind, at one moment barely more substantial than the wisp of voile at the bathroom window
and the next crystallised, cemented, into something with
all the vivid solidity it merits as the first building block of
their marriage. Their own personal creation myth: Anne
Boleyn, divested of her green velvet, wandering the City
streets with this worldly-wise man who had taken an
inexplicable interest in her.

She smiles at him now. Her smiles are more pinched,
more scarce, these days, but Jim's response gives no sign
of that.

'Do you like it?' he asks.

'It's perfect.'

'Easy to let, I agree.' He turns, looking out over the
little patch of garden with its spiral-paved patio. 'Shall
we make an offer, then? If the sums add up?'

Cath doesn't reply at once. She wants to own this
house very badly, but she has a sudden sense of apprehension: a presentiment almost tangible in the hush of
the double-glazed bedroom.

It's as if she's giving up her last wish, she thinks. As if
letting this house be her heart's desire means that

everything else she longs for will never come to pass. And there's something else that matters much more than the house. Something that looms so large that the rest of life is flattened against the edges of the room.

Something she'd give anything, everything, for.

Jim

Jim's early for his ten o'clock appointment, so he parks near the river and walks the last bit. It's a beautiful January day, chilly but bright, with a dazzling blue sky. He likes being outside: it's one of many things about his job that he's grateful for. Even after fifteen years on the *Gazette* he still marvels at how rural Surrey is, his photographer's eye caught by a sunken lane of silver birches or the green sweep of a valley. He's lucky, too, that he sees so much of it: his photoshoots span the county, taking him deep into suburbia and out to farms at the end of mud tracks.

Today he's going to a primary school a couple of miles from home whose pupils have won an environmental competition. Jim likes schools: the children excited when he arrives, the staff bustling them into order, the walls filled with pictures and well-meaning slogans. *We are kind to each other. We do our best.* Occasionally he thinks back to the old days on the *NME*, when the slogans were rather different, the faces too, and wonders what he's doing taking pictures of under-fifteen football teams and hundredth-birthday parties. But he's not one to complain. It's paid the bills all these years, and the *Gazette* isn't going under just yet.

Cath has always found that frustrating, he thinks now, as he follows the path along the riverbank. His phlegmatism. And he's always recognised the irony of people seeing Cath as the sensible one, the steady primary school teacher who married the seat-of-the-pants photographer. But perhaps something has been out of kilter all along; perhaps neither of them was playing quite the roles they thought they were, even before things started to go wrong. He considers this thought for a moment, then lets it drop. There's no point, he tells himself. No point looking back.

The photoshoot is quicker than he expects – break is at ten thirty, and the teachers are keen to get to their coffee. When he's finished, handed in his visitor's lanyard and waved goodbye through the playground fence, Jim takes a different route back to the car and finds himself passing the end of St John's Street. On a whim he turns left, and in a couple of minutes he's standing outside the little house.

It's a nice property, he thinks, with a prick of proprietorial pride, though primped and prettified within an inch of its life: the nineteenth-century occupants would hardly recognise the bright rooms, the grey-tiled bathroom. A good investment, he'd said to Cath the day they signed the contract, and she'd agreed, though with a little tweak of a smile that twisted the words into something less straightforward.

Secretly, though, Jim is ambivalent about the plan, even if it's a sensible proposition and the asking price was almost exactly, uncannily, the amount his father left them. What Jim aged nineteen, punk rock wild child, would think of Jim aged fifty-nine as a rentier doesn't bear thinking about. But it's true that they could do with some extra income: after the years of part-time working and then stopping earlier than they'd bargained for, Cath's pension is tiny. The rent from St John's Street will be very welcome, especially if he doesn't want to work until he's seventy. Besides, buying the house has perked Cath up, and he's glad of that.

Like all his feelings about Cath these days, his gladness is shot through with complication, but it's sincere, nonetheless. He'd hoped the cake-making business she'd planned to launch would give her an occupation, a diversion, but that idea never really took off. For a few weeks after she resigned from St Mary's they ate almost nothing but cake, and Jim entered into the spirit of it, pleased to see her so full of purpose. Cath had always been good at baking, her birthday cakes the envy of other mothers: fairies, dinosaurs, dragons, following the fads of childhood. It took Jim a while to realise that her run of practice cakes last year was reproducing them, one by one. The pirate ship alerted him at last: he remembered photographing that one, with Emma's smiling face behind the Jolly Roger. He didn't say anything as the birthdays sped past in an accelerating rush of fondant icing, but he waited in apprehension for the series to grind to a halt.

The last one was a plain chocolate cake, wrapped in a bow. Jim remembers that one. Oh, he certainly remembers that one.

When he gets home that evening, Cath is waiting, hovering in the kitchen. Her face is bright, excited, and for a moment hope catches in Jim's throat – but it's not that. Of course it isn't.

'The agents called,' she says. 'They've got a potential tenant already.'

'But we're not completing for a fortnight,' he says. 'We're not ready for tenants yet, are we?'

'The vendors don't mind if we start viewings. Wouldn't it be good to have someone all set to move in?'

'Sure,' he says. 'Sure.'

'We could meet them tomorrow.' There's a glimmer of uncertainty in Cath's face now, a tremor of concentration as she wills him to go along with her.

'Sure,' he says again. 'I mean, yes, of course.' He takes a step forward, puts an arm around her. 'It'll be fun,' he says. 'We can play the evil landlords. Remember when we were in their shoes? Mr Boss, was it?'

'Bosch,' says Cath. 'Like the fridge.'

She leans against him, and he holds her tight for a moment, his fingers toying with the ends of her hair. *It'll be all right,* he wants to tell her. *Everything will be all right.* But he can't say it.

'Shall we go out?' he says instead. 'Celebrate?' He hesitates. 'A curry, like we used to in Leytonstone?'

Cath's face hovers, again, between emotions. Like a photo loading on a screen, Jim thinks, its pixels uncommitted, wavering from black to white.

'How about tomorrow?' she says. 'After we meet the tenants?'

'OK.' He smiles, although he knows enough not to count on tomorrow evening, either. Cath has slipped out of his arms now, and he opens the fridge, looking for a bottle of wine. 'Do you know anything about them?' he asks.

'They're called Mr and Mrs Smith, apparently.'

'Better than Polkinghorne.' He waggles his eyebrows at her, and at last her face relaxes.

'Not everyone's got my courage,' she says. 'Not everyone's idiotic enough to throw in their lot with someone even Rumpelstiltskin couldn't guess the name of.'

Lara

They're late leaving, and Lara's mind fills with misgivings as she gathers up keys, purse, phone. Neasden's not exactly the centre of town, but it's only a few miles from work and the West End and the different corners of London where their friends live. They've got a life here, the grown-up life they were determined to create for themselves: jobs, flat, routine. Carefully shaped pleasures like their Friday evening *bibimbap*. The thought of throwing in those certainties, still fresh and new enough to be thrilling, makes her anxious. Lara knows what it means to leave behind a life you know.

But Nick's right: the Tube might run all night but it takes an hour to get anywhere from here. And it's a dump, where they live. An expensive dump. They'll never be able to save up for a deposit if they stay put, and they don't want to be stuck in rented accommodation for ever.

Nick's done his homework. Along the commuter lines to Surrey there are several places, only forty minutes from Waterloo, where they could live in a nicer flat for less money, even taking the train fares into account. And they can walk to the office from Waterloo: that's the clincher. He showed Lara the calculations last night, and when she agreed it made sense, it was certainly worth thinking about, he told her he'd arranged three viewings for this morning.

'Already?' she said.

'Why not? Strike while the iron's hot, eh? We haven't signed the lease renewal yet.'

And then he made her a gin and tonic, opened a bag of the expensive crisps he loves, and they spent the evening fantasising about a new life in the country: long walks and proper pubs, away from the traffic and the pollution. By the time they went to bed, Lara believed in it. Walking home from the station in the evening along a tree-lined lane; waking up on Saturday morning to birdsong and lawnmowers. Definitely an improvement on the perch they've established here, clinging to the capital and to financial solvency by the skin of their teeth.

This morning, though, the picture has shifted again. They're only twenty-six: it feels too soon to give up city life and turn into commuters. It feels, frankly, too early – too cold – to be getting out of bed on a Saturday morning.

'Couldn't we leave it a month or two?' she wheedles, when Nick brings her a cup of coffee.

'We're only looking,' he says. 'It's an adventure. If we hate the idea by the end of the day there's nothing lost, eh?'

'OK.' Lara smiles, steeling herself for the jog to the tube station, the slog across London to Waterloo. An adventure, then.

There's just time to buy bagels before they leap on to the train. Sliding into window seats, they grin at each other. A recorded message lists the stops in a singsong voice that makes them sound like a poem: Haslemere, Petersfield, Havant, Fratton, Southsea.

'Did you have Miffy when you were little?' Lara asks. 'This is like Miffy going to the seaside. We should have brought our buckets and spades.'

'We could go to the seaside from Lingford,' Nick says. He raises his eyebrows, the way he does when he's offering her a treat, or a kiss, and she feels a little squeeze of pleasure.

The first property they see is disappointing. It's an apartment in a new block, right opposite the station, and despite the double glazing it's noisier than their flat in Neasden. Smaller, too.

'No point coming to the country to live somewhere like this,' Lara says, and the agent smiles thinly and says she understood they wanted to be near the station.

The next place is the ground floor of a terraced house. There's lots of space, a ramshackle garden out the back, but music thumps through the ceiling and it's definitely more than the twelve minutes from the station the description claimed.

'We could get bikes,' Lara says, seeing the disappointment on Nick's face, 'it would be fun to have bikes,' but they can both see it's no good.

She's more convinced, now, that this isn't what they should be doing, and there's a pleasing sense of reassurance about that. Reaffirming the status quo, she thinks. They'll just have to try harder to save money, take one step at a time. She glances at her watch: if they cut the final visit they could be home by two. They could call Val and Pete and suggest a film tonight. Remember the joys of London life.

'I wonder,' she begins, when they've shaken the estate agent's hand and set off up the road. 'Perhaps we should—'

But Nick has stopped in front of a little café. Not as chic as the places that pepper Dalston or Shoreditch, but quirky, with an enticing array of cakes in the window. A couple their age are just coming out, the girl carrying an armful of tulips, and they smile as they pass.

'Hungry?' Nick asks. 'We've got a few minutes before the next viewing.'

She *is* hungry, Lara realises, despite the bagel. As Nick pushes open the door, a waft of coffee and vanilla greets them. Three young women sit at a corner table, each holding a toddler smeared with orange icing. Despite herself, Lara's eyes are drawn to the little tableau, the mothers' hands full of wet wipes and sippy cups, and she feels a twist of something she can't, or won't, explain.

'Look at them,' says one of the women, mock-despairing, and another says, 'It's carrot cake, Lindsay. Carrot cake's a vegetable.'

'Have you lived around here long?' Nick asks the man behind the counter, as the coffee machine hisses. 'What's it like?'

'We're meeting the owners at this one,' Nick says, as they head on down the street ten minutes later. 'I wouldn't say no to landlords you can put a face to. It's left here, then … Wow. That must be it.'

Across the road, a 'To Let' sign is planted outside a little terraced house, set back behind a pretty front garden. There are two windows on the left and a door on the right, topped by a flourish of decorative brickwork.

'It's a house,' says Lara. 'Is it the whole house?'

'Yes.'

'It can't be less than we're paying now, then. It really can't.'

'The agent said it was competitively priced,' Nick says. 'She said the owners want the right kind of tenants.'

Lara stares at the house for a moment. She's not sure about being looked over by the landlords. She's not sure she wants to be the right kind of tenant; certainly not the wrong kind.

'Best foot forward, then,' she says.

January

Before they reach the door it opens, and there's a woman on the doorstep, smiling. She's maybe fifty-five, sixty, greying hair still streaked with black. One of those weary-looking women you see on the Tube, Lara thinks, who gaze at their phones with a frown of concentration.

'I'm Cath,' the woman says. 'And this is my husband Jim.'

Nick

The house is perfect. It's hard to imagine anywhere more perfect: the immaculate kitchen and bathroom, the main bedroom overlooking the back garden and the other room they can use as a study, or for guests. Friends who come down for the weekend. Not to mention the living room, with its fireplace and polished floor and clean white walls. Nick wants to live here so badly he can feel the adrenaline rush he gets sometimes coming home to Lara: and it's the same thing, he thinks, the same longing to look after her, to be certain of their future.

'So you both work in London?' the woman's saying – Cath.

'Yes,' he says. 'For the same company. That's how we met, actually.'

'What kind of company?' Jim asks.

'IT,' says Nick. That's usually enough for people their age, but he can see Jim's searching for another question, so he says, 'It's a boutique firm that provides bespoke software solutions for small businesses. Lara's on the programming side, and I'm in marketing.' He feels a flash of pride, as he says it, for the fact that Lara's the technical one.

Jim smiles, the you've-got-me smile of someone who has no idea what you're talking about. He looks younger than his wife, though he probably isn't. His hair's still thick, longer than Nick's, and he smiles more than Cath.

'I really love the house,' Lara says. 'I'm sure you'll be inundated with people wanting it, but I just want to say I really love it.'

Lara's very quiet on the way home, staring out of the train window with that vacant, troubled look she gets when her mind's busy. Nick watches her, enjoying the pleasure of letting his eyes travel over her. Sometimes he pretends to himself that they're going to be parted, and that he has to memorise every detail of her. That's how they used to teach people to draw, someone told him: they'd have the models on one floor and the easels on the floor below. The students would have to run up and down the stairs every time they wanted to check the angle of a mouth or the shading of a cheekbone. It was supposed to train their memories. He's no artist, but he thinks now that he wouldn't need Lara in front of him to draw her. Her hair curling thickly over her shoulders; her high cheekbones and narrow nose and those hooded eyes that seem to change colour whenever she laughs or frowns. The first time he saw her, when he came for his interview at Mordant, she was in Ted's office, showing him something on a screen. Leaning over slightly so the line of her back looked like a piece of sculpture, and discussing firmware and bitcoin in the tone of voice his mates use for football results. And then she turned, caught sight of him, smiled, and a phrase fell into his head as though someone was writing a script for the movie of his life: *the most beautiful woman I've ever seen.*

Until that moment, he'd always kept women at arm's length – the classic commitment-phobic twenty-something male. With better reason than most, but even so. He was good-looking enough, confident enough, that he never had trouble hooking up with women, but it never lasted more than a few weeks. They always knew, his girlfriends: sometimes they read the signs soon enough to dump him first. But when he saw Lara, something happened. Something completely beyond his control. It was as though all the loose parts rattling around inside him, like an Ikea box of dowel rods and barrel nuts and locking screws, had suddenly found their right places and bolted themselves together, and bingo – there he was, suddenly grown up. A man who knew what he wanted.

It took him a few weeks to pluck up the courage to ask her out, and a bit longer to know how uncannily right that first instinct had been. But looking back, it still feels as simple as it did that day in Ted's office. They were after exactly the same thing, he thinks now – and that little house ... that little house is just as right for them as they are for each other.

When his phone rings, Lara's eyes swivel towards him. 'Hello?' he says.

It's the agent, not the landlords – the Polkinghornes – but he's ringing with good news. Nick listens, a smile unrolling across his face.

'That's great,' he says. 'I'll have to talk to my wife, of course' – he grins at Lara: it still gives him a thrill to use those words – 'but I think she liked it as much as me. I think we'll be really happy there.'

FEBRUARY

Cath

When she reaches the door, Cath feels suddenly nervous. The curtains are closed and the warm yellowish light showing through them seems to draw her in and shut her out at the same time.

It was theirs for such a short time, she thinks, before they handed it over to Lara and Nick. She'd imagined she and Jim might spend an evening or two here – taking a break from scrubbing floors, perhaps, to open a bottle of beer – but there was never any reason for it. The place was left spotless. And she couldn't bring herself to suggest an evening of make-believe, sitting cross-legged on the floor as though they were moving in themselves. However brightly she talked about inventories and management fees, she caught Jim looking at her once or twice with that slight frown she's come to recognise.

She hesitates, letting an alternative reality hover about her for a moment, and then she knocks on the door and steps back, composing her features into a smile.

'Oh, hi!'

It's Nick who opens the door, his hair as tousled as hair that short can be, wearing a T-shirt streaked with dust.

'A little house-warming present,' she says, holding out the bottle of Prosecco.

'That's really kind.' Lara has appeared behind him, wearing jeans and a hoodie that make her look more like a teenager than a married woman. 'The flowers and everything – you've been so kind already.'

'Do you want to come in?' Nick asks. 'There are boxes everywhere, but ...'

'No, don't worry,' Cath says. 'Unless there's anything I can do? Anything you need?'

'You're very kind,' Lara says again. 'We're so happy to be here. We can't really believe ... It feels as though we're staying in someone else's house.' She blushes – remembering, perhaps, that it *is* someone else's house – and her face changes, filling with a tantalising glimpse of emotion. For a moment Cath can't take her eyes off her: she wonders whether she dares to offer help with the unpacking. But then she smiles, and digs her hand in her pocket for the car keys.

'I'll leave you to get used to it,' she says. 'Good luck with the boxes. We'll stop by again sometime and make sure everything's OK.'

'Thanks.' Nick holds out a hand to shake hers, and Cath takes it, a little surprised by the gesture. They must think she's ancient, a different species. She smiles again, resolutely, and turns away as the door shuts behind her.

'Been out?' asks Jim. There's something loud on the CD player, and a good smell which she recognises as last night's lasagne reheating in the oven.

'I called in on the tenants,' she says. 'I took them a bottle of wine. A house-warming present.'

'Oh yes?' Jim's sitting at the table cleaning a camera lens; Cath stands for a moment, trying to decide whether his casualness is affected. It would be safer not to say any more, but she can't help herself.

'They were a good pick, I think. They're nice.'

'How are they settling in?' Jim asks, and she shrugs, not turning to face him.

'I didn't go in.' She moves towards the cupboard. 'Shall I put some peas on?'

The water splashes into the pan when she turns the tap on, and she slops it slightly as she carries it to the hob. The weight of the pan, the solidity of the steel handle, give her a sort of courage, and while it lasts she says, 'She reminds me a bit of Emma. Lara does.'

It's not true; Lara looks nothing like Emma. Jim knows that, and he'll know why she's said it, too. That she's daring him to call her out.

February

When she steals a glance at him he's zipping the lens back into its pouch. She feels anger welling up inside now, and she knows Jim will sense that too.

'A bit, I suppose,' he says eventually. He stows the pouch in his bag, shuts the clasp. 'They remind me of us, back in the day.'

Cath freezes, staring at the surface of the water as it trembles over the flame. Jim's tone of voice was matter of fact, but even so she's moved. She feels the nascent anger subsiding, leaving behind the gnawing sadness which is the most reliable, the most familiar emotion she has left.

Jim looks up, smiles at her.

'I'll just put this away,' he says, 'then I'll lay the table.'

Sometimes Cath loses track of how long it's been. Never for long, though. Like a prisoner scratching out the days on the wall of her cell, she never stops thinking about it for long enough to forget. She remembers counting off the time when she was pregnant – advancing through weeks and then months, then back into weeks again as the end approached. But there's no certainty of an end, this time, and it's already been more than a pregnancy's worth. Almost a year, she says to herself, shaping the phrase carefully, so that it sounds decorous and dignified, a thing you could share without making people wince. Not that she does share it. In one sense there's nothing to share: no news, no announcement; no painful moral to be drawn. Just nothing, since Emma's ...

vanishing, might it be called? Without any explanation to shape their understanding, they've never known what to call it. They say her name when they need to, can't bear not to, and that's more than enough to evoke the grief they share, in the empty space that was once occupied by their daughter.

This evening Jim is gentle. He's always gentle, Cath thinks, but there are different shades of it. Sometimes it feels more like helplessness, and that's the worst kind, an indicator of narrowly disguised despair. But this evening his gentleness is calm, infused with some of the assurance he had at the beginning, back when she was Queen Anne Boleyn and he was a raffish twenty-four-year-old, and it soothes her a little, although she resists being soothed, almost can't bear it. He has to tread carefully, and he does.

'Coffee?' he asks, when they've finished eating, and she shakes her head. 'Shall we take Rover out for a pee, then?'

The dog's name is Hector, the name he came with from the rescue centre, but Jim has always called him Rover. A joke so old and worn it's lost its shape: Cath hasn't laughed at it for years, but it confirms something, she thinks. Something going on the same, despite everything.

'OK,' she says.

And then they're outside, and the simmering tensions of the evening are muffled as they pull their coats around them. Pinprick stars press through the invisible clouds, and the dog – ancient now, shuffling on arthritic hips – snuffles at the dank leaves on the verges. The world smells very real, Cath thinks. Earth and rain and trees and frost. In the dark you can almost believe it's benevolent, straightforward, unspoiled.

Jim

It's been raining for a week – even trying to snow, a couple of times, but the temperature has hovered just above freezing, turning the incipient snow into slushy, skin-soaking sleet. February is always a dismal month for news, too. Jim has covered traffic accidents and dog thefts and planning applications, dutifully turning in images of nondescript roadscapes festooned with police tape, bereft owners (a lucky break with a freckled five-year-old) and indignant neighbours. Once upon a time his Live Aid photos were on the front page of *The Times*, he reminds himself – though even that seems, in the dreary light of February, in his sixtieth year, pretty inconsequential as achievements go.

No, he thinks, peering past the lugubrious sweep of the windscreen wipers to the sodden world beyond, the iconic image of his life was his first sight of Cath's face, smiling out from that garish float. He doesn't have a photograph of that, but he doesn't need one: the memory has remained bright. Her dark hair swept up in that velvet headdress, the glow in her eyes. The shadow of it is still there when she smiles at him, despite the overlay of worry and disappointment and age. He doesn't mind those things: it touches him more than he can express to see the young Cath beneath them.

They haven't done so badly, he thinks now, on the richer and poorer, the sickness and health, but the better and the worse have been unfairly balanced for them. The unkindness of Fate has undone something in Cath: something he still hopes will heal, but which feels like a spreading stain, the brush of plague.

The house, and that young couple – Lara and Nick – have cheered her up more than he could have bargained for, though. *They remind me of us,* he hears himself saying. He didn't mean it, didn't think it was true when he said it, but perhaps it is. A kind of truth. An alternative story, unfolding from the beginning again.

This morning he's going to meet a woman in Dorking whose artisan cosmetics business has grown to a turnover of nearly a hundred thousand within eighteen months. He's read her publicity material, with its gushing celebration of flower extracts and natural oils, and he's got a picture of her in his head: a carefully made-up forty-something with blonde hair and tight-fitting jeans. So it's a surprise when he rings the bell of a red-brick semi and the door is opened by a woman closer to his own age, short and smiling and not, as far as he can tell, wearing any make-up at all.

'Hi,' she says. 'You're from the *Surrey Gazette*?'

'Jim,' he says. 'Jim Polkinghorne.'

'That's quite a name. Almost as good as mine. Dido Barnes.'

She holds the door open and he steps into a cheerful chaos of books and boxes, infused with the scent of rose and violet.

'Do you want coffee? I've made some gingerbread. Helps with the nerves, I find.'

'Gingerbread?'

She laughs. 'No, cooking. Come through.'

The house has been extended backwards across the garden, the far end transformed into a glass-walled work-shop which is evidently the hub of the business operation. There are steel pans on hotplates, a computer half-buried beneath piles of paper, glass jars overflowing with dried flowers and herbs. The rose-and-violet scent mingles, now, with the smell of baking. Before he's quite taken it all in, he has a cup of coffee and a slice of gingerbread in his hands. Dido is still talking, explaining some detail of the recipe, and Jim's eyes stray to the garden with its crowded rockeries, maturing apple trees and scattered cold frames. Gravel paths wind through it, as though it were the walled kitchen garden of a grand house rather than the modest plot of a Surrey semi. The expansiveness of it, the whole-heartedness, is irresistibly pleasing.

'Do you grow everything you use for your products?' he asks.

She laughs. 'Lord, no. But I include home-grown ingredients when I can. It appeals, you know. To me, anyway. And it's all organic, what I buy in.'

Turning back to her, he catches her eyes on him. She looks like a good witch from a fairy tale, brewing potions in her kitchen: a beguiling mix of wholesome and seductive. Can he capture that impression, he wonders, for the paper?

'I suppose I ought to have dressed up,' she says now. 'I suppose you want me in the photos?'

'I do, really,' Jim says. 'You need a human being in a human-interest story. But you look fine.' More than fine, he wants to say, but he can tell she doesn't need the reassurance. She's moving things around now, stacking pots and packages. 'Let's see how the light works if we have you here,' he says, setting down his coffee and unpacking his equipment.

The shoot goes well. Her face has the spark of engagement that always makes for a successful photograph, and – consciously or not – she knows how to use it. He spends longer than he needs to trying different backgrounds, different props, and Dido laughs and chats, feeds him anecdotes about how she came to give up her job as an estate agent to set up the business. Selling a different type of dream, Jim thinks, remembering the house in St John's Street.

'You'd think the market was overcrowded,' she says, 'but it took off almost overnight. It was a risk, going for the top end, but it meets a need. My products make people feel good. Life's complicated. People need to feel good.'

He wonders whether the journalist writing the copy has been here. More and more they do the interviews by phone, or even email, but it would be hard to write about Dido without seeing all this for yourself. And even then, it would be easy to leave out some essential ingredient: the smell of flowers; the abundance; the ease of her manner.

As the time rushes on towards the hour he can reasonably spend with her, he struggles to turn his mind to his next appointment – at a wildlife sanctuary which has launched an appeal to protect hedgehogs. It's the kind of thing he enjoys, usually.

'That was fun,' Dido says, when he finally packs the camera away. 'I wasn't expecting it to be fun. Thank you.'

'My pleasure,' he says. 'I don't know how many they'll use, but there's plenty to choose from. The picture editor should be pleased.'

'I'm at a craft fair at Fulford town hall on Saturday,' she says. 'Just in case you've got nothing better to do.'

'Thanks.' He zips up the camera bag, hesitates a moment. 'I might bring my wife,' he says. 'She likes that sort of thing.'

'Do.' Dido smiles at him, something dancing behind her eyes, then she ducks across the room, hands him a little box. 'Take her this. My top seller. Whet her appetite.'

But when he reaches out to take it she doesn't let go at once. She looks straight at him for a second, two, three, and then she says, 'You don't need to go right away, you know.'

Jim gazes at her. He can feel things melting and tumbling inside him, pooling at his feet, so that he couldn't move them even if he wanted to. It's not the first time someone's propositioned him on a shoot – but is that what this is? It could be simpler than that: an invitation to have another cup of coffee, another piece of gingerbread. Her words echo in his head – *Life's complicated,* he hears her saying; *People need to feel good* – and he's overcome with yearning for whatever it is that fills this kitchen: whatever it is that Dido creates here. He can't bear to let it go, now he's glimpsed it.

'I'll stay, then,' he says. 'Shall I?'

He has no idea, in that moment, what will happen next. Perhaps he'll settle in the rocking chair and watch her measure ingredients into one of those steel cauldrons, or follow her through the glass doors to pick herbs from the garden. Those things would be enough, he tells himself. But they wouldn't. They're not. The physical has a way of colliding with the metaphysical; he should know that.

'Let's go upstairs,' she says.

Her face hasn't changed, nor her voice. There's no deception in her, Jim thinks. No pretence. And that thought sinks the last of his misgivings. He's been pretending for too long: for longer than he can remember.

The Shadow Child

Not about the big things, but the little things have grown and grown until they've dwarfed him. Him and Cath.

He follows Dido back along the passage towards the front door, then up the stairs.

Cath

It's been a wild night: the kind of storm that almost makes you believe there's something alive outside, shaking the trees and hammering at the windows and then whipping away on a furious whim. Cath isn't sure how long it's been going on. The clock says four thirty, but she remembers it saying two something, three something. She's slept in fitful bursts, her dreams merging with the wind and the rain.

For a while she lies still, listening to the storm and to Jim's quiet breathing beside her. She can't see him, except in her mind's eye – his smile, amused and ironic, and his young face with its smooth, hard outlines, as it was thirty years ago. More than thirty years: so hard to countenance.

Jim's breath catches again and he sighs, stirs, then turns his head a fraction towards her.

'How long have you been awake?' he asks.

'Not long.'

Woowooh! shrieks the wind, as though it too has been disturbed, and a flurry of rain, sharp as pebbles, dashes against the window.

'Do you remember the big storm?' Jim says. 'The week we went to the Isle of Wight?'

'Yes.' Everyone remembers that storm, the one the weathermen got wrong. Cath remembers curling up with Jim in a tiny bed in a tiny cottage and feeling safe. 'We got up and made breakfast in the middle of the night.'

'So we did.' Jim grins, but Cath can feel tears rising in her eyes now, and when Jim reaches a hand towards her one spills over and runs down her temple, leaving a little trail through her hair.

'We could do that now,' Jim says. 'I could cook you breakfast.'

He pushes back the covers and she turns her head.

'You're not really getting up?'

'Just for a pee,' he says, 'but if you want bacon and eggs, I'll make it.'

'No.'

But perhaps he can tell she means yes, even before she knows it herself.

They put on all the lights in the kitchen, but it still feels dark and shadowy. An uninhabited hour, Cath thinks, when the room wasn't expecting them.

'Scrambled?' Jim asks, and she nods.

February

'Bacon?'

'Why not?'

There's a kind of awkwardness between them that reminds her of long ago – long, long ago, when neither of them was certain of the other. As Jim beats eggs in a bowl, Cath feels suddenly skittish. No, not quite that: she feels released from something, let off the familiar weight of worry and guilt, because this is not their usual life. The usual them. Perhaps Jim understands, because neither of them says anything more for a while. Cath sits in the rocking chair that was a wedding present from her parents and looks out through the window at the night in the garden, the darkness tempered by a partial moon. She could find her way around it without even the moonlight, she thinks: she knows every shrub, every lump in the lawn.

And perhaps it's this thought – the remembrance of what she knows intimately, even in the dark, even if she never chooses to explore it – that makes her speak.

'I never told you this,' she says, and she sees Jim register the words and what they might herald, sees his shoulders stiffening, and knows she has to go on now. Which is what she must have meant, of course: to commit herself. 'She used to steal. Emma. When she was little. I never told you.'

Jim turns. 'Steal what?'

'Sweets. Stickers. Rubbers.' Cath meets his eyes. 'Never anything valuable.'

She waits for him to say, *Why didn't you tell me?* But he doesn't.

'It was around the time your mother was ill, when you were going up to Scotland a lot,' she says, conscious that she's not picking her words quite carefully enough. 'It wasn't a big deal. Emma didn't want me to tell you, so I didn't. Lots of kids steal things.'

'Was it always when I was away?'

'I can't remember. I don't think so.'

He nods slowly, and she can see him wondering whether to push it any further.

'Why are you telling me now?'

She shakes her head: *I don't know.* There's silence again for a bit, just the sizzle of bacon in the pan, and then she says: 'It'll be a year soon.'

'Yes.'

'Had you forgotten?'

'How could I?'

She shrugs.

'Did you think I had?' he asks. 'Did you think I could?'

'No.'

'I keep looking,' he says. 'You know I do. Online. All the time.'

'Yes.' And then: 'The eggs,' she says, 'have they caught?' – and he swivels round again.

'Damn.'

'My fault. I distracted you.'

He stirs vigorously, then reaches for the plates. There's a faint smell of charring, but he spoons the egg out and plunges the pan into the sink.

As they sit down, Cath feels something else: the little thrill she used to get on the rare occasions when Jim was roused to anger. The sense that things might go in any direction now. Phrases jostle in her head like signposts.

After a few moments, Jim puts down his knife and fork.

'Do you think there's a connection?' he asks. 'With the stealing?'

'A connection with her leaving, you mean?'

'Yes.'

'Why would there be? It was years ago. She stopped; things were fine again.'

'Maybe she didn't,' Jim says. 'Maybe she moved on to other things. Maybe she got better at not getting caught.'

He looks, now, as though he has things to say too – secrets, for want of a better word, although secrets, in their marriage, have usually been things they both know but don't discuss.

He stares at his plate as if he can't remember what was on it, or why they're here, and Cath watches him, remembering the peacefulness of his breathing in bed, the wildness of the storm outside.

'I nearly forgot,' he says then, pushing back his chair. 'I've got something for you.'

He brings her a tiny pot of hand cream, its label vaguely familiar. A tangling of leaves and plain black lettering – *jasmine and bergamot*, she reads. She's seen it in a shop somewhere, this brand. Seen the price tag. It smells wonderful.

She looks up at him. 'How kind of you.'

Jim shakes his head, embarrassed. 'I went to photograph her today,' he says. 'The woman who makes this stuff.' He hesitates. 'She gave it to me,' he says. 'For you.'

Nick

Nick rolls over to turn off the alarm with a groan of reluctance. It's cold this morning. It's cold every morning: they're keeping the heating low, terrified of the bills they might be racking up. And it's early. They've taken to catching the six thirty-two train, because you're more likely to get a seat, and it means they can come home earlier, too. In a month or two they'll be able to sit out in the garden after work, he thinks, under the fledgling apple tree.

But for now he doesn't want to get out of bed, even for the pleasure of the luxurious shower in the little bathroom next door, or the porridge they cook every morning.

'I had such a weird dream,' Lara says sleepily. 'We were on a beach, and there was a lion, rolling in the sand. Then it got up and galloped off towards the sea, and a wave broke over it and it was gone. One moment it was there, splashing in the water, and the next it had vanished.'

'Hmm.'

'What do you make of that?' she asks, her breath warm against his neck.

'Maybe it was the storm.'

'Was there a storm?'

He laughs. 'A huge one. Didn't you hear it?'

'Perhaps it means we should get a pet,' she says. 'A cat. We could have a cat.'

'I'm not sure if we're allowed pets.'

'We could ask them tonight.'

'Ask who?' He threads an arm under her neck.

'Cath and Jim. They're coming for dinner.'

'Is that really tonight?'

'I thought you could make that pasta dish,' Lara says. 'The one with olives. Bagsy first shower.'

She leaps out of bed before he can kiss her again, and he watches her skitter across the cold floor, then hears the water being turned on, the whine of the boiler as it springs into action. A moment later he follows her, heading downstairs to put the kettle on, but he halts on the landing: the bathroom door is open and he can see her in the shower, the sharp curve of her back as she tips her face up towards the water. She looks so young, he thinks, with her hair wet, slicked smooth against her neck. Vulnerable, somehow. He can't get used to seeing her in this beautiful house: she looks, sometimes, like a child who's found her way into a luxury hotel room, and he wants very badly to make her feel at home. He wants the years to pass until they're beyond the invisible fence that still stands between them and safety.

He can tell that this evening's dinner is important to her, and although he wishes it wasn't – wishes the Polkinghornes weren't coming – he resolves to do his best. Not that pasta dish, he thinks: he'll buy some beef. They can open the last bottle of wedding champagne. They can be grown-ups.

Two Hearts

Jim is almost late. Cath's been here since half past, having allowed an absurd amount of time for the bus to be held up and for her to get lost on the way to the ultrasound department. Although there's still five minutes to go before her appointment, she feels a dart of anger when she spots Jim coming down the corridor. Didn't he realise she wanted him here early, to wait with her? Doesn't he understand what's at stake, after all the anxious years of waiting? That if there's something wrong with the baby, they might not get another chance?

Nothing to worry about, the midwife said when she saw her yesterday, but I think we'll book you a scan. But Cath has invented a hundred reasons for the midwife's disquiet. The worries have multiplied overnight, rearranged themselves frenetically in her mind during the last half-hour. Almost all the other women in the waiting room are more pregnant than she is, which makes her feel like a fraud, and fills her with doubt about whether she'll ever get to that point. Perhaps she's been kidding herself. Perhaps she'll never be a mother.

When Jim sits down beside her and takes her hand, electricity surges through her. Relief, reassurance. What Jim does. As her annoyance seeps away she leans against him, grateful for his steadiness. For him being there: she still hasn't learned to take that for granted. Whatever's coming, she tells herself, they'll face it together. They'll get through it together.

'So, you're fourteen weeks now by dates,' the sonographer says, when Cath's settled on the trolley, 'but your midwife just wants us to check that.'

'Why?' Cath's sure of her dates: her cycles have always been regular.

The woman doesn't answer at once, busy squeezing cold jelly on to Cath's stomach. Lying on her back, with her midriff exposed and the slight medicinal smell of the room, the chipped institutional paintwork and the crush of equipment, Cath feels strange. Not quite herself any more, but absorbed into the ambience of the hospital, turned into a part of its workings. It seems more likely to her now – more than likely – that there's something wrong with the baby.

'Let's have a look,' the woman says. She presses the probe on to Cath's skin and the screen beside her fills with patches of black and white, swirling shapes that make no sense to Cath.

'Can you see it?' Cath asks, straining her neck. 'Can you show me?'

Jim's on the other side of her, perched on a stool. Maybe he has a better view, or maybe he's just more used to looking at pictures.

'Oh my God,' he says, just as the woman halts the probe and says, 'There: do you see?'

'Is that the baby?' Cath still doesn't get it. There's some fluttering on the screen, among what looks like a small collection of potatoes, and she feels something leap in her chest. 'Is that the baby's heart?'

'Two hearts.' The sonographer smiles now. 'Two babies.'

She adjusts the position of the probe, and uses a pointer to show Cath what's there: two heads, four arms, four legs. Two hearts.

'Two babies,' Cath says stupidly. 'Is that why ...?'

'The midwife thought you were large for dates,' the woman says. 'And now we can see why.' She looks at Cath, then at Jim. 'Congratulations,' she says. 'Are you ready for twins?'

'Oh, Jim!' Cath still can't think straight. She gazes at the screen, at the outlines of the two tiny beings curled together. As the sonographer moves the probe, fingers come into focus, then the blurred contours of a face. They look as though they're floating in outer space, miles away from her, but they're unmistakably human already.

'Are they all right?' she asks. She wants to know what Jim's thinking, to look at his face, but she can't drag her *eyes away from the image on the scanning machine. 'Are they both all right?'*

'They seem to be,' the sonographer says. 'I'll measure them, have a good look. We'll be keeping a close eye on you from now on, of course, but there's really no reason to worry about twins these days.'

'Twins!' Jim says now, as though his mind has been spinning too, absorbing the news. 'My darling, you never do things by halves, do you?'

Cath giggles. The reprieve and the surprise have made her light-headed: the hospital feels like a place of miracles now. The anxiety of the night has been swept away. Jim has taken her hand, and she pulls him closer, close enough to feel the scratch of his jacket on the bare skin of her belly.

'Can you tell what they are?' she asks. 'What sex?'

Maybe she shouldn't ask; maybe two healthy babies is all she should dare to hope for. But she wants to know. She wants to be able to imagine them: her babies. Her children.

'It's a bit early,' the woman says, 'I shouldn't speculate, really.'

'But if you had to?' Jim asks.

She looks at him, smiles. People always warm to Jim.

'I think you've got two little girls,' she says.

Jim

Guilt doesn't feel like Jim expects it to. It doesn't lurk in the shadows; it wreathes itself around him, calling attention to itself, and he doesn't fight it. He knows he ought to feel regret, shame, self-hatred, but somehow he doesn't. Instead he feels a heightening of his senses: an impression of seeing things more clearly.

There's no reason what he's done should hurt Cath, he tells himself. Perhaps the opposite. He remembers the storm last night, and the tenderness he felt for her then. There's been nothing like that for years – getting up in the small hours; the hint of playfulness. Like being young again, freeing themselves from something. And then the way Cath spoke about Emma: the fact that she spoke about her at all, telling him things he hadn't known, secrets saved up from her childhood. Stealing.

What does stealing mean? Were there things that Emma wanted, things she couldn't have? Or did she just want to take things that weren't hers?

It must have been hard for her, Jim thinks now, in those early years. Did they think enough about that, when she was little? It was Cath he always worried about. And when Emma left, should they have thought then – but maybe Cath did. Maybe she never stopped thinking about it. Looking back, he can almost see the shadow between them, stretching back, and it fills him with pain.

He has a lot of driving to do today, from one end of the county to another. Usually he listens to the radio, but today he drives in silence, remembering Cath driving heedlessly around after Emma left, driving God knows where. And then later – almost worse – sitting for hours at a time at the kitchen table, not even a book or a crossword to hand. Does she still do that? Jim has no idea. Sometimes he feels she can't wait for him to leave the house – so she can stop pretending, perhaps. Because the anguish they can express to each other is constrained, somehow: because each of them wants to be comforted, and to comfort the other, but at the same time they need to hold on to the molten sorrow that burns inside them.

There's another sharp stab of guilt, then: a feeling so painful it's almost pleasurable. The truth of life is in plain sight just for a moment, the tragedy of it, but it's not bearable for longer than that. Riding it out, his hands clench on the wheel – and as it passes there's Dido, waiting quietly just outside his field of view, busy with her perfumed oils and dried petals. Surrounded by the smell of lavender, roses, ginger; infinitely soothing. And then there's a crashing wave of desire, so powerful it blinds him for a moment, and as it recedes a devastating undertow of remorse. What he should have felt yesterday, he realises. What he would have felt, perhaps, if he'd been capable of it.

He grips the steering wheel harder, shaken by the enormity of his feelings, and then he pulls over into a gateway and stops the engine. He can hear himself breathing, his pulse throbbing, and there's a choking sensation in his chest that grips him tighter and tighter.

My God, he thinks, is this a heart attack? A nervous breakdown? Is this what it feels like: Jim Polkinghorne of the *Gazette*, of the *NME*, coming to a sudden halt in his car in a country lane?

A tiny part of him feels relief at the prospect of giving in to it; of admitting there's something wrong. Not just for his sake, he tells himself. How can he go on being, doing, what Cath needs when he's been ignoring this great chasm inside himself?

And so for a long while he sits, waiting for something to happen, to shift, to become clear. But nothing does. All he can see is bare trees and ploughed earth, and the sky grey, seamless. No one comes; nothing moves.

So what, then: start the car and drive on? Follow the road towards his last appointment of the day, and then dinner, God help him, with that young couple in St John's Street, so brimming with youth and hope that he can hardly bear the thought of them?

And finally that stings him into action. He turns the key in the ignition, looks at the time on the dashboard, pulls back on to the road and swerves into a three-point turn.

Dido smiles when she opens the door. Is she surprised to see him? Jim wonders. Pleased? He can hardly remember, now, what they said to each other yesterday; whether she could possibly be expecting him.

'Hello,' he says.

She steps back from the door to let him in, and he inhales that rich amalgam of scents again: a different inflection today, but still a base of rose petals, as though she has strewn them up the stairs in anticipation of his arrival.

He doesn't explain himself, and she doesn't ask any questions. He follows her through to the kitchen, and she pours him a glass of wine.

'I'm celebrating,' she says. 'I've invented a new recipe.'

'What's in it?' he asks.

'Trade secret. See if you can guess.'

She hands him a bowl containing a thick, pale cream. The smell is intoxicating: some exotic flower or tropical fruit, perhaps.

'Delicious,' he says. 'Congratulations. A new bestseller.'

She smiles, setting the bowl down. Her movements are easy, uncomplicated: everything about her, he thinks, is straightforward, and the thought makes him want to cry again. He's been deceiving himself, thinking she's not beautiful. But it's not conventional beauty; nothing so obvious. It feels like something he's discovered for himself.

'Dido ...' he says.

And then her hand is on his shoulder, and his hand is on hers, his head twisting towards her bosom. She smells of wax and honey.

'Hey,' she says, 'it's all right. It's all right ...'

'Tell me about you,' she says, as they lie in her bed. Cushions are strewn about them as though someone has designed this scene. Dido. Has she foreseen all this?

'There's not much to tell,' he says, and she makes a little noise of amusement.

'OK,' she says. 'That's fine.'

He turns to look at her. 'There really isn't,' he says. 'I'm a photographer. I take photographs.' He hesitates. 'I'm married.'

'Yes.'

'I don't ...'

'No.'

'Never,' he protests. 'Never before.'

'I'm flattered.'

'I didn't mean to come back today.'

'I didn't expect you.'

'I don't mean ...' He shuts his eyes, remembering the grey sky, the emptiness. 'This afternoon,' he says, 'I thought – I don't know. I thought my life was ending.'

She doesn't speak, but her eyes rest on him: her face is calm, composed.

'I think I met you in the nick of time,' he says.

'I'm very glad.' She lifts an arm, touches his face. His eyes are tracing the line of her neck, her shoulder blade, but he feels suddenly shy.

'Our daughter Emma ...' he says. His breath almost stops in his throat. No, he thinks. No. And then he notices the clock beside the bed; notices that it says six o'clock. Bloody hell.

'I have to go,' he says. 'I'm sorry.'

'It's all right.'

'Why are you so nice?'

'Why not? Why not be nice?'

He laughs, pulling himself upright. 'I'm sorry. Thank you. I don't know quite what to say.'

'Then don't.'

He takes her in his arms then, the only woman he's held like this, apart from Cath, in thirty years. More than thirty years. He wants her to know he's glad it's happened. But he won't come back again, he thinks. Twice was wonderful, more than wonderful, but he won't come back.

Before he lets her go, he says: 'Our daughter Emma left home, a year ago. She was seventeen. She had – a bad experience. Nothing to do with us, but a terrible thing happened to her and she ran away, afterwards. She left us.'

'I'm sorry.'

'It's been very hard for Cath – for her mother. Life hasn't been the same, for either of us.'

He feels as though he's laying something down: layers of gauze, brushstrokes of paint.

'It's not fair, telling you. I don't want you to think ...'

'It's all right, Jim,' she says. 'It's – I'm fine. I don't want to make your life more complicated. I hope I haven't.' Her hand grasps his for a moment. 'Please don't feel ... Please don't worry about me. Don't feel you have to come back.'

'It wouldn't be because I didn't want to,' he says.

But he pulls away then, and she lets him go. In that moment he sees clearly what he's done – but it feels to him, still, as though this is happening in a different realm, under different rules. The separate parts of it – the magic potions, the sex, the confessions – are unconnected pieces, and none of them have anything to do with Cath, any more than the photography session did. Why can't that be so?

As Dido watches him dress, Jim imagines the eyes of the young couple on him later. Lara and Nick. For the first time he's glad they'll be there, and that Cath will see him through their eyes tonight. Dull but reliable: he'd settle for that.

Lara

'Mrs Dalloway said she would buy the flowers herself,' Nick says, as Lara comes through the door with an armful of daffodils.

'Well,' Lara says, smiling, 'since you're cooking, I thought I'd better do something. They're not too bad, are they? They always sell them so closed up, as if everyone buys flowers several days before they actually want them.'

She puts the flowers in the sink and opens the cupboard beside the fridge, then frowns.

'We might have to choose between water and daffodils,' she says. 'We only have that one jug.'

'You could use the teapot,' Nick suggests. 'Like Val did that time?'

The daffodils have to be trimmed by several inches to stop them falling out of the teapot, but Lara is delighted with the result. She's delighted with everything: with Nick chopping vegetables, and the house looking bright and welcoming, and the smell of pudding in the oven. Even Nick quoting Virginia Woolf: she gave him *Mrs Dalloway* for Christmas, and he's been reading it, dutifully, on the train every morning.

But even so, when she thinks of Cath and Jim coming through the door in half an hour, she feels queasy. It's like a rite of passage: like having your parents round to your own house for the first time. Like it might be, if—

Too late, she wonders if they should have had a starter. Crisps, even. They forgot all that.

Cath and Jim have brought a bottle of Prosecco, and they sit in the front room, using up all the chairs, raising their glasses to each other.

'We love the house,' Lara says. 'We feel very lucky.' But then she remembers saying exactly the same when Cath came to the door that time, and she blushes.

'And how do you like commuting?' Jim asks.

Lara looks at Nick, lets him answer that one. They have a stock of commuting stories already: the day no one could get to work because of the snow; the guard who's on the early train sometimes who tells jokes over the loudspeaker. She listens to Nick telling them Lingford's great because there are always seats available, before Fulford with its great crush of commuters. That they've been to Fulford a few times at the weekends, for shopping or the cinema or the leisure centre; that they didn't realise what a big town it was. A university town – a cathedral town, even. And Cath and Jim, who know all this, nod, pleased.

'What do you do, Cath?' Nick asks next, and Lara's proud that he's asked Cath first, then scared it might be the wrong question.

'I was a primary school teacher for years,' Cath says. 'I retired last summer. Since then – well, I thought about starting a cake business.' She hesitates, glances at Jim.

'So far I'm the only customer,' Jim says. 'Not that I'm complaining.'

He smiles, but there's a silence after that, and Lara decides it *was* the wrong question. Perhaps they shouldn't ask questions.

'Something smells good,' Cath says, and Nick gets to his feet.

'Give me a couple of minutes,' he says. 'Finishing touches.'

The food is amazing, as she knew it would be. Nick's made Beef Wellington, and it looks and tastes more than good enough for Cath and Jim. While they eat, conversation rolls along happily – Jim tells stories about their early efforts in the kitchen, Cath chips in with reminders of the ingredients you couldn't find in the shops back then but take for granted now, Nick talks about his trip to Japan a couple of years back and the sushi he ate there. Then he produces his apple tart, and Lara looks at it and realises that's two lots of pastry in one meal, but Cath says something admiring, and even though it's a bit soft on the bottom it tastes lovely and they're all teasing Nick, in a flattering sort of way, about going on *Masterchef*.

'Oh, I can't be bothered with all that fancy stuff,' Nick says. 'Tea-smoked duck, or whatever.'

'Maybe it should be Cath going on *Bake Off*,' Lara says. 'What sort of cakes do you make, Cath?'

'Nothing grand enough for *Bake Off*,' Cath says. 'Just ordinary cakes, really. Christmas cakes, birthday cakes …'

'Some of them weren't ordinary,' Jim says, and Cath frowns, anxiety streaking across her face.

Lara pretends she hasn't noticed, but the questions she might have asked next fizzle out. Birthdays? she wonders. Children? She doesn't know whether they have any.

'That kitchen's a dream to cook in, though,' says Nick, and Lara shoots him a grateful smile.

'We can't claim any responsibility for that,' Jim says. 'It was all there when we bought the house. But when I think of the kitchen we started out with …'

'Where was that?' Lara asks.

'A dilapidated corner of East London,' Cath says. 'Leytonstone, out along the Central Line. We didn't know what we were about really, did we, Jim? We had a terrible old gas cooker; half the rings didn't work. I'm sure it would be condemned now.'

'It was fun, though,' Jim says. 'We had fun.'

Cath looks at him, and there's that same sense of something lying there, unsaid. A whole collection of things, perhaps. What must it be like, Lara wonders, to have been married for as long as Cath and Jim? To have all that time behind them, instead of ahead? It's Cath, she thinks, who's Mrs Dalloway, not her – and she feels suddenly anxious about whether the evening has gone as well as she hoped.

'Coffee?' Nick asks, but Jim glances at Cath and shakes his head.

'We should go,' he says. 'It's late.'

It's only ten thirty, and tomorrow's Saturday, but Lara doesn't protest. She's exhausted. She can't explain, now, why she was so keen to invite the Polkinghornes round. But they've carried it off, haven't they, she and Nick? They're a good team. A perfect team. And now her chest thrums with pleasure at the thought of having him to herself again.

MARCH

Jim

Jim's driving up Fulford High Street when he sees her. She's walking down the other side of the road with cars passing between them and the pavements busy with pedestrians, so he only gets a glimpse, but he's certain it's her.

'Emma!' he calls out, before he can stop himself – but of course she can't hear him. He looks wildly over his shoulder, searching for her in the wing mirror, but she's disappeared.

Fifty yards on he turns into a side road and parks on the double yellow line, then he leaps out and dashes across the road, dodging between prams and shopping trolleys as he chases after her.

'Emma!' he shouts again. He can't see her, but she was walking and he's running, so he should be able to catch her up. But she could have gone into a shop, he thinks, or off down one of the side streets; he might have passed her already. He slows, glancing through the windows of cafés and clothes shops and upmarket chemists, wondering which she might have chosen, what sort of errand she might be on. Is she visiting friends in Fulford, or ... His breath catches in his throat.

At the bottom of the hill he stops, panting. There's no sign of Emma. Perhaps it wasn't her after all – but somehow he's sure it was. Impossible to mistake your own daughter, surely, even if her hair is shorter, her clothes different. Even if you only see her for a second.

He leans against the wall of the shopping centre and shuts his eyes.

Emma, he thinks: whatever happened, sweetheart? What on earth is going on?

She was a sweet child, Emma. A round-faced, smiling, responsive little girl who was still affable, amenable, at fourteen and even fifteen: the first half of fifteen, anyway. It was the lily-pond cake that birthday, Jim remembers. Fondant lilies and a little marzipan frog. He can conjure, now, a tiny shadow over that day, a suggestion of impatience, but he isn't sure whether he really remembers that or whether he's edited it in, in retrospect. In the light of what followed. They bought her a new phone and hair straighteners, and she bought herself a black eyeliner from an expensive brand she was mad about.

Gradually, she became more mysterious to them. The hours she spent up in her bedroom didn't translate into achievements at school: quite the opposite. The friends they'd known, the Maddies and Izzies and Livvies, faded from view. But Cath took it in her stride, and Jim admired her for it. She'd seen it all before, her former pupils' parents rolling their eyes when she asked after them at fifteen and sixteen. She'd seen them emerging a few years later, heading off to university with a clutch of A levels and the future in their sights.

And that, surely, is what would have happened to Emma, Jim has kept telling himself. No one could blame her, or them, for the catastrophe that overtook them. Except that Jim can't help feeling that the seeds of it all, of her disappearance, had been sown well before that. He can't help feeling that Emma had been hiding herself away in plain sight for a long time.

Is that true? he wonders now, staring hopelessly back up Fulford High Street through the crowds of shoppers. And if it is, could they – should they – have done things differently? Perhaps Emma should have been their priority, right from the beginning. They were torn, he thinks, pulled in different directions, and they did their best. It was never easy; they never let themselves off the hook. But even so, he's caught between guilt and a desire – surely forgivable – not to judge themselves too harshly. For Cath's sake, especially. Cath, he knows, is caught between simpler emotions: hope and despair.

They first heard about the murder on the news. For Jim, it meant work: a scramble to get himself out to the scene, on to the next place the investigation threw up. A dash from woodland to petrol station, from the girl's front door on a Fulford housing estate to the police press conference. He's ashamed to remember, now, how exciting it was: the biggest news story to break in south-west Surrey for years. The national press was all over it, and his local knowledge was valuable to the photographers from *The Times* and the *Daily Mail*; he relished the chat and speculation as they all hung around, waiting to get their shots.

They had no idea, he and Cath, that Emma knew the victim. They were at different schools, lived in different towns, and she was older, Julianne Roberts. She was nineteen, and Emma wasn't yet seventeen.

It was clear from the outset that Julianne was no angel, but the media didn't play that up: she was the innocent victim of a horrific crime that made you want to lock up your daughters. Her father owned a shop in Fulford and her mother was a midwife – those were good visuals, the shopfront (an old-fashioned toy shop) and the maternity unit. Julianne had been found on Clorley Common, a hundred yards from a car park, strangled and mutilated, with evidence of appalling sexual violence. She'd only been missing for twenty-four hours, and she'd been seen getting into a car with a man identified by her parents as an ex-boyfriend. The investigation moved fast: within a couple of days the chain of events was pieced together, the journey he'd taken her on and what he'd put her through before dumping her body.

His photo, his name, were everywhere, but the first time the police turned up on the Polkinghornes' doorstep he hadn't been arrested yet.

The shock of it is branded on Jim's mind. Looking back, it feels unreal – like something that would happen to someone else – and that was how it felt at the time, too. There must have been a mistake, they said: they didn't believe Emma could have anything to do with it. They hadn't noticed her reaction to the news being any different from what you might expect – but then they hadn't paid particularly close attention to her over those few days. That was the first thing Cath would blame herself for. They'd told Emma, of course, that she must be careful, not take any risks, while this man was on the loose, in the same way every parent in Surrey must have done. If she'd looked paler or more expressionless than usual, they'd attributed it to a grudging recognition that they had a point, for once.

There'd been nothing in the media, at that stage, about what the police had found on the boyfriend's computer: the photographs they showed to Cath and Jim, and to Emma. Photos described by the judge, ten months later, as among the most horrifying she'd ever seen. Julianne Roberts trussed up, naked, with stab wounds and slashes of lipstick all over her body. With her head in a noose, knives to her throat, her hands and feet bound. Some of them real, taken during the nightmarish interval between her abduction and her death, and some of them painstakingly constructed with photoshop. Those were almost worse, the images created from his imagination: the violence was more extreme, the meticulous editing sickening. The cold-blooded fantasies he meant to make real.

And the worst thing of all, the thing Cath and Jim couldn't begin to make sense of, was that some of the photoshopped pictures featured not Julianne, but Emma. Emma's neck with chains around it; Emma's face smeared with blood. A half-dismembered corpse with Emma's head.

At first Cath and Jim had thought this monster must have downloaded images of Emma from social media sites – Facebook, Instagram, Snapchat, all the places she scattered photographs of herself. (Kyle Jenkins, his name was. Kyle Jenkins, 22, a lifeguard at Fulford leisure centre. That was an irony: he'd been employed to save lives.) They'd assumed he'd picked Emma by chance, perhaps among several other girls, before doctoring the pictures to show her being tortured and raped. And they *were* doctored images, the ones of Emma: the police were at pains to point that out. But they said they'd heard, they'd been told, that Emma knew him.

And to Cath and Jim's astonishment, Emma admitted that she did. That she knew Julianne as well as Kyle. They were friends, she said.

Cath and Jim stared at her. Emma knew Jim had been covering the case. They'd talked to her about it – those warnings to take care – and she'd said nothing, revealed nothing.

'How?' Cath asked. 'How did you meet them, love?'

Emma shrugged, more resistant to her mother's questions than the police's. 'At the pool,' she said.

'When was that, Emma?' the more senior police officer asked. She was plump, fortyish, a sensible-looking person.

Emma shrugged again. 'August?'

'You met them both then? Kyle and Julianne?'

'Yeah.'

And so the story filtered out. Not much of a story – not to hear Emma tell it. She'd met them, become friends with Julianne, spent time with her. With them both. Shopping; hanging out; swimming at the leisure centre when Kyle had a shift. Cath and Jim remembered the swimming: remembered with dismay their pleasure that Emma was doing something so wholesome. After Kyle and Julianne had broken up she'd seen him a few times on his own, she said. Hung out at his flat with him.

'Alone?' the police officer asked, while Cath and Jim sat frozen with horror.

'Yeah, sometimes.'

A muffled sound from Cath: almost like a labour pain, Jim found himself thinking.

'And what did you do with him, Emma? What did you do while you were in his flat?'

'Nothing.'

'You mean you didn't have a sexual relationship with him?' asked the police officer, unflappable.

'No.' Emma's snort of derision made Jim's spirits rally, until he caught himself. His daughter had spent time alone with a psychopath who'd raped and murdered his girlfriend. What the hell did it matter whether Emma had had sex with him?

They'd played games, Emma said reluctantly. Online games, she meant: computer games. They'd watched stuff. Not porn, she insisted. Violent stuff, maybe, sometimes. He'd been depressed, after Julianne broke up with him. Sad more than angry. Why had Emma visited him then? Had he asked her to? Yeah, she supposed so. Had she liked him? Kind of. Had she ever been frightened of him? Not really. Had he ever shown her any alarming pictures, perhaps talked to her about – fantasies ...?

'She'd hardly have gone round there again if he had,' Cath burst in, unable to contain herself any longer. 'Where is he now, this Kyle? How are you going to protect Emma?'

Because it was clear, by then, that Emma had been in danger. No matter that Julianne had dumped him and Emma had been a shoulder for him to cry on. The photoshopped images of both girls were very similar, the police admitted. It was entirely possible that if Kyle hadn't managed to get Julianne into his car that evening, it might have been Emma instead.

He was arrested the next day. Jim would never forget the hours before that, though: the uniformed police officer outside the house all night while they tried to talk to Emma, then let it go, telling each other she was in shock, that there was plenty of time. That they'd be there when she was ready. When the news of Kyle's arrest came through, Emma wept in Cath's arms, and Jim watched, full of the same uncontrollable emotions as the night Cath had given birth. The terrible, wonderful responsibility of parenthood. The brutal mercy of Fate, once again.

But after that thaw, Emma withdrew again, more thoroughly than before. He and Cath stood alongside her through the long, long process of the investigation and the trial. They spent their evenings talking in hushed tones, wondering what they should do, what they could do, while Emma skulked upstairs in her room. Her other friends seemed to have fallen away; she hardly went out, except to school. They tried to persuade her to accept some counselling and bit their tongues when she refused, insisting that she was fine, Kyle was locked up, wasn't he, and he'd never laid a finger on her. They waited, when it was all over, for things to go back to normal. Patience, they whispered to each other, late at night in the dark, or when Emma refused to come down for meals; when she slammed out of the house without speaking. She's dealing with it in her own way. It's a terrible thing she's been through.

And then, one day, she didn't come home from school. It was a year, almost to the day, after Julianne died, and at first they assumed she was having some kind of memorial vigil with friends. As the hours passed, he and Cath prepared themselves to tread carefully when she returned, to be ready with love and sympathy if this was the moment for it, at last.

But she didn't return. Instead, a postcard arrived a couple of days later – a bizarre form of communication for their digital-age child. Ten words, in Emma's curly, childlike handwriting: *Please don't look for me. I'm fine. Love you, Emma.*

She was seventeen, still at school. Not look for her? How could they not? But although the police were sympathetic – the Julianne Roberts case was still fresh in everyone's minds – it turned out there was surprisingly little they could – or would – do. She was nearly an adult, legally, and in any case, they explained patiently, given the circumstances Emma was defined as 'absent', not 'missing'. Her disappearance was unexpected, but not totally out of character: it turned out her attendance at school had become erratic, that she'd regularly rung the absence line pretending to be Cath. Most persuasively of all, she'd sent her parents a card, told them she was fine.

But how could they be sure it hadn't been written under duress? Cath had demanded. Surely they could understand – what if one of Kyle Jenkins's friends had taken her, lured her into a trap? Had she stayed in touch with his friends, then? the police had asked – and Cath and Jim had shaken their heads in bewilderment. Their answers to every question were hopelessly inadequate: they had no idea who Emma's friends were any more.

The police offered statistics that were designed to reassure: over two hundred thousand children went missing every year, most of them teenagers. The vast majority came home of their own accord within a few days. Abductions were very rare, murders even more so: Cath and Jim should try not to worry. The police searched Emma's room, took her laptop, but found no clues. They promised to check hospitals and hostels, to notify the Missing Persons Unit. Was Emma on Facebook? Instagram? Cath and Jim supposed so – she certainly had been in the past – but when the police looked for her accounts they drew a blank. Perhaps she'd deleted them all after Julianne died, they suggested. But surely they had experts who could try to trace her online? The answer was non-committal. They'd do what they could. But there was no reason, the police assured them, to think Emma had come to any harm.

When another card arrived, two weeks later, with almost exactly the same message, the police took it as confirmation that Emma had left home voluntarily, intentionally, and their interest dwindled further. Cath and Jim waited and hoped; they cancelled their holiday in Spain in case Emma called, or appeared on the doorstep, or sent another postcard, but there was nothing more. Not that whole spring or summer, and not since.

Jim gets back into his car, his heart still thumping with the adrenaline of the pursuit, and sits for a moment staring back towards the High Street, towards the place he saw Emma – or Emma's shadow – pass.

Does everyone who's lost a child feel the same sense of helplessness? he wonders. There's a nagging voice in his head telling him they should have shouted louder, looked harder. They didn't organise searches, or print posters, because how could they when Emma had said she was fine, that she didn't want to be found?

And everything they tried was so little use. Jim worked out how to get on to Facebook, Twitter, Instagram, and he searched for Emma there, but with no more luck than the police. For weeks Cath drove endlessly, fruitlessly, around the countryside in the forlorn hope of seeing Emma. *I can't just sit here,* she'd say. *I have to do something. She must be somewhere.* She'd head straight off from school, most days, and not get back until late at night, and she could never say where she'd been, how far she'd driven. Jim would come home from work not knowing whether she'd be there: he'd imagine her criss-crossing the county, getting out to wander the streets, maybe; it drove him nearly mad with worry. *What if you have an accident?* he'd ask. *What if I lose you, too?* Eventually she did have an accident – not a serious one, just a prang, when she braked suddenly and someone ran into the back of her, but after that the expeditions stopped. After that she took to sitting like a statue at the kitchen table, as though she'd lost hope.

They thought – several times they thought – about hiring a private investigator, but for one reason and another they never did. The police advised against it in the early days: if Emma didn't want to be found, they said, then employing someone to track her down might be the worst thing to do.

She'll come back, the nice female sergeant said. *Give her time.*

But time went on, weeks and then months, and Emma didn't come back. Cath and Jim were encouraged to join a support group run by a national charity, but the first meeting was so heartbreaking they never went again. Other people's situations were so much worse – their children were younger, or had a history of drugs and self-harm, of selling naked photographs online or abusive boyfriends years older than them. They were sympathetic about the connection to Kyle Jenkins, but they couldn't hide their envy, their incredulity, when Cath told them about Emma's postcards. In the car afterwards, Cath said it had felt as if they were making a fuss about nothing. But when they got home, passed Emma's empty room on their way to bed, the worry and grief came flooding back, and with it Cath's terrible fear that Kyle had been part of a network of psychopaths; that those appalling photos of Emma were out there somewhere on the internet, and someone had seen them. Someone who'd got to know Emma, and then taken her.

Jim rang the police the next morning, and was told the nice sergeant they'd dealt with had gone on maternity leave. A painful irony. Someone called him back, a young constable who knew nothing about Emma but had looked up the case file and recited the details Jim already knew by heart. It was clear that nothing had been added for some time – that the file was on a shelf, gathering dust. Jim tried reason, then pleading; he came close to losing his temper. Emma had been caught up in a horrific murder, he'd shouted, and she'd been gone for three months now. Surely the police could understand that they needed to know she was all right? But Emma had informed them she was safe, the young man said. He repeated the statistics they'd heard so many times; the message that this wasn't a high-risk case. Emma was eighteen now, and had a legal right to disappear.

Jim didn't tell Cath he'd been in touch with the police again, because he couldn't bear to tell her they weren't looking for Emma any more. He went back to checking social media: the same routine each time, and each time the same flutter of expectation, rapidly dashed. And meanwhile, contacting a private investigator required either more hope or more despair than either of them could allow themselves to feel.

Hope and despair, Jim thinks. That was what they felt eighteen years ago; what they've lived with all this time. It shouldn't be so hard any more. But it is.

The Statistics of Love

Emma has been more settled since Rose came home from the hospital four days ago. She's been waking less in the night, crying less in the day; her little body no longer clenches up every time they change her nappy. She must have missed her sister, Cath thinks, having been so close for all those months in the womb. She must have felt as though part of her had been removed: for both of them, the world must have been a scary place to find themselves, all alone. It's wonderful to be able to put them down beside each other in the same cot, returned at last to each other's comforting presence.

In fact, Cath thinks, they've all been more settled since Rose came home. Their family is complete now, after the scary weeks when Rose was in the Neonatal Intensive Care Unit, and it feels as if the rollercoaster they've been on for the last six months has slowed to a halt at last. Sitting up in bed on this peaceful morning with the babies in her lap, pillows propped around her as the midwife suggested and sunshine flooding in through the bedroom window, Cath can almost trace a straight line back to that first scan at fourteen weeks when no one knew anything was wrong; when she began to imagine her two little girls being born, growing up.

They're both asleep just now, their tiny faces peaceful, and she feels such a surge of love and joy that tears spring up in her eyes. Motherhood, she thinks. She can call it that now: she's a mother. Not a patient, or an anxious bystander, or a clinical curiosity. She's at home with her baby daughters, and the sun is shining. Just for now, just in this moment, everything is all right. This, she thinks, is the reward for everything they've been through.

She's trying not to think too much about all that, though: the second half of the pregnancy, after the problem was discovered, or the first weeks after the girls were born when Rose's life hung in the balance. It feels like a bad dream, the memory of a kidnap or a hijacking. What she remembers is statistics: 50 per cent chances and 85 per cent chances; clinical stagings and success rates; prognostic indicators from academic papers. Nothing to do with their real lives, with the squirming babies growing inside her.

The operation the doctors recommended was less dramatic than they had expected. Cath was only in hospital for one night, and the whole thing was done through tiny tubes a few millimetres across. She didn't feel any different afterwards – she was almost tempted to think they'd done nothing at all – but the next scan was better, and the next better still. The babies both survived, seemed to be thriving, and when the talk turned to planning for delivery, Cath and Jim allowed themselves to relax at last. The worst was over, they thought. They could put it behind them and start to count their chickens, just like other expectant parents. They bought tiny car seats and a pram and a cot, filled a chest with baby clothes and painted the little spare room primrose yellow. The date of the Caesarean section was marked on the kitchen calendar with an unassuming star.

The doctors had always said there was a chance of brain damage, but it was a small chance, much less than the odds they'd beaten already. Cath and Jim weren't prepared for it. Looking down at Rose now, her face so calm and sweet, Cath feels another unsteadying gush of love. Emma is stirring, starting to produce those gurning noises that make Jim laugh, but Rose is still asleep, her little body relaxed. She looks so perfect, and she's feeding better than anyone expected. Cath can't bring herself to believe what they've been told about her future.

There are no statistics for love, she thinks suddenly, stubbornly. No scientific papers to measure the effect of the fiery passion that fills her heart every time someone looks at Rose with that sympathetic expression she hates so much. If she loves both girls the same, surely they'll follow the same path? If she loves Rose a little bit more, even – but she doesn't, she couldn't. They are both so precious, so sweetly fragile: she could never, never choose one over the other.

But perhaps – perhaps she loves Rose a little differently. Perhaps she needs to do that. She can't explain it exactly, but she wants to hold Rose closer, to fold her back inside her, to keep her safe from all harm. Most of all, she doesn't want to think about the future. She wants to stop time right now, right here, with her little girls in her arms and the house warm and silent around her, so that nothing can ever go wrong again.

Cath

In the week or two after their evening in St John's Street, Cath finds it hard to put Lara and Nick out of her head. A little voice has settled there, reminding her of them, suggesting things. Encouraging her on. She stops by with a thank-you card one evening, but they're not in, so she posts it through the door and lingers for a moment outside, inspecting the paintwork on the windows. The next Saturday, when Jim's working, she calls in with a cake on which the front of the house is recreated in fondant icing. *You were asking about my baking,* she says: *I thought I'd make you a house cake.*

Driving home, she replays their effusive thanks in her head, and then the evening they spent together. How did they come across, she and Jim? Were they asked out of duty, or because Lara and Nick wanted to get to know them? She's already decided she'll ask them back, but she doesn't want to rush it: she doesn't want Jim to suspect that any undue importance is attached to the invitation. *We really ought to have the tenants round,* she imagines herself saying, in a few more weeks. *It's rather awful that we've left it so long when they went to so much trouble.* Perhaps she'll invite some other people first, some of the friends who've more or less given up on them, these last couple of years.

One day the following week, she passes the new florist in Lingford, its window full of pale sheaves of narcissi which remind her of the ones on Lara and Nick's table, spilling artfully out of an old teapot. She's never particularly liked narcissi, but there's not much else available at this time of year, unless you want exotic blooms air-freighted from sunnier climates.

But then she stops, overtaken by an idea. It would be nice to have an excuse to drop in at St John's Street now and then, she thinks, without having to think of a reason each time. Little things for the house are tricky, because it's let unfurnished, but the garden is a grey area. Of course Lara and Nick could plant things if they wanted, but why should they, if they'd have to leave them behind when they move? Much better, surely, if the garden needs a little more colour – and it certainly does – for Cath to provide it? It's their garden, in the end, hers and Jim's. And she has the time. Lara and Nick both work all week; their leisure time is precious.

For the rest of the day, she savours, mulls, plots. It would be good to see the garden again before buying any plants, and that means asking first. But if they say no, tell her not to worry, then what? Eventually she settles on a plan: she'll buy a couple of pots and plant something spring-flowering in them – camellias, perhaps – and take them down to St John's Street as a fait accompli. Then she can help take them through to the terrace, help decide where they might go, and while she's there she can offer to do more: suggest some annuals in the little flowerbed beside the terrace, a clematis or two on the back fence. How could they object to that?

That evening she's in a good mood. She makes shepherd's pie for supper – Jim's favourite – and finds a bottle of the nice red they drank at Christmas to go with it. She's had another idea about the garden project, too: a way to make the work at St John's Street seem like an overspill of horticultural enthusiasm.

'I thought I'd go to the garden centre tomorrow,' she says. 'I thought we could put some new shrubs in where the sycamore fell last year.'

'Great,' Jim says.

'We could do with a few new bulbs, too,' Cath says, 'and maybe some hanging baskets.'

Jim grins. 'Go for it,' he says. 'I'm all for keeping Squire's in business.'

She can see he's pleased, genuinely pleased, but as the evening goes on she watches him, her curiosity aroused. It's funny how things work in a marriage, she thinks. You're like two cogs in a mechanism, a clock that keeps ticking, turning, marking out the days. If one of you's out of kilter, you might not notice it if you're off balance your-self – but this evening, when she's happier than she's been for a while, she can tell Jim's got something on his mind. But whether it's something new or something old, the old news they both live with all the time, she couldn't say.

When Jim puts Talking Heads on after supper, and gets out an old photography magazine, she's reassured. Perhaps he's just being careful with her, not wanting to read too much into her good mood. These days they both watch each other, she thinks. Walk on eggshells. It's a long time since they've been as easy together as Lara and Nick are.

The next morning Jim sets off late: his first appointment has been cancelled. He brings Cath tea and toast in bed, and she sits up, tray on her knees, as he pulls back the curtains.

'Much more of this treatment and I'll get suspicious,' she says, but he doesn't hear her: he's looking out at the garden.

'Over there, do you mean, for the shrubs?' he says, over his shoulder.

'Yes, where the tree was. Any preference? Camellias?'

'If you like. Yes, camellias.'

Jim turns again, bends to kiss her before he leaves, and Cath feels a little surge of pleasure. An unfamiliar feel-ing these days, and it comes with a kickback that hits her as he closes the bedroom door behind him. Guilt, poi-soning the simple comfort of that kiss.

Guilt at feeling pleasure when Emma is gone. When Rose is gone, too.

She stares at the window, at the spot where Jim stood a moment ago, and lets the turmoil roll through her, the heat and cold of it, spinning her heart like a bicycle wheel upended in the road. Silence, stillness, all around, and the sickening gyre of calamity in its midst.

People said the worst would pass, that she'd come to accept it, but Cath didn't believe them. And it hasn't passed; she hasn't accepted it. She can't understand how anyone could. The rational part of her – the part that says when something bad happens to you, something terrible, you have to find a balance, somehow, between the past and the future; you have to accommodate to a new sort of life – that part does battle, all the time, with the raw pain of loss. The fact that they don't even know what they are accommodating to – desertion, abduction, death – ties them, still, to that first bewildering shock. To the empty room kept ready; the constant, exhausting half-expectation.

But the days have to pass somehow. Days of driving wildly around in search of Emma; days of sitting motionless for so long that her thoughts slowed to a sluggish, dreamlike crawl; days filled with frenzied cleaning, baking, walking. Sometimes, now, she almost doesn't notice the effort of living through them.

Perhaps it's this: her mind hasn't accepted it, but her body has got used to living like this. From the outside, you might not know anything was wrong. Lara and Nick don't know: the Cath they see is ordinary, friendly, competent.

And if she can take pleasure in that, Cath tells herself now – take pleasure in being an ordinary person, and in Jim bringing her tea and toast, kissing her goodbye – isn't she allowed that? Don't they both deserve it?

She slides the tea tray away and gets out of bed. Standing at the window, she looks out at the garden, at the scar where the sycamore tree was. Definitely camellias, she thinks. Something that will flower soon and fill that space with colour.

Jim

Jim has held to his promise not to go back to Dido. For two weeks he's hardly allowed himself to think about her, even when the article about her finally appeared in the *Gazette* and people in the office were talking about how striking his photos were and what great comments there'd been on the piece. *Thanks,* Jim said, and he moved the conversation on to plans for Easter coverage, did his best to enthuse about passion plays and Easter bunny picnics.

His resolve nearly broke the day he thought he saw Emma in Fulford. He badly wanted to tell someone, and he knew it couldn't be Cath. Cath was the only person who would understand the wild flaring of hope during that mad dash down the High Street, but he didn't dare to risk unsettling her, especially just when she seemed a bit brighter.

Jim was cautious about that at first, assuming it was one of those brief flickers of gaiety which have deceived him before, and which always leave Cath more despairing than ever when they burn out. But this time the buoyancy has lasted longer. This time she's seemed different: more engaged, more purposeful. And although Jim can't help seeing the purchase of the house in St John's Street as a turning point, Cath's good mood doesn't seem to hinge on Lara and Nick. She's planting things in the garden, inviting people for supper.

The painful irony, though, is that the upswing in Cath's spirits hasn't summoned an answering rise in his own. The fact that he has things on his mind that she can't know about is somehow harder to bear when Cath is cheerful; when he'd like to be cheerful with her. And the stakes are higher, too, because she has further to fall. He can't bear the thought of what it might do to Cath if she finds out about Dido. Or if he raised her hopes about Emma, only for them to ebb away again.

All of this revolves in his head as he sets off for the dullest day's work he's had in a while: covering a symposium at the university on sustainable IT solutions. How he's supposed to get a good visual out of that, God knows. The sun's shining for the first time in weeks, too: he should be outside, photographing spring lambs.

By one o'clock he's none the wiser about sustainable IT, but he's managed some shots that might lift the science editor's coverage of the event. Some young boffins looking excited around a giant screen, and a great image of an ancient computer that's been brought out of the university archives – a digital-age Tyrannosaurus rex. He's heading for the door when someone hails him.

'Jim!'

He turns, confused. A woman's voice: one he recognises, but can't place. And then, heading towards him across the foyer, he spots Lara. St John's Street Lara. IT, he thinks. Of course.

'Are you here to take photographs?' she asks; then she points at his camera and mimes stupidity.

'I have been,' Jim says. 'I'm on my way out, actually.'

'Oh, you'll miss my presentation!'

'Well, I could …'

'God no, don't stay. I'm going to bore myself, even.' She grins. 'You could take my photo though, if you like. The face of sustainable IT. Mordant would be dead chuffed if it got in the paper.'

'I certainly could. Sustainable IT could do with your face.'

Jim raises an eyebrow, wondering if that's an acceptable remark, but Lara must get worse than that, working in a world of geeky men. She looks different in work mode – it's not just the elegant trouser suit, but the air of purpose and energy. Her hair is swept back in a ponytail which changes the shape of her face somehow. She's very photogenic, Jim thinks.

Lara nods towards the symposium's banner display near the entrance.

'There?' she says. 'It's quite funky, the banner.'

He catches her almost before she's ready, a spontaneous smile that makes it look as though she's advertising a theme park. That'll definitely make the cut, Jim thinks. Much better than the other pictures.

'Give me your company's name again,' he says, 'so we can make sure we spell it right.'

'Will you really use it?' she asks. 'I was joking, about putting it in the paper.'

She looks shy now, an expression he recognises from that night they went for supper. And Jim feels awkward too, suddenly. The mortification of that evening, playing the dependable husband for Lara and Nick when he'd been in Dido's bed all afternoon, is something he won't forget in a hurry.

'You've been so kind, you and Cath,' Lara says. 'We feel so fortunate to have – well, you feel like more than landlords.'

Jim pulls a face. 'I'm not sure we'd have liked landlords who were more than landlords at your age. Ours kept his distance. Especially when something went wrong.'

'Oh no – we like the fact that Cath pops in,' Lara says. 'She's so thoughtful. You both are.'

Cath pops in? Jim thinks. He's on the point of asking more – how often? what for? – but Lara's already answering.

'She brought us a lovely cake last week,' she says. 'You were right about her baking. Did you see it? It had the house on top, in icing. So clever.'

*

Driving away, Jim ponders. A cake, he thinks. A house-warming present, a few weeks back. Perhaps other things, other thoughtful touches: would they have thought to ask the landlords round, otherwise? Maybe it doesn't matter. It's harmless enough, fussing over the tenants, and they seem appreciative, but ... He sighs. It's a terrible thing, losing children. If it *is* the tenants who've cheered her up, shouldn't he be grateful? Lara and Nick must have their own parents: they'll know how to keep her at arm's length. And she's not stupid, Cath.

So why does it bother him, then? Is he jealous? Certainly it worries him that she hasn't been entirely upfront about it, but perhaps she knows he'd disapprove. Worry. Well, he mustn't be cross with her. Mustn't resent them. And he's not; he doesn't. But it all feels like such a tangle: none of his emotions are what they should be. He longs for calm and reassurance. For consolation.

Before he knows it, he's turned on to the Dorking road. There are fields, he tells himself. There might be lambs. But he knows perfectly well where he's going.

Lara

Lara sees Cath's car pulling up a few minutes before the doorbell rings. It's a Sunday morning, and she and Nick are still in their pyjamas with cups of coffee and the Sunday papers. Nick has always liked paper papers, spread across the sofa, and she's been thinking what a perfect scene this is. *Hygge.* That word's all over social media at the moment, and they've got it to a tee. There's even something a little bit Danish about the house, now she comes to think of it. All the bare wood, the white paint, the checked curtains.

So she feels a twinge of annoyance when she sees Cath's car – not so much because of the scene being interrupted as because it reminds her that it's not really theirs, this idyll. They're just borrowing it, living it for a while. But then, she tells herself severely, there's all the more reason to be grateful to Cath. So she pushes herself up out of her chair – 'Cath's here, Nick' – and goes to the door, pulling it open just as the bell rings.

'You must think I'm an awful nuisance,' Cath begins. 'But I was at the garden centre yesterday and I thought you could do with a couple of pots out the back. On the terrace.'

'Oh, that's kind!'

'The weather seems to be settling,' Cath says. 'We might even get a spring, eventually. You'll be able to sit outside soon, and I just thought it looked a bit bleak.'

'We've hardly been out there yet,' Lara admits. 'Nick keeps talking about the apple tree, though. I think he's hoping for a crop.'

'Blossom, before that,' Cath says. 'You ought to get some blossom.' She pauses, taking in Lara's pyjamas. 'I'm sorry; I shouldn't have come so early. I'll just – let me get the pots, and I'll—'

'Nick can do that,' Lara says. 'Don't you lift them.'

Nick's upstairs: she knows he'll be funny about Cath turning up when they're not expecting her, when they're both in their pyjamas, and she wants to make sure Cath doesn't get wind of that. Cath's already protesting, but Lara insists.

'Nick!' she calls again, her voice brighter, louder. 'Cath's brought us some pots for the garden. Can you give her a hand?' She smiles at Cath. 'Come in and have a coffee, while he's sorting himself out.'

The pots look great: there are three of them, one bigger than the other two, and they position them in a triangle in the corner of the terrace so you can see them from the kitchen window. They've each got the same kind of bush planted in them, with dark, glossy leaves, and different coloured buds on each one. Red, white, pink. So pretty. *Hygge* for the garden, Lara thinks. Nick's gone back inside to answer his phone, but she and Cath stand for a moment, admiring them.

'They're beautiful,' she says. 'How clever of you. I don't know anything about plants, I'm afraid.'

'They're camellias,' Cath says. 'They should flower for several weeks. It's nice to have a bit of colour in the garden at this time of year.' She moves over to inspect the dead-looking bushes at the side. 'I think this might be a ceanothus,' she says. 'A Californian lilac. Autumn-flowering, but that's rather nice. There's not always a lot of colour in the autumn, either. Bright blue.'

'It's exciting, not knowing what's coming,' Lara says.

'That's what happens when you move into a house in the winter. Surprises all the way. Not that there'll be many here: it's a bit sparse, I'm afraid.' Cath looks around. 'It could do with a bit more planting, really,' she says. 'A clematis or two on the fences; maybe a nice shrub in that corner.'

'We're not really gardeners,' Lara says, 'but I suppose we could learn.' For a moment she imagines them, her and Nick, digging and harvesting: another strand to the country-living dream.

'I'd be happy to do the planting,' Cath says. 'If we'd had the place for a bit longer before you moved in, we'd have tackled the garden.' She pauses. 'I could come during the week, while you're at work. You don't need me intruding on your weekends.'

'Are you sure?' Lara hesitates. She's not sure how hard she should protest. But it's their garden, she reminds herself – Cath and Jim's. If Cath wants to plant things in it, so much the better for them.

Nick reappears then, his coffee cup crooked in his arm, and Lara smiles at him.

'Cath's going to do some work on the garden,' she says. 'Isn't that nice of her?'

Nick

Nick waits until he's at his desk to open the letter. He found it in the pile of junk mail when they got home the night before, then shoved it in his pocket and forgot about it until this morning. All the way to London he ignored it, but now he takes it out and looks at it for a moment before slicing it open with a pen.

His mother's writing. No one else writes him letters by hand, but even so he couldn't mistake it. In his mind, it forms notes stuck on the fridge, propped against empty wine glasses, stuffed under his bedroom door. The content of the notes hasn't changed much, he thinks. Explanations, apologies, requests. The emotions they elicit haven't changed much either.

He likes to think his own marriage is the silver lining to the cloud that hung over his childhood, but it could easily have gone the other way, he knows. Some children – boys, especially – shy away from marriage when they've seen it go so wrong. That was him, wasn't it, until he met Lara? He certainly didn't want to run the risk of behaving like his dad. And his mum – he loved his mum; loves her still. He never blamed her, except that it's hard for kids not to blame their mothers when they're not like other mums. Not coping.

He remembers the moment he told Lara: their first date, a few weeks after he'd started at Mordant. *My dad left when I was five,* he found himself saying, over a gin and tonic in the bar she'd suggested. *Just took off, left us in the lurch.*

Lara's eyes had widened then, and Nick felt her sympathy flowing through him, percolating back through the years.

'What did he—' Lara began.

'Another woman,' Nick said. 'Younger, of course. He had two kids with her, then left them too, three years later. He went to the States, she said. She came looking for us, thought we might know more. Bastard.'

'How awful,' Lara said.

'It was really tough on my mum,' Nick said. 'You'd think it'd be better to know it wasn't just you, that he'd done it again, but it wasn't.' He drained the gin, stared at the empty glass. He'd never said any of this to anyone before; never even framed it in his mind, really, as something you could say. 'She struggled. Drank. There were lots of men. Some for a while, a few years. Not very nice, most of them. I used to be glad I was a boy, and big for my age. I tried to make things easier for her, but I couldn't wait to leave home. I used to dream about it. I went as far away as I could to college.'

There was a little silence after that, just long enough for Nick to register that Lara was going to say something important too. He remembers that moment – feeling the energy of it rising inside her.

'My parents died when I was seventeen,' she said. 'A car crash. I've been – well, on my own, really, ever since.'

'God.'

Nick felt terrible, then, for complaining about his parents. Stupid arse, he thought. What would Lara think of him now? But she was smiling at the dismay in his face: a slightly strained smile, but definitely a smile.

'Don't worry,' she said. 'You weren't to know. And it's OK, really. I'm OK. They were – well, we didn't – they were very religious.'

She didn't like to talk about her parents; he discovered that pretty quickly. That was probably the longest conversation they'd ever had about them. But at the time, it sealed something between them. Nick made some clumsy comment, and then he blushed, and Lara laughed, and in a few moments they'd moved through laughing and crying and into kissing. And that was that, really.

It's easy, he thinks now, when you meet the right person. He and Lara are a perfect fit: they need each other, and they want the same things, the same life. And he'll never leave her. He'd like to keep her in a little bubble, just the two of them, shut off from the rest of the world. That's what he thought the house in Lingford would be, a place no one could get them. But his mum's letters keep coming, wanting to see him. Wanting affection, attention. Forgiveness.

And there's the landlords, too. Cath especially, turning up on Sunday mornings with pots of flowers. Nice of her, Lara said, and of course she's right, but even so Nick wishes she wouldn't. Wishes his phone hadn't buzzed at just the wrong moment, so he wasn't there when Lara agreed to let her come back and do things in the garden. He wants it to be their place, not to be reminded all the time that it's not. He doesn't want there to be strings attached: he resents the suggestion that they need help, that there should be space in their lives for Cath and Jim, or for anyone else.

He mustn't overreact, he tells himself, as he scans his mother's letter. There's no point getting worked up. And anyway, his mum's not asking for anything this time. She's going on a cruise with someone called Robert. The way she refers to him makes it sound as though Nick ought to know who he is, but he's pretty certain he hasn't heard the name before. *Let's get together when I'm back*, she says. *Hope all's good with you.*

Nick reads the letter twice, looking for a catch, then tears it in half and throws it in the bin. A cruise, eh? In his mind's eye he sees himself opening the empty cupboards, looking for something to eat before school. Their children won't have to do that: another promise. They'll have bike rides and picnics and days at the seaside. He can give them all that. He and Lara.

APRIL

Jim

Jim's feelings for Dido are so different from his feelings for Cath that it's hard to see what he's doing as a betrayal. They occupy separate zones in his mind and his heart, as well as his life: as different, he thinks, struggling to explain it to himself, as the feelings you have for a friend, a parent, a child. A spouse, a lover ... his conscience completes the list, goading him, but it's not like that, he tells himself. Not like the cliché – the thrill and sexual charge of a mistress versus the dreary familiarity of a marriage. Sorrow and misfortune are not dull, and what he has with Dido is less piquant than the word *affair* suggests. There's a powerful sense of soothing, unburdening. Healing. He feels like an injured knight who has stumbled into the bower of a benevolent enchantress.

Dido's story is simpler than his. She's been married, but never had children. When the divorce was finalised two years ago she took stock of her position and decided to follow her dream with the cosmetics business. And here she is, she says with a smile, as she finishes this brief sketch of her history. Here she is, ready for Jim to arrive out of the blue: her situation perfectly designed, he thinks wonderingly, to offer what he needs.

He's under no illusion that he can give what she deserves in return, but life has made her self-reliant. She doesn't want another husband – she doesn't spell that out, but he infers as much. What would she do with one at this point? Her business is flourishing, and she's tried marriage once. But that leaves Jim wondering what she might want from him. She likes sex, certainly, and that he can give. Sex with Cath has dwindled, like so many other things, and he's been surprised how little, how relatively little, that has mattered to him. But as the weeks pass, he realises he's missed it more than he thought. It's delicious, sex with Dido: as delicious as her gingerbread hinted, that first time they met. It's warm and supple and richly spiced, and there's always more of it, a ready supply for these lazy, clandestine afternoons. Her body is more youthful than he expected, unblemished by childbirth. It's stocky, sturdy even, but soft, too; dark hair sprouts unrestrained in her armpits, between her legs, even around her nipples – curling strands that brush his lips when he kisses her, and makes her back arch and twist luxuriously.

Everything else, he realises, she is accustomed to providing for herself. Coals to Newcastle, she tells him gently when he asks, clumsily, what her favourite per-fume is. She likes scarves; she wears them often, wispy lengths of silk or muslin that she flicks out of the way as she stirs the pots on her hotplates, but she has plenty of those, too. She doesn't expect presents. And that's a relief, he admits, because bringing gifts would feel like too much of a stereotype for this delicately balanced arrangement. But even so, he feels a little guilty.

'What can I do for you, Dido?' he asks her, one after-noon. His fifth visit: he's still keeping count.

'Right now?' Her hand slides down his flank; she grins.

He lifts his hand to tuck a lock of hair behind her ear. 'Right now, or in general.'

'What makes you think you're not doing enough?'

'Am I?'

She shakes her head lazily, and the lock of hair falls forwards again.

'I don't know why you keep asking. Do you feel bad about it? About coming here?' She hesitates. 'On my account, I mean. I know ...'

'No,' he says. There's a stab of guilt then, but it's true. Coming here makes him feel anything but bad.

'Well then.'

'But I mean – would you like to – go out for lunch?'

A frown presses down her eyebrows. Her face isn't used to frowning, Jim thinks. It doesn't fold itself into worry lines the way most people's do at her age.

'Is that what you'd like?' she asks. 'Wouldn't it be a risk?'

'Yes,' he says. 'But if—'

'Ssh.' She touches her finger to his mouth, to his chin. 'Don't let's complicate things, Jim. We're safe here. No one can find us.'

And so that's that: their space, their time. A time out of time, Jim thinks; a space capsule that could carry them forwards through the years with nothing ever changing inside it. Dido will never grow old, cocooned in her bower with her balms and lotions, and perhaps the Jim who visits her won't either. If only their time together could be made to disappear from the workaday calendar altogether, they would be untraceable. But, as it is, things are as well arranged as they could be. His schedule is his own, and as long as he fulfils his assignments no one asks him to account for hours and minutes. And if Cath wanted him, she would call his mobile phone, and he'd answer.

But they're circumscribed, even so, these carefully camouflaged hours. Stretch them too long and the disguise will falter; the embezzlement will be suspected. Jim leans forward to kiss Dido once more – an unhurried kiss, lingering in the secret places he's still exploring – and she understands what it means.

'I'm away, next week,' she says later, as he pulls on his clothes. 'At a trade fair in Derby.'

'Derby,' he says. 'Well, I'll have to survive without you, then.'

Cath is happy again that evening. He can almost see it, Jim thinks, floating around her – a shawl of happiness brushing her shoulders. Is it entirely down to St John's Street, to Nick and Lara? Has she been down to see them again?

But as he watches her stirring soup, something else occurs to him. If it *was* Emma he saw that day in Fulford – if she's really that close to home – perhaps she's been in touch with Cath. Surely, though – surely Cath would have told him? He didn't tell Cath that *he'd* seen her, of course, but that's because he wasn't certain it was Emma, and he was afraid of offering Cath false hope. But if Cath had met Emma, spoken to her – might something prevent her from telling him? A baby, perhaps? Why would either of them want to keep that from him? A man, then; a man Emma might not want her father to meet. But no – Cath would tell Emma that was nonsense. This whole idea is nonsense.

They don't talk much while they eat, and Jim's more conscious, tonight, of the bits of his day that have to be filleted out. He notices the particular pieces of silence they might have occupied. And then he thinks of a reason why Cath might not have told him, if she'd heard from Emma. A reason happiness might hover around her, rather than filling her up.

He stops eating, a spoonful of soup resting on the edge of his bowl.

Adultery. The word sounds in his mind for the first time as he looks into the face of his wife.

If Cath knew – if she suspected that he was seeing someone else, sleeping with someone else – what would she feel? What would she do?

He thinks of her as fragile, vulnerable, but she's used to bad news, to bearing things. She might brush it off, not want to know for sure. She might. But might she not feel, if a consolation was offered to her, that she deserved to keep it for herself?

He breathes in, out; takes up his spoon again. If Cath has noticed the pause, she doesn't comment on it. No, he thinks. She's not cruel, Cath. And she's no actress: she couldn't sit here with him, drinking soup and talking about the garden, if she had such a secret.

And then he looks down at his hands, the fingers that traced the line of Dido's ear, her mouth, only two hours before.

Perhaps this is what happens to deceivers: they see deception all around them. Their own treachery, reflected back at them in the eyes of the people they betray.

Cath

Tuesday and Thursday have become Cath's gardening days. The idea of working on both gardens in parallel pleases her: for one thing, their own has been neglected this last couple of years and deserves some attention, and for another, it ekes out the time she can spend at St John's Street. The garden there is so small that even the most elaborate plans couldn't be dragged out for long, but if she spends an hour there for every three or four at home, she'll be kept busy for weeks. And this way, working on her own garden feels like part of the same project; part of the same secret pleasure. When she can, she buys the same plants for both gardens. Sometimes they're on special offer, three for two, and she has the satisfaction of getting something for St John's Street free.

She takes her time choosing plants that will work well together and cover as long a season as possible: a

late-flowering Polish Spirit clematis, which should produce velvety purple flowers against the back fence from
midsummer, and a row of climbing roses – Queen of
Sweden, a pretty pink – along the side boundary. An
easy-care deutzia and a dwarf forsythia, tucked in beside
the ceanothus at the edge of the terrace. A pair of currant
bushes, black and red, in the far corner, where she hopes
they'll get enough light to flourish. And an array of bedding plants – geranium, impatiens, petunia, lobelia – to
fill every inch of the beds with garish colour. Hanging
baskets would be lovely too, but there are no brackets,
and whether she put some up herself or asked Jim or
Nick to help her, it would seem, she fears, a step too far.
Better to stick to what can be done with the appearance
of minimal effort.

Lara has given her a set of keys so she can let herself
in – there's no side gate, so it means coming through the
house each time. She and Jim have a key anyway, of
course, stashed away in the box file with the papers for
the house, but Cath uses the ones Lara gives her, and she
leaves a note in the kitchen each time so they know she's
been. The first time, made thirsty by her digging, she
finds a glass for water, then washes it up and puts it back.
The next time, a cold day, she decides it would do no
harm to make herself a cup of tea, and while the kettle's
boiling she has a quick look in the cupboards to see what
they have in the way of cooking equipment. In case she
ever needs an idea for a present, she thinks. The sight of
their pans, their mixing bowls, their colander and sieve

and scales, tug at her heart. So new, so carefully chosen. She straightens a cushion on the sofa on the way out that day, patting it down so it'll be more comfortable when Lara or Nick sits down that evening. It's not the kind of cushion she would buy – a ring of roses and *Home Sweet Home* in loopy writing in the middle – but it makes her smile.

The time after that, she needs a pee before she leaves, so she climbs the stairs and tiptoes into the bathroom, as though the neighbours might hear her. The bathroom smells good. She looks at the row of bottles on the shelf while she's washing her hands, but she doesn't touch them, and afterwards she scuttles downstairs, feeling slightly shame-faced. The next time, she comes straight through the house when she arrives and straight out again at the end, to prove to herself that she's not on a slippery slope. There's no harm, anyway, she tells herself. In the normal way of things, they'd come and inspect the house formally once a quarter, and she has no intention of doing that.

That day she stops at the farm shop on the way home to buy eggs, and while she's queuing to pay for them her eye is caught by a display of jams. Shades of red and purple: strawberry, raspberry, boysenberry. She stops.

Boysenberry.

A vivid memory, not here, but somewhere … Emma, aged five or six, spelling out the word delightedly – *boys and berries!* – then chanting it all the way home. For weeks after that, every time Cath asked her what she'd like for breakfast, she said, 'Boys and berries jam, of course. I only eat boys and berries.' Cath had to keep buying it, going back to the same place – where was it? – to stock up. And then, as these things do, the phase passed and the phrase slipped away, lost between the cracks of memory. Cath hasn't thought about it for years. There must be a hundred other incidents, other little anecdotes, that she doesn't think of any more.

And then it occurs to her, with a shock she feels like a sudden pressure in her chest, that she hasn't thought about Emma at all today. What about yesterday? When did she think of her yesterday? She can't remember. She's never not thought of her before.

And if she hasn't thought of Emma for a couple of days, how long is it since she thought of Rose?

She feels queasy now. She's allowed herself to be distracted, she thinks. She's allowed herself to be happy. Too happy.

She almost leaves the eggs on top of the jam display, but she's at the front of the queue now, so she fumbles in her purse for the right change so that she can hand it over and get out of here. When she gets home, she sits down at the kitchen table and lets the tears she's fought all the way home fall unrestrained. The dog heaves himself out of his bed and shuffles over to lay his head on her knee, tail beating uncertainly against the table leg, and she lets her hand rest on his back, glad of his warmth and the animal smell of him. For fully half an hour, she weeps silently, with Hector silent, staunch, beside her.

And then she gets up, goes upstairs, opens the hatch to let down the loft ladder and climbs up into the darkness. The dog, who rarely tackles the stairs any more, lumbers after her and stands at the bottom of the ladder, confused. As she fumbles for the light switch, Cath can hear him whining.

'Lie down, Hector,' she says, surprised to hear her voice sounding steady. 'Good boy. Lie down.'

It's colder than she expects up here, and dusty. But she finds the switch and fills the space between the sloping rafters with cloudy light. Jim spent some time sorting and organising last summer, she remembers: he took some old furniture to the dump to make room for the stuff he brought from his father's house. Where would he have put the baby boxes, the most precious of the loft's contents?

There. Two large plastic boxes with clip-down lids, bright blue. Did Jim open them, she wonders, when he was up here? If he did, he didn't tell her.

At first she can't work out how to get the lids off, but then she finds the right place to squeeze and lift, and the top comes away from the first box. This is the earlier one: the one she's after. At the top are a sheaf of pictures Emma did when she was four or five. She loved drawing, Cath remembers. When did that stop? Here's the house, look, with the dog outside – not Hector but Rex, his predecessor. And this one – she can't tell what it's meant to be, but on the back, in Cath's handwriting, it says, *Bees that make honey*. And another: *Fairies in the woods.*

And then – a self-portrait, she thinks, a smiling figure with spiky hair and a striped blue dress and beside her, lying on the ground, a black outline of a girl wearing the same striped dress. Her heart jolts. On the back, in her handwriting, it says, *My shadow's called Rose, and she's got a blue stripey dress on too.*

She can feel tears rising again as she puts the shadow picture back with the others. Below the sheaf of drawings there are letters, nursery school reports (*Emma socialises well and is learning to share*), a few pieces of clothing she couldn't bear to throw away – though not that blue dress. Tiny gloves with clown faces on the fingers; a pair of shoes, scuffed at the ends, with tight buckles. Children don't wear buckled shoes any more, she thinks. They all had Velcro fastenings at St Mary's. On down: yes. Letters from the hospital, from the physios, from Children's Services. A little cardigan that wasn't Emma's. And near the bottom, two red plastic baby record books. Two pink wrist bands: *Female infant 1 of Cath Polkinghorne; Female infant 2 of Cath Polkinghorne.*

She sits back on her heels, her hands trembling. How little they've kept, she thinks. Photographs, in the albums downstairs. Official documents in the filing drawer in the study. Otherwise … But there were no drawings, of course. There were no school reports, no letters to Father Christmas or notes for the tooth fairy. Looking at the evidence in these boxes, you could be forgiven for thinking that they'd hardly noticed Rose's existence.

But that wasn't how it was. If anything, Rose took too much of their time. The tears that start to fall again now are tears of regret for the years when she could have immersed herself in Emma, savoured every moment of her childhood, and tears of guilt, equal and opposite, for the suggestion that she resented any of the time and energy and anguish she gave to Rose. Tears of frustration and sorrow that she had to make that choice.

Losing Emma was ... it felt like a double loss, she thinks. A blow upon a bruise. They always knew Rose might die, but it never occurred to them that Emma might run away. And Rose – Rose was always a shadow of herself. A shadow of Emma. The image of Rose, of who she might have been: Emma took that with her, too.

Fairy Babies

When she comes into the twins' room, Cath's heart jumps. Emma's leaning over the side of the cot, her hands reaching towards her sister.

'What are you doing, darling?' she asks.

'I'm talking to Rose.'

Emma straightens up, and Cath can see Rose now, lying in her cot, exactly as she left her.

'I'm telling her a story. She likes stories.'

'That's nice of you. What story are you telling her?'

'Oh, just one about fairies. There are fairy babies in it.'

Cath smiles. Fairies are the flavour of the month: she is under instructions to make a fairy birthday cake this year, and Emma has built a fairy house at the end of the garden, for use in bad weather.

'There are two fairy babies called Emma and Rose,' Emma goes on. 'And Emma isn't very well.'

'Emma *isn't very well?*' Cath asks, before she can stop herself.

Emma shakes her head solemnly. 'Emma is poorly, and Rose has to look after her.' She lowers her eyebrows, daring Cath to contradict her. 'Rose is telling Emma a story.'

'I see. That's kind of her.'

Cath hesitates for a moment, then she sits down in the armchair, a little way off from the cot. Sometimes it astonishes her what goes on in Emma's mind. Is it the same with all children? she wonders. She thinks of an article she read recently about stem cells, the extraordinary potential they have before they're channelled in a particular direction – and she thinks, too, of Brave New World, *with its categories of citizen, shaped from birth to fit the requirements of society. Is that what happens to children? By approving some ideas and actions, and censoring others, we shape them into useful citizens who accept the status quo?*

Not Emma, she thinks; she won't let that happen to Emma. In any case the status quo, for Emma, is more complicated than it is for most children. Cath feels a surge of affection for her, so great that she has to resist the desire to whisk her into her arms and kiss her.

Emma is speaking again now, in a squeaky tone Cath assumes at first must be meant as a fairy voice.

'Do you know that, Emma?' she says. 'Do you know 'bout fairy babies? They are borned in the garden, fairy babies, and when they're poorly they sisters has to make them better.'

There's a tiny pause, and then Emma resumes, in her own voice.

'I don't know that, Rose,' she says.

'Yes, they do,' the squeaky voice says. 'They always has to make them better.'

'How do they make them better, Rose?' asks Emma's voice.

A longer pause. 'I will tell you, Emma,' says Rose's squeak. 'But first I got to tell you a story. Once upon a time, there was – there was …'

'Tell me one about Emma and Rose,' suggests Emma's voice. 'Tell me once upon a time there were two sisters called Emma and Rose.'

From where she's sitting, Cath can see Rose's face, blinking, impassive. They don't know whether she can hear; the doctors think she probably can't. Certainly she can't see. But when Emma speaks to her, touches her, she blinks.

Lara

Some days they don't notice Cath has been until they find her note, propped against the kettle. *I've put in a couple of currant bushes in the corner. If it stays dry, could you bear to water them? Or Clematis on the back fence has lovely purple flowers. I hope you'll get a few this summer.* Other days there's a sign – the post picked up from the floor and placed on the coffee table, or a shopping list that has fallen out of her pocket. Each time, when Lara realises she's been, she goes out into the garden to see what Cath has done today.

The day the flowers appear in the bed beside the terrace she's home before Nick: she wasn't feeling well, she told them at work, and she left early. It's strange being here without him. The house feels smaller, somehow. It ought to be the other way round, but he brings it alive, she thinks. Without him, the rooms are just empty spaces, white walls.

But it's easier to think without Nick here, and she needs to think. She stares at the flowers – lots of different kinds, and lots of different colours, their petals drooping slightly and flecked, here and there, with earth. Not properly rooted in yet, she thinks, so it would be the work of a moment to pull them up again.

She hasn't done a test yet, because once she does, she'll have to tell Nick. And then she'll have to tell him other things, and he'll wonder why she hasn't told him those before. She hopes he'll understand, feels sure he will, but even so she dreads telling him: dreads telling him any of it, which is terrible, because this news, the new news, should be happy. The news she's kept to herself for a few weeks now, counting off the days and measuring out the symptoms.

But the way things are going, she can't put it off much longer. A couple of mornings feeling off colour; a couple of early nights; one day crying off work early. Nick will start worrying about her, and she wants to tell him before he guesses.

So there are things she needs to think through. Things she needs to work out.

She goes back into the house and puts the kettle on. She can't face coffee or tea; that's happened already. Herb tea, though. Camomile. She takes a cup up to bed and climbs under the covers – such a comfort, to be in bed. Her own bed in this dear little house that they both love so much. All she wants to do now is sleep, but she mustn't, not yet.

What has she told Nick? Start there. Can she remember how she put it, when they first met? *My parents died when I was seventeen. I've been on my own ever since.* Yes, something like that. Not: *They threw me out. They disowned me.* She'd wanted to tell him that, wanted him to understand the hurt and the abandonment, but there'd have been too many questions, too much to explain. It had been easier to lie. She was used to the lie, used to thinking it was harmless – but she'd already known, by then, that Nick was more important than other people. With him it wasn't just about keeping things simple, guarding her privacy. She should have told him the truth, after a few weeks, a few months. But the truth was complicated. She hadn't dared; hadn't known where to start.

They were very religious. Yes, he knew that. He'd grown up without religion, Nick, without any at all, not even church at Christmas, so it wouldn't have taken much to convince him that her parents were crackpots. Fanatics. But they'd been loving parents too, convinced their way was right. She knew what it had cost them, cutting their only child out of their lives.

She's crying now, soaking the beautiful white pillowcase with tears. *I left home because I got pregnant, had an abortion.* She can't say that. She can't even say it to herself, out loud. The undertow of her childhood pulls the words out of reach whenever she tries to speak them. *I had to choose between my family and my freedom.* That sounds brave, admirable. But perhaps, she thinks now, it was cowardice, not courage, that carried her away from her parents. If she'd dared to stand up to them in little ways ... but she never had. And with no leeway, no middle ground to explore, she'd let her mind wander into the wilderness, where bad things could happen. Bad things like Jacob Turner, son of one of the elders in their community, a boy graced with such beauty that Lara had been half in love with him for as long as she could remember.

A boy of Jacob's lineage was to be trusted absolutely, and certainly allowed to walk Lara home after youth-group meetings. Of course it was Jacob who'd taken the initiative: Lara had been seventeen, a bashful, blushing seventeen, barely cognisant of the facts of life, even if the currents of desire running through her were adult enough. No, it was Jacob who'd taken her hand and led her through a gate in the winter darkness, across a field towards a tree which cast a deeper shadow over the ground beneath it as his hands touched her, raising a quivering rash of lust and fear wherever they went.

But it was Lara who was blamed. Immorality came from Eve; everyone knew that. She didn't even dare to name him: she'd have been accused of lying, or of seducing an innocent young man; perhaps of both. If there was any truth in their teachings, Jacob would be punished in good time – and if he believed any of it, he would have to live with that.

Resting her cheek against the cool cotton, Lara remembers what it felt like. Not what she did with Jacob: the aftermath. The next morning, it had been as though nothing had happened. The waters had closed over it, in her mind, like an obscure verse of scripture she half remembered reading (although that, for certain, was a sacrilegious thought). It was what came next that she remembers: the sickness, the lethargy, the lack of bleeding; all of it noticed, fretted over, by her mother. There were prayers and tonics, rest and then hard work. There was weeping, perplexity, anger. It was the work of the devil, she heard her parents saying, when they thought she was asleep. Exorcism was mentioned, in hushed tones, behind closed doors.

And then Lara felt better. There was still no bleeding, but she lied, pretended she'd had a little, and that satisfied her mother. She ate and ate, regaining the weight she'd lost when she was sick, and her parents nodded in satisfaction. She gained a little more, and they reminded her of the sin of greed. She was eighteen weeks pregnant by the time she could no longer deny what was happening.

Her parents were incredulous. If she'd told them she'd been visited by an angel, Lara thought later, they would have believed her. The idea of natural conception, the desecration of her body, was almost impossible for them to grasp. And Lara denied any immoral behaviour. She'd certainly shown no signs of it, either before that evening with Jacob or after: he had never touched her again, and his manner towards her hadn't changed. He, too, had let that evening slip into dreamland, Lara thought. He had needed to know what it was like, perhaps, just once, and then the muffling blanket of scriptural teaching had settled back over his mind.

So puzzling was the situation to Lara's parents that they were almost ready to accept that the baby was an anomaly – a gift from God, even – and to raise it, quietly and discreetly. But that, Lara saw, would be the end of her life. To live in this community was bad enough: to live out of sight in it was impossible.

So when they took her to see a doctor, she told him she wanted an abortion. With her parents out of the room, she said that she'd been raped by someone in the community and that her parents were covering it up. Once she'd stated her case, she was unshakable. And after that terrible night, the arguments and tears and accusations that tore them all apart once the doctor confronted her parents, she never saw them again. She vanished not just from their lives but from her own: she changed her name from Ruth (a terrible irony for a child who proved to be so ruthless) to Lara, and changed her story too. A car crash was simple; it made people feel sorry for her, but not in the same way the truth would have done. It drew a line under the past.

Sometimes, in the months that followed, Lara longed to turn back. The reality of life as a lone seventeen-year-old, without the protections or the certainties of the community she'd grown up in, was harder than she could have imagined. The route from the gynae ward at the hospital in Salisbury to her job at Mordant is easy to describe – a sequence of sentences – but living through it was daunting, even with the kindnesses she received from unexpected sources along the way. The charity that housed her while she worked her way through her A levels by cleaning offices six hours a day; the teacher who helped her apply for financial support at university; the lecturer who noticed when she was struggling – not with the course, but the sudden liberties of university life.

Nick knows some of this. The sequence of sentences: the cleaning jobs, the route through university. It seems to Lara that the rest is barely part of her any more, but even so, she knows she has to tell him. The doctors need to know about the termination, the blood loss afterwards, and she can hardly keep that information from her husband now it's relevant to her antenatal care. To the safety of their baby.

Jim

The week Dido's away passes very slowly. Jim is sharply conscious of the hours he might have spent with her – the times when he could have wound up an appointment early or delayed going to the next – and it makes him feel his life has always had these gaps in it; that there's always been space for Dido, waiting to be filled. At the same time, it seems utterly fanciful that he should be doing this: conducting an affair in plain sight. But the voice of his conscience, incredulous at what he's done, is crowded out by astonishment that Dido might want him, anxiety that she might not. He longs for her to be back, to re-assure him.

It doesn't help that it's an uneventful week at work. With Easter behind them, there are no more cheery events to punctuate the familiar round until the May bank holiday. The best of it is a feature on the prettiest

Surrey villages, and an afternoon spent in pursuit of bluebells. But tramping through woodland, Jim can never help thinking of Julianne Roberts, dragged among the trees and left there to be found by a Jack Russell terrier. The sea of blue feels like the battlefields' poppies: a dazzle of colour to remind you, forever, of atrocities.

Meanwhile, Cath has been busy in the garden, planting currant bushes and azaleas and a swathe of bedding plants. She never does things by half, Cath: coming home to find bags of compost piled at the side of the house, Jim feels a prick of disquiet, but he tells himself it's a healthy preoccupation. Better than hanging around St John's Street, mentioning Lara and Nick in every other sentence; much better than sitting at the kitchen table hour after hour. The gardening phase will peter out, he expects, just as the cake-making did, but every phase carries her forwards a little – or so he hopes. And his panic the other night has passed: if Cath has noticed anything out of the ordinary about his behaviour, found any evidence of Dido in his pockets or in slips of his tongue, she hasn't mentioned it.

He knows there's a ravine beneath him, something deep and dangerous he's skirting around all the time, but pretending it's not there is part of the spell. It seems to him a good thing that he doesn't feel guilty: it means he's not giving away anything that belongs to Cath, and that his attitude to her isn't distorted by over-carefulness. If he feels an extra burst of warmth towards Cath from time to time, it arises as much from relief that she's less sad, just at the moment, as from the prospect of Dido's return.

And in any case, there's nothing so unusual about offering to take Cath out for supper. That's what he'll do, he decides, one afternoon towards the end of the week: text her from Gomhurst (number seven in the list of prettiest Surrey villages) and suggest a curry tonight. Or whatever she fancies. If she's been gardening, she ought to have an appetite.

Cath doesn't reply, but that's not unusual. Her phone's probably in a coat pocket. Jim's planned to cut the day short – he started early, this morning – and get home in time to admire whatever she's done in the garden, perhaps have a glass of wine before they go out. So when his phone rings at four thirty, he's already back in the car. He glances down at it while he's looking for a place to pull over and sees a number, not a name. A number he hasn't saved on his phone just in case Cath ever has a reason to look through his contacts. Without stopping the car, he flicks the screen to accept the call.

'Hello,' he says. 'How's Derby?'

'Dull,' she replies. 'Which is why I've come home early.'

It's the first time he's lied to Cath, and even this is a small lie. Another text, to say he's been held up, but he'll be back by seven; they can still go out, if she fancies it.

Dido is wearing different clothes from usual. *Conference clothes*, Jim says. *Estate agent clothes*, she replies with a smile, and Jim has a sudden image of the two of them in an empty house, someone else's house, and him removing the little navy jacket, the silk blouse, the skirt that sits snugly, curvaceously, around her thighs.

'Don't,' he says, a groan of a word, and she looks at him curiously, amusedly.

'You missed me,' she says. 'That's dangerous—' But he's kissing her by now and the words are half-lost, a movement against his mouth that makes him groan again and draw her towards him, her body warm beneath the thick wool of the suit.

If there's been any hesitation before, any moderation, it's gone now. They're head to head in the gallop towards consummation, pulling and pushing at each other until they're both naked, tumbled on the bed, finding their way together.

'Bloody hell,' Jim says, when they're done. 'Sorry, I ...'

'No sorries,' Dido says. 'That's the rule.' In the evening light she looks like a pre-Raphaelite Madonna, her eyes half-shut. 'I didn't even give you a cup of tea,' she says.

'I've been thinking about that.' Jim grins. 'I've been thinking it was pretty inhospitable of you.'

She smiles too, but she still doesn't open her eyes.

'Do you want one?' she asks. 'Or a glass of wine?'

'No. Thank you.'

'You need to go.'

'Not just yet.' He looks across at her alarm clock: five forty-five. 'Not for a while yet.'

'Good.'

He hesitates, watching her. She looks more like a wife than a mistress, he thinks. It's Cath who's the beauty – who has been, anyway. That fact has been part of his absurd rationale, he realises. This can't be a love affair, because Dido is plump and uncomplicated, while Cath still has her temptress eyes and the emotional turmoil to go with them.

'I don't want to make things difficult for you,' Dido says.

He turns, sees that she's looking at him. Can she read his face so well?

'You don't.'

'Maybe not yet. But maybe I'm starting to.'

'Oh, Dido ...'

'It was always going to happen,' she says. 'There's no future in having your cake and eating it. Things get spoiled.'

'Are you speaking from experience?' he asks.

She shrugs. 'You love your wife.'

'You think I've been using you.'

'No, no.'

'Playing.'

'Only in the same sense that I have. Indulging a whim.'

'It feels like more than that.'

'That's what's dangerous. Isn't it? Because you can't fall in love with me.'

Jim pushes himself up on to one elbow. 'You're very extraordinary, Dido. I've never met anyone like you.'

She laughs. 'Is that a compliment?'

'It's a conundrum. Because the more calmly you explain to me why I can't fall in love with you, the more likely it becomes that I will.'

'I'd better not speak, then.'

'Not about that,' Jim says. 'Not about us.'

'There isn't a logical solution, so there's no point talking about it?'

'That's about it.'

'That's called sticking your head in the sand,' she says. 'But OK. For now.'

'Good,' he says. 'I don't want to be talked out of your bed. Not just yet.'

Another laugh. But she doesn't speak again, as promised.

'Tell me about the conference,' Jim says, after a bit.

'Trade fair.'

'Tell me about the trade fair.'

She shakes her head. 'Very, very dull,' she says. 'There's the wacky bunch and the commercial bunch, and I'm somewhere in the middle, so none of them want to speak to me.'

'How foolish of them,' Jim says.

'Tell me about your work.'

'Bluebells, today. And Surrey's seventh prettiest village.'

'No interesting entrepreneurial women offering you gingerbread?'

'Sadly, no. That's why I came when you called.'

'Hotfoot from Surrey's seventh prettiest village.'

'Indeed.'

There's a silence then, a longer one, as though they've talked themselves out. Exhausted their supplies of ready wit, anyway. Jim doesn't mind the silence: Dido is an easy person to share it with. And it's all they have. There's nothing to do but curl up and let the minutes tick by.

'You could tell me about your daughter,' Dido says, after a while. 'If you'd like to.'

'I thought I saw her,' Jim says, before he can stop himself. 'A few weeks ago. I was driving through Fulford, and I saw someone I was sure was her.'

'But it wasn't?'

'I don't know. By the time I got out of the car she'd vanished.'

He promised he wouldn't tell Dido any of this, he reminds himself. Perhaps not quite promised. But it's a relief: he's never talked about Emma, about her disappearance, to anyone except Cath and the police.

'Might you be able to find her, if she's living in Fulford?' Dido asks.

Jim's driven down Fulford High Street often enough since that day. Up and down, looking. Asking himself again and again if it really was Emma.

'I don't think she wants to be found.' He hesitates. 'When she left we had two postcards, saying she was fine and didn't want us to look for her.'

'How long ago was it?'

'Just over a year.'

There's barely a hesitation; no shocked intake of breath.

'That's time enough for things to change,' Dido says. 'People get out on a limb. I read something in a magazine, the other week. It's more common than you might think, children walking out like this. Late teens, early twenties. Cutting off ties with their families.'

They've heard all this many times, but Jim's touched that she's read up about it. Not by chance, he thinks.

'They don't always come back,' he says.

'No,' she says. 'I don't imagine it's that easy, when you've been gone for a while.'

But how could they make it easier for Emma? Jim wants to ask. What on earth could they do?

He doesn't feel angry with Dido; none of this is her fault. But his mood has changed, even so. He shouldn't have come tonight, he thinks, when he'd promised to take Cath out. Dido is occupying Cath's time: he's never felt that before.

But perhaps Dido has. Perhaps that's why she asked about Emma. *That's called sticking your head in the sand,* he hears her say again. She's right: she's always right. They can't go on with this. They really can't.

It's only six thirty when he gets home, half an hour ahead of the time he gave Cath, which feels like a small vindication.

'Cath?' he calls. 'I'm home!'

There's no sign of her downstairs: perhaps she's gone up to change. He climbs the stairs.

'Cath? Are you up here? Did you get my texts?'

The bathroom door stands wide open: for a moment, a horrifying moment, he hesitates, then peers inside, sees it's empty.

And then he notices that the loft door is open, although the ladder has been pulled up. He stands beneath it, craning his neck. There's no light up there.

'Cath?'

'I'm up here.'

'In the loft? Where's the ladder?'

There's silence for a moment, and then he hears her moving, coming towards the hatch, and there's a scraping sound as she pushes the ladder towards him. He grabs it and pulls it down. What the hell's going on? he wonders. What has she ... And then he realises. He heaves himself over the lip and on to the boarding, reaches for the light switch. Cath is sitting beside the plastic boxes where the girls' memorabilia is kept.

'My love, how long have you been up here?'

'I don't know.'

'You've been looking at Emma's things.'

His tone is as gentle as he can make it, but she shakes her head.

'Rose's. Emma's too, but – there's so little of Rose's. We kept so little of her.'

He doesn't know what to say. 'There are photographs,' he says, 'lots of photographs. She had a dad who's a photographer, don't forget.'

Cath nods, just once.

'There aren't …' He hesitates. 'There aren't drawings and things, I know, but …'

Cath's lip trembles. 'When she died, it was like – nothing had gone. Nothing had gone from the world – just from me.'

'From all of us,' Jim says. 'From me. From Emma.'

She says something he can't hear, and Jim moves closer, puts his arm around her. Cath turns her head into his neck. 'I want her back,' she says.

'I know, love. I know.'

He doesn't know whether she means Emma or Rose, but – it's not the same, he thinks, not exactly, but he sees clearly now that it's all part of the same loss. The daughter who was never going to leave, never going to go anywhere – who'd have been a burden and a care forever, a baby needing her mother until she was old enough to be a mother herself – and the daughter who lived and loved and laughed, who made up for everything. And then ran away.

Nick

It's odd getting on the train alone. Nick feels more like a commuter this evening: when he and Lara are together it always feels like a day trip, even if there's nothing but work in the middle of it. He notices the other people more than usual – some of them familiar by now – and he wonders, as he usually doesn't, what they do. What kind of work they go in to, and what kinds of homes they come back to. None, he suspects, are as happy as his.

It's still light when he gets out at Lingford. How fast the spring is coming on, he thinks, looking up at the cherry blossom which transforms the row of humble houses into something to catch the eye of a Hollywood location scout. A street of candyfloss, he thinks. And then his mind turns to Lara, waiting for him inside number 2. *It's nothing,* she said at lunchtime. *Just a headache.*

I haven't been sleeping well. Odd, he thinks now, because he's woken in the night a bit himself this week, and Lara has been fast asleep each time. Perhaps they've been taking turns to lie awake. Anyway, he's thinking of a takeaway tonight, something easy. There's a fish and chip shop round the corner that they haven't tried yet.

'Lara?' he calls, as he comes in.

There's no answer. She hasn't replied to the text he sent from the train, either. Perhaps she's asleep. He tiptoes upstairs and into the bedroom. In the bed, Lara stirs.

'Sorry – did I wake you?'

'I don't think so.' Lara's curled on her side, the duvet pulled over her.

He hesitates. 'Shall I leave you alone? Do you want anything?'

'No, don't go.' She turns over then, manages a smile. She looks pale, he thinks. 'Come and sit with me. I need to tell you something.'

His heart bumps in his chest. 'Something good?'

'Yes,' she says. 'Something good, and—'

He's across the room before she can finish the sentence. Only a couple of steps, but he seems to fly, reaching the bed and gathering her in his arms.

'Oh, darling,' he says. 'Tell me. Tell me quick.'

Her head is buried in his neck, her hair warm and thick under his hands. There's a muffled laugh: 'I can't tell you anything like this,' she says, and he loosens his grasp, laughing too, so he can see her face.

'I haven't done a test yet,' she says. 'I was going to wait until then, but I feel so shattered, and I'm weeks late now, so – I'm pretty sure I'm pregnant.'

For a moment Nick thinks he might cry. He thought nothing could feel better than falling in love with Lara, but – to be a dad, he thinks. To have the chance to bring up a baby, a child, together. A proper family. How funny that when he thought about all that a few weeks back it never occurred to him it could happen so soon.

'That's the best, best news,' he says. 'The best in the world. I love you, Lara. I love you so much.' He takes her hands now, looks into her eyes and sees a shadow of doubt there. 'Were you worried about what I'd think?'

'Only that—'

'I know it's sooner than we planned, but it'll be fine. It'll be wonderful.' He kisses her forehead, her cheeks. 'I promise you, Lara, you can rely on me. I'll never, ever do what my dad did. Till death us do part, remember?'

'Yes.'

Lara looks less certain than he'd like; less elated. She's not feeling well, he reminds himself. And this isn't the moment of revelation for her, of course, but even so sharing it with him ought to be—

'You are happy about it, aren't you?' he asks.

'Of course I am.' She manages a smile.

'I'll look after you,' he says. 'While you're feeling poorly I'll do everything. And then when …' He hesitates: neither of them has said the word aloud yet, he realises. He takes a deep breath. 'When the baby comes, we can share everything. I can take paternity leave; we can work everything out between us.'

'Yes,' she says. 'Thank you.'

Nick laughs. 'I was going to suggest fish and chips,' he says, 'but maybe that's not what you're feeling like.'

Her face softens. 'Actually,' she says, 'that would be perfect.'

MAY

Cath

Cath's enthusiasm for gardening has ebbed away. There's no more to do at St John's Street, and although their own garden could do with more attention, ongoing attention, she hasn't had the heart for it since that afternoon in the loft. The idea of growing things feels unbearable, suddenly. Pointless, she thinks viciously, when they'll only die, or wither, or run away. What was she thinking? How could she have deceived herself?

But the trouble is that now she's seen through her own trickery, there's no point in trying any more. The hole in her life feels more conspicuous than ever. She has no idea what to do with herself, how to fill the days. It's easier to forbid things: there's a sharp pleasure in that. In self-denial, and in self-protection. No baking; no planting; no visiting Lara and Nick. She hasn't allowed herself anywhere near St John's Street for a couple of weeks.

So when she sees Lara in Boots in Fulford she does a double take. It's a Friday morning: surely Lara should be at work? She hesitates for a second, then ducks into another aisle. But Lara has seen her.

'Cath!'

She turns, mimes surprise.

'How are you?' Lara asks. She's got a couple of plastic bags in her hands and she looks – bedraggled, Cath thinks. Weary.

'I'm fine.' Cath's heart is thumping now with the idiocy of her behaviour. 'Fine. Have you got a day off?'

'I'm working from home today, actually. I suppose this is my lunch break.' Lara pauses. 'Have you eaten?' she asks. 'We could ... there's a nice café next door. Let me buy you lunch. A thank you for all the gardening. Or – maybe you haven't got time.'

Lara looks doubtful now. Because of her reaction, Cath thinks. Poor Lara, it's not fair to ...

'No, that would be nice,' she says. 'That would be lovely, if you're sure.'

Cath orders a Caesar salad, and Lara, who has barely glanced at the menu, asks for the same. She looks better now she's sitting down, Cath thinks, but when the waitress has gone, she says, 'Oh dear – I don't think I do want a Caesar salad, actually.'

'Would you rather have something else?' Cath asks. 'I can call her back.'

'No, no, it's fine. I'm just – I'm not very hungry. It was your company I wanted.' She blushes slightly with this admission, but Cath is touched. She looks at Lara more carefully.

'Are you all right?' she asks. 'You look a bit pale.'

Lara responds with a flush that spreads from the neck of her jumper up to her hairline.

'I'm – well, I'm pregnant, actually,' she says. 'We haven't told anyone yet – work, or anything – but I suppose – you'll have a new tenant.' She stops, looking suddenly alarmed. 'I hope that's OK. I mean – the tenancy agreement ...'

'Of course it is.' Cath beams at her. 'It's wonderful. I'm thrilled for you.'

She is, too. Unreservedly. Sitting here smiling at Lara, everything else seems suddenly ... It's as if the sun's come out, she thinks, and you can't help but feel warmed by it.

'I'm sure you'll want to buy new things,' she hears herself saying, 'or your parents will probably have stuff – but we've still got a cot up in the loft, and a pushchair. But they'll be very old-fashioned by now, I'm afraid.' Pushchairs, these days, are more highly designed than aeroplanes, she knows. Space-age baby-transport systems.

'That's so kind.' Lara looks tearful now: Cath remembers that, the ricocheting emotions. 'I didn't know – I mean, I've never asked whether you have children.'

'Grown up now,' Cath says. There's a little stab of betrayal, but what else could she say? 'So have you told your parents yet?' she asks.

'No.' Lara frowns slightly. 'No. Not yet.'

'A happy surprise for them,' Cath says.

Lara forces a smile. 'We, um ...' she hesitates, then shakes her head. 'How old are your children?' she asks.

'Nineteen.' No one has asked Emma's age for a long time, Cath thinks.

'At university?' Lara asks, and Cath shakes her head.

'Not yet,' she says. 'But she's not living at home any more.'

'A daughter?'

'Emma.'

'That's a nice name. I'd thought of Emma for my baby, actually, if it's a girl.' Lara blushes again, perhaps feeling that it's tempting Fate to be thinking of baby names already.

'Where do your parents live?' Cath asks. 'Are they near enough to come and help?'

'Near Salisbury,' Lara says. 'But ...' She hesitates again. 'I don't see them any more. We – fell out.'

Cath feels the shock of those words like a jolt in her chest. She stares at Lara, and for a moment she sees not her face but Emma's: she hears Emma's voice, speaking those words to a stranger. *I don't see them any more. We fell out.* Is that what Emma would say? There's a gush of sympathy, now, for Lara's parents. What if Emma got pregnant and didn't tell her? If Cath had a grandchild she didn't know about?

She knows her dismay is showing in her face, but she can't help it. She thinks again of the hours she spent in the garden at St John's Street, the furtive exploration of the kitchen cupboards, and she feels suddenly sick. Trying to worm her way into their lives, to take the place of a mother. Someone else's baby, she thinks. Another daughter who's run away from home. The irony of it feels devastating.

Lara's looking at her in alarm now – alarm and something else, Cath thinks. Supplication. Another irony: that now, when Lara wants something from her – wants a substitute mother, even, possibly – she can't bear to give it. She makes a show of looking at her watch, forces a smile.

'I'm so sorry, Lara, but I've just remembered I'm supposed to be—'

'Please,' Lara says, 'don't go.'

She looks distressed; despite herself, Cath hesitates.

'It must sound terrible to you,' Lara says, 'a daughter not being in touch with her parents. But it's not what you think. They weren't bad people, but they had very strong beliefs. They couldn't—'

To Cath's horror, Lara's weeping now, more violently than Cath could have believed possible a moment before. At the next table, a middle-aged couple have turned to stare at them.

Cath stands up. 'Come on,' she says. 'Let's go home.'

'Thank you,' Lara says, as they turn out of the car park. Her tears have stopped, but she looks blotchy and exhausted. 'You're being very kind.'

'You don't have to keep saying that,' Cath says. 'I'm not a very kind person, really.'

Lara laughs, despite herself. 'You seem it to me,' she says. 'How are you not kind?'

Cath doesn't reply. Guilt tweaks at her, but she pushes it away. At the traffic lights she flicks on the indicator and pulls on to the Southford Road.

'We're out in the sticks,' she says.

'It's beautiful.' As they drive, Lara stares out at the woods, at the sudden views of the valley, green and lush in the May sunshine. 'I can't believe it's like this so close to Fulford.'

'We should have moved here sooner,' Cath says. 'We lived in London until Emma was five.' It's a peace offering, that sentence, although Lara may not recognise it. But she covers it up, almost at once, with a change of tack.

'It's not easy, being pregnant, is it?' she says. 'It certainly wasn't for me. It's a bit of a shock, the first time. The early stages.'

'It's not the first time.'

'Sorry?' Cath turns to look at her.

Lara takes a deep breath, then lets it all out again in a shuddering sigh. 'It's not the first time I've been pregnant,' she says. 'I need to – I have to tell someone. I don't know what to do.'

Lara

If Lara had tried to imagine a house for Cath and Jim it would have been just like this: a little house up a lane, surrounded by woods. It's made of red brick and tiles and everything about it seems to slope, as though it's been built from a set of triangular blocks. Inside, it's shabby and old-fashioned, with beige wallpaper and worn carpets and furniture that doesn't match.

Cath takes her into the kitchen, which is painted bright yellow and has a wooden table in the middle, a bit too big for the space it occupies. A black dog gets up from a basket in the corner and comes towards her.

'Do you like dogs?' Cath asks. She's putting the kettle on, taking mugs out of a cupboard.

'I haven't met many,' Lara says. 'He's sweet.'

She strokes the dog's head and he looks up at her with big brown eyes.

'He's going deaf,' Cath says. 'Would you like tea?'

Lara hesitates. 'Do you have herbal? I can't—'

'Of course.' Cath opens another cupboard and takes out a selection of boxes. 'Here, take your pick.'

While the tea's brewing Lara inspects the clutter of bills and magazines that fills one end of the table. It has the look of a space well used to confessional talks, she thinks.

'Shall we go through?' Cath says.

Most of the rest of the downstairs is taken up by a living room with a fireplace at one end and a television at the other. Between them, French windows lead on to the garden. Lara spots several of the glossy bushes with big soft flowers Cath planted at St John's Street. Camellias, she remembers. If you half shut your eyes, they turn into a green embroidery adorned with red knots. The garden's not much longer than theirs, but it's wider and there are trees in the corners that blend in with the woodland beyond, so it feels like a cottage garden from one of those fairy tales where children grow up deep in the woods and sneak out through the gate to meet wolves.

Cath gestures at the chairs near the French window and drags over a little table for their teacups. Lara sits down in an armchair that is less comfortable than it looks, and picks up the mint tea Cath has made her. The smell of it is soothing, almost medicinal.

'Better?' Cath asks, and Lara nods. She wants to thank Cath again, tell her how much her kindness means, but instead she searches for a way into what she wants to say.

'My parents' house was nothing like this,' she begins eventually. 'It was – narrow. Literally narrow, like – no, not like St John's Street, because it was very dark, always, but … it was very plain.'

She glances at the walls of Cath's living room. There are pictures everywhere: blown-up black and white photographs that might be Jim's and framed posters from art exhibitions; in one corner, smaller photographs of people that she can't see clearly. Their daughter, presumably. She feels a flash of envy for her, growing up here. Lara's parents' walls held nothing but verses from scripture. Graven images were prohibited, and almost anything risked being a graven image. *Any likeness of any thing that is in heaven above, or that is in the earth beneath,* she remembers. There are no photographs of her as a child, and even drawings were discouraged.

'They were religious,' Cath prompts, and Lara nods. She feels a tug of – disloyalty? No, fear. A terror of divine retribution, like a lingering trace of superstition. *Honour thy father and thy mother: that thy days may be long upon the land which the Lord thy God giveth thee.*

'We belonged to a community,' she says. 'A Christian community. Not a sect, a …'

'Brethren?' Cath asks.

'Something like that.' She doesn't want to speak aloud the name they used. 'They're good people, but …' This feels like more of a betrayal because Cath is a mother; because Cath has brought up her own daughter in the spirit of whatever beliefs she has. She takes a deep breath.

'Misguided,' she says. 'Not – I don't mean it's wrong to be guided by the Bible, but where it guided them, what it made them.'

'So you – escaped?'

'I had to leave,' Lara says. 'I had an abortion.' There: another impossible word, spoken out loud. 'No one knows. Not even ...'

'You haven't told Nick?'

Lara is trembling now. 'Nick thinks my parents died in a car crash. That's what I've told everyone, all along. I didn't want to lie to Nick, didn't mean to let the lies carry on, but – there was never the right moment to take them back.' She bites her lip, harder than she means to. 'One minute it was too soon, and the next it was too late, because we'd told each other everything already. And I suppose – I suppose I was frightened it would change his view of me.'

Cath nods. 'I can understand that,' she says.

Lara looks up at her gratefully, and then, in a rush, she says: 'He doesn't even know my real name.'

Cath says nothing, and Lara blushes. She didn't mean to go that far. She wonders, suddenly, whether this is a terrible idea, telling Cath. Whether it might change Cath's view of her – or worse, whether Cath might do something, tell someone. Tell Nick. But Cath's face is full of compassion.

'How did it happen?' she asks. 'The abortion?'

Lara swallows. 'It was a boy in the community. He used to walk me home from meetings, youth groups, and one evening he took me into a field and ...'

'That sounds like rape,' Cath says, and Lara shakes her head fiercely.

'I didn't try to stop him. I wanted it.'

'What happened to the boy?'

'Nothing. As far as I know. I never told anyone who he was.' She laughs, a tiny laugh, as something occurs to her. 'They didn't even ask me. It didn't matter. It was my sin.'

'Doesn't the commandment cover both parties?' Cath asks.

'That's a matter for him,' Lara says. *'He that committeth fornication sinneth against his own body.'*

'You don't believe that now?'

'No,' Lara says, 'of course not.' She shakes her head, to convince herself as much as Cath. 'They were going to keep me, my parents. Me and the baby. Wrap me up in shame and disgrace but keep us both and – I don't know, raise the baby as a more God-fearing child than I'd turned out to be. I couldn't bear that.'

'I'm not surprised.'

'When I told the doctor I wanted an abortion my parents tried to argue, to claim I was a child, a minor, that they could forbid it. The hospital staff had to drag them out, denouncing me as they went. And that was the last time I saw them. *Thou shalt not kill.* Abortion is even worse than fornication, in their minds.'

'You poor child.'

Lara can feel Cath's eyes on her, her sympathy and outrage, and it's almost too much to bear.

'The thing is,' she says, 'I have to tell Nick now. I have to tell him about the abortion, because the doctors need to know. And I have to tell him about my parents, too.'

'Do the doctors really need to know?'

Lara nods. 'There was a lot of bleeding, after the abortion. They kept me in hospital for nearly a week. They said it was important to mention it if I ever got pregnant again.'

'And you couldn't ask them not to tell Nick?'

'You keep your medical notes with you,' Lara says. 'Nick might look at them. Anyway, he ...' She stops for a moment, trying to grasp at the swirl of thoughts in her head. 'I've had to remake my life, you see. Remake myself, so all that – stuff – can't keep dragging me down. And Nick's at the centre of it. Of *me*.'

Cath doesn't say anything for a while. She looks out of the French windows, and Lara follows her gaze. A pheasant struts across the lawn, bright as a soldier, his tail cocked behind him.

'I understand,' Cath says eventually. 'I do understand. But perhaps ... perhaps if you haven't told him before, there's a reason. Sometimes, in a marriage – even in the best marriage – there can be things you choose not to tell.'

Lara stares at her. 'But what if there was a problem with the baby, the pregnancy, and he didn't know ...?'

'I'm not saying you shouldn't tell him,' Cath says, 'I'm just saying it should be your choice.' She hesitates. 'It seems to me you haven't had enough choice about – things to do with your body.'

'This is my choice,' Lara says, putting her hand over her belly. 'And Nick. I couldn't have been luckier, finding him.'

'No,' Cath says. 'I can see that.'

'The thing is, though – Nick's been through a lot too. His dad abandoned his family when he was five, and Nick hates him for it. He's always said he'd never do that to me. Never. But ...'

'You're worried if you tell him you lied about your parents – about the abortion – he might see it as a betrayal? A breach of trust?'

Is that it? Maybe it is, although the baldness of the words takes Lara's breath away for a moment.

'Isn't it worse not to tell him?' she says. 'I could explain it, make him understand why I didn't say anything before. If I don't do it now, it's like another door shutting that I can't open again.'

'That's true.' Cath's finished her tea now: she puts the cup down on the table. 'That's very true. But just remember that once you say something, you can't unsay it. Until you do, you still have a choice. You still have control.'

Lara nods, but she feels distraught. Somehow she imagined that telling Cath would make everything better, but it hasn't. It feels as though the stakes are even higher than she realised.

'It's up to you, Lara,' Cath says, her voice very gentle. 'I'm sure if you tell Nick ... I'm sure everything will work out.'

'But what if it doesn't?' Lara asks. 'What if he can't forgive me?'

Cath's looking out of the window again. Lara waits, but Cath doesn't say anything more; doesn't turn to face her. And then at last she reaches for Lara's hand.

'What was your name?' she asks. 'Would you tell me that?'

Jim

The strange thing is that now he and Dido have agreed that it's impossible for them to go any further, they have settled into a steady state of almost-farewell. It isn't an affair any more but the aftermath of an affair, Jim thinks, when he finds his car turning towards Dorking one afternoon in the second week of May. It's never really been a full-blown affair, in fact: they went straight from the early stages, when it was a transient, uncertain entanglement, to something they've signed off from, which now stretches out indefinitely, less troubling to his conscience than the *medias res*.

Since that day – that same day – when he came home to find Cath in the loft, things have been different at home, too. It's as if a layer of pretence has been removed. Cath has been sometimes more abrasive and sometimes more affectionate, but in either case more herself, and Jim tells himself this must be another step forwards.

That evening, they sat for hours over the boxes of keepsakes, and then the photograph albums, turning the pages with a kind of wonder. He'd forgotten how similar they looked when they were born, the girls. One of them whole, and the other – never really there, he thinks now. As Emma developed, Rose just grew. Two babies lying side by side in the same incubator, in the same cot, and then one sitting, standing, talking, running.

Maybe there's more that can be done, nowadays: twenty years must have made a difference to the management of twins like theirs. But at the time it had been a small miracle that they were both born alive, and they had been duly thankful. That's a habit they learned the hard way, he thinks: thankfulness for what they had. Thankfulness for Rose, for her sweet oblivion, her lack of resistance to love. Thankfulness for what she taught Emma: those agonisingly touching moments when she hung over Rose's crib, talking and singing and stroking her face. But did she teach Emma other things? Jim wonders now. That she wasn't complete on her own; that her parents – her mother, especially – would always have half a mind on her sister, even when the crib was empty, the shadow sister gone?

He's never arrived at Dido's house and found it empty before, but today he does. Of course he knows that Dido goes out, does things he knows nothing about. He can't really have imagined her waiting at home for him, except that just now he feels a pang for the loss of that illusion. He rings her mobile and Dido's voice, friendly and efficient, asks him to leave a message. He doesn't. For a minute or two he stands outside the house, feeling it triumph in its emptiness – a fancy he scoffs at as soon as it takes shape – and then he gets back into his car.

He could go home now, but he'd rather not make up a lie about an appointment being cancelled. Instead he heads for the *Gazette* office. It's an opportunity to show his face, he thinks, to have a word with the picture editor about the summer weddings feature. He takes a circuitous route through the town centre, a habit he's fallen into without any realistic hope of seeing Emma. But as he turns down the High Street, scouring the pavements almost absently, he spots her. Or rather – he sees someone who could be Emma, who looks like the glimpse he had before of someone he was sure was her. A young woman with short hair, wearing jeans and a sweatshirt, walking purposefully round a corner into a side road. He slows down, but he can't turn back: he has no choice but to drive away from her, past the shops readied for summer with colours that evoke blossom and bunting. This time it isn't even worth shouting her name at the windscreen. Anyway, he tells himself, there's really nothing to say it was Emma. He feels less certain, this time, that it could have been. Just a young woman of roughly her age and height, he thinks, one of hundreds like her in Fulford.

If the last sighting left him unreasonably hopeful, this one casts him into gloom. A gloom augmented by Dido's absence, although he tells himself it's the wasted journey that goads him – or the fact that he wouldn't have had that tantalising glimpse of Emma's doppelganger if Dido had been at home.

He's briefly cheered by finding a parking place outside the *Gazette*, but the office is half-empty, the picture editor not at her desk. He halts, thrown again. And then he settles at one of the hot desks, opens up the computer.

There's always a moment, after he types in Emma's name, when he thinks he'll find her this time. Like that ridiculous hope every time you buy a lottery ticket. But it's exactly the same as usual: five or six Emma Polkinghornes on Facebook, none of them his. Some of them feel like old friends now, their looser privacy settings giving him a window into their lives: Scottish Emma, US Navy Emma, Middlesborough Emma. He tries Twitter, then Instagram; then he sits back in his chair, riding the familiar wave of disappointment. Idiot, he thinks, to allow himself to expect anything else. But the thought that Emma might be close by, might have been within reach all this time, taunts him. *Might you be able to find her, if she's living in Fulford?* he hears Dido saying. Surely there must be a trace of Emma somewhere on social media? Surely there must be a way to find her?

He glances covertly round the room: most of his colleagues are younger than him, and must know more about social media than he does. But he can't bring himself to ask for their help. They're journalists, after all: he can't bear to have their professional prurience focused on his family.

The flicker of protectiveness this train of thought elicits nudges his mind towards Cath. He should go home. He turns off the computer, nods towards the knot of people gathered in the kitchen when he passes, and heads for the exit.

There's a sense of energy in the house when he comes in that puts him on the alert. Sometimes, often, it warns him that Cath is in a state of mind he has to manage carefully. But this evening she seems fine: cheerful rather than frenetic, stirring something at the stove.

'Good day?' he asks, crossing the room to kiss her. 'That smells good.'

'Chilli con carne,' she says. 'I bought some mince at the nice butcher in Lingford.'

'Lingford?' He can't help the note of uncertainty in his voice, and Cath doesn't miss it.

'Lara was here today,' she says. 'Lara the tenant' – as though there could be some doubt about which Lara she means. 'I ran into her in Fulford, and she wanted to talk.'

'Oh.'

Cath puts the lid on the casserole and turns to face him. 'Drink?' she asks.

They take their wine glasses through to the living room, and Cath makes for the pair of chairs facing the French windows.

'We haven't sat here for ages,' Jim says. 'The garden's looking lovely.'

'Yes.'

Jim waits: she's brought him here, sat him down, for a purpose, he thinks.

She leaves it a few more moments, and then she says, 'Lara's pregnant. Just pregnant – it's not public knowledge yet.'

'Ah, that's great!' Jim smiles, mustering enthusiasm. Great that she's told Cath at this early stage is partly what he means. That explains the energy, the staging of this drink. 'Was it planned?'

'I didn't ask. Welcome, I think.' Cath takes another sip of wine.

Jim's sure there's more – a twist to the story, perhaps, or something entirely different, to which Lara's pregnancy is a preamble – but if there is, Cath doesn't produce it. He watches her looking out across the lawn, listening to the evening chorus coming through the open windows, and it strikes him that they make a picture of contentment: the comfortable, long-married couple, sitting in the shabby armchairs they've had for a quarter of a century, sharing a glass of wine while birds sing in their garden. Might that picture be as truthful for them as it is for anyone? he wonders. Can they – just for this moment, this evening – lay claim to that?

Later, in bed, Cath lies closer to him than usual.

'It's been a nice evening,' he says. 'Delicious chilli.'

Cath doesn't reply, but she shifts a little, sleepily, so that her hip nudges against him. He lifts his arm to stroke her hair – she used to love that, he remembers, when she was pregnant – and she makes a small, an almost imperceptible, sound of pleasure. He's sleepy too, and gradually his hand slows, stills, resting against the side of her head, and he can feel them both slipping towards sleep. But sometime, somewhere, Cath stirs again, and he feels her taking hold of his penis, holding it like a comforter, the warmth of her hand enclosing him deliciously. He's got an erection, he realises, still half-asleep at first, and then drawn slowly, slowly, up towards consciousness by burgeoning arousal. Cath squeezes him gently, but he can't tell whether she's awake, whether the movement is deliberate, and so he lies still, keeps his eyes shut, as waves of desire rise through him – desire for Cath, only for Cath.

Does he dare roll towards her, murmuring suggestions in her ear? Might that resolve something, somehow, between them, as well as … No, he tells himself. It's enough that she remembers he's there. For a while he wonders whether he'll be able to control himself if she keeps hold of him like this – and then her grip slackens, and he's both relieved and disappointed. After a few moments he reaches his hand down and closes her fingers around his penis again, shutting his eyes tight to imagine her stirring and tightening her grasp, making those pleasurable noises again. Somewhere between waking and sleeping his fantasies spill over in his mind, and she rises towards him, drawing him down …

When he wakes in the night, Cath is lying with her back to him, and he wonders whether he dreamed it – her hand, his erection, that sense of possibility. He's wide awake now, his mind filled with the idea of sex, but not, just now, the need for it. This is new, he thinks. When he was younger, the slightest thought sprang instantly to urgent desire. This detachment isn't altogether welcome, but it's helpful in disentangling things: the reasons, for example, for the decline in their sex life; the difference between sex with Cath and sex with Dido. In this unfamiliar territory between thinking and feeling it's possible to examine these things more closely – and more safely – than he expects.

He can remember when he and Cath last had sex – not so very long ago, in fact – but not when the frequency of it began to decline. Before Emma's disappearance, surely. Before Julianne's murder. Some downturn must be normal, but how much and when he's not sure.

Perhaps it's the lack of history that makes things simpler with Dido? And the lack of expectation? There's an element of surprise, each time, that allows instinct to lead them. There is, he thinks now, something oddly chaste about the whole business: they're like two primitive people, meeting each other in a cave, doing what their bodies insist on without any sense of the emotional complication later millennia will impose on sexual intercourse. And he likes it. Oh, how much he likes it.

It should feel like an irony that he can enjoy sex so easily, so straightforwardly, with Dido, but not with Cath.

May

It should feel like more of an irony that he can lie beside his wife, desire for her still recent enough to have left its imprint on him, and think about sex with another woman without feeling ravaged by guilt and confusion. Men, he remembers his father telling him in a rare moment of intimacy, don't think about sex the same way women do. He has never believed this, but he wonders now if it's true. Married men and married women: would that make the adage more accurate? But he's never strayed before; never really been tempted. And he refuses still, with a stubbornness that both pleases and dismays him, to see what he has with Dido as infidelity. Not in the sense he has always understood it, the sense of a threat to his marriage. That, he tells himself, is the other thing about Dido: he likes her, he's grateful to her, he would hate to hurt her, but he doesn't care about her.

But even as this thought lays its reassurance over his weary, dead-of-night mind, he knows it's not entirely true.

Light and Dark

Cath is dozing in the chair beside Rose's bed when Jim arrives with Emma. Cath's eyes open at once when she hears the click of the door, but for a second – a fraction of a second – she's not sure where she is: there's a blessed instant before the anguish of the last few days comes back into focus. Rose, lying inert on the hospital bed, her face distorted by the breathing tube and the tape that holds it in place. The click and hum of the machines and the scribble of neon across their screens.

The faint whisper of despair that fills the room.

Jim wasn't sure it was a good idea to bring Emma to the hospital, but Cath insisted. She knows there's a chance that Rose won't come home again this time. A substantial chance. Things have never been this bad before. She's sure Jim knows it too, even though neither of them has admitted it to the other. It's like a spell they can't bear to break: as though speaking it aloud makes it more likely that the worst will happen. And Emma needs to understand. Maybe this shouldn't be her last sight of her sister – but it surely won't be how she remembers her, Cath tells herself. Rose is lodged too deep in Emma's consciousness for this scene to overshadow five years of memories. They're joined, still, by the beating of Cath's heart, the rush of blood through their shared placenta.

So here she is, dear Emma, wearing her best dress to visit her sister. Cath hasn't seen her since yesterday morning, when Rose was rushed off in the ambulance, and she registers a little shock now, seeing Emma's face: seeing Rose's features, which she has been gazing at for the last twenty-four hours, untwisted, animated, filled with light. Seeing them as they might have been. And then Emma throws herself into Cath's arms – Mummy! Mummy Mummy Mummy! – and a great flood of emotion sluices through her. Love, mainly. Sorrow. Guilt. Anger. Dread. A desperate, pleading hope. Not just for Rose, but in that moment for Emma, too. For the ineffable, the almost painful joy of her presence.

'Darling Em,' she says. 'How are you? Have you and Daddy been all right on your own? Have you had a nice breakfast?'

Emma nods, snuggling into Cath's lap, sliding a thumb into her mouth as her eyes turn towards her sister. For a moment she takes in the wires and the tubes, and then she leans forward to stroke Rose's hand.

'Poor Rosy,' she says. 'Is she very sad?'

Tears start in Cath's eyes. 'I don't know,' she says. 'I don't think so, darling. The doctors have given her lots of medicine to make her feel better.'

'I 'spect she'll feel better now I'm here,' Emma says, and Cath's lip trembles.

'I'm sure she will, darling. You always make her feel better, don't you?'

Emma nods, satisfied. 'I do. I'm good at lookaftering to her.'

Jim puts his hand on Cath's shoulder, squeezes hard. He knows, Cath thinks. They both know they have to prepare Emma.

'The doctors are good at looking after her too,' she says. 'They're doing their very best.'

'I don't like their lookaftering,' Emma says, eyeing the medical paraphernalia that surrounds Rose's bed. 'Why do they need all these things when they could just give her medicine?'

'Because Rose is very poorly, my love,' Jim says. 'She's very, very poorly, I'm afraid.'

'Rose has always been poorlyish,' Emma says. 'Not like me.'

Cath bites her lip hard. But does it matter if Emma sees her crying? she wonders. Maybe it's better if they don't pretend.

'Poor Rose,' she says, her voice quavering. 'It's bad luck, isn't it? Bad luck that she's so poorly. But she's lucky to have such a lovely sister.'

For a moment Emma doesn't say anything, and Cath longs to know what she's thinking, what she's feeling. And then she slides off Cath's knee and on to the edge of the bed, and finds a little space to curl up next to Rose. She lays her arm gently across her sister's chest, brushes back her hair and murmurs into her ear in that strange language that belongs only to them: a language of infant secrets and twin-to-twin communion that they've shared since they first lay beside each other in the cot and maybe – who knows – before that. For a long moment there's no sound in the room except the purr of Emma's voice, and Cath leans her head back against Jim's leg and looks at her two girls, at their heads close together, and Emma's hand holding Rose's.

And then Emma looks up at her parents and smiles.

'It's all right,' she says. 'Rose isn't sad any more. I've made her happy now.'

Nick

The private clinic is on the outskirts of Fulford: a non-descript place that could easily be an office block. It's early – the Saturday slots get booked quickly, the receptionist told them when they rang, but there was one left at eight, if they didn't want to wait another week. And they didn't. Nick's impatience to see the baby, to be assured that everything's OK, is almost overwhelming.

As they park, he smiles at Lara.

'This is so exciting,' he says.

'Yes.' Lara takes his hand for a moment. Nick keeps imagining she looks different, moves differently: he longs for the stage when the bump will show and he can steer her through crowds, make sure she gets a seat on the train.

'Mr and Mrs Smith?'

'Yes,' Nick says. 'Really. No aliases.'

He grins, but the receptionist looks taken aback; the joke doesn't always work. Lara squeezes his hand again, and he turns the grin towards her.

'Take a seat,' the woman says. 'The nurse will call you in a moment.'

There's one other couple in the waiting area, slightly older than them.

'First baby?' asks the woman.

'Yes,' Nick says. 'First baby. We're very excited.'

Lara looks a little anxious now. He sits down beside her, gestures towards the pile of magazines, but she shakes her head. Is she worried that there might be a problem? he wonders. That thought has niggled at him too, though he hasn't dared mention it to Lara. Perhaps they should have discussed it. Would they consider an abortion, if ... But he hopes they'll never have to face that question.

And then the nurse appears, and before he knows it they're in the scanning room, Lara on her back with jelly spread across her stomach and him on a stool, holding her hand, both of them craning their necks to see the black and white screen on which lines and spaces flicker.

'About eight weeks, you think?' asks the sonographer.

'Yes,' says Lara. Her face is tense; Nick strokes her arm.

'That looks about right,' the woman says. They both stare at the screen, astonished that she can detect anything on it, but then something swims into view – something more like an ant than a baby, a pair of white bobbles in a lopsided puddle of black.

'Is that it?' Lara asks. 'Is that the baby?'

'That's the baby.' She smiles. 'That bean shape there is the head, and this is the body. See? Let me just do some quick measurements ...' Yellow crosses ping up on the screen, lines tracking between them, as the sonographer taps at her keyboard with one hand, keeping the other one steady on the probe against Lara's pelvis. 'Sorry,' she says, as Lara winces, 'full bladder, I know. We can't see the baby without it at this stage. Luckily we've got a good enough view this way, though. We won't need a trans-vaginal scan. So' – she clicks another button, and the screen changes – 'a single intrauterine pregnancy. Congratulations, Mum and Dad. Everything looks tickety-boo. It's telling us eight weeks and two days. A Christmas baby.'

'Is it all right?' Nick asks. 'Can you tell if the baby's all right?'

'I can show you the heartbeat – hang on a moment, though, that's a nice picture ...' Another click on the screen, and a piece of paper whirs out of a printer on the far side of the room. 'You can put that up on the fridge,' she says. 'OK – see that oscillation there? That's baby's heart.'

Nick stares, wonderstruck. They have a child with a beating heart.

'Lara,' he says, and she looks at him, her face filled with the same raw joy. The sonographer lets the probe hover where it is for a few moments, but Nick can tell their time is nearly up.

'What about ...' he begins. 'Is it called the – nuclear translucency?'

'Nuchal translucency,' the technician says. 'The test for Down's? It's a bit early for that. Eleven weeks, usually. You'll be offered it on the NHS, though of course you can come back here if you want.'

She lifts the probe away, and the screen goes blank. Nick feels a bizarre sense of loss, as though the baby is unreachable now. Until the next scan, he thinks. But as Lara gets up from the couch he imagines the baby nestling inside her as she pulls her jumper down, and he wants to wrap her in his arms so he, too, can keep hold of it, keep it safe.

They go for a coffee afterwards in town. A coffee for him, anyway: Lara has a glass of orange juice and a blueberry muffin, made hungry by the early start and the emotional ride of the scan. Nick watches her eat, struggling to contain the desire to touch her.

'That was wonderful,' he says, hoping to map his feelings on to more recognisable territory by attaching familiar words to them.

Lara smiles, her mouth full of crumbs. 'It's lovely to have a picture,' she says. 'It was a bit of an extravagance really, but it was worth it.'

'Definitely.'

She offers Nick the last bite of muffin, but he shakes his head.

'Have you thought when we might tell people?' he asks.

'Who? Work?'

He shrugs. 'I was thinking about my mum, actually. It would be nice to tell her.'

He's been feeling more warmly towards his mother these last few weeks; feeling a bit guilty about his reaction to her last letter, and about not being in touch with her. She must be back from her cruise by now.

'Of course we can,' Lara says. 'I should have thought – I should have said.'

'I wouldn't have wanted to until we'd had the scan, though.'

A brief frown creases Lara's forehead. 'I told Cath,' she says. 'I hope you don't mind. I met her in town the other day. I didn't ... I hope you don't mind.'

Nick swallows. 'Of course not,' he says. He does mind, in fact, more than he expects. But not having a mother must be especially hard for Lara just now, he tells himself. Women turn to their mothers when they're pregnant, don't they? And he wouldn't expect Lara to turn to his mum. Wouldn't want it, even.

Lara gets on fine with his mother. She has a way of taking people at face value which he finds – almost always finds – touching. The version of his childhood he's told Lara missed out some of the grittier details, and he tries to live with that version now. But the version of his mother Lara sees – well, truthfully, it's a bit hard for him to accept. The woman who goes on cruises with men called Robert; who works for social services and goes to salsa classes. Does he begrudge his mother those things, or the visits every few months? Of course he doesn't. Nor the pleasure she'll get from having a grand-child. She'll be the only grandparent the baby has: the only one it sees, at least. He'd rather it saw his mum than Cath Polkinghorne, he admits. But even so, he'd like to protect Lara from both of them. From everyone.

'Penny for your thoughts?' Lara says, and he leans across the table and brushes a crumb from her chin.

'I was thinking we've got the whole weekend ahead,' he says. 'We're not usually even up by now on a Saturday. What do you want to do?'

JUNE

Cath

Cath is careful not to take too much advantage of the pretext Lara's pregnancy gives her for dropping in with gifts, but she allows herself to buy a little baby blanket in one of Lingford's more chi-chi shops. It's crocheted in blue and yellow squares, an old-fashioned design she hopes Lara will like. The assistant wraps it in tissue paper, and the feel of it, the soft, warm rustle of the parcel, tugs at some nostalgic string inside her – but it's a good feeling, not a sad one, she thinks. And June has brought the garden into glorious bloom, too: every time she comes home the pale blue clematis on the front of the house seems to spread its arms in welcome.

It occurs to her one morning that it might be all right – might be *right*, even – to invite Lara and Nick for supper now. It's more than three months since their dinner at St John's Street, and surely they're on certain enough terms these days. She and Lara are, at least. She finds her diary, puts a hopeful question mark beside the following Saturday, and digs a card out of a drawer. She can deliver it when she drops in the blanket, she thinks. It's late enough notice that they can easily say no if they don't want to come.

But they don't.

Cath has never taken so much trouble over a supper party before, but half of the trouble is concealing the other half of it from Jim, making the arrangements seem effortless, almost accidental. The pretty napkins someone gave them for their silver wedding, which they've never used and which take half a day to find. *Look what I came across, Jim. Bob and Clare gave them to us, do you remember?* The African violets she plants in dark blue pots and strews around the house. *My mother always had African violets in the house. They were on special offer at Squire's and they reminded me so much of her; I couldn't resist.* The elaborate nibbles she makes, three or four different fillings wrapped in filo pastry, spooned into vol-au-vent cases or baked into tiny tartlets. *I've had such fun playing in the kitchen today. Not quite like the ones on* Masterchef, *but never mind.* Flowers from the garden, carefully culled so that they don't leave obvious gaps, and their old silver candlesticks painstakingly scraped out and polished. *That used to be your job, Jim* – a hint of reproof which he will take, she knows, in good part.

And for the menu itself, deceptive complication. A soup which requires pulses to be soaked, stock to be brewed, peas to be shucked. A fish pie with eight separate preparatory steps, combined eventually in a plain white dish and concealed beneath mashed potatoes and celeriac, smoothed blandly flat on top. Home-made ice cream, two different sorts, each of which require hourly stirring before returning them to the freezer, and biscuits made with crushed pistachios and olive oil, the dough rolled into a cylinder, chilled and then sliced like fat pieces of salami. She plans to make chocolate truffles – she has a recipe from years ago – but decides in the end to buy some: a final sleight of hand. *I ought to have made them, but it's such a palaver ...*

She rejects the idea of a new dress, too, and instead spends an afternoon rootling in her wardrobe for something to wear. She's always congratulated herself on her thrift in keeping so many clothes but she wonders now, pulling things out, why she's allowed some of these things to take up space for so long. A pile accumulates for the charity shop – a happy side effect, and another red herring for Jim – but she finds a cream silk blouse she used to love, used to think wonderfully elegant, and lays it out on the bed.

Lara and Nick turn up in jeans, and Jim, of course, is wearing exactly the clothes he always wears. Chinos in some indeterminate shade between beige and brown, and a checked shirt that doesn't, now Cath looks at it properly, really go with them. He's offered to put a tie on, and has donned a cardigan instead.

'What a pretty blouse,' Lara says. 'I'm sorry we haven't dressed up. I'll be in maternity tents soon, so I'm wearing my jeans while I still can.'

Cath waves a hand dismissively. 'I've just rediscovered it,' she says. 'I did a big chuck-out and found it buried under a heap of things I hadn't worn for years.'

'It's lovely. Such a nice colour. Here – we brought you some chocolates.'

'Come through,' Jim's saying. 'What will you drink?'

Despite all her planning, the evening begins awkwardly. Have the preparations been too meticulous? Perhaps she should have left more to chance, appeared at the door flushed with steam and wearing an apron. Too late now. The nibbles are laid out in the living room and the kitchen table is all ready, candles waiting for a match and embroidered napkins rolled inside the silver rings they never use.

'Lovely house,' Nick says, as Jim pours him a glass of wine. *Don't let on that you know about the baby,* Cath insisted, so Jim offers Lara a glass of wine too, and she turns it down with a little blush.

'Cath didn't tell you, then?' she asks, and Jim has to mime surprise when she explains why she's not drinking. Unconvincingly, Cath thinks. Damn it: why did she have to marry someone who can't tell a lie?

'I've got elderflower cordial,' she says. 'Would you like that? Oh, and help yourselves to these. Those are crab, and those are chicken. And the tarts are tomato and basil.'

'How delicious!' Lara beams appreciatively. 'Am I allowed crab, Nick? Can you remember?'

'The rules have got more complicated, I expect,' Jim says. 'In our day it was all a bit simpler.'

Cath smiles jauntily. It wasn't at all simple, she thinks, but let's not get into that, please, Jim. Let's not terrify these poor young things with our horror stories.

After that things settle down, but the food is centre stage all evening, and Cath's sorry about that. Somehow her deceptive simplicity has failed to deceive.

'This is amazing,' Lara says, a few spoonfuls into her bowl of soup. 'I wish I could cook like this.'

'It's really not difficult,' Cath says, but of course it is, and even her simplified explanation silences them. 'You can cut lots of corners,' she finishes. 'Ready-made stock, frozen peas, tinned chickpeas.' But then it's obvious that she didn't cut those corners, and the soup – just soup, she'd hoped, delicious but not at all noteworthy – has been elevated to a status beyond, even, what it deserves, and the scene is set for the fish pie to be equally admired, equally dissected.

Cath can tell from the way Jim's grinning at her across the table that he's pleased: he assumes she meant them to notice, she thinks. He's happy that she's made an effort, proud that they've noticed her skill. She isn't, honestly, much of a cook, but each time she protests they all smile knowingly. They have become a united front, now, determined to applaud: it has drawn the three of them together, not exactly against her, but so that she is left alone to demur. And denying her skill leaves only the fact that she has made an enormous effort.

'Stop,' she says eventually. 'You're embarrassing me. It's just supper. I won't even bring out the pudding if you go on like this.'

Jim smiles again, certain that she's being coy, that she's enjoying herself.

Is she? Cath wonders. Isn't this what she hoped for, in all those weeks when she resisted the temptation to invite Lara and Nick over? She has served them a sequence of exemplary dishes, and they have eaten them with relish. Even Nick, who looked so uncertain to begin with, has become animated. What is it, then, that feels disappointing? She pushes the question aside, gets to her feet.

'All right,' she says. 'Pudding.'

Jim responds to his cue, rising to gather the dirty plates and carry them to the dishwasher while Cath opens the freezer. She should have got the ice cream out sooner, she thinks; she should have scooped it into pretty bowls. Never mind: the more normal and homely the better, at this stage. The biscuits, nestled in a tin, look exquisite. The ice cream too, actually, moulded on the surface like miniature icebergs and frozen to delicate pastel shades of pink and yellow.

'This one's strawberry and rose,' she says, 'and this one's a sort of honeycomb.' It took three goes before the honeycomb worked; three lots of pans to soak and scrub.

Even Cath has to admit the result is delicious, though. The flavours complement each other perfectly, the rose and the honey and the pistachio; the fine crumb of the biscuits and the edge of crunch from the nuts are a dream with the velvet texture of the ice cream.

And at last, now, there's a conversation about something other than her food. Nick, in a burst of garrulousness, is describing a walking holiday a couple of years ago which involved more mishaps than seems entirely plausible, as though the story has been embellished by frequent retelling. They all laugh at his imitation of the dour Scottish hotel-keeper, the appearance of a bottle of whisky at an inopportune moment, the final disastrous breakdown of the aged Skoda. Jim asks Lara if she saw her photo in the paper – Cath had forgotten that: Jim meeting her at a conference he was covering – and she makes a joke about the company producing a calendar next year.

But then, just as Cath is beginning to relax and enjoy herself, Lara is catching Nick's eye, and he's making a waggish comment about sleep being her favourite activity these days, and so Cath is forced to urge them not to stay any longer than they want before Jim can even suggest putting the kettle on, or searching out the bottle of brandy that usually only comes out at Christmas but which Cath had imagined him offering Nick tonight. (She'd almost envisaged an old-fashioned scene in which she and Lara would retire to the living room and Jim and Nick would cradle a glass of brandy at the table, but she can see now that that was an absurd idea).

In the hall, Cath hands Lara her pashmina while Jim makes a last-minute attempt to engage Nick in some kind of male banter, asking his advice about an IT issue.

'Any time,' Nick says. 'Lara's more expert on the programming side, to be honest, but if it's just a matter of … And she's got enough on her plate, just at the moment,' he finishes fondly.

'Thanks,' Jim says. 'And thanks for coming. We've enjoyed it.'

'We have too.' Lara beams, wide-eyed with sincerity, and Cath is pierced by a pang of yearning and loss that takes her breath away.

'Honestly, such fantastic food,' Nick says, and Cath forces a smile, and a moment later they're gone.

'Well,' Jim says, 'that was great, wasn't it? A triumph, thanks to all your hard work.'

'Good,' says Cath. She turns back into the kitchen and starts collecting bowls from the table. She can feel Jim watching her. He's registered that something's amiss, she knows. Weariness and anticlimax, he'll think. And perhaps it is. Perhaps that's what you'd call it.

'I'm rather tired, I'm afraid,' she says, with an effort, and Jim comes up behind her and puts his hands on her shoulders.

'Leave the clearing up,' he says. 'It's Sunday tomorrow. I'll get up and do it.'

'I was thinking …' Cath stands irresolute now, caught in the flux of a change of heart. 'I could rather do with a whisky,' she says, and Jim squeezes her shoulder.

'In here?' he asks, 'or next door? Or take it up?'

'I don't mind. Take it up, maybe.'

She's hardly aware of climbing the stairs, taking off the silk blouse (hopelessly frumpy, she can see now), getting into bed. Jim sets a glass of whisky down beside her and disappears into the bathroom. No, she thinks, don't go. Don't leave me alone, or it'll be too late. As the bathroom door clicks shut, the first tear rolls down her cheek. But he's back in a moment.

'Oh, Cath,' he says. 'What is it? You've exhausted yourself. Such delicious food, but …'

She shakes her head, her lips trembling. 'I'm a fool,' she says. 'You understood that before I did.'

'A fool? Why are you a fool?' He climbs into bed beside her, still wearing all his clothes.

'They think I'm a fool,' she says.

'Lara and Nick? Of course they don't. They had a lovely time.'

'I don't know what I was thinking. I wanted – I thought if we gave them a really nice evening—'

'And we did. You did.'

Cath shakes her head again, more vigorously. 'It doesn't matter,' she says. 'They don't – It doesn't mean anything.' She takes a tissue out of the box beside her bed and mops her eyes. 'Oh God,' she says.

Jim doesn't reply for a moment. 'I think it matters to them,' he says eventually. 'Maybe more than you think. More than I thought.' Cath makes a scoffing sound. 'No, really,' he says. 'I think they're very touched by your kindness.'

'*Kindness.*'

'Yes, kindness. You've been very kind to them, and they're touched by it.'

'It's not that simple.'

Jim hesitates again. 'I think it is to them,' he says. 'To Lara.'

'It's not at all simple for Lara. She – she doesn't see her parents any more. For good reason, but even so ...' Cath reaches for another tissue and twists it between her fingers, struggling to shape the next sentence. She's reached the point where she can't tell which words are going to come out until she speaks them. 'And it's not simple for me. You know that. You knew it from the beginning.'

Jim puts an arm around her and she doesn't resist, even though just now she feels as though she hates him for seeing her like this, humiliated. Maybe it would have been better if she'd shouted at him downstairs, on some pretext, so that he'd left her alone.

'What did I know?'

'That I was – trying to turn the clock back.'

'Is that what ...?' He sounds moved. 'I thought you liked the idea of spending time with younger people,' he says. 'I hoped—'

'You thought they wouldn't want to be friends with us. With me.'

'We didn't know anything about them,' he says gently, cautiously. 'But I thought they'd taken your mind off things. I thought they'd cheered you up.'

Cath feels very small now, her voice barely audible and the rest of her deflating, sagging against Jim. She feels like one of those women who steal babies from prams. She fights back her tears, not letting her shame be softened by a display of remorse. It's all right for him, she thinks, for sane, blameless Jim.

Her tissue is shredded, sodden, but she doesn't want to reach for another. She can feel Jim's breath in her hair; a little scalding heat from each exhalation, then a sudden chill as he breathes in again.

'Do you think she'll ever come back?' she asks at last. There's a long pause. 'I hope so.'

'Oh Jim, what did we do wrong?' she says, on a sob. 'She was such a sweet little girl. What did we ... ?'

'We didn't do anything wrong,' he says. He holds her tight, repeating the words over and over until they become just words, just sounds, and meaning and truth float away, out into the night. 'We didn't do anything wrong, my love. We didn't.'

Mummy and Daddy and Emma

There's a new picture on the fridge when Jim gets home.
A familiar sort of picture: a house, a tree, a row of fig-
ures. There are names beneath them, these days, in
Emma's proud Reception class hand: Mummy, Daddy,
Emma, the letters carefully formed, correctly assem-
bled. It takes him a moment to realise what's strange
about this picture, and when he does it stops his heart
for an instant. This is the first picture that shows their
family without Rose.

Cath is upstairs, putting Emma to bed; he heard the
sound of their voices when he came in. He should go up,
before they wonder where he is – they'll have heard the
front door – but he can't drag himself away from the
picture. It's attached to the fridge door by a pair of but-
terfly magnets, and he takes it off to look more closely
at the faces. All three of them are mottled with pink dots

that he took initially for a kind of shading, but he can see now that they might be tears. He notices some marks showing through from the back of the sheet of paper and he turns it over, expecting perhaps an abandoned draft of this picture. And that's what he thinks it is at first, a building with a tall roof and one figure below – but this figure is lying down, and it's not a sketch but a detailed, finished portrait, as far as Emma's current skill goes. There are fingers and toes, ten of each, flowering like twigs from the hands and the feet; there's hair, curling around the head, and ears as well as eyes, nose, mouth. A red mouth, turned down in sadness. And the building, he realises, doesn't just have a tall pitched roof but a spire. There's a thump in his chest that might be his heart starting again, or thudding out of its settled rhythm.

He puts the picture back on the fridge and climbs the stairs to find Emma in the bath, her small body shining and perfect among the Matey bubbles.

'Daddy!' she shouts.

'Hello, my darling.' He bends to kiss her, and she throws wet arms around him, leaving blobs of froth that make her laugh when he stands up again. He's glad of the excuse to wipe his face, swabbing away the tears he'd rather she didn't see, even if she has added them carefully to her picture of him. Tears, he thinks, of joy as well as sadness, wonder as well as loss. For the fragility of life; for the tiny chances that divide one twin's destiny from another's, when they both started from the same

cell. For the unimaginable contingencies that might take Emma away from them, too.

She's ready to come out of the bath now, and he seizes a towel from the rail with a practised flourish and lifts it in front of him like a screen, preparing for the familiar charade.

'Where has Emma gone?' he asks, his voice teasing, roguish. 'Where can she be? She must still be in the bath, because she can't get out on her own, can she? She's not big enough to climb out on her own, without—' And then, as she scrambles slipperily over the edge of the tub and snatches the towel away from him, the stagey fake surprise tinged this evening with a thread of genuine astonishment at her presence, her realness, her competence: 'Oh my goodness, there she is!' And a gathering up, a swaddling, a hugging to him; damp limbs and soft skin and that smell of baby shampoo and applemilk childishness that he so loves.

'Daddy,' she says, when he's lying beside her in her bed, story book at the ready.

'Yes, my darling?'

'Did Rose die because she couldn't talk?'

He lifts a finger to stroke her cheek. 'No, my love.'

It's been three months since Rose died, and the house still feels hollow without her. Although the strange thing is that because she didn't speak, couldn't move, it's very hard to believe that she's not still here somewhere. Lying in her bed, sitting in her wheelchair, behind a closed door. Sometimes, when he comes into the house, Jim feels a pressing need to check that they haven't left her alone, got on with their lives while she waits patiently for them to come and find her.

'Are you sure, Daddy?' Emma asks. 'Cos everyone needs to talk. Don't they?'

'Talking is important,' he says, 'but it doesn't keep you alive.'

'What does?'

'Eating. Drinking. Breathing.'

'Rose could breathe,' she says. 'And she could have her special food.'

'Yes.' There's a pause. 'Poor Rose had things wrong with her brain,' he says. 'With her head.'

'Like she couldn't talk.'

'Yes.'

'So that is why she died.'

'I suppose it sort of is. But the things that were wrong with Rose – the things that made her not able to talk, or walk, or draw pictures – they made her poorly, too. In the end she got very poorly, didn't she? She had to go into hospital, poor Rose.'

'And the doctors couldn't make her better.'

'No.'

There's another pause, longer this time. 'So if you can talk, then you won't die?'

Jim feels agonised now. 'Everyone dies in the end, Em. When they're old.

'I know that,' she says scornfully. And then, in one of those bewildering turns that children specialise in: 'I *don't want that story. Tell me about you and Mummy, in the beginning.'*

Jim puts the book down on the bedside table and gathers her tighter in his arms. She wriggles, settling herself comfortably.

'It was the Lord Mayor's Show,' Jim begins, 'and it was a wonderful sight. There were floats and floats and floats, covered in flowers and models and people dressed up—'

'Did Rose die because of me?' Emma asks. 'Because I had all the talking?'

'No,' Jim says. 'No, no, no. It was nothing to do with you.'

'But she was borned wrong,' Emma says. 'If we were borned together, why was she borned wrong?'

'It was an accident,' Jim says. But that's the wrong word: it sounds like something Emma might have done wrong without meaning to. Spilling something, dropping something. Stealing her sister's blood. 'Not an accident, a – mistake. A problem that happened in Mummy's tummy.' He's never spelled this out before, and he's worried about getting it right, but he can't duck away now. 'It's a problem that happens sometimes when there are two babies in a mummy's tummy at the same time.'

'Twins,' Emma says.

'Yes, twins. Both the twins need blood from the mummy—'

'Blood?'

'Yes, that's how babies get their food in the mummy's tummy.'

'From blood? Eugh.'

Jim smiles. 'They're part of the mummy, really. She feeds them. But sometimes when there are twins, one baby doesn't get enough blood.'

'So I took Rose's blood?'

God, she's quick, Jim thinks. 'No,' he says firmly – although of course that's the nub of it. Twin-to-twin transfusion syndrome. 'Things were just connected up wrong. The pipes that brought the blood from Mummy.'

Emma thinks for a minute. 'If I didn't get enough blood, would I be like Rose?'

'Maybe,' Jim says. 'But you did. You were all right.'

'I can talk,' Emma says. 'Like you, Daddy. Tell me the story now.'

'This story?' Jim asks, holding up the book. 'Or – shall I tell you your own story?'

'My story?' Emma looks pleased.

'Your very own story. About when you grow up.'

She needs to think about the future, he thinks. He needs to remind her there's a future for her, not just the past she shared with Rose.

'When you grow up,' he says, 'you're going to be a beautiful woman, just like Mummy. Maybe one day you'll be in a parade, and someone will spot you in it. Someone who'll notice just how beautiful you are.'

'Will I be a teacher like Mummy?'

'Maybe.' Jim smiles. 'You can be anything you want, sweetheart. And you'll have your own babies, too. You'll fall in love and live happily ever after, just like Mummy and Daddy and Emma.'

Emma looks at him, pleasure and puzzlement mingling in her face.

'Do I have to do that?' she asks.

'Not if you don't want to,' Jim says.

Emma says nothing for a few moments,

'I don't think I want to be in a parade,' she says, and Jim laughs. Emma laughs too, pleased by his reaction. 'But I think I will have babies,' she says. 'Lots of babies, and lots of bunnies, too.'

Cath

The morning after their supper party for Lara and Nick, Cath wakes feeling as agitated and as desperate as she did in the first weeks after Emma left. She hides under the covers for a while, then throws them off. Jim's working this morning, covering a charity event, and she's glad of it. It would worry him, seeing her like this, and she couldn't stand that.

The bathroom mirror throws back her reflection: the red blemishes of exploded blood vessels, the brown blotches of moles. Dark stains under her eyes like bruises. Cath wants to turn away, but she forces herself to look. Here she is – a woman whose only surviving daughter has abandoned her. A woman who no longer has a job, or children, or even interests she can sustain for more than a few weeks. Recipe books – party cakes, healthy cakes, easy cakes – gather dust on the kitchen shelf. The garden needs weeding: the ebullience of June has roused bindweed and ground elder and nettles, and the new shrubs are being choked.

She can't face any of that today. Can't face the dog, even, with his old, sad eyes. She pulls on some clothes – not that stupid blouse, sitting on the back of a chair – and grabs the car keys. She has no idea where she's going, but she remembers the exhilaration of driving off into empty space from those first months after Emma left. The same feeling people describe when they cut themselves: the clarity of mind that comes from stepping over a boundary, beyond what the world expects of you. She's missed this, she thinks, as she pulls out of the drive. Missed the thrill of escape. She feels wild, angry, alive.

She makes for the A31, the A3 – the trunk roads that carve the county into segments, linking it to London and the coast – and heads south. A long road to drive along, going nowhere, detaching herself. Letting her thoughts loose to roam where they will.

It's her children, of course, that her mind turns to, and thinking about them, as the road speeds past, delivers a cocktail of comfort and release and pain that feels right for this morning. The early days: the struggle to feed Rose; the growing contrast as Emma bloomed and smiled and Rose lay, day after day, in her cot. The devastating fact that such a simple mishap, an accident of plumbing, could lead, step by unavoidable step, to that final scene: to Rose's sweet, blank face, near the end, distorted by the tubes and wires that made her seem more helpless than ever.

She never loved Rose less than Emma, but she never loved her more. Did Emma understand that? It worries her, that thought. Might Emma have felt like second best? Not enough of a compensation when they lost Rose?

Cath hid her grief, when Rose died, just as much as she thought right. Emma needed to see that she was sad, that Rose's death was a terrible blow, but watching them grieve for Rose mustn't make her feel that she mattered less; that her own hold on her parents' hearts was less secure. Although Cath was conscious, too, that there was a danger in clinging too hard to Emma: in making her feel she had to do all the work of two twins herself.

Did they misjudge it? Cath wonders now, as she coasts down the dual carriageway, barely aware of where she is. Were they too careful, or not careful enough? Did they fail to explain things in a way Emma could understand? Perhaps it's wrong – pointless, self-destructive, even self-indulgent – to re-examine all this, but she can't stop herself. Whatever Jim says, it's clear that they – that she – did something wrong. Something much worse than the thousands of other bad parents in the world; something so terrible that Emma was forced to run away, stay away, never come back.

Don't look for me. Don't look for me.

But Cath can't find herself, without Emma. For almost twenty years, she poured her energy, her time, her love – everything she had – into being a mother, and she has failed. She carried her worry and her vigilance deep in her bones, to no avail. Both her girls have gone. There's nothing left but the empty space they used to occupy, the hours they used to fill. What's left of her, without them?

And the sorrow, the self-hate, the anguish and desolation that comes with that thought is more than she can bear. More than she can allow herself to think about, or she'll tumble into the abyss. It would be easy, on the road. A tweak of the steering wheel; a slip of the pedal. The end of all this. Does she have the courage for that?

For a moment she lets go of the wheel, and the car veers sharply towards the crash barrier – and then she grabs it again, her heart pounding. No, no, no. Emma might still come back, she tells herself. There's still a chance of that – a chance to make amends, to understand. How can she let that go?

There's an exit ahead, and Cath pulls off the dual carriageway, turns into a garage. Her heart's racing, her head spinning with dust and grief. She's had nothing to eat or drink, and the car's almost out of petrol. She fills it up, buys coffee and a pastry, eats it sitting in the driver's seat. She pulls down the mirror to brush away the crumbs, and her face stares back at her again: the same tracery of lines and creases; the same weariness and suffering in her eyes.

And suddenly she feels furious with herself – with the version of herself that has given way to despair and self-pity.

It's easy, she thinks savagely, to allow herself to be buffeted between the winds of misery and guilt. It's easy to sit here and wonder why life has been so cruel to her; to count her losses. But she has just enough self-knowledge left to know that it would be insufferable not to acknowledge her blessings, too.

How does the pyramid of human needs go? Food, shelter, warmth, love, leisure. Something like that. She has a house, a garden. The dog. She has Jim. How could she explain to a Syrian orphan, a Palestinian living under daily threat of bombing, that this life isn't enough for her? Neither of her daughters has been raped or murdered. She doesn't have to contend with poverty or political oppression, cancer or torture or adultery. On the grand scale of things, she's among the fortunate. She has everything she needs to survive: food, shelter, warmth, love. Leisure.

There's someone behind her now, wanting the petrol pump. Beeping. Fuck off, she thinks – but she turns the engine on, noses out of the garage, turns back towards the dual carriageway.

Leisure, she thinks. There's the rub. *This* is the rub: nothing to stop her spending the day driving pointlessly, recklessly down this long road, burning up petrol for no reason. Unremitting leisure is a mixed blessing. Worse, perhaps, because it's one she's brought on herself. But resigning from her job felt like the right, the only, thing to do. How could she go on teaching other people's children when her own had fled? How could she conceal her

despair, day after day? Much better, so much more graceful and self-knowing to leave decorously at the end of the
year, a few months after Emma vanished into thin air,
with less notice than she ought to have given but with the
blessing, the warm wishes, of the Head. Who was probably, frankly, glad to see the back of her, Cath thinks
now. What sane Head would want Cath in their school
when they could have a bright young Ms Butterfly or Mr
Jaunty, fresh from their PGCE and cheap as chips?

She misses it. She misses the sense of purpose, the
filling of her days – even having something to grate
against, to complain about. Some days she regrets her
haste. But she couldn't go back. It was a blessed relief to
give it up, that's the truth. She simply didn't have enough
left to give.

She's almost at the south coast now, and for a moment
she feels a longing for the sea, the limitless reach of the
horizon. But she forgot to feed the dog; she needs to collect Jim's prescription, call the plumber, put a wash on.
Those are the things that tether her to the world now –
and the best she can do, she tells herself as she turns the
car towards home at last, is to manage the life that's left
to her with grace. To tend the garden, read books, make
a cake now and then. Hold on to the fragile thread of
hope. She's got by for all this time: surely it can't get any
harder?

And then, despite herself, she laughs out loud. She ran
into an old colleague the other day who was raving about
yoga. The thought of herself in Lycra, twisted into knots,

is absurd, but what is there to lose? Better passing fads than none at all, she thinks, as she passes the first sign for Fulford. Yoga might do her good, stave off the creeping pains in her back. It might even ease her mind.

Jim

Jim's timing is lucky: Nick's at home on his own when he rings. Or soon will be, anyway: Lara's going swimming. Some kind of pregnancy class, Nick tells him. Aquanatal.

'D'you want to pop over now?' he asks.

Cath's out tonight too. She's been persuaded to go to a yoga class with an old colleague from St Mary's, and Jim's pleased about that. Don't rush back, he said as she was leaving, stay for a drink if you want, and she tipped her head: *Maybe.*

'This is kind of you,' he says, when Nick opens the door.

'No problem.'

Nick leads him through to the kitchen. He's different without Lara around; more straightforward, Jim thinks, man to man.

'So ...' Nick says. 'Social media, was it?'

Jim hesitates. He's going to have to tell Nick more than he'd like to, he realises. He's been congratulating himself on his quick thinking at the end of the supper party, asking if Nick would mind helping him, but he hasn't really thought through the practicalities.

'The thing is,' he begins, 'our daughter – left home. She hasn't ... We haven't heard from her for a while. I don't know whether Cath has mentioned it. We don't talk about it much.'

'I'm sorry,' Nick says. Jim can see him processing this. Shifting his view of the situation, and placing himself at a safe distance.

Jim smiles, attempting not nonchalance but a degree of detachment. 'It's been tough on Cath,' he says. 'And we ... I've tried looking for her on social media, but I've never found a trace. It occurred to me that you might be able to give me some pointers. A fresh pair of eyes, anyway.'

'Do you know what platforms she was on, your daughter?'

'Facebook, certainly. And Twitter, I think, and Instagram. I've tried all those. I thought you might ... What do you use?' He meets Nick's eye for a moment. 'Emma's a little younger than you. Nineteen.'

Nick shrugs. 'We're on Facebook, Lara and me. Most of our mates are. But there's – well, yes, Instagram, Twitter. Snapchat. Things like Tumblr. We can try those too, but no harm starting with Facebook.'

'I've got an account,' Jim says, 'a profile, or whatever you call it.'

Nick opens up his laptop, clicks to launch Facebook.

'There are several Emma Polkinghornes,' Jim says, as he logs in, 'but none of them are her.'

'Sure?' Nick asks. 'Let's try again, just in case.'

But the search confirms Jim's findings.

'OK, so if she's on here still, she's probably using an alias,' Nick says.

'An alias?'

'Facebook lets you choose your username,' Nick says. 'You could have called yourself anything you wanted. Jim Smith, for example.'

'So searching for Emma Polkinghorne – that wouldn't find her, if she's using a different name?'

'No.'

Jim could kick himself. How could this not have occurred to him? Because he's a dinosaur, he thinks. He thought he'd cracked social media. He thought it was like the phone book.

'But if she could be calling herself anything she likes, how on earth can we ...'

How many accounts are there on Facebook? he wonders. Millions, maybe billions. How can they search through all of them?

Nick rests his hand on the touchpad. 'I can think of two ways in,' he says. 'One is through her friends. If we can find any of them, we can scroll through their friends list and see if Emma's there.'

'Can you do that?'

'Depends on their privacy settings, but – yeah, usually. The point of social media is to connect, after all.'

He looks expectantly at Jim. Those friends from before, Jim wonders – Ellie and Izzy and Jess – would Emma still be in touch with them? He's not sure how much she saw of them after she met Julianne, and he can't recall their surnames, offhand. He'd have to ask Cath.

'What's the other way?' he asks.

'Trying other names she might use. Her middle name, perhaps?'

'Louise,' Jim says. There are more Louise Polkinghornes than Emmas, but they draw a blank with them, too. After that they try variations of Emma, variations of Louise, combinations of initials, all to no avail.

'A different surname?' Nick suggests. 'A nickname?'

So they try Cath's maiden name, Cath's middle name, a couple of pet names from Emma's childhood. Nick is just about to close Facebook, suggesting they try Twitter, when Jim has another idea.

'Try Rose,' he says abruptly. 'Try Rose Polkinghorne.'

And there she is. Almost immediately, there's Emma, looking out slantwise from her profile picture.

'My God,' Jim says. He feels dizzy suddenly.

'Is that her?'

Jim nods. Shorter hair, like the person – the version of Emma – he saw in Fulford. Thinner, he thinks. Older. He feels a painful pressure in his chest: the relief, the anguish, the pride, is almost unbearable. His darling girl, alive.

Nick says nothing for a few moments. He sits back, letting Jim study the photograph of Emma.

'I'm sorry,' Jim says eventually. 'It's a bit ...' Using Rose's name, too: that's almost unbearably touching to him.

'Her privacy settings are very tight,' Nick says. 'Her friends are hidden, and most of her posts.' He types something, clicks, hunts. 'No contact info, no personal details, no places or work or events. Not much to go on, I'm afraid.'

'Wait,' Jim says. 'When did she update her – what's it called? The photo there?'

'In February,' Nick says.

So she's alive, Jim thinks, with an almost physical thump of relief. She was alive in February, which means there's every chance she's alive still.

'We can see her old profile photos,' Nick says. 'That's pretty much all we can see, but ...' He clicks on the photos one by one. A couple of them have comments on, or likes. 'We can check out these people who've commented on her photos,' Nick says, showing Jim how to bring up the list. 'In a moment we can see where that takes us. But let's just have a look ...'

'There,' Jim says, stabbing at the screen. 'That one there – that was taken in Fulford, I'm sure it was.'

'That was two and a half years ago,' Nick says, clicking again. 'All these other photos are from a while back.'

Two and a half years ago, Jim thinks. Before Julianne died.

'So – has she been off Facebook most of that time?'

'We can't tell,' Nick says. 'Sometimes people don't change their profile pictures very often. Someone Emma's age, though ...'

Jim is putting things together in his head. It was March when he thought he saw Emma in Fulford, just after she changed her Facebook photo. Coincidence, maybe. But evidence, possibly, of ... what? A new start?

'Might she have changed her name then too?' he asks. 'When she changed the photo?'

Nick shakes his head. 'We can't tell that, either. Whether she's changed it, or when. Sorry.'

Nick's still looking at the screen, but Jim can tell he's losing interest. Other people's lives, Jim thinks; other people's problems. But he's got a lead now. That was what he wanted, what he's been longing for. And he knows Emma's alive: he knows there's hope.

'Thank you,' he says. 'Thank you so much.'

The first thing Jim sees, when he leaves the house, is a full moon. Not just any full moon: it's huge, faintly traced with pink veins, hanging still and heavy over the church spire at the end of the road. Perhaps it's one of those super moons that seem to occur so often these days.

While he's gazing at it, his phone beeps. A text from Cath: *Going to the pub. Back by eleven.* Jim replies: *Have fun.* Then he types: *Have you seen the moon?*

Might pop out to take some photos. He opens the boot and grabs the small camera he always keeps in there, takes a couple of shots from where he is and a couple more from further up the road.

And then he gets back in the car.

He's not sure, at first, where he's going. He feels as though he's circling himself, circling the news he's been waiting more than a year for and still can't quite believe: Emma's face, looking back at him from the computer screen. A trail of clues he can follow. He wants to – but what does he want? To celebrate? To fulminate against his own ignorance, his stupidity at not asking for help sooner? Just like a man, Cath would say – but he can't tell Cath, not yet. He needs to – she won't be back until later anyway, and he needs to let things settle, get his thoughts straight.

He hasn't seen Dido for a while now. Things have slid into a kind of limbo since the day he turned up in vain on her doorstep, and he can't explain what he's been thinking: whether he's been waiting for her to call, or shying away from opportunities to visit her. It's been harder to deceive himself, he thinks, since that night; since the supper party for Lara and Nick. He's felt more conscious of what's at stake. But the full moon ... He doesn't believe in signs, he tells himself, but even so: if he goes all that way again and Dido's not there, maybe that means something.

As he drives, he feels his resistance strengthening. Now he's got a whisper of Emma's voice in his head, things feel different: the kaleidoscope has turned again, he thinks. He almost hopes Dido will be out; he imagines himself standing on the doorstep, then turning away.

But she is there.

'Hello.' Her expression is exactly the same as ever: pleased; unsurprised.

'It's been a while,' he hears himself saying, as he follows her through to the kitchen. Not what he meant to say.

'Yes.' Dido goes down to the workshop and starts closing packages, putting on lids. 'I'd begun to wonder whether you were coming back.'

'I'm sorry.' For the first time, there's an awkwardness between them. This feels suddenly like a tipping point – resuming after a break, coming back for more when he could easily not have done.

But Dido turns, smiles. 'I'm glad you came tonight,' she says. 'I was feeling a bit low.'

The words catch him off guard: she's never said anything like this before.

'Any particular reason?' he asks. 'Anything I can help with?'

She puts a hand on his collar. 'There is,' she says. 'Actually, there is. If that's still on the menu.'

Jim shuts his eyes, feeling the blood rush down to his crotch. It doesn't take much, he thinks. All those noble sentiments ...

And then he follows her up the stairs, into that familiar, flower-scented lair.

*

The guilt is worse, afterwards. Guilty sex is supposed to be exciting, but he enjoyed it more when he managed not to feel guilty. Does that make him a better person, or the opposite?

Dido lies beside him, her eyes on his face.

'Better?' he asks, and she nods, running a finger down his arm.

'So what were you feeling low about?'

'Oh, just ... lack of company.'

A little dart of pleasure at this suggestion of his importance to her is followed immediately by wariness. Needing him is Cath's territory.

As if she can read his mind, Dido chuckles. 'Not just your company,' she says.

She raises an eyebrow, then stretches, comfortable and unconcerned, but something in her tone has snagged Jim's attention. The emphasis of that phrase. Not just *your* company. Could she mean ...? He thinks back to his first visit, then his second, his third. How spontaneous it all felt, how natural. But – could it have been a familiar pattern for her?

His heart's racing now. What has he thought all this time: that she likes sex without strings. Likes sex with him. Did he imagine there'd been no one else since her divorce? No one else, at least, since that day he walked through her door with his camera.

'Are you OK?' she asks. 'Something on your mind?'

'No.' He forces a smile. 'It's late, though. I need to get back.'

'Mmm.' She doesn't move. 'I've got an early start too.'

He gets dressed, kisses her goodbye, breathes in the tantalising smell of her. Makes no promises as he leaves.

The moon hangs low over the horizon as he drives home. He can hardly quiz her, he thinks. It's none of his business, for one thing, and for another, if he's not the only one – if there've been a string of Jims, perhaps even others at the same time – she'd laugh at him for thinking she'd been laid on for his own especial pleasure, and he'd feel foolish. Selfish. Hypocritical.

But isn't he all those things already?

Lara

'So what did Jim want?' Lara asks, later that evening.

They're in bed, she and Nick, and she feels deliciously sleepy after her workout in the water. Most of the other women are much more pregnant than she is, and she loves the sense of limbering up for what's to come. And the biscuits and hot chocolate afterwards; the earnest weekly chat about pain relief or home births.

'He wanted to find someone on Facebook,' Nick says.

'Who?'

'Their daughter. She's missing. Out of touch, anyway.'

'Really? Since when?'

'A while, I think. More than a year.'

'How awful.' That explains Cath's reaction when she told her she didn't see her parents any more, Lara thinks. Poor Cath.

'Haven't they tried Facebook before?' she asks.

'He had, but he hadn't had any luck. He thought I might be able to help.'

Lara's conscious of a twinge of pique that Cath hasn't said anything about her daughter, given how much she's told Cath. But perhaps Cath reckoned she had enough to think about already.

'What did he say to you?' she asks. 'Jim. About the daughter.'

'Not much. Just that she hadn't been in touch for a while. That it had been hard on Cath.'

For a moment, Lara imagines her own father speaking those words. Has her absence been hard on her mother? They were close, when she was younger. She never meant Lara any harm. Quite the opposite: she was in terror for Lara's immortal soul long before Lara gave her any reason to be.

'Poor things,' she says aloud. 'Poor, poor things.'

Nick assumes she means Cath and Jim, of course. He wouldn't understand her sudden compassion for her own parents, even if he knew the truth. Nick sees things in black and white: that's the legacy of *his* childhood. His dad was the villain; his mum – for all her self-pity, her letting him down – was the victim.

'We found her, anyway,' Nick says.

'Cath and Jim's daughter? Really?'

'She was using another name. Rose. A middle name or something. She's on Facebook as Rose Polkinghorne.'

'So he's in touch with her now?'

'Not yet, but he knows she's out there.'

'That was kind of you, to help him.'

Nick shrugs off the compliment. 'It wasn't entirely altruistic,' he says. 'Doing something for them makes us less – under an obligation.'

'Is that what you feel?' Lara's voice sounds sharper, more surprised, than she expects.

'It wasn't very difficult, anyway,' Nick says. 'I'm surprised he … You'd think they'd have tried harder, if she's been gone all this time, wouldn't you? Classic boomers, though: useless with technology.'

'I suppose.' Her parents wouldn't have a clue about social media, Lara thinks. They certainly wouldn't search on Facebook if they wanted to find her. If they ever …

'What's weird, though, is that he asked me not to say anything to Cath, if I saw her. About looking for their daughter.'

'Protecting her, I suppose,' Lara says. 'Sparing her feelings. In case he doesn't find her.'

'But he has,' Nick says.

'Maybe he'll tell her now?'

'I hope so. She'd want to know her daughter's alive, don't you think?'

Lara doesn't reply. *She'd want to know her daughter's alive …*

Nick strokes her hair, oblivious. 'I can't imagine not sharing something like that with you,' he says. 'Promise me we'll never be like that. Never keep things from each other, even after thirty years.'

Another leap; another plummet. Oh God. It's almost as though he knows, Lara thinks, and he's twisting the knife deliberately. But Nick would never do something like that, would he?

She moves her leg, easing herself into a more comfortable position. The baby's already making its presence felt. Asserting its claim, she thinks, and she feels her mind shift, too, as she finds the right angle for her body. She's a mother herself, now. That's the most important thing in her life. And she needs Nick. Needs him to support her, to look after her, without conditions and contingencies.

So alongside the guilt Nick's words cause her, there's anger, too. Anger that Nick makes it impossible for her to say what she needs to say: that he leaps to his own assumptions, and there's never room for her to edge through with the delicacy her story needs.

This is the moment for it, she tells herself. This is absolutely the cue she needs. But what if she can't make Nick understand? That's what she was worried about in the first place, and there's so much more to understand now. Not just what happened to her, but why she lied about it. Why she's gone on lying. Every day the tally goes up, as though she's being extorted by some terrible loan shark.

And then, while her head is still spinning with arguments and reservations and protests, she realises that Nick's asleep. Just like that: the sleep of the virtuous. There's a brief moment when self-righteous fury burns so bright inside her that she knows it would carry her through the few minutes it would take to wake him up and tell him the bare facts, but she knows that's not the right way to do it. It's not Nick she's angry with, not really. It's not his fault his opinion of her is too high. She's deceived him: isn't that how he'd see it? She's sucked him in because she wanted someone good and true and honest. Someone who believed she was too.

Jim

After the night of the full moon, Jim is determined not to think any more about Dido.

When he got home that night, there was a moment when he thought Cath had guessed what he'd been up to, and the reality of the situation came sharply, shockingly into focus. There was a question in her face he couldn't bear to see; a reflection of himself that filled him with self-loathing. It's been four months now: four months of double dealing. He can't undo that – but certainly he must, surely he can, stop now. There can't be another scene like that, standing at the bottom of the stairs, warm from another woman's bed, while his wife looks down with doubt and fear in her face.

So when Dido texts him, a few days later, to say she's going to a trade fair in Frankfurt, it feels like a reprieve.

June

The right way forward will present itself, he tells himself. The opportunity for a proper ending.

Meanwhile, he gets used to the different kind of stealth associated with following Emma online. Making amends, he tells himself. He dreams of banishing Cath's sadness in one fell swoop. She never believed he'd find Emma online: if the police IT experts couldn't do it, how could he? she used to say. And now – well, he's found her, and yet he hasn't. He still has no idea where she is or what she's doing. He won't tell Cath until there's something more substantial to report, he's decided – but he's determined to find it. To find the next clue, and the next, until they lead him to Emma.

He takes to getting up early, while Cath's still asleep, and firing up his laptop for a spell of cyber-sleuthing. Emma's privacy settings mean there's precious little to see on her Facebook page. *Send Rose a friend request to see what she shares with friends,* the programme suggests each time he visits. No; he can't do that. He can't let Emma know he's found her, or she might disappear all over again. But thanks to Nick, he's got the names of ten friends who have liked or commented on her profile photos, and some of them have a laxer approach to privacy than Emma, which means he can see their posts, read the comments others leave on them, see who likes their photos. Each morning, he scrolls through the trails of messages between Emma's contacts and their friends, clicks on events they're interested in, studies the faces tagged in their photos.

He doesn't really know what he's looking for, except Emma's name. Rose's, he corrects himself. Emma's shadow. Emma/Rose liking a photo, commenting on a post; evidence that she's out there somewhere, and possibly a clue to what she's doing or thinking. But morning after morning he recognises nothing – no names, no faces – and it occurs to him gradually that this might be a wild goose chase. These people with their wide-open accounts aren't the kinds of friend Emma is likely to engage with any more. Not if she's trying to hide. Or perhaps there's a simpler explanation? If she's careful about privacy, would her comments on other people's feeds be hidden from him anyway?

Jim doesn't know enough about how Facebook works, and he can't bear to ask Nick again. He reads all the information Facebook provides about privacy settings, and a couple of online articles that aim to expose shortcomings in them, but they're all written for Facebookers who want to protect themselves. None, for good reason, are designed for someone coming at it from the other side.

One morning, he hears Cath's footsteps overhead when he's still immersed in Facebook, and he rushes to sign off, to open another page. His colleague Ken's daughter is getting married on a beach in Greece – it's been the talk of the *Gazette* for weeks – and that's the first thing that comes into his head. When Cath appears at his shoulder, he's perusing a website for villa holidays.

He turns, miming being caught in the act.

'I was thinking,' he says. 'Maybe we should book a holiday? Somewhere warm, in September?'

Now he's said it, he's delighted with the idea. But a glance at Cath's face proves him wrong.

'Maybe.'

He thinks of Cath on a beach, in the sun. *It would do you good,* he wants to say. *It would do us both good.* But he doesn't.

Perhaps he should tell Cath what he was really doing, he thinks. He's found out that Emma's alive. That she was alive in February, at least, and doing something as ordinary as posting a new photograph of herself on Facebook. Cath would want to know those things, wouldn't she? That she's using Rose's name: that's a bit more complicated, but Cath could cope with it. Of course she could.

But if he tells her right now, and the Facebook trail never leads them any closer, would it really be better for Cath to know that Emma was out there, living her life quite happily, God knows where? No: better to wait until there's a bit more information, more than this frustrating dead end to show for his efforts. Until he can tell Cath where Emma is, what she's doing.

He needs to look harder, though. He needs to redouble his efforts, think creatively. So in the middle of the night, when Cath is asleep, he climbs out of bed and creeps downstairs to the computer.

He's got to know the small band of Emma/Rose's friends he's been stalking quite well. There's Darcy Graves, who was at school with Emma and is now at university in Coventry, and whose page features a mixture of neon-lit party photos and political posts. Holly Dugdale, Aynoor Khan, Livvy Parker, all eerily similar, off at universities around the country. Then there's another group who are still, as far as Jim can tell, based in or near Fulford, working in pubs or shops: fewer political posts, but the same party shots. Jade Bell, Josh Lee, Hayley John. He knows what music they listen to, which fast food they prefer, whose parties they've been to. It feels even more grubbily voyeuristic, even more pointless, following the lives of these strangers in the depths of the night, and he's on the point of telling himself he should give it up, that there's no way it's ever going to lead him to Emma, when he comes across the first glimmer of an interesting lead.

There's a fun run in Grove Park in Fulford the following Sunday, to mark Midsummer Day. It's become a bit of an event locally over the last few years: a day of celebration, sometimes blessed with sunshine and sometimes not. There are bands, stalls, picnics, sideshows. Families gather and old friends congregate. Most of the Facebookers Jim has been tracking have marked it as an event they're interested in or going to.

If there's anywhere Emma might be, over the next few months, it's surely there, he tells himself. And the *Gazette* will want photos, of course. He can be at the finish line of the fun run; he can spend the whole day wandering around the park with his camera. He sits back, filled with an unfamiliar emotion. Not quite optimism, but a sense of things moving forwards. At last he has a plan.

Lara

It's too hot to be in London this midsummer weekend, but the outing has been planned for ages. Nick bought the tickets for her birthday: an early showing at the BFI and then an evening ride on the London Eye. They joke about the fact that they've turned into tourists since they moved out of town. They never went to anything when they were living in Neasden – museums, the theatre – but now it feels like an adventure to come up to London, with the added bonus that they can use their season tickets to travel free on the train at weekends.

It's still stifling at six o'clock when they join the queue for the Eye – a long queue, edging forwards patiently in several caterpillar-like chunks. Nick slips off to buy Diet Cokes, and Lara looks up at the huge circling structure in front of them, the pods rising slowly into the air. A small girl follows her gaze upwards, then smiles shyly at her, and Lara feels a lurch of longing and disbelief. Is it really possible that she'll have a child like this soon? A little girl with dark curly hair, wearing her best dress for a trip to London? She smiles back as the queue shuffles forwards. It'll be an extra treat to watch her reaction to the ride, she thinks.

But they find themselves sharing a pod with a group of American tourists, not the little girl and her family. Lara's disappointed, but she can hardly explain that she wants to stay near a stranger's child. As the doors shut, Nick leads her to the rail. He's been on the Eye before, for a friend's stag night, and he's looking forward to showing her the sights.

For now, all they can see is the architecture of the wheel. It looks, Lara thinks, as though it's been made from Meccano – one of the few toys approved by her parents. She remembers, suddenly, going to the fair with her father, years ago: another birthday treat. She remembers the exhilaration of the Ferris wheel, whirling round and round, defying the normal laws, as though for a few moments anything was possible. That stuck with her. Seeded something, perhaps. She takes Nick's arm. This, she realises, is her last birthday as a childless woman. There won't be many more trips like this, just the two of them.

'Can you see St Paul's?' she asks, as they start to climb. 'The Shard?'

'There's a guide, if you want to know what everything is,' Nick says. 'But what's really cool is seeing the whole city laid out. Like a map, with the river winding through the middle.'

She smiles. 'That's very poetic.'

The pod moves more slowly than she imagined, but gradually the view opens up. The river frontage on both sides is familiar – the panorama of the Houses of Parliament – but Nick's right that it's the pattern of the city, shifting steadily as they climb, that's most compelling: a jigsaw out of which emerges, now and then, a familiar landmark, like one of those children's puzzles where some of the pieces are shaped like a real object: a car or a cow or a castle. St Paul's and the Shard, yes, and Buckingham Palace, picked out of the background. Lara gazes down, imagining the people working, walking, talking far below: all the hidden life of the city. This *is* poetic, she thinks. A poem-in-motion: the ascent over London.

As they near the top of the arc, Nick touches her arm and points to the east, along the snake of the Thames, towards the curving horizon of Essex and the North Sea beyond.

'Isn't it amazing to think of the Vikings sailing up there?'

'Did they come this way?' Lara asks. 'Up the river?'

'Of course they did. And the Romans.'

'Gosh.' The things he knows, Lara thinks. Maybe it's a boy thing, like the football teams, the band members. She stares down at the river, a grey slug-trail beneath.

'I feel rather small, up here,' she says.

'It puts things in perspective,' says Nick. 'Makes your worries smaller, too.'

Lara looks at him, surprised. Can he tell she's had something on her mind? That's *not* a boy thing – not a Nick thing, she'd have said – but perhaps he's noticed more than she thinks. She's not sure what to say next: she hears herself laughing uncertainly.

'Maybe.'

The silence stretches out again, and Lara is both relieved and sorry. She wants Nick to tell her more about the Vikings, or the city's landmarks – but there's another bit of her that wants him to follow up that last remark, and her non-committal reply, with a question.

Because, quite suddenly, she feels a terrible urge to pour it all out: the darkest shadows of her childhood; the night Jacob led her through that gate; the awful months that followed. She feels like a fairy-tale princess cursed with a terrible secret. She stares out at the shreds of cloud, high above the city. In a moment the pod will start descending again towards the platform and she'll have missed her chance. Nonsense, some part of her says, but she knows it's true. Trying to reason things out rationally has only got her tangled in more and more elaborate knots. What's left but to succumb to an impulse?

She glances at Nick, and realises he's not looking at the view, but at her. And then she feels a great surge of emotion, as though something that has been battened down for years has been released at last.

'Nick,' she says. 'I've made a terrible mistake.'

'About what?' He smiles, as though he can't imagine any mistake too terrible for him to sort out for her.

'There's something I should have told you.' Her heart's racing now, and she feels a flicker of doubt. This is the wrong way to go about it. But it's too late. 'I didn't because – I don't know. I was ashamed, I suppose. Frightened.'

He hasn't moved, but she can see wariness in his face now. What's he imagining? That she's met someone else?

'It's nothing – about now,' she says. 'Nothing to worry about.'

'Something from the past,' he says. He looks relieved: her past is a box of terrors, in his view. Well, so it is.

'I should have told you,' she says again. 'I meant to, but – I've never found the right moment.'

'So tell me now.' She wishes he'd come closer, touch her, but he doesn't.

She sighs, then turns it into a wry laugh.

'I feel as though I'm playing with fire,' she says.

'What have you done?' He looks alarmed now. 'Tell me, Lara,' he says. 'You're scaring me.'

Where to start? At the beginning, surely.

'Something happened to me when I was younger,' she says. 'When I was seventeen.'

'I know,' he says. 'You lost your parents in a car crash.'

'No.' She shakes her head. 'That isn't what happened. I – Please let me just say this, Nick. Please let me tell you.'

'I'm not stopping you.' His voice has an unfamiliar edge to it.

'My parents were very religious,' Lara says, trying to ignore the sound of Nick's voice, the boiling fear in her stomach. If she can get everything out in the right order, she tells herself, he'll understand. 'We lived in a community with very strict rules about what you could do and say. It was – I found it very hard, as I grew up. I was so protected, so restricted.' She stops. God, this is difficult. 'And then ... I got pregnant. A boy in the community – one night, on the way home from a youth-group meeting – and I didn't want to keep it. I was seventeen; I didn't want a baby. My parents—'

'You were pregnant before?' Nick says, two steps behind her in this helter-skelter narrative. 'You—'

'I had an abortion,' Lara says. 'I couldn't – I know I should have told you, Nick, but I honestly couldn't bear to. I didn't want you to think ...'

'What?' he says. 'What didn't you want me to think?'

Lara feels like crying now. They've kept their voices low because of the Americans clustered on the other side of the pod, but Nick's last question was loud enough to attract their attention. Lara flinches as a couple of them turn to look.

'So your parents—?' Nick asks, as though his mind has just processed that bit of the story.

'Let's wait,' she says. 'We'll be down in a few minutes. Let's ...'

'No,' says Nick. 'Tell me now.'

Lara turns away to stop him seeing her tears. She was right to hesitate, she thinks. Wrong, wrong to give in to that mad impulse. She hears Cath's voice: *Once you say something, you can't unsay it. Until you do, you still have a choice.* There've been so few choices in her life; so few chances of happiness. Nick was the best choice she's ever made.

'My parents didn't die,' she says, 'but when I – they threw me out. Or I threw myself out. I—'

'So where are they?' Nick asks.

Lara shakes her head. 'I don't know. Probably in the same place still. I don't know.'

'You haven't heard from them? They haven't tried to find you?'

Lara swallows. 'I changed my name,' she says. 'They don't know who I am.'

There's a silence then.

'And who are you?' Nick asks at last. 'Do I know who you are?'

'Of course you do.' Lara can feel her whole body shaking: part of her wants to wrench open the door of the pod and jump out. That would be a simple answer, she thinks. She can't bear the coldness in Nick's voice, the edge of sarcasm. 'I'm Lara,' she says. 'I'm myself. Of course you know who I am. It was just easier not to have to tell people everything. It was so messy, and—' She takes a deep breath. 'I was called Ruth,' she says. 'I wasn't – I couldn't go on being Ruth.'

Nick doesn't reply. He doesn't meet Lara's gaze, either, but when they reach the platform and the doors open, he turns to check she's coming, holds out an arm to steer her. Not, Lara thinks, in a tender way; more like a tour guide making sure he hasn't lost his charges. When they emerge into the evening bustle on the South Bank, he stops.

'Let's get a drink,' he says. He looks at her then, and she can see that he's taken aback by her tear-stained face.

She follows him along the tree-dotted riverside walk, towards the bridge and the square bulk of the Festival Hall beyond. On their right, people are lounging in the little park, spreading picnic rugs and opening bottles of wine. Lara would dearly love a glass of wine, but she can't, of course. Instead, Nick buys lemonade at a stand, and they find a bench to sit on. Lara waits: she can tell he's gearing up to speak. But before he does, he takes her hand. A few minutes ago she would have been more than grateful for the gesture, but now it almost makes her recoil. He hasn't understood in the way she hoped he would; that much is clear. Taking her hand feels like softening the blow of what he's going to say. Worse, it feels like her father, holding her tight while he passed judgement on her.

'Lara,' he says – and then he stops again, as though he's thinking about her name, about the implications it carries now. 'I don't understand why you didn't tell me. I just don't understand it.'

There's some fire in Lara's belly now, and she lets it fuel her. 'Look at your reaction,' she says. 'Is it any surprise I was worried?'

'But—'

'I've been trying to persuade myself it wouldn't be a big deal, that you'd understand, but I was clearly wrong.'

'It's a pretty big deal,' he says. 'An abortion, and a new name, and your parents not being dead. It's a lot to take in. But it's you not telling me I really don't get. We're married. I'm your husband. Didn't you trust me?'

'Trust you to what? Not act like some fucking patriarch?' Her upbringing has left enough of a trace that it still gives her a thrill to swear. She glares at him, sure of her ground for a moment.

Nick's stung into raising his voice.

'You know I'm not like that, Lara. I believe in women's rights. A woman's right to choose.'

'Doesn't that give me the right to choose what to tell you?' she demands. 'Or does being so enlightened give you the right to know every single thing about me?' Nick opens his mouth, but Lara hasn't finished. 'Have you told me everything that's ever happened to you? Every last little thing?'

He frowns. 'I've told you everything important,' he says, 'but—'

'But you get to decide what's important enough for me to tell you?'

'You were raped and had an abortion and that's not important?'

'I wasn't raped.'

'You said you'd made a mistake,' Nick says. 'You admitted it was a mistake not to have told me. All I'm saying is, yes it was, and—'

'I have the right to make mistakes, too,' Lara says. 'I've made a mistake telling you now, that's for sure.'

She stops. This is so unfair. No one led Nick through a gate instead of walking him home. No one tried to make him have a baby he didn't want. His father left, and that makes him inviolable. The perfect man. She swigs the rest of her lemonade and gets up.

'Cath was right,' she says. 'I shouldn't have said anything.'

'Cath?' he asks. 'What's Cath got to do with this?'

She shakes her head, turns away.

'Lara,' he says, 'don't run away. We need to—'

But she's started walking now; she can't stop. One step then two, three, four. *Sometimes, in a marriage,* Cath said that day, sitting looking out at her garden, *there can be things you choose not to tell.* Lara didn't want to believe that: she thought her marriage was different. Better than other people's.

'Lara,' Nick calls after her. Is he going to follow? It seems not. She imagines him explaining her behaviour to himself – *Women do this kind of thing when they're pregnant; fly off the handle* – and it makes her even angrier.

She's walking in the wrong direction for the station, but never mind. She doesn't want to go home. She keeps moving with the crowd, slowed by Saturday-evening leisureliness: a great mass of bodies ambling along, with the sun still warm overhead. Why not let herself be swept along by them? Just for once, let the current carry her somewhere unexpected, unplanned.

But when she gets to the bridge, she stops. This is mad. She doesn't have anywhere to go, unless she turns up on the doorstep of a friend, or a colleague, and there's no one she can think of who wouldn't ask questions. Who'd say the right things.

She thinks about that little girl in the queue for the Eye, about the baby inside her. She hates mess and complication, but walking away won't solve it. Better to go back and finish the conversation. She turns, and starts to beat her way back towards the bench where she left Nick.

It doesn't occur to her that he'll have moved. But as she gets nearer, she can see an unfamiliar figure on the bench where she left Nick, a large woman in a bright orange dress. Perhaps Nick's beside her? But he's not. Lara stops a few feet away, staring, then comes closer.

'Excuse me,' she says. 'There was a man sitting here ...'

The woman looks at her, smiles, shakes her head.

'You didn't see him?' Lara asks. 'You didn't see which direction he went?'

The woman shakes her head again, and Lara understands that she doesn't speak English.

Damn it, Lara thinks. Damn Nick, and damn her temper, and damn Cath for ... But she has nothing to blame Cath for, she thinks. And in that moment it occurs to her that there is someone she can go to. Someone who'll say the right things.

Cath

It's not late when the doorbell rings, only ten thirty, but Jim's already in bed, ready for his early start the next morning. Cath's lingering downstairs, putting things away in the kitchen. It's unusual for anyone to come to the door: her mind always flies to Emma, of course, although she's schooled it not to. Probably a delivery, she tells herself. They come at all hours, these days.

But it's Lara, standing alone on the doorstep.

'I know it's late,' she says. 'I'm sorry, I ...'

'Come in,' Cath says.

Lara looks as though she might burst into tears at any moment. She comes into the house, into the kitchen, and Cath shuts the door behind her. Not so much to avoid disturbing Jim, she thinks, as to avoid him coming down. It doesn't look as though whatever Lara's come about is for his ears.

'Do you want tea?' she asks.

Lara nods. Cath puts the kettle on, and pulls out a chair for Lara.

'I'm really sorry, Cath. I didn't ... I'm in a bit of a mess.'

She looks so young, Cath thinks. Too young to be married and pregnant.

'We went to London,' Lara says. 'Nick booked it all, for my birthday. The cinema and then the London Eye. And something made me – while we were up there, looking down at the city, I had this feeling that I had to tell him.'

'About – the abortion?' Cath prompts. 'About your parents?'

Lara nods, her lip trembling.

'It was stupid of me, I know. I should have taken your advice.'

'I didn't ...' Cath turns away for a moment to pour hot water on to a teabag. 'I said it was your choice, didn't I?'

'You said I didn't have to tell him. You said sometimes it was better, in a marriage, not to say things.'

Something twists inside Cath.

'And what happened?'

'He was angry,' Lara says. 'He said he didn't under-stand why I hadn't told him before, why I didn't trust him. And then ...' She bites her lip, gathers herself. 'I was angry too, and I walked off. You know how when you're pregnant, you get – but I was only gone a few minutes, and when I came back, he'd gone.'

'And you couldn't find him?'

Lara shakes her head.

'Have you been home? Tried calling him?'

Lara shakes her head again.

'And he hasn't called you, or texted?'

'No.'

Cath gets up: she's spotted a stray teacup on the far side of the kitchen, and fetching it gives her an excuse to think. Part of her – the sensible part – doesn't want to get embroiled in a marital tiff. What can she offer, anyway? Her marriage – her life – has hardly been typical. She knows how hungrily she pursued these young people, how much she wanted to befriend them. And she also knows now why it was a bad idea.

But poor Lara, she thinks. She's touched that Lara came here.

'He said he supported a woman's right to choose,' Lara says, 'and I said I had the right to choose what I told him, too.' Her voice breaks. 'I thought it would be OK, but it wasn't. It really wasn't.'

'I'm sure it will be,' Cath says. 'You love each other, that's obvious. If this is the worst thing that happens in your marriage ...' It won't be, she thinks. Don't kid yourself. But she's not going to say that.

'The thing is', Lara says, 'that neither of us has an example to follow.' She twists her hands around her tea-cup. 'I mean – my parents are married, but it's ... a weird sort of marriage. No arguments. No *feelings*. And Nick – his mum was left on her own, and she had a rough time, and he – he had this ideal in his head all the time about what marriage should be like. What his childhood should have been like. And ...'

'He wants an ideal marriage,' Cath says.

'Yes. The two of us and the baby, and everything perfect.'

'Marriage is never perfect,' Cath says. It feels like such a trite thing to say, but it's true. 'The point is ...' She hesitates, about to give advice she hasn't always taken herself. 'You have to keep trying. You have to—'

But then there's another ring on the bell, startling them both. Cath gets to her feet, and Lara follows, both of them suspecting, hoping for, the same thing, Cath thinks. And sure enough, it's Nick.

'Hello,' Cath says. 'I thought it might be you. Come in.'

'No, thank you.' He stares at her, and Cath is disconcerted by what she sees in his face. He looks angrier than she could have imagined. He's always seemed so amiable when they've met, but there's an ugliness in his eyes now that frightens her. There's a taxi waiting at the end of the drive, its engine running: it feels like a scene from a thriller.

'I take it my wife's here,' he says, and Cath almost laughs at the clichéd line of the cuckolded husband – but that would be a mistake, she thinks. She needs to stay calm. It occurs to her suddenly that he's angry enough to hurt Lara.

She looks round: Lara is standing in the kitchen doorway now, her bump very obvious as she leans against the frame.

'She's just finishing a cup of tea,' Cath says. 'Why don't you come in and—?'

'I knew you were behind this,' Nick says. 'I knew it was too good to be true.'

'I beg your pardon?'

'The cheap rent. The friendly dinners. The little presents. I should have guessed what you were up to. I should have known you just wanted to ...'

'To what?'

'Interfere,' he says. 'Put ideas in Lara's head. Come between us.'

'No,' Cath says. But even to her ears the denial sounds unconvincing. She *has* interfered, right from the beginning, hasn't she?

'Were you jealous of us?' Nick says. The words are fired like little pellets. 'Is that it? Couldn't you bear to see us happy?'

Listen, she wants to say, *none of this is my fault* – but she can't speak. Her heart is beating very fast; she feels a little dizzy. Frightened, too.

'I'm her husband,' he says. 'She shouldn't be here with you.'

'Stop it, Nick,' says Lara. Cath turns round. Lara's coming towards her, towards Nick. She looks frail and tired, but she doesn't look scared. Her tone of voice suggests that she's recovered her sangfroid. 'Just stop it,' she says. 'You're embarrassing yourself.'

'And you're not?' he says. The edge of danger has faded a little; he sounds wounded now, almost plaintive.

'No.'

Nick starts to speak again, but Lara pushes past Cath and grabs his arm.

'Stop,' she says. 'I don't know what the fuck's going through your mind, but this has nothing to do with Cath and Jim.'

Nick opens his mouth to answer, then thinks better of it. He looks awfully young too, Cath thinks, suddenly less like a hard man than a teenager out of his depth in an adult argument. But she can't match the thought with the pity, the forgiveness that ought to follow. She's numb, still, from his accusations, the bitterness and aggression in his voice.

And before she can gather herself, Lara is bundling Nick off down the drive and into the taxi, muttering apologies to Cath, and Cath is staring after them into the dark.

For a few moments after the taxi pulls away, Cath doesn't move. A tiny breeze rustles the trees on each side of the drive, but otherwise everything's still and quiet. The chill of the night touches her face, her bare arms, and she shivers.

Perhaps if she tries hard enough she can pretend none of this happened. She can stick Lara's teacup in the dish-washer, turn off the lights and go up to bed. Maybe Jim will stir, and she can curl up against him. *Did I hear shouting?* she imagines him saying, and her saying, *No, just the television.* Falling asleep beside him, and waking up to think of it as a bad dream. But she's trembling. Shaking.

The irony is that she can see Lara and Nick coming through this: Lara's got enough balls, enough sense, for both of them, and Nick will have to accept the new version of Lara's past. Lara had plenty of time before they even saw the house in St John's Street to tell him her secrets, and she didn't. He'll have to face that. He'll have to deal with the flaws and fault lines that make them both human, but they've got years to work things out. They've got the rest of their lives ahead, and by the time the baby's born all this will be in the past.

But she can't imagine the four of them recovering ... what they had, she thinks. Whatever the hell it was. And she won't recover her dignity, not entirely. All those hours planting things in the little garden; the surreptitious slinking around the house; the ludicrous effort that went into the dinner she cooked for them. What was she thinking? What *was* she thinking?

She was thinking about Emma, she admits. She was wishing she could do those things for Emma. And Emma is in her mind again now: all the time Lara was talking, Cath was imagining Emma having a conversation like this with someone else, some confidante. Emma pregnant, perhaps; confused; battling with the past. Emma telling people her parents are dead. Is that what she does?

Eventually she turns back into the house, and does just what she imagined: puts on the dishwasher, turns off the lights, climbs the stairs, gets into bed. But Jim doesn't stir. She lies awake beside him, still trembling, and listens to him snoring gently.

She never forgets the gratitude she owes Jim for his kindness and understanding and patience. And she *is* grateful. Every day she's grateful. But gratitude is corrosive: gratitude and grief act together, she thinks, not to mitigate each other but in a terrible corrupting alliance. They have eroded so much, these last couple of years – these last twenty – that she feels sometimes as though the slightest tap might make everything crumble. As though what's left for them is more a matter of shadows than of substance.

She wants Emma so badly, just now, that the pain of it keeps her awake long into the night.

Jim

Jim's up early on the morning of the fun run. He arrives at Grove Park before seven, in time to photograph the first wave of volunteers setting out route markers. There's a scattering of marquees up already, and the St John's Ambulance arrives while he's standing on a little rise at the edge of the park, followed by a steady trickle of food vans. Ice creams, burgers, kebabs, chips; crêpes, noodles, pizzas, pies. A portrait of modern Britain in mobile catering, Jim thinks. He finds a van selling bacon sandwiches and coffee, then goes back to sit in the car for half an hour.

At eight, runners start arriving to register. They wander around the park in their numbered vests, some stretching with *who, me?* self-importance and others looking blithely unprepared for their exertions. Some are 5K-ers, running for a laugh, others 10K-ers whose route will take them out of the park and across the dual carriageway footbridge into the farmland beyond. Jim shoots a few pictures, takes down names, smiles – the *Gazette*'s ambassador, on days like this.

The first runners start at nine. As Jim wanders towards the start line, the marquees and gazebos begin to pump out music. The park's pretty full already, brewing up a festival atmosphere. Community support officers and committee members with hi-vis jackets and walkie talkies patrol the crowds, and the mayor comes on to the PA to declare the day open.

The early heats include family groups: mums and dads, children – some as young as four or five – and grandparents. Some are in fancy dress, or wearing sashes declaring their support for various charities. The commentator – a local radio presenter, his voice familiar – celebrates their efforts and the good causes they're supporting. Between heats, he informs the assembled merrymakers that the Fulford morris dancers will be performing later, and a marching band drawn from local schools. And there'll be an opportunity to take your pooches round the fun-run course at the end of the day – which is a good moment for a reminder that all dogs must be on leads, please.

Normally, Jim would be thinking of sloping off soon, returning to catch the tail end of the proceedings, but today he's determined to stick it out for the duration. There must be a thousand people here already, maybe more, but he somehow feels sure that if Emma comes today, he'll see her. And so he stands by the finish line for every heat, and in between he wanders between the stalls and displays, taking photographs and keeping his eyes open.

By the time the lunch interval arrives, he's hungry. He spotted a Thai food van earlier, and he goes to look for it now, his stomach gurgling in anticipation.

He's in the queue when he hears his name – 'Jim!' – and turns to see Dido approaching. Pleasure and apprehension hit him at the same time. He's never met Dido in public before.

'Hello,' he says. 'Are you running?'

A stupid question, since she's wearing a dress, a flowing silky dress that flatters her curves, but she laughs cheerily.

'No chance,' she says. 'I've got a stall, over near the Portaloos. I take it you're here on official business?'

Jim gestures, unnecessarily, at his press lanyard.

'Why don't you bring your lunch over?' she asks. 'I've got a couple of chairs.'

Jim hesitates, caught between definitions of reasonable behaviour, different versions of what he wants. Might this not be a chance for a civilised farewell? And is there any harm, if they're both here on official business, in being seen together?

Dido's looking at him coyly, amused by his indecision.

'Don't if you don't want to,' she says. 'I realise you've got a job to do.'

'Of course I will.' He smiles. 'I've never seen your wares set out in their full glory.'

Dido's stall manages, somehow, to recreate the atmosphere of her kitchen: among the stacks of pots and jars there are flower heads in narrow vases, bowls of dried herbs and a steel pan in which she's apparently been demonstrating her manufacturing methods. She takes a second deckchair out of the back of her van, along with a Tupperware box of sandwiches.

'How've you been?' Jim asks. He's trying to think how long it is since they saw each other. Ten days, perhaps, but it seems longer. Now he's with her, that old sense of the harmlessness of it all is sneaking back. Her manner is so light, her smiles so ready; she's like an old friend, he thinks.

'How was Frankfurt?' he asks.

'Interesting,' Dido says. 'There's a possibility of an export deal.'

'That's exciting.'

'We'll see.' She takes a bite of her sandwich. 'I'm flying out to Poland next week to meet a distributor.'

This is good, Jim tells himself. Polite, professional chat in the open air: a final coda. When he walks away, there'll be a tacit understanding that this is how things are being left. But he can't help thinking about Poland, about the distributor, about Dido's ready smiles being bestowed on them. He can't help thinking about her body underneath her dress, and the fact that he might never see it again.

'It feels like the right thing,' she says, and for a moment he's not sure what she's talking about. 'Nothing ventured, and all that. I might as well seize the chance.'

Silence falls, and Jim lets it extend, almost as though it's a calculated risk.

'How are things with you?' Dido asks, after a few moments. 'Did you try looking for Emma online?'

Jim doesn't want to talk about Emma. He should never have mentioned her to Dido. He's still framing an answer when the PA system wheezes into action again. The running will resume in a few minutes, the MC's voice announces, so finish up your lunch and come and cheer on the serious runners: it's the 10K up next.

'You'd better go,' Dido says.

'I had.'

'Come back later, if you like. I'll be here 'til the bitter end. Come and say goodbye.' She smiles, tilts her head, and Jim feels something slip inside him.

What does she mean by *goodbye*? he asks himself as he walks back across the park. Does she know – has she guessed, perhaps even decided for herself, that it's all over between them? Or does she mean the kind of good-bye that seals the next meeting?

The afternoon passes slowly. There's no sign of Emma among the runners or the supporters, and Jim has more than enough pictures already. He dutifully photographs the winners, the brave souls running in burdensome costumes. He climbs the hill at the edge of the park once more to take pictures from above. He captures the morris dancers and the marching band, the line of dog owners setting off around the course, a small child with an ice cream.

By the time the national anthem is played over the PA in what seems to him an incongruous gesture of nationalism, he's exhausted. He should go home now, he tells himself. He shouldn't go back to see Dido: the fact that he wants to makes him ashamed. But it doesn't stop him crossing the park again to find her stall.

Dido's almost finished packing up. She's leaning inside the van, and Jim picks up one of the boxes still stacked on the grass and waits for her to reappear. When she does, she looks startled for a moment, and then she laughs.

'I wasn't sure you were coming,' she says.

'Well, here I am.'

She comes towards him, as if to take the box from his hands, then leans over the top of it and kisses him. Just a quick kiss, a friendly kiss, and then she's loading the box into the van, and Jim picks up another. A longer kiss this time: he glances around when she pulls away, but there's no one else about. When the final box is loaded, he takes her by the shoulders and steers her around the side of the van.

'Jim ...' she says, but it's not a protest, not even a warning. She lifts her face, and he shuts his eyes as his lips meet hers. For a moment he feels perfectly poised between desire and fulfilment, but he's already thinking about following her home, about what he can say to Cath, about—

'Dad!'

He wrenches away, spins round.

Emma is standing there, just a few feet away, her face riven with dismay and disgust.

PART 2

JANUARY

The mornings are Emma's favourite time of day. Waking in what was once a maid's room in the attics, she's surrounded by birdsong. She never used to notice the dawn chorus, but it's hard to miss it here: the house is circled by trees, and her little room is at the same level as the birds, high in the branches. There are many more of them in the summer, a bewildering profusion of different voices, but even now, when there's frost on the ground each morning, there are still a few birds awake before dawn to greet the day.

Emma doesn't know their names, but she prefers not knowing. They could be tree sprites, she thinks sometimes, invisible but raucous, each with their own distinctive song. Every morning, when she wakes up, she lies in bed for a few minutes, imagining there's only her left in the world, her and the tree sprites – and then she tiptoes across to the tiny window and looks out at the garden, rambling and chaotic, and at the woods beyond, stretching away as far as she can see.

FEBRUARY

The days start early at Larkmore. Emma's usually awake by six, and she's lost the habit of staying in bed for half the morning. One of the things she loves about being here is the sense of being useful, endlessly useful; there are jobs to be done from first light until well after dark.

She sometimes thinks about the maids who used to sleep in the little room she shares with Jeanie, how they'd have been up at dawn to lay fires and scrub floors, and she's grateful that what awaits her is the babies. There are four of them on bottle feeds at the moment: Jonas, Addy, Lukas and Daisy. If they're quiet when she passes the nursery on the first-floor landing, Emma creeps down to the kitchen to make up their bottles before they wake, but often one or more is grizzling, and then she scoops them out of their cots, shushing and soothing, and brings them down to sit in the big playpen while she boils the kettle and measures out the powder.

The nursery is one of Larkmore's quirks: a throwback to her Victorian childhood, Penelope says, with a wry smile. The mothers can have their babies in their own rooms, of course, but most of them use the nursery at least some nights, so they can sleep better – and strangely enough, the babies often sleep better there, too. Emma volunteered early on to do the morning feeds. She loves the babies, and loves being trusted with them, too. Jonas is her favourite, although she tells herself severely that she's not allowed favourites. He's only five months old, but bright as a button and already trying to crawl, and his mum, Courtney, is happy for Emma to spend as much time with him as she wants. Addy is a screamer, and Daisy's mum mostly looks after Daisy herself; Lukas is a darling boy, solemn and silent, but it's Jonas whose smiles call Emma out of bed in the mornings. Jonas and the birds outside her bedroom window, singing their welcome to the day.

Emma thinks of her position here as being somewhere between staff and resident, but no one at Larkmore really uses terms like that. The house belongs to Penelope, so most of what happens here comes down to her – and even if it wasn't her house, the sanctuary her idea, there's something about Penelope that would still make you feel she knows best. Emma is in awe of her. Afraid is the wrong word – she's not a scary person – but she's so strong and calm, as though nothing that could happen would be beyond her competence. In another life, if she wasn't the lady of the manor, she might have been prime minister, Emma thinks. She's got that kind of voice, that way of talking. But what she says doesn't sound much like a lady of the manor or a prime minister, and the things she cares about aren't what you'd expect either. Her life, like everyone's here, is focused on Larkmore. The outside world is kept at a distance. The past, too, Emma thinks, with a flash of gratitude. It's today that matters, Penelope always says.

Penelope is up before her today.

'Morning,' she says, as Emma comes into the kitchen.

'Morning.'

'No babies awake yet?'

'I don't think so.'

Penelope looks smarter than usual: perhaps she's going out somewhere, Emma thinks. Penelope looks good whatever she's wearing – she's tall, wide-shouldered, her greying hair neatly bobbed – but today, in a navy suit and a pale striped blouse, she looks ready to put the fear of God into anyone who crosses her. Emma feels a little thrill at being alone with her, especially just now, dressed like this.

'Can I make you breakfast?' she asks, but Penelope smiles and shakes her head.

'I've had some toast,' she says, 'but I'll sit with you while you eat.'

'I'd better get the bottles made,' Emma says reluctantly.

'Come and sit,' Penelope insists. 'There's a pot of tea made.'

Everyone knows Penelope's story, or at least the version of it that's been passed from person to person for however many years it is now. Penelope grew up in this house, and it's belonged to her ever since her parents died when she was young, but she married an unfaithful bully who tried to take it off her – the house, and plenty more besides, people say darkly when they tell the story. But he'd reckoned without Penelope's fighting spirit. She hung on to the house, and her money, and from then on no men have been allowed at Larkmore, ever. The women who find their way to Larkmore have all suffered at the hands of men, Penelope says, and they need to feel safe. She's like a character from a children's book, Emma thinks: one of those wise, eccentric, benevolent figures who turn up when you need them most.

And that's exactly what happened to Emma. That day, that terrible day when she thought she couldn't go on any longer, she stumbled through the door of the crisis centre in Fulford and there was Penelope. She'd come to see someone else, but while Emma was waiting for one of the Haven staff Penelope sat beside her, took her hand, listened, and Emma poured out her heart. And even though she was more or less incoherent with grief and rage and guilt, Penelope got enough of the gist. *You can come to us,* she said. *You can come today, if you want. We're there if you need us.* Emma wept in her arms, wept with relief that someone understood even when she couldn't explain anything properly. It was as if an angel had reached down and gathered her up, lifting her out of the muddle and distress of her life.

'How's the course going?' Penelope asks now, as Emma pours herself a cup of tea.

'Fine, I think. I've nearly finished.'

The online child development course was Penelope's idea, of course.

'You're enjoying it?'

'Yes. I've got two more modules, then I have to write up a case study.'

'On Jonas?'

Emma smiles. 'Probably.' Her ears strain, then, for the sound of crying from above, but there's silence still. It's nearly seven: late for the babies to sleep.

'And you're happy, Emma?' Penelope asks.

'Yes, I'm ... Yes.'

Emma glances up to meet Penelope's eyes, then looks away. Penelope's an easy person to be with, but this morning Emma's aware of being watched. Studied. There's that uncanny feeling she's had before: that Penelope's reading her mind. Not just reading it, but – almost fishing out thoughts she hasn't even had yet.

She *is* happy, of course she is, but ...

Emma feels suddenly queasy. She'd like to push away the question, pretend it hasn't been asked. Penelope's still looking at her, still sitting in that particular way she has, motionless and attentive, like a Zen master.

'I have to go out,' Penelope says now, 'and you've got babies to feed. But later, perhaps, we might talk?'

The rest of the day passes very much like normal. Emma's roommate Jeanie comes down while Emma's still juggling babies and bottles.

'You don't need to do this on your own, you know,' Jeanie says. 'I keep telling you, their mums can do it.'

'I like doing it,' Emma says. 'And it means they get a break.'

A break from what? Jeanie might say, but she doesn't today.

Jeanie's been at Larkmore for two months, having run away from a children's home. *Hated it,* she says darkly, whenever she mentions the place, and she's fiercely grateful to be at Larkmore now. She's the only person here, apart from the children, who's younger than Emma, if only by a few months. Emma likes not being the youngest any more, but Jeanie's also the only person who asks questions Emma would rather she didn't. Questions that seem to come from nowhere, sometimes.

'Have you ever been pregnant?' Jeanie asks now.

'No.' Emma snorts as she tucks the bottle back into Daisy's mouth. Still half of it to go: Daisy's being slow this morning. 'Why would you think that?'

'I wondered if it was why you liked babies,' Jeanie says.

'Would it make me like babies?'

Jeanie shrugs. 'I dunno. Just wondered.'

There's a silence then. Jeanie's waiting, Emma knows, for her to ask a question, but she doesn't. Has Jeanie been pregnant? She doesn't really want to know, even if Jeanie wants to tell her. Other people's stories alarm her, and Jeanie ... she likes Jeanie, but sometimes Jeanie alarms her too.

'D'you want to get out the breakfast things?' she asks.

Jeanie gets up with a show of unwillingness, rolling her eyes, then smiles to show she doesn't mean it. She's tiny, Jeanie, hardly bigger than a child, and she's wearing something green and shapeless this morning that looks huge on her skinny frame.

'Is that the dress you were making?' Emma asks.

Jeanie halts, a pile of bowls in her hands, and does a sort of curtsey.

'D'you like it?'

'I like the colour,' Emma says. It's a strange green, dusty, like dried herbs. 'It's the same colour as your eyes.'

'Penelope gave me the material,' Jeanie says, and she turns away to hide her pleasure.

Later, Emma takes Jonas and Addy for a walk in the double buggy, then she helps Kadisha make soup for lunch. The winter spinach has gone mad and they have to keep finding ways to use it. Emma's getting to be a good cook: she likes opening Penelope's old recipe books – Delia Smith, Elizabeth David, Constance Spry – and finding things they can manage. There isn't much money for expensive ingredients, but for most of the year there are more vegetables than they can eat, and eggs from the chickens. And everyone who stays at Larkmore long enough learns to make bread and jam and gets to peel a million apples from the ancient twisting trees in the orchard.

At five o'clock Penelope comes back from wherever she's been, and Emma sees Courtney getting out of the car with her, but she moves away from the window and goes into the kitchen to offer help with supper. Friday is roast chicken night, and there's always a load of potatoes to peel.

Her conversation with Penelope this morning has been pushed to the back of her mind all day, but it's been sitting there, simmering. Usually the prospect of a private chat with Penelope after supper would be exciting, but it doesn't feel like that today. It's not even as though Penelope asked her anything difficult – just whether she was happy here – so she knows the dread and reluctance all comes from her, and that makes it more complicated.

The thing is, she thinks, safely installed behind a small mountain of potatoes, all the things that make Larkmore good are also ... She can't think of the word; she can't even think what she means, really. Just that nothing else seems to matter when you're here, nothing outside, and after a while that makes you feel you couldn't live anywhere else. That you're not quite a whole person any more, maybe.

No – not that. She's more of a whole person now than she ever was, Emma thinks: a person who can be relied on, who can do things, who's the equal of anyone. But something slips into her mind then, a memory of peeling potatoes in another kitchen. It makes her shudder, this reminder that she used to be someone else, that she belonged somewhere else, and her mind freezes, shutting it out.

There are twenty-two of them around the table that evening. Emma counts them, as if she's taking stock. She notices the wallpaper, too, for the first time in ages – an old-fashioned swirly flower print in pinks and browns that she'd probably hate if it was anywhere else – and that the table is much grander than she's realised, with elaborately carved legs and a once-shiny top, all of it battered and scuffed and stained by years of children's feet and hot plates and spilt water. She looks at Penelope, who's changed out of her going-out clothes and back into a familiar blue dress that hangs loosely from her shoulders. Penelope never sits at the end of the table, but wherever she does sit feels like the focal point, Emma thinks, the place everyone turns towards.

After the chicken there's a bread-and-butter pudding, made by Jeanie. Stodgy puddings are Jeanie's weakness, but no one ever gets tired of her pies and crumbles. There are no men here, Emma thinks smugly, to make them feel bad about eating them.

And then everyone's clearing the table, and Courtney and Abigail are groaning about the washing up, and Penelope catches Emma's eye and raises an eyebrow, and

Emma follows her slowly across the hall to her study –
the only room in the house no one would go into without
being invited. Penelope shuts the door and crosses to a
cupboard in the corner. For a moment Emma thinks
maybe Penelope's got a file on her, on each of them, but
when she turns round again she's got a box of chocolates
in her hand. She smiles, opening the lid and offering
them to Emma.

'Milk Tray,' she says. 'I've always loved Milk Tray.
When I was a little girl, my mother would only allow
dark chocolate in the house.'

'Thanks.' Emma takes a chocolate at random and eats
it so quickly that Penelope laughs and holds the box out
again.

'Have another.'

Emma takes a second chocolate, but she keeps it in her
hand this time. She shouldn't feel nervous, she tells herself. Penelope won't make her do anything she doesn't
want to.

'Did you want to talk to me?' she asks.

Penelope tilts her head to one side. 'I thought maybe
you wanted to talk,' she says, 'but if not, that's fine.'

Emma puts the chocolate in her mouth. It's a nougat,
her least favourite, but it occupies her for a bit, and while
she's still chewing, before she has to say something,
Penelope speaks instead.

'Larkmore is a wonderful place,' she says. 'I couldn't
have dared hope that it would be so wonderful when I
started out. The idea I had – it seemed outlandish, in the

twenty-first century. A place outside the world. Outside time, almost.'

'It is,' Emma says. 'It's exactly that.'

'But it's not quite real life, what we have here, is it? And that's fine; that's the point, in a way. Sometimes people need to escape real life for a bit. But I always think it's dangerous to forget that real life exists.'

Emma doesn't take her eyes off Penelope's face.

'It's easy not to think about anything else, you mean? While you're here.' She hesitates. 'It's today that matters.'

Penelope smiles. 'Today always matters,' she says, 'but for you there's tomorrow, as well. What I don't want, Emma, is for you to miss the right moment to take stock.'

For a while then, quite a long while, neither of them says anything, but Emma's mind is moving fast, skimming over thoughts and feelings in a way she doesn't often allow it to. That moment, earlier – that thought ...

'I ...' she begins. 'I'm not sure ...'

Penelope takes another chocolate and offers her the box again. Emma shakes her head; the taste of the nougat is still cloying in her mouth. Penelope eats another couple, and then she looks at Emma again, and Emma can tell she's going to do the talking after all. There's a flurry of anticipation, then a flurry of dread. But Penelope's voice is unhurried, casual.

'When people arrive at Larkmore,' she begins, 'I sometimes think it's as though they've been dropped from a balloon. They land here clutching a bag or two of belongings, or maybe nothing at all. Sometimes they couldn't even tell you how they got here. They've stepped out of a kind of mist, and they don't want to look behind them for fear of what might be there still.'

She raises an eyebrow, and Emma nods. She remembers that first day, getting out of the car and stumbling up the steps to the front door with almost no idea where she was. Just for a night or two, she'd thought, when Penelope suggested it. But she slept for most of the first week, pottered around the house numbly for the second, then wandered into the kitchen during the third and had a tea towel put into her hands. After a month she couldn't imagine being anywhere else. It was such a relief, such a blessed relief to be in a place where she felt … normal. To be condensed down to the core of herself, and of life.

When Penelope goes on, her voice is even gentler, almost as though she's telling a story.

'But eventually,' she says, 'the moment comes when you can start to understand what's happened to you. When you can see back along the path that brought you here. And when that moment comes – you need to look. Think. Talk, maybe. Because then there's a chance you can see the way out again – not along the same path, but navigating by it in some way or another. Picking up landmarks.'

The way she looks at Emma then, with her eyes wide open, completely focused on Emma's face, makes her want to cry.

It's been a long time, she thinks. A long time not looking back along the path. And she's not sure she wants to find the way out: she's not sure about that at all.

'Shall we talk more another time?' Penelope asks, when another silence has spooled out for a minute, or two, or three. 'It's late; you're tired. You were up early, feeding those babies.'

Emma is relieved, but also disappointed: part of her badly wants to stay here, under Penelope's spell, eating Milk Tray and listening to her talk in metaphors that colour the air as much as clearing it; that leave a sort of veil hanging between them that makes Emma feel soothed and impatient at the same time. But she can hardly sit here all evening saying nothing, can she?

Besides, the thought of another evening like this with Penelope, another day to look forward to it and to dread it, is enticing too.

'OK,' she says. And then, plucking up her courage: 'Tomorrow, maybe?'

Emma wakes late the next morning: it's almost eight o'clock when she opens her eyes. Oh God, the babies! They'll be screaming the place down. Then she notices that Jeanie's bed's empty. She throws herself into her clothes and runs down the stairs. In the kitchen, Jeanie and Penelope have a baby each on their knees, and Jonas is sitting in the playpen, watching.

'Good sleep?' Penelope asks.

'I'm sorry,' Emma says. 'I don't know what happened.'

'There's nothing to be sorry for. You're very devoted to these babies, but they're not your sole responsibility.'

Emma picks up Jonas, who reaches his arms towards her with a shriek of pleasure, then settles on her hip with a familiar, pleasing weight, bouncing gently against her and making earnest burbling noises. As though he's trying to tell her his dreams, Emma thinks. What would they be like?

'Has he had his bottle?' she asks.

'He hasn't finished it. It's on the side.'

She pulls a chair round so she can sit near Jeanie and Penelope – the three of them in a circle, each with a baby on their lap – and she feels contentment settling over her like the sun coming out. Jonas leans back in her arms, his beautiful dark eyes gazing up at her as he sucks and his tight curls tickling her skin.

Why would she want to think about the path that brought her here, she thinks, if it might show her the way out again? How could she possibly leave Jonas? Jonas makes small noises of pleasure as he gulps down his milk, noises Emma had never heard before she came here, and she holds him a little tighter, absorbing herself in the sight and sound and smell of him.

On Saturdays, when the weather's good enough, they take their lunch outside and have a picnic on what was once the lawn and is now more like a meadow. This is the first picnic Saturday of the year: an unseasonably sunny, almost spring-like morning, like a gift after a fortnight of rain and wind. The ground is damp, but they've laid groundsheets and rugs, made cheese sandwiches and sausage rolls, and when they've eaten them Jeanie is pressed into organising games for the children. Emma would prefer to sit with Jonas on her knee, but the older children, a motley crowd of half a dozen between the ages of two and ten, are clamouring for her to play forty-forty-in, so she hands Jonas back to Courtney and scrambles to her feet.

It's nice for them to live like this, she thinks, with other children to play with. Whatever they've been through, Larkmore is a happy home. They fight too, of course, but just now the scene feels idyllic: the trees in a protective ring, laughter echoing and small bodies scampering across the grass. Jeanie's running in happy circles, and Kadisha gets groaning to her feet now too, dragging Abigail with her.

Emma scoots behind a tree as the hunter counts to forty. She can see Penelope among the little group of women still clustered on the picnic rugs, taller and more upright than anyone else so that her head and shoulders are always visible, like the carved figurehead of a ship, and for a moment Emma wants to run back, to throw herself down on the rug beside her, but instead she slips further into the shade of the trees and presses herself against the rough trunk of the oak whose top branches she can see from her bedroom window.

'Coming!' she hears, and she freezes, listening for the swish of grass, the muffled panting, that will tell her the chase is closing in.

It's not easy to find peace and quiet at Larkmore, but there's a room on the first floor which is occasionally used as a bedroom, when the house is very full, but which is otherwise a sort of quiet retreat. Apart from an ancient sofa, it contains a bookcase with a bizarre collection of books (a row of Enid Blytons, some battered self-help manuals and a few red-leather-bound tomes with gold titles) and a desk with a computer on it. There's no rule about internet access here, but it's slow and people don't use it much. There are a couple of laptops for the children – the ones who are being home-schooled – but this computer usually sits idle.

Emma has been doing her childcare course in here, but that's not why she's come today. She hasn't been on social media for – it must be months, she thinks. She's not sure why she's doing it now, except that maybe it has something to do with her conversation with Penelope. As if there's something to find out, something to try out, before this evening.

It feels very strange, logging on to Facebook. She changed her username to Rose when she arrived at Larkmore. At first she thought about asking people here to call her Rose, because she wanted to think of herself as a new person, a different person, but that felt too weird. On Facebook it's good, though. It makes her harder to find. She'd already deleted her other social media accounts and shut her security settings down tight on Facebook before she came to Larkmore, and it feels like visiting a museum now – a random display of other people's posts on her feed that don't seem to have anything to do with her. Does anyone look at her page any more, she wonders? On a whim, she uses the computer's camera to take a photo of herself and uploads it as a new profile picture. Her face, deadpan, and the bookshelf in the background, slightly blurred. She stares at it for a moment, then clicks it away.

Before she logs off, she goes to Julianne's page, just to check it's still there, that Julianne really existed. Like visiting her grave, Emma thinks, a ritual she can't resist but still has to force herself to bear. People still post on Julianne's page sometimes, memories and *miss you* messages and occasionally an old photo they've found. Julianne on World Book Day in primary school, dressed as a wizard. Julianne in a bikini, holding a slushy.

No one knew how close they were, she and Julianne. No one knew how much they'd known about each other, what plans they'd had. What secrets. After Julianne died, the only thing to show for their friendship was Emma's number in Julianne's phone: without that, no one would have been any the wiser. No one except Kyle.

She can hardly bear to think about any of it, but she lets the words into her mind now: *if Julianne hadn't died.* There's no point, she tells herself. No point imagining how things might have been. But as she sits in front of the old computer, the shock and grief fill her again, the hate and fury and fear and desolation.

The enormity of her feelings in those first few months was terrifying: the sense that nothing else would ever stand a chance against the horror of it all. She had recurrent nightmares about Kyle, about herself being trussed and tortured. Chains, knives, gags, blindfolds. Gashes of red that might be lipstick or blood. The nightmares stopped when she came to Larkmore: that was the first miracle of the place. But sometimes she still dreams about Julianne. Julianne alive, laughing and joking – and it should be wonderful, but Emma's always crying, in those dreams. *What's wrong?* Julianne asks. *I thought you'd be happy.* And Emma can't bear to tell her – *You're dead; you're not really here; this isn't what happened* – so she tries to smile, but the tears keep falling.

For a few minutes she lets herself sit, looking at the photographs of Julianne. Not many of her smiling, but most of those were taken by Emma. A secret smile, just for her. When she feels the tickle of tears on her cheeks, she clicks the log-out button and wipes her face on her sleeve.

There's an argument, at supper time, between Courtney and Kadisha, over some stupid thing to do with the cooking. They argue often, and although they seem to enjoy the drama of it, chucking insults at each other and letting themselves get heated and angry, no one else does. Kadisha's little boy starts crying, and some of the other children giggle, wide-eyed, with fists stuffed in their mouths. Penelope lets it run for a bit, then cuts in quietly – 'Enough, I think' – and the row diminishes, moves into the kitchen with the dirty plates, and simmers on, muted now, while everyone clears and disperses.

'Emma?' Penelope says then, and Emma nods and follows her.

There are no chocolates this evening, but Penelope's cut some flowers – semi-wild ones, pink and orange and lilac, that grow in clouds in the falling-down greenhouse at the side of the house – and their smell fills the room. Almost like incense, Emma thinks.

'Sweet peas,' Penelope says. 'I used to grow them, and now they grow themselves. They come earlier and earlier each year.'

'They're beautiful.'

'I've always loved them.' Penelope leans towards them and inhales, and then, after a moment, she sits down in the same chair she took last night. 'Have a seat, Emma.'

Emma sits, feeling Penelope's eyes on her.

'It was a nice picnic today,' she says. 'The children had fun.'

Silence again. This feels, Emma thinks suddenly, like being with the counsellor they made her see after Julianne died. The counsellor didn't speak for ages, and then she'd ask some stupid question which Emma wouldn't answer. After the first couple of times she refused to go back. Penelope isn't likely to ask stupid questions, but Emma decides to get in before she does tonight.

'What do you think of me?' she asks.

'I think you're a great asset to us,' Penelope says. 'I think—'

'I'm not ready to leave,' Emma says. 'Do you want me to leave?'

'Good Lord, no. I don't ever – Well, no, very occasionally I encourage people to leave. Ask them to, even, when there are good reasons. But ...'

'What?' Emma asks.

'But you're very young,' Penelope says. 'Your experience is – different to some of the other people here.'

Emma is suddenly apprehensive. That morning at the crisis centre, the Haven – did she say more than she remembers? She casts her mind back: *I can't go on. I can't be this person any more.* That's what was going round and round in her head. Might she have said other things as well? *My friend died. They said I was in danger too but it was her who died.* Did she say that to Penelope? Could Penelope have worked out who she was, what had happened to her?

She can't explain why it matters, except that she's felt anonymous here, and that's been important to her: being a new person, a different person, without a past. And there's that sneaking feeling, the one she pushes desperately away, that she might not – that Penelope might not ...

'What do you know about me?' she asks. 'About my experience?'

'I know very little,' Penelope assures her. 'Except what I see in you.'

'And what do you see?'

Penelope screws up her face, as if she's selecting the right words with great care. 'I see someone who's been loved,' she says. 'And who has loved. Who has love to give.'

Emma feels her eyes filling with tears for the second time today.

'There are people here I can give it to,' she says. 'The babies.'

'Certainly. And you do. But not quite in the way I mean.'

'You mean a man?' Emma produces the word with a dousing of disbelief.

'Not necessarily.' Penelope looks straight at her now. 'I think you've lost someone, Emma. Someone who mattered to you. I think life was very difficult for you for a while.'

Emma nods, not daring to speak. Just for a moment, she longs for Penelope to know everything without her having to tell it. The people she's loved; the people she's lost. The agonies she's been through. If Penelope could understand all that ... But she couldn't, Emma tells herself fiercely. She wouldn't. Better to keep it locked inside her. Better not to risk her place here, and her peace of mind. Penelope's good opinion.

'It's nearly a year since you arrived,' Penelope says. 'Do you realise that?'

Emma shakes her head, but her stomach lurches. A year. She can't tell whether it feels like less than that, or a lot more.

'What I want to be sure of,' Penelope says, 'is that Larkmore helps you.' She stops, frowning slightly. 'Some people stay here a long time. There isn't a time limit, you know that. It's a sanctuary: it's here to help people for as long as they need it. But there's more for you in life than being here, Emma.'

'So you do want me to go?' Emma says. There's a note of aggression in her voice now that she knows isn't fair.

'Only when you're ready. But I don't think you'll know when you're ready unless you think about it. Unless you consider the possibility.'

Emma stares down at her hands, noticing the traces of earth beneath her fingernails, the fraying cuff of her jumper.

'The real world hasn't worked out so well for other people here,' she says, although she knows it's a flimsy argument. 'I could do more. Help more. You could train me. I could ...' She hardly dares voice this thought. 'You'll need someone to take over, eventually.'

Penelope smiles. 'Like Willy Wonka and his chocolate factory?'

'Yeah, we could do with a chocolate river here.' Emma smiles too, relieved that Penelope isn't offended.

'I don't need you to do more, Emma. I don't need you to do anything, except – dip your toe in the water. Go out a bit. Remind yourself that there are people out in the world who are happy.'

'How would I do that?'

'With me,' Penelope says simply. 'You could come out with me, sometimes. Would you be up for that?'

'OK,' Emma says. Her heart's beating faster than it was earlier, running through the trees to escape the hunter in the game. 'OK, I suppose so.'

MARCH

Over the next few weeks, Emma goes with Penelope whenever she has errands to run. Taking the cat to the vet; sending a parcel to a woman who left Larkmore last year. It occurs to her, standing in the queue at the Post Office, how long it is since she last saw a man. She's like a fairy princess shut away in a tower. The man behind the screen takes her money, unaware of his significance. There are male children at Larkmore, Emma reminds herself; it's not such a step. But it feels like it.

She's on the lookout for outings cooked up by Penelope just to get her out of the grounds, but if that's what Penelope's doing, she's cunning about it. And each trip turns into a little treat: they go to a garden centre to buy seeds for the vegetable garden, and Emma chooses a little cactus for her room. They take the car to be serviced and have lunch in a café round the corner while the mechanics are working on it. Then one day Penelope asks her to come along to the chemist to collect a prescription, and they're so busy talking about something else that Emma doesn't notice at first that they're going further than the village. When they pass a sign for Fulford, she swivels round.

'What are you doing? Where are we going?'

'To Boots,' Penelope says.

'There must be a chemist closer than this.'

'I wanted to go to the big Boots. I thought we could have a look in some clothes shops, too. Buy you something, maybe?'

'I don't want any clothes.' Emma can feel panic flaring. She hadn't realised how close they were to Fulford. Ten miles, the sign said. 'Are you going to leave me there?'

'Of course not.' Penelope glances at her. 'I'm not leaving you anywhere, Emma. You can stay in the car if you want to.'

But when they arrive in Fulford, the lure of the place is too great to resist. It's impossible to say what it makes Emma feel: something loud and bright, clanging in her head. As she walks down the High Street beside Penelope every step sparks a memory, and she has to fight to keep them out.

'Here we are,' says Penelope, as she turns into Boots. 'Coming in? Or do you want to wander? There'll be a wait, I expect.'

'I'll come in.'

Emma stays close behind Penelope, but she can't help seeing the racks of cosmetics, exactly where they've always been. Can't help hearing Julianne's voice, just over her shoulder: *What d'you reckon to silver sable? Shall I give it a whirl?* Julianne laughing, posing. *Try this one, Em – ice pink is perfect for you.*

And then she stops sharp in front of the shelf of pregnancy tests.

'I think I'll go back to the car,' she says. 'I feel a bit …'

Penelope looks at her. 'Do you want me to come with you?'

'No,' Emma says. 'No, just – can I have the keys?'

'Of course. I'll be as quick as I can.'

Emma doesn't run, but she walks fast, keeping her head down. The High Street's busy, but she doesn't notice the other people, or the shops she's passing. Her mind is in another time. Smears of eye shadow on the backs of their hands; Julianne slipping a lipstick into her pocket with a wink.

Then halfway down the hill something catches her attention – a shout, a laugh – and she looks up briefly. And just at that moment there's a car passing on the other side of the road, a car she recognises – and there, staring out at her, is her father. A little older, a little greyer, but definitely her father. Eye to eye, barely five metres away.

Emma freezes, her heart thumping to a stop. *Dad!* screams a voice inside her head. But he's gone already, long gone before she can take it in, before she can be sure of it.

A tumble of emotions floods through her, disbelief and yearning and regret and others too complicated, too compromised to name. Her father's face lingers in her mind's eye, a split-second image of his hands on the steering wheel. She remembers how he used to drive, his fingers flexing now and then as he spoke, almost as though he was playing the piano. She remembers herself beside him – the old Emma, before any of this happened. Before everything went wrong. The traffic flows past, another car and another; people jostle around her on the pavement. No one noticed: no one cares.

Emma tries to walk on, but she stumbles, and an elderly couple veer away from her, their faces disapproving. A few metres on she ducks off the High Street, along the passage that leads to the back entrance to the multi-storey car park. She remembers the smell in here: urine and disinfectant, the half-dark and the low ceilings. She hears laughter echoing, glass smashing, feels the swirl of alcohol behind her eyes. She can hardly breathe now, and her heart is hammering so loudly it fills her whole head. It takes her a while to find the car – she didn't think to notice where they parked. She struggles with the key, then the door, her hands shaking.

Stupid, stupid. She shouldn't have come; shouldn't have got out of the car. She hunkers down in the back seat and locks all the doors from the inside.

It wasn't her dad in the car, she tells herself. It couldn't be. The first time she's been back to Fulford and he just happens to drive past? So her imagination, then. Wanting to see him.

Her eyes fill with tears, and for the first time in a long while she lets them come. Crying is good, she thinks. If you let it, it takes you over, stops you remembering what you're crying about. Like pricking your finger, cutting your arm, blotting out what's behind. And she needs to do that; she can't let herself go there. It's too much, too hard.

She's not sure how long she's been in the car, curled up on the back seat, when Penelope knocks on the window.

'Emma?' she calls. 'Emma, are you in there?'

Emma uncurls herself slowly. She reaches up to unlock the door and Penelope opens it. For a moment she stands looking down at Emma's tear-stained face, then she lays a hand on her shoulder.

'Are you all right?'

Emma gives a tiny shrug. In Penelope's eyes she can see the reflections of all the other women Penelope has seen like this, all the times she's offered the same compassion. And Emma wants very badly to accept it, but it feels more complicated than it did that first day; than it has felt all these months since then. There's a voice inside her head telling her that she doesn't deserve Penelope's compassion.

'Do you want to come in the front,' Penelope asks, 'or are you happy there?'

Emma climbs out of the back seat and slides in beside Penelope. They sit like that for a while, side by side, and

Emma's sure Penelope's going to say something, ask something, but she doesn't. Instead she sighs.

'How about a drink?'

This is a surprise: there's no alcohol at Larkmore, but it doesn't sound as though Penelope's talking about a coffee.

'OK,' Emma says. 'I mean, yes. Please.'

Penelope turns the key in the ignition and backs out of the space. The traffic's bad – it always is in Fulford – but soon enough they're on the road out of town again. After a couple of miles, Penelope pulls off into the forecourt of a pub.

'This takes me back,' she says, with a little laugh.

The pub is empty; it smells of scented candles and deep frying. Penelope orders a gin and tonic, and after a brief hesitation Emma does the same. Part of her wants to swig it back and ask for another, and then another, but instead she follows Penelope towards a table in the corner and sits down with the glass cradled in her hand, watching while Penelope opens a packet of crisps and sets it on the table between them.

'Better?' Penelope asks, after a minute or two.

Emma nods. She can still feel the adrenaline swirling, the sickening tumble of emotions, but she can feel the gin, too, spreading a soothing numbness through her body. She ought to say something now, she owes Penelope that, but none of the sentences in her head lead anywhere. *It was ... I felt ... I saw ...* No: that's impossible. She's never mentioned her parents, her home, to Penelope, and it strikes her now, with a terrible lurch of guilt and confusion, that Penelope might think her parents are dead. And then there's such a pressing need to bury that thought that she manages to speak at last.

'It was just – it was really strange, being back in Fulford.'

And somehow those words make a bridge between the muddle in her head and the solid reality of the Emma who's sitting here in the pub with Penelope, the Emma who wakes to the dawn chorus at Larkmore. She feels her shoulders drop, the pent-up breath being released from her chest.

'I understand,' Penelope says, and Emma manages a tentative smile, because at least that means Penelope isn't going to ask any questions. But there's a flash of disappointment too, because she's caught between wanting and not wanting; between longing and dread. Just to speak their names now: her parents' names, and Julianne's, and Rose's. What would that feel like? She imagines it as jumping off a cliff, not knowing where you might land.

'It made me feel sad, going there,' she says.

Penelope nods once, twice, slowly, and then she says: 'I'm sorry. I'd like more than anything to see you happy, but I know ...' She sighs. 'Sometimes sadness – heartbreak, even – sometimes it gives you a greater capacity for happiness in the end. But it can take a long time.'

Emma swallows, feeling tears rising again.

'I don't expect that makes any sense,' Penelope says. 'But I think – we all have our shadows, Emma. Things in the past we can't push away for ever. It's not easy, I know. It takes courage. But I'm here to help. I'm always here, if you want to talk.'

Emma nods. She wants to touch Penelope's hand, but she can't. Can't find the right gesture or the right words. The sentences that spring up in her mind now are different: they're too long, too dangerous. Winding paths she doesn't dare to step out on to.

And then the moment's passed, anyway, and Penelope's looking at her watch.

'I'm afraid we must go,' she says. 'It's almost five. Have you finished your drink?'

Emma is grateful to get back to Larkmore that evening, grateful to wake the next morning to the birds singing and the distant sound of a baby crying. But things aren't quite the same after that day. As daffodils fill the garden at Larkmore, images of Fulford, and of her father's face, keep drifting into her mind's eye. Lying in bed at night, she hears Penelope's voice – *we all have our shadows* – and she imagines them circling her bed as she sleeps. Her devotion to Jonas doesn't falter, but when Lukas, in a sudden burst of progress, hauls himself to his feet and takes a step towards the cat before tumbling over, she doesn't rejoice as loudly as she would have done a few weeks earlier.

She finds herself drawn more and more to the solitude of the little computer room, where she's supposed to be working on her childcare course but instead starts cautiously, tentatively, looking up old friends to see what they're doing. Just a glimpse, at first, of their lives, but then more: following the trail of messages on their walls, clicking on events they're interested in. She lingers over photographs of places she knows; lets memories take shape, cautiously, inside her.

Jeanie, perhaps sensing the change in her, grows curious. Even more curious than she used to be, and petulant with it, getting on Emma's nerves.

'Did you have a boyfriend, before you came here?' she asks one evening.

'No,' Emma says.

'I bet you did.'

Emma shrugs.

'It's no big deal, you know.'

'Then why are you asking?'

And then another day, when they're chopping onions in the kitchen: 'What d'you do up in the computer room, then? I thought you'd nearly finished your course?'

'None of your business.'

'You're sly, you know. That's what my foster mum would call you. Keeping secrets.'

'Everyone has secrets here,' Emma says – but her conscience is pricked, all the same.

She and Jeanie have been roommates for nearly three months now, but they haven't really got any closer over that time. Jeanie's always asked questions, and Emma's always had the feeling that Jeanie wants to tell her things, and she's resisted both. She looks at Jeanie now, clothed in another of the odd dresses she's been making – this one rust-coloured, with big pockets at the front. Her thin neck and her round childish face stick out at the top like a straggly plant growing out of a pot, and her eyes are fixed on Emma's as though she's desperate to be noticed.

She could have been nicer to her, Emma thinks. Could still be. Jeanie's so needy, she tells herself sometimes, as though that's an excuse. Jeanie's taken to changing in the bathroom, as though she wants to draw attention to the fact that she's not a child any more, that her boobs are growing, maybe. *It's not as though you've got anything to hide,* Emma said this morning, and Jeanie blushed so deeply that Emma hated herself for it. Maybe she should give her a hug, she thinks now, but her hands stink of onion, and … People are careful with each other at Larkmore, she tells herself. She's careful with people. That's all it is. But when Jeanie lifts her board to sweep a pile of onion pieces into the pan, Emma smiles at her, tilts her head in a conciliatory gesture, and Jeanie beams back.

'Have you got any brothers or sisters?' she asks.

Emma grins again. It doesn't take much to encourage her, she thinks. 'Where'd that come from?' she asks.

Jeanie shrugs. 'I dunno. Just thinking.'

'Have *you*?' Emma asks, in case that's what Jeanie wants, but she shakes her head.

'I asked first.'

'I had a sister,' Emma hears herself saying. The words ring in her head. How long is it since she's talked about

Rose? That moment of guilt has drawn it out of her, she thinks. Not just that, though. Her mind has been turning that way, hasn't it? She feels a surge of energy; a strange sort of energy, almost self-destructive. 'She died.'

Jeanie turns big eyes towards her. 'What of?' she asks.

'She had problems with her heart,' Emma says. 'We were twins, but she wasn't – she was born with lots of problems. She died when she was five.'

'That's really sad,' Jeanie says.

'It was.' Emma's lip trembles; she feels light-headed suddenly. 'She was called Rose.'

'That's a pretty name.' Jeanie prods at the onions in the pan with little jerky movements. 'Do you miss her?' she asks. 'Is that why you like the babies here?'

A picture comes into Emma's head then: Rose lying in her cot, when she must have been three or four, and Emma standing with her face pressed against the bars. She remembers suddenly, sharply, the feeling she had in that moment: that part of her was on the other side of the bars, lying in the cot. That she and Rose had been prised apart against their will. That if she wished it hard enough, she could enable Rose to get up and stand beside her: to walk, talk, play.

She shuts her eyes.

'It was a long time ago,' she says. 'I was only five.'

She nudges her onion pieces into a pile with the edge of her knife and slides them into the pot to join Jeanie's.

'Do you have brothers and sisters?' she asks.

'I dunno. I was in care. They said I didn't. But I always wanted a little brother – I dunno why.'

'What happened to your mum and dad?'

'Dead,' says Jeanie matter-of-factly. 'When I was a baby.'

'I'm sorry.' Emma absorbs this: the fact that Jeanie's always been on her own. That she's grown up without a family. She remembers that Jeanie ran away from the children's home, and she wonders why, but she doesn't ask, even though she knows she ought to.

'Have you got a mum and dad, then?' Jeanie asks.

'Yes.'

'Couldn't you stay with them? Is that why you came here?'

'No, I could. I mean, I could have stayed, but I . . .'

'What did they do?' Jeanie asks.

'What do you mean?'

Jeanie frowns, as though it's obvious what she means. 'What did they do to you so you had to leave?' She cocks her head, curiosity getting the better of her. 'Do they know you're here?'

Emma stares at her. 'None of your business, OK?'

'OK.' Jeanie shrugs again, with an edge of bravado. She's hurt, Emma thinks, but she can't deal with that. She can't deal with Jeanie's dead parents and her wanting a little brother; with her hungry curiosity about Emma's family.

She grabs a wooden spoon and stirs the onions more vigorously than she needs to, and Jeanie starts opening the tins of tomatoes sitting ready on the side.

'Not yet,' Emma says. 'Don't put them in yet.'

'OK.' Jeanie hesitates, watching her. 'Shall I get some herbs from the garden?'

Bouquet garni, says a voice in Emma's head, but she pushes it away.

'OK.' She manages a smile. 'Anything that's growing in the herb bed.'

Jeanie heads out of the door, her ponytail swinging. She looks like a little girl from behind, Emma thinks, bouncing along on her old trainers. Emma shakes her head, trying to settle everything back into place. When Jeanie brings the herbs Emma tells her she can manage on her own now. Jeanie hesitates for a moment, then runs off down the garden towards the swing that hangs off one of the trees, and Emma watches her with a dart of resentment that she knows is unreasonable.

She tips the tomatoes in with the onions, chops up the herbs and chucks them in too; then she puts the lid on and leaves the pot to simmer. She was going to add other things, but she can't be bothered now. Tomato pasta sauce – that'll be fine. Everyone will eat it. And now she's sent Jeanie away she'll have to make the pudding on her own.

As she gets out the ingredients – eggs, butter, sugar, flour – she's conscious of her mind conducting a battle with itself. For a while the part that insists nothing's wrong seems to be winning, but the other part keeps circling back, wrong-footing her with little stabs and volleys: her father's hands on the steering wheel; Rose in her cot; the cosmetics counter at Boots. Bouquet garni: little Emma trying out the strange words, mangling them into a phrase that made everyone laugh.

The thing is, she thinks, as she cracks the eggs on the side of the bowl – the thing is that those images, those memories, are only the beginning. You might tell your-self that you can look back and just see the surface of the past, position yourself at the right angle so that the light glances off it and it looks smooth and solid and safe, but underneath – underneath is all the pain, all the regret, all the guilt and yearning and horror and hopelessness. Once you let the memories in, there's no saying where they might lead you.

And in that moment, Emma sees Julianne diving into the pool, her outstretched hands cutting through the surface of the water and the rest of her body following in a ring of spray and admiring glances, and her mind erupts.

That first day, Julianne was showing off. Diving off the top board, stretching herself tall and then plummeting down, a bright flash in her yellow bikini.

She couldn't do any of the fancy stuff you see on the telly, but she could dive straight and fearless, hitting the water with barely a ripple. There were always queues for the top board, but people let her pass – gormless boys blushing when she brushed past them on the steps, then chucking themselves off with shrieks and whoops, hop-ing she'd notice and smile at them. She dived maybe ten times – ten that Emma saw – and then she strolled over to the high chair where Kyle was sitting and propped herself against it, her hips angled so that her flat stomach was stretched taut.

Not that Emma knew it was Kyle yet, just as she didn't know it was Julianne. She was at the pool with Izzy and Jess, because they were bored and it was raining, a miserable summer day in the middle of the holidays. They'd idled in the shallow end, splashing each other and laughing. They'd swum lengths, counting the calories they'd burned, racing each other even though none of them could do crawl properly, so that they all ended up spluttering through mouthfuls of water. *Try butterfly*, Izzy had said; then, *Try backstroke*. Jess had done handstands, waving her legs in the air. Emma had floated on her back like a star, imagining herself swimming off a yacht in the Med.

And then she'd noticed Julianne – looked up at just the right moment to see her falling towards the water in the roped-off diving section – and felt a thrill of admiration, and of disgust at her own childishness. She'd pitched back on to her front and swum towards the rope barrier, attempting a more graceful breaststroke, as though she wasn't going anywhere in particular, and then she tilted up her head to watch Julianne climb the steps again and launch off. She came up, that time, a few feet from Emma, blowing the air from her lungs as she surfaced and then grinning in Emma's direction, as though she knew Emma had been watching. When she turned away,

Emma ducked underwater, then bobbed up again with the chlorine stinging her eyes.

'There you are!' Izzy's voice, just behind her. 'What is this – hide and seek?'

'Just swimming,' Emma said. 'It's a swimming pool, isn't it?'

'We're going to get something to eat,' Jess said. 'I'm getting cold.'

'You won't if you swim,' Emma said.

'I'm bored of swimming,' Jess said. 'You coming? They do hot chocolate in the café.'

'In a bit, maybe. You go if you want.'

The good thing about being in a three, Emma thought, is that two could always go off together. Usually that wasn't a good thing, actually – usually you spent your time trying not to let the other two go off, or even have a joke you weren't part of – but it meant if you didn't want to hang out with them any more, you weren't leaving anyone on their own. She pushed herself into a glide, glancing up just in time to see Julianne leaping off the board again, her body curving through the air, legs straight and taut like a ballerina. She watched her circling round – surfacing, climbing, diving – not hurrying, but not lingering either. Emma thought of the tiger she'd seen at a zoo, pacing up and down in enraged boredom, and she watched more intently then until Julianne stopped, sauntered over to the lifeguard's chair and leaned casually against it, lifting her head to speak to him.

And then Emma took fright. What if the girl realised she'd been watching all this time? Or what if that mad bit of her brain that did stuff without thinking suddenly got the idea of going to speak to her? She swam to the other side of the pool, near the changing rooms, so she could scramble out without passing the lifeguard's station and follow Izzy and Jess up to the café. She expected they'd still be there. Izzy would have drunk her hot chocolate and Jess would have played with hers; she'd push it across the table towards Emma – *Here, finish mine, I've had enough* – and Emma would try it and pull a face because it was almost cold, but she'd probably drink it anyway and then Jess would laugh at her – *You worked up an appetite, then* – and …

'Lost your friends?' said a voice behind her as she stood under the shower, and she turned to see the diving girl. Julianne. Emma was startled to realise that she'd noticed them, her and Izzy and Jess.

'Yeah,' she said, and Julianne stepped under the shower head next to her and stretched up her arms as though she was going to dive again. She was shorter than Emma, not that thin but – narrow, somehow, her skin a couple of shades darker than Emma's, spectacular against the yellow bikini.

'Kyle's not off shift for half an hour,' she said.

'Oh.'

'Kyle's the lifeguard.'

'Oh, yeah.'

'He's my boyfriend.'

Emma nodded. 'I saw you talking to him.'

Then: 'I'm Julianne.'

Emma wasn't sure, really, why it was a big deal, Julianne talking to her. She was the queen of the swimming pool, though; the one all the boys gawped at. There was something about the way she showed off without a qualm, pushed past them all on the steps, let them watch while she flew through the air. And here she was, shaking out her hair so the ends of it flicked over Emma's shoulders, her skin smelling of coconut and pepper.

They parted after the shower, heading for lockers at opposite ends of the changing area. Emma usually took her time getting changed, but she rushed today, bundling her wet stuff into her bag and barging out into the reception area as fast as she could. No Julianne. Had she been even quicker than Emma, or was she still getting dressed? She wasn't going to wait, Emma told herself, that would be weird, but she might buy something from the vending machine. She stared at it, making a slow decision between crisps and a Twix, then digging out her purse, counting out the coins—

'You don't wanna buy any of those,' said Julianne. 'They've been there for years, some of them. If no one buys them they just leave them in there.'

'Oh.'

'You're better off in the café. You can check the sell-by dates up there.'

'OK.'

Julianne smiled then, a sudden flash of light in the dingy lobby.

'I'm going up there to wait for Kyle,' she said. 'You can buy me something if you like. I haven't got any money.'

Emma felt a stab of disappointment. So that was what she was after, then. Well, never mind. No harm in standing her a packet of crisps.

'D'you live in Fulford?' Julianne asked, when they were sitting down. She'd ordered a milkshake and a portion of chips for them to share and steered them to a table beside the glass wall that overlooked the pool. She stared out for a moment or two when they arrived, and Kyle looked up, lifted a hand.

'Not far away,' Emma said. Izzy and Jess had gone: she was glad about that. 'Towards Lingford.'

'Oh.'

'Good chips.'

'Yeah, I love chips.'

'Which school are you at?' Emma asked, and Julianne threw back her head and laughed.

'I'm at *college*,' she said. 'When I bother going.'

'Oh.'

'What about you?'

Emma blushed. 'Stavelands,' she said.

They ate the chips and ordered another portion, and when they'd finished those Kyle appeared, still in his lifeguard's T-shirt. He was shorter than he looked at a distance, square and darkish blonde. Not very talkative.

March

'This is Emma,' Julianne said, as Kyle slouched into a plastic café chair with a can of Coke.

'Hi,' Emma said, and Kyle lifted his chin in a so-what, that's-cool-with-me acknowledgement.

Julianne chattered on for a bit, saying things about the other people in the pool, about the chips, about the top she'd seen in town, a bright sparkle of conversation that seemed to sustain itself without the need for anyone else to join in. But when Emma replied, saying something boring and stupid like *yeah* or *that sounds great*, Julianne grinned at her as though she and Emma were in on a secret.

When Kyle had finished his Coke, Julianne pushed back her chair. 'Emma's coming back to ours,' she announced, and Emma nodded, a sweet soft core of pleasure opening up inside her.

'Are you all right, Emma?'

Emma feels herself start. For a moment she has no idea who's speaking to her, where she is, and then the present comes back to her in a rush of agitation and relief.

Penelope. Penelope's voice, and Penelope's face, with a little smile as though she's caught Emma fast asleep in the middle of the day. But no – she's awake, and here's the cake batter half mixed, the pasta sauce simmering, the sounds of a Larkmore afternoon around her. Shouting and laughter, a baby wailing, the hum of the hoover.

'I'm fine,' she says. 'I'm nearly done.'

'Are you on your own?'

'I told Jeanie I could manage.' Emma glances at the clock: it's nearly six. Nearly supper time. She shivers, throwing off the memory of chlorine and vinegar, the curdled pleasure of that afternoon. Lucky, she thinks, that Penelope came in when she did. A lucky escape. Don't go there again.

'Shall I help?' Penelope asks. 'Shall I butter the tin?'

'Thank you.'

Emma reaches for the cake tin at the same time as Penelope, and their hands collide, and then Penelope grasps her fingers briefly, gives a little squeeze of reassurance Emma is hardly sure she means.

'It smells good, whatever's in that pot,' she says.

APRIL

Emma thinks of the routine at Larkmore as a comforting cocoon. People come and go; there are arguments and crises and niggling problems that run for a few weeks before fizzling out. But when you look back over a week or a month, the texture of life here is always the same. Not much disturbs the predictable pattern of it.

Not much. And usually, perhaps always, it's people who disturb it. People like Naomi, whose arrival at Larkmore in the second week of April causes more fluster than Emma has seen in all the time she's been here.

Naomi is beautiful. She has the kind of face that looks a little haughty, with high cheekbones and full lips and a perfect nose, but when she smiles she raises one eyebrow as if she's inviting you to share a joke. The women at Larkmore aren't much given to admiration, but everyone wants to sit next to Naomi, to be on the duty rota with her, to show her how the washing machine works or where to find clean towels.

Towards the end of her first week at Larkmore, Naomi comes into the kitchen one morning while Emma's feeding the babies.

'Is this your job, then?' she asks. 'Nursemaid to the little ones?'

'Only because I like it,' Emma says, a touch defensive.

She has held back, during the early rush to befriend Naomi. She's told herself people like Naomi aren't worth the trouble. But she's flattered when Naomi pours her a cup of tea and comes to sit with her while she spoons porridge into Jonas and Lukas.

'Can't say I've ever wanted a baby,' Naomi says, 'but these two are cute.'

'Aren't they?'

'Maybe they'll win me over,' Naomi says.

Emma gives her a curious glance. She doesn't usually wonder about the other women, about where they've come from, what they've been through, but Naomi looks as though she could have walked in from anywhere – a High Street shop, or an office. A suburban house with a brand-new kitchen. Emma's conscious of an unfamiliar urge to ask questions; of an even more unfamiliar urge to be asked them.

Naomi only stays in the kitchen for a few minutes, but somehow Emma feels the effect of her presence for the rest of the day: a vague sense of things being a little bit more interesting. She tells herself they've all been in need of some new company. The conversation at supper time is more lively than usual: they manage a long riff on *Gavin and Stacey*, and it turns out that Kadisha does a brilliant Welsh accent, and that Jeanie, little Jeanie, has Gavin's mum's Essex twang to a tee. Emma grins at her across the table, and Jeanie catches her eye and grins back, and later that evening they giggle together, up in their room, as Jeanie repeats some of her best lines.

Before she falls asleep, Emma allows herself to notice that the circling shadows have troubled her less these last few days, and to feel a guilty sort of relief about that. And then she thinks that perhaps she'll ask Naomi if she'd like to go for a walk tomorrow.

While Emma is feeding the babies the next morning, she hears voices in the garden. It's a beautiful spring day, and the kitchen window frames a view of cherry blossom, powder pink against a blue sky. Even from here Emma can feel the warmth of the sun, and she's itching to be outside: such a perfect day for a walk, she thinks, remembering her plan. There's blossom in the woods too, and such greenness on all the trees.

Whoever's in the garden is heading towards the house now, along the path to the kitchen door, and Emma is ready to smile at them, to say something cheerful. Then one of the people laughs, and she recognises Jeanie's voice. And even before they come through the door, she's guessed that it's Naomi who's with her.

'Morning!' Naomi says. 'What a gorgeous day.'

'I haven't been outside yet,' Emma says. Jeanie is looking at her, smiling, her face flushed from the spring air.

'Oh, you must!' Naomi says, turning away to pour tea from the big pot. 'Jeanie and I have had such a lovely walk.'

'That's nice,' Emma says. She's conscious that she's being childish, but she puts down Jonas's spoon with a little clatter, as if to draw attention to the fact that she's been working while Jeanie and Naomi have been out enjoying the early-morning sun. Stupid, she tells herself. Naomi doesn't belong to her, and nor does Jeanie. Jonas is looking at her with big, worried eyes, waiting for his next bite, and she smiles at him.

'More?' she says. 'Are you still hungry, you guzzler?'

Naomi pours herself a cup of tea and takes it upstairs, but Jeanie stays, hovering near Emma with that bright look still about her.

'It was really lovely out,' she says. And then, with a slight edge of nervousness, 'I wish you'd come.'

'I would if you'd asked me,' Emma says, and then she wishes she hadn't, because Jeanie looks even happier now at the thought that Emma might have been sorry not to be asked.

'We can go out later if you like,' Jeanie says.

'Maybe.' Emma shrugs. 'It's no biggie.'

Jeanie looks at her for a moment. 'Did you mind me going with Naomi?'

'Of course not.' Emma makes a *duh* face. 'Why would I mind that? You can do whatever you want.'

'OK.'

But Jeanie goes on looking at her, goes on hovering, and there's a sort of lump in Emma's chest now that makes her feel edgy and breathless, and she wants to say *shoo*, not just to Jeanie but to everything. The day, the kitchen, all these stupid people around her. She gets up to fetch another jar of baby food, and Jonas eats the whole lot, but then he's sick all over the high chair and Emma has to wipe everything down and take him upstairs to find some clean clothes.

By then she's almost forgotten about the walk, and the cherry blossom, but she meets Naomi on the stairs and Naomi's beautiful nose wrinkles up at the sight of Jonas.

'Yuk,' she says. 'Rather you than me.' She's wearing a long leather coat, the kind of thing that isn't often seen at Larkmore, and when she sees Emma looking at it she says, 'I'm going shopping with Penelope.'

Emma manages a smile. It's been a while since *she* went anywhere with Penelope.

'Have fun,' she says.

Naomi's coat is too hot for today, she thinks. She's wearing it because she wants everyone to know she's got it.

Penelope and Naomi aren't back by lunchtime, and Jeanie's gone back to bed with a stomach ache. Everyone's a bit subdued except the older children, whose squabbling gets on everyone's nerves. Kadisha sends them outside as soon as they've finished eating, and the sound of them running and screaming and laughing echoes back into the dining room as the adults clear the table. Emma's supposed to be washing up, but she offers to take Jonas and Addy out in the double buggy instead, and Courtney takes her place.

It feels good to get out of the house. Emma doesn't go towards the woods, but turns off the drive along the path that skirts round the border of the Larkmore grounds, passing the old sheds that are half hidden among brambles and nettles. They look a bit scary on a winter evening, but today they catch at Emma's imagination. There are several of them, one with a door still hanging in its frame, another with a skeleton of beams where the roof used to be. If Jeanie was with her, Emma thinks, they could make up a story about a mad old woman living here. Keeping pigs, maybe – feeding them scraps and talking to them as if they were people. Maybe she's forgotten human language, it's been so long since she spoke to anyone. Emma peers around the door of the last shed, half expecting to see someone inside, scaring herself enough to make her laugh.

But then it occurs to her that she doesn't really know whether Jeanie does made-up stories like that, doesn't know whether she'd get the idea of it. Addy starts complaining and Emma shushes him impatiently, and the fun of it melts away and they're just old sheds, falling down bit by bit.

She pushes the buggy on along the path, reaching the bit under the trees that's still muddy, and the pushing is harder work. Both the babies are whingeing now, and suddenly it doesn't feel like a spring day any more. When Emma looks up through the trees, the sky isn't blue now but grey. But it feels as if the change is inside her head: as if the mud and the grey sky are things she's made to happen. As if she's spoiled the day.

She stops, shuts her eyes, ignoring the wailing of the babies. She remembers this feeling, the panicky feeling that everything bad in the world is her fault. It's a long time since she's felt it, but now it's back it's as though it's never really gone away; as though she's been kidding herself, pretending everything's OK. And then she thinks of Jeanie coming into the kitchen with Naomi and she feels a tug of grief. Not for Jeanie, and certainly not for Naomi, but for—

For that summer, she thinks. That shining summer with Julianne, when nothing else mattered, and she felt like someone. Felt like she had a life ahead of her.

After the day when she met Julianne, the holidays fell into a pattern. At first, Emma made Izzy and Jess come with her to the pool, but she always ended up leaving with Julianne and Kyle, and after a bit Izzy and Jess lost interest and Emma went on her own. Julianne tried to teach her to dive, but Emma was useless at it: they both preferred it when Julianne dived and Emma watched. After the pool they'd hang out in town, or at Kyle's flat, which seemed to be Julianne's flat, too, although there wasn't much to mark it out as a place she lived.

When he wasn't being a lifeguard or smoking weed, Kyle spent a lot of time gaming. Call of Duty and Fortnite seemed to interest him more than Julianne, at least when Emma was there, but that was fine with Emma. Kyle was OK, but he was older than the other boys she knew, and she was a bit in awe of him. She liked it better when he wasn't around.

'Me and Emma are going out,' Julianne would say, and Kyle would look up and nod. When they got back he'd stop for a bit and open beers for them, and sometimes they'd watch a film – usually one he'd streamed from somewhere, more hard-core than Emma was used to, but she didn't mind. She wasn't squeamish.

Emma didn't talk to her parents about Julianne or Kyle. They didn't ask many questions: they were pleased she was getting out of the house, especially to go swimming. They were OK, her parents, but they were the kind of parents you had to protect from things they didn't need to know about. Kyle was twenty-one and Julianne was nineteen; that would have worried them. Emma didn't want them to be worried, so it was easier to let them think she was with Izzy and Jess, or any of the others.

When school started again, Emma saw Julianne, and sometimes Kyle, after school and at the weekends and sometimes, not very often, during the school day. Julianne offered to ring up the school absence line and pretend to be Emma's mum, but Emma thought she could do it more convincingly. It was a recorded message, and Emma had to think of something to say that would make Julianne giggle but wouldn't make the school suspicious. For some reason, Julianne thought *Emma's asthma's very bad today so I'm taking her to the doctor* was hilarious. Everyone at school knew Cath was an anxious mum. And Emma never skived more than one day at a time.

Julianne was fun to hang out with. She was cooler than Emma, of course, but she didn't laugh at her, after that first time when Emma asked her which school she went to. She worked part-time in a restaurant in Fulford and she had endless funny stories about the customers and the boss. Men were always making passes at her, and she was always outsmarting them. *Hashtag me bloody too,* she'd say. She was supposed to be doing hospitality and tourism at Fulford College, but she didn't like the course much. She was thinking of switching to hair and beauty, and she spent lots of time doing new make-up looks on Emma. Emma would pretend to be a snooty client – *I'm thinking* subtle, *darling* – and she'd sit looking up at Julianne's face through her eyelashes while Julianne bent over her with her wands and brushes. Julianne had such a look of concentration, so different to her familiar jokey face. More like the focused look she got when she was diving, Emma thought.

It took Emma a while to realise that things weren't going well between Julianne and Kyle. One day when she turned up at the flat she could hear them arguing through the door, and she waited outside for a bit, hoping they'd stop, then slipped away. Julianne texted her later: *what happened 2 u?* and Emma replied, *sorry not feeling well.* There was a little gap after that, and Emma was worried Julianne was angry, but then another message pinged up: *Emmas asthmas very bad today.* She sent back a row of laughing-crying emojis and *cu sat?*

For a while Julianne hardly talked about Kyle, and then she talked about him more than she ever had – whole afternoons harping on about the pros and cons of Kyle, or something he'd said or done. There seemed to be more cons than pros, but Emma suspected there were things she didn't understand. She was bored by it all, was the truth. She wished they could talk about other stuff, that things could go back to how they had been. Kyle on the lifeguard's chair in his red and yellow T-shirt, and Emma and Julianne in the pool, or the café, or heading out into town.

Christmas came and went. Julianne went home to her parents' house for Christmas and didn't go back to the flat straight afterwards, which made things more complicated because it seemed to be understood between the two of them that their parents' houses were off limits. Instead, they met in town, in pubs and parks, although it was too cold that winter to hang around outside. They went to the cinema and bought huge boxes of popcorn and sniggered in the back row. Julianne was sometimes a bit quiet, but at other times she made up for it by being louder and crazier than ever.

April

And then things happened quite quickly. Julianne and Kyle had a massive argument, and Julianne told Emma that was that, she'd broken up with him. Julianne cried a lot, got drunk a lot, laughed a lot. Kyle, for the first time, messaged Emma and asked her to come over, and she was touched, even though he didn't say much when she got there. She played Fortnite with him, which basically meant watching him play. It was odd seeing him without Julianne there. It didn't make her feel anything: it was almost as if he was an avatar, like the ones on the screen, invented by Julianne to be her boyfriend. A Sims lifeguard, watching the pool and blinking slowly, then left sitting in his flat on his own to stare at a screen. He texted her again the next week, and Emma thought maybe he'd talk to her more this time, but it was just the same. After that she ignored his texts, or replied *soz, busy tonight*, hoping not to hurt his feelings.

And then it was Valentine's Day.

Emma's phone buzzed in the middle of double French, and she looked at it surreptitiously under the desk. *What u doing 4 valentines?*

Emma grinned, gazed earnestly at Miss for a few minutes, then flicked her gaze back to the phone. *Can't decide between my beaus*, she wrote. They'd watched *Gone with the Wind* over Christmas and had taken to using Scarlett O'Hara speak in their texts. *Fiddle dee*

dee, Julianne wrote back. Then: *Parents away, come to mine.*

It was the first time Emma had been to Julianne's parents' house. It wasn't what she'd expected – somehow the idea of Julianne actually having parents was hard to get her head around. It was the kind of house most of her friends lived in, a bit smaller than hers but nearer everything, shops and buses and things, in a cul-de-sac where there'd always have been kids to play with growing up. Inside it was very tidy, with colourful pictures on the walls of flowers and bits of countryside. In the living room, there was a photograph of Julianne as a baby – the same smile, even then – and one of her parents' wedding. Her mum darker than Emma expected, and her dad pale and gawky-looking.

'She's pretty, your mum.'

Julianne grinned. 'Where I get my looks,' she said.

Up in Julianne's room, things started out the same way as usual. Julianne put some music on – one of the trashy bands she liked. That was one way Emma felt superior to Julianne: she liked bands not many people had heard of, plaintive singer-songwriters less mainstream than Julianne's beloved Ed Sheeran and Justin Bieber. But Emma loved that about Julianne – the way she wanted to be a bad girl, but always stuck to the safe choices. Domino's, Top Shop, One Direction. Kyle Jenkins. Julianne's room still looked like it must have done when she was twelve, pink puffy hearts hanging over the bed and a row of plastic horses on the mantelpiece. The two of them sat on her flowery duvet drinking vodka and lemonade out of Easter-egg mugs, singing along to the chorus of Julianne's latest favourite song – *I want you to go, no don't go – I beg you to stay, no don't stay* – and then Julianne said: 'So guess what?'

'What?' Emma wasn't as used to vodka as Julianne; she was already a bit woozy.

'I'm having a baby.'

Emma turned her head: she was sitting so close to Julianne that she couldn't see her expression properly, just a side-on view of her mouth, closing again after saying those words.

'You're pregnant?'

Julianne pulled back a bit then, so she could see Emma better. She was smiling, the same smile as on that first day when she'd said *I go to college.*

'Are you shocked?'

'Surprised,' Emma said. 'What does Kyle think?'

'I haven't told Kyle. Haven't told anyone. I only did the test yesterday.'

Emma remembered that text in French, imagined Julianne typing it with the test strip still in her hand, and she felt suddenly breathless.

'I need to do another test,' Julianne said. 'It says you should check again. I thought we could do it together. I mean, I could do it while you're here.'

'OK.' Emma couldn't manage more than that for the moment. *I'm having a baby,* Julianne had said. Not *I'm pregnant.* Is that what she meant? She tried to imagine

Julianne and Kyle in his flat with a baby, and couldn't. Call of Duty and weed and nappies.

'OK then.' Julianne launched herself off the bed and took a small box out of the top drawer of her bedside table. It was a Boots one, with reassuring blue and white packaging. 'Back in a sec,' she said, as she banged out to the bathroom. In a moment she was back, holding a thing a bit like a highlighter pen.

'What's it say?' Emma asked.

'You have to wait. Actually, though, you can see it already. Look – if there's a plus sign you're pregnant.'

She waved the stick under Emma's nose, and sure enough, there was a faint grey cross in a little window.

'Wow.' Emma looked at her. Julianne was grinning, but was that because she was pleased, or because it was ...? Not a joke, she couldn't think that.

'You know what's funny,' Julianne said, as though she'd read Emma's mind, 'my mum's a midwife.'

'Will they—' Emma began. 'Are you going to—'

'I dunno.' Julianne flopped down beside her on the bed again. 'Don't tell anyone, will you?'

'Of course not.'

Emma could hear the waver in Julianne's voice now, the jokey bravado slipping.

'Maybe you and me could bring it up, Em,' she said. 'You could leave school, get a job. We could get a flat. Tell the council we're lezzies.'

Emma felt something drenching through her then, as though she'd been poisoned, or—

April

'I bet lezzies get to the top of the list,' Julianne said, and then she laughed. 'God, don't look like that, Em. I didn't mean it.' She picked up Emma's hand and shook it gently.

'We could, though,' Emma said. 'I wouldn't mind helping with the baby.'

'What would your mum say if you left school?'

Emma shook her head. 'I could go to college in the evenings,' she said. 'I could do my A levels that way.'

'God, you've got it all planned.' Julianne laughed again, but there was an edge to her laughter now. Fear, Emma thought.

'I'm serious, Jules. I'll help you, if you want to have the baby. Unless ...'

'I dunno.' Julianne sighed, her mood suddenly deflated, then tipped the rest of her drink into Emma's cup. 'Better not have any more, had I?'

Emma put both their cups down on the bedside table. She'd had enough too: her head was swirling, and she needed her wits about her. Julianne stopping drinking was more serious than anything she'd said.

'Fancy a pizza?' she said. 'We could order Domino's. Or I could nip out for something.'

'Yeah, I'd better eat,' Julianne said. 'I'll be sick otherwise.'

'Are you?' Emma asked. 'Being sick?'

'How d'you think I knew?'

Emma thought back to the tears and the raging and the hysterical laughter over the last few weeks. She'd thought it was all about Kyle, but it struck her now that Julianne had never really cared that much about Kyle.

'How far on are you?' she asked, reaching tentatively for the right terminology.

'Dunno exactly. Three months, I reckon. Due in August.'

So she'd worked out ... 'Have you been to the doctor?'

'Not yet.' Julianne sniffed, an attempt at nonchalance that didn't work. 'Will you come with me?'

The sound of Jonas and Addy yelling drags Emma back to Larkmore, to the muddy track and the heavy weight of the buggy.

'Shush,' she says, leaning forwards over the handle. 'It's OK.' She lets the buggy stop and squats down beside them. A fresh crop of nettles, pale green and whiskered with stings, brushes at her bare calves. 'Shush,' she says again. 'Shush now. Don't cry.'

Addy waves his fists like a tiny boxer, his face screwed up and angry, but Jonas just looks at her with his big dark eyes, as though he can tell something's wrong. And Emma avoids his gaze, hardening herself against the comfort of his affection because she knows, now, what she loved in him; what he's been a substitute for. Julianne's baby, who vanished into thin air while Emma was still dreaming up names. And Rose, sweet Rose. A picture forms in her mind: small Emma, gripping the handle of a buggy as big as her, determined to push it herself – *See,*

Rose, I can take you for walks now – and Rose blinking at her when she stops to draw breath. Rose's sweet, empty face lifted to the sun.

It feels suddenly as if something has been taken from her, a fragment of peace and normality and purpose she's been hoarding as though, if she treasured it up, that and other scraps from Larkmore, it might add up to enough to sustain her. Enough to balance out the losses and the joys and the catastrophes of that other life she can't seem to keep out of her mind any longer.

She leans her weight hard against the buggy, forcing it onwards.

'Home soon,' she says to the boys. 'Home soon.'

If she cut across the lawn now they'd be back at the house in five minutes, but instead she follows the path in the other direction, round behind the old pond. And as the house falls out of sight again, there's a terrible sort of relief in letting her mind slip back again to Fulford and to Julianne; to the dread and despair that's waiting for her.

It was a delicious time, that fortnight when Julianne's pregnancy was their secret. Emma loved being the person Julianne trusted, loved the feeling that she was involved in something more important than school or make-up or music, or any of the other things that used to fill her life. Something real.

They went together to the doctor, not long after Valentine's Day, and Emma sat in the waiting room while

Julianne was being seen. She came out looking serious, not saying much, but they went and had a milkshake at the new smoothie place in the shopping centre and Julianne perked up a bit.

'I'm worried my mum's gonna find out,' she said, slurping the last dregs of her Oreo Dream, 'once I'm on the system.'

'Where does she work?'

'At the hospital. But I expect it's all the same system.'

'Did you ask?'

Julianne shook her head. 'Didn't want them to know I haven't told my mum.'

'But you're nineteen,' Emma said. 'You don't have to.'

'Bit awkward living at home, though.'

'Yeah.'

'Want another one?' Julianne asked, and Emma shook her head. 'I'm going to. Eating for two, aren't I?'

While she was at the counter Emma stared at her back, her heart beating fast. When she came back, Emma said: 'So you're definitely keeping it, then? You're definitely having it?'

'Looks like it,' Julianne said. 'Got a scan next week. You can come if you like.'

At the weekend they went to Mothercare and looked at baby clothes and cots, changing units and maternity bras and colourful toys you could string across a pram. Everything was really expensive, and you seemed to need so much. Emma wondered if her parents had anything in the loft, but she could hardly tell her parents when

Julianne hadn't told hers. She wanted to buy a little pair of bootees, just a token thing to give to Julianne, but she didn't dare. Julianne was unpredictable these days. Most of the things Emma wanted to do or say she kept inside.

Then there was the day of the scan, up at the hospital. Julianne was terrified: mainly terrified her mum would see her, but also that there would be something wrong with the baby. Or perhaps, Emma thought, that there wouldn't: that it would be alive and healthy, waiting to come out and lie in one of those frilly cots in Mothercare. Emma held her hand while she lay on the table. She'd never done anything this exciting. She was enthralled by all of it: the technician in her white uniform; the black and white picture coming into focus on the screen; the baby like a curled-up tadpole with a heart beating very clearly, very fast, in the middle of the picture. And Julianne's hands clutching hers tight: the hands she'd first seen plunging into the swimming pool from the diving board.

Afterwards, Julianne was a bit tearful, but happy tearful. They walked back into the middle of town and went to the cinema, on the spur of the moment, to watch a Disney film about cavemen. In the dark, Julianne reached out her hand for Emma's again and they sat like that, surrounded by small kids and their parents, until the film finished.

'I'm gonna tell Kyle,' Julianne said afterwards.

'Really?'

Julianne sniffed, then nodded.

'Yeah. I should. He's the dad.'

Emma's heart was thumping now. 'D'you want him to be the dad?' she asked. 'As in ...?'

Julianne shrugged.

'D'you want me to come?' Emma asked.

'No.'

'Are you sure?'

Julianne shook her head.

'I'll see you tomorrow,' she said.

Emma hesitated. 'Text me after,' she said.

Julianne laughed then, her face suddenly clearing.

'It'll be fine,' she said. 'It's only Kyle.'

Emma's managed not to think about Kyle for a long time. Not the Sims lifeguard Kyle but the other one, whose photo was printed in the paper below huge shock-horror headlines. And she won't think about him now, she tells herself fiercely, as Larkmore comes back into view again on the other side of the pond. She'll stop the reel there, with the sweet, stale smell of popcorn and Julianne's hand holding hers in the dark and the Disney soundtrack playing over them, the kind of soundtrack that tells you nothing can ever really go wrong. With Emma going home on the bus, hugging the secret to herself, and then lying on her bed waiting for Julianne to call. And when she didn't, imagining she'd patched things up with Kyle, and that he wanted to be a proper dad to the baby. Feeling jealous, God help her. Thinking damn Julianne and her lack of conviction.

No. She won't think about any of that. She'll take Addy and Jonas home now, back to Larkmore, and she'll offer to help whoever's cooking this evening. She'll watch the telly afterwards with the others and she'll be nice to Jeanie, nicer than she was this morning, but not too nice because she can't let it happen to her again. Not ever.

MAY

Naomi's stay at Larkmore is brief, in the end. Not long after May has ushered out the cherry blossom and ushered in the hawthorn, she appears at breakfast one morning with a suitcase, and looks around the room as if she's gathering her audience to her.

'Well, girls, it's goodbye from me,' she announces. 'It's been great knowing you all.'

She slides on to a chair at the end of the table then, and helps herself to a cup of tea, but she waves away the plate of toast with a deprecating smile. Going back to the suburban house with its new kitchen, Emma thinks, with a dash of viciousness. Waving goodbye to Larkmore as though it's an eccentric boarding house where she's had an unscheduled holiday. Naomi's smile is as dazzling as ever – but is there, Emma wonders, a hint of sheepishness in the glance she catches? It gives her some satisfaction that the response of the assembled Larkmore women is less effusive than Naomi might have hoped. They're not good at pretending, Emma thinks, and there's something about Naomi's departure, as there was about her presence here, that feels ... off key.

'Did you like Naomi?' Jeanie asks that evening, when they're both in bed.

Emma hesitates. 'Did you?' she asks.

Jeanie shrugs. 'Yeah. She was nice to me.'

'Are you sorry she's gone, then?'

'Kind of.' Jeanie's lying on her back, her knees drawn up so the sheets make a tent over her belly. 'She made things more fun. But I'm glad she's gone home.'

So she *has* gone home, then? Emma thinks.

'Yeah,' she says, matching her tone to Jeanie's: casual, careful. 'She was always going to, I suppose.'

'I s'pose.'

You've still got me, Emma wants to say, but she doesn't. Instead, she lets the silence run on, and after a couple of minutes she hears Jeanie snoring gently. Nothing comes between Jeanie and sleep; not even the loss of her idol. Just as well, Emma tells herself. She has nothing to offer Jeanie. Better for her to dream of Naomi.

Naomi's name is hardly mentioned again. That's how things are here, Emma thinks, one morning a couple of weeks later. She's awake early, and as she lies in bed watching the first glimmers of light sneaking beneath the curtains she finds herself thinking about how people come and go at Larkmore, and how quickly the water closes over them. How other people's stories don't matter – can't matter – that much.

But even so, it seems to Emma that everyone at Larkmore has been a little bit different since Naomi left. A little bit sadder, or angrier, or more argumentative. Naomi gave everyone here a glimpse of a life most of them will never have, she thinks. They'd forgotten lives like that existed: lives garnished with leather coats and expensive haircuts and the air of confidence that goes with them. It's made Larkmore seem shabbier and less magical. Less safe, too, perhaps. But that might be her own private feeling.

Emma turns on to her side, pulling the covers up over her shoulders. It's very early still: too early. Across the room, Jeanie's fast asleep, her back hunched towards Emma. Emma envies her. The birds are in full voice now: they start singing at five o'clock, or even four thirty, calling for a mate and calling Emma relentlessly from sleep. She can't bring herself to get up at this hour, and so she lies awake, on these cold, pale mornings, counting off the minutes, while her mind tosses and turns.

Although it provides a convenient cover, Emma knows her growing restlessness doesn't have much to do with Naomi. She can trace it all the way back to that day in Fulford when she thought she saw her father, and when the door she'd shut on the past was first nudged open; through the long bouts of remembering that have followed. If Penelope believed that letting that happen would be helpful, Emma thinks, she was wrong. All it's done is to make her realise that even at Larkmore there's no peace to be found, because what she thought was peace was just a kind of numbness. Simplicity, usefulness, routine – being among other people who have suffered as much as her, and often more – had lulled her into a false sense of security.

The days have kept passing in the same way as they always have, rolling invisibly into weeks. Emma has kept getting up in time to feed the babies. She's kept helping with the cooking and the gardening, hanging out the washing, mopping floors. At mealtimes, conversations flow past her as though they're in a foreign language. She's felt Penelope's eyes on her from time to time, but she avoids her gaze, and shimmies away when she senses that Penelope is going to speak to her. Her dreams have become more and more terrifying: not chains and blood and rape any more, but the dark boom of a tomb-like place that she realises slowly, stupidly, is a womb.

She shuts her eyes again now, pushing the shadow of the dream away. Did it come back again last night? She can't remember. But the space it occupies in her head – the space it draws her into – is always there, deep in her mind. The womb where Julianne's baby lived and died; the womb she shared with Rose. She used to think about that, after Rose died. She remembers the terror and loneliness and guilt: lying alone in her bedroom, frozen with panic, thinking of Rose in her little coffin. Thinking of the part of herself that was buried with her twin.

And thinking, too, of the blood she stole from Rose as they grew side by side in that dark womb which should have been a safe place for them both, but which wasn't so safe for Rose after all. She remembers how grotesque it sounded to her when her parents tried to explain; remembers thinking how unnatural she must have been, how greedy and selfish and savage. For a long time Emma longed to ask more, but she never dared, for fear it would remind her parents of the part she'd played in Rose's illness, and her death. Murderous Emma, who had her parents all to herself now, but who had lost the most important part of her.

She takes a deep, shuddering breath. Outside, the birdsong has reached a frenzy. A dozen different melodies sound against each other, and over the top of them all is a repeated note like a siren, growing louder and louder until Emma thinks it must be inside her head, and that she might explode with the pressure of it. She can't distinguish, any more, her grief and guilt for Rose and her grief and guilt for Julianne. It's as if, like the siren bird, they're all the same thing, the same note. The same repeating pattern, over and over again. *She she she*, the bird chants, leaning on each note more heavily than the last. *She she she she she.*

And suddenly Emma can't stand it any longer. She throws off the covers, grabs her dressing gown from the back of the door and slips out of the room. The kitchen will be darker, warmer, quieter. She needs to think. She needs to let her mind go again, let it slip back into the past, or the struggle to stop it will drive her mad.

She hasn't let herself think about Julianne since the day of the cherry blossom, when she pushed the double buggy around the pond and remembered the scan, the cinema, the evening of suspense that followed. Her mind sets her down again now not on that evening or the next – there's a searing, frozen horror to those memories that won't let her back in yet – but a few days later. As she pushes open the door to the familiar Larkmore kitchen, its high window still full of night, her mind's eye alights on an image of herself huddled in her bed at home, poring obsessively over the news reports. Staring at Julianne's name, printed over and over again in big letters and smaller letters, in sensational tabloid headlines and sober editorials.

After the first day or two, they stopped using Julianne's surname and attached adjectives instead. *Tragic Julianne. Murdered Julianne. Local girl Julianne, 19.* There were photos too, a bland smiling one that Emma recognised from Julianne's college ID card and others from when she was younger, with short hair and no make-up. But the news reports never mentioned the baby. That was a mystery to Emma: there were pages and pages about Julianne but no whisper of her pregnancy as a possible motive, or an extra layer of tragedy, or merely a salacious detail to serve up to the millions who were following the case by now. Maybe no one knew, she'd thought, but she'd seen enough police procedurals to know that they would have found out, one way or another.

Had Julianne's parents asked them to keep the baby quiet? Had they been allowed to keep that private bit of grief as their secret? Theirs and Emma's, although they didn't know it. And more hers than theirs, she'd told herself fiercely, remembering Valentine's Day, only a few weeks before. Remembering the way Julianne had tipped her vodka into Emma's cup because she didn't want to hurt the baby. *Maybe you and me could bring it up, Em.*

Had Julianne meant that? Had she believed it might really happen?

Had she had any idea how much Emma had wanted it?

Emma didn't know. There were so many things she didn't know, and would never know now. That was almost the worst thing, during the weeks and weeks when she woke up thinking of Julianne and went to sleep thinking of Julianne and had Julianne in her mind all day long, like a black veil between her and the world. Not knowing, and feeling so far away from Julianne, almost as if their friendship had never happened. They'd been closer than anyone knew, she'd kept telling herself, closer than Julianne had been to anyone else, but the story of Julianne's life that appeared in the news reports never mentioned Emma.

And Emma had missed the vital, the fatal moment. She knew what Julianne had done every day for weeks before she died, but that last night of her life was a total blank.

What had been in Julianne's mind? And what had happened after she left Emma to go and meet Kyle?

Those questions, and others, circled her mind for months, never letting her out of their grip. And they've never gone away, Emma thinks now, sitting in the silent kitchen at Larkmore. She's tried not to think about them, but they've always been there, haunting her. What did Julianne really want? How did she imagine things turning out? And what did she say to Kyle that evening that made him so angry?

She gets up and fills the kettle, not because she wants tea but because sitting at the table any longer is unbearable. Coming down here morning after morning to feed the babies; peeling potatoes and chopping onions; going for walks in the woods – how could she have imagined any of that would change anything?

Because even in the depths of grief she was tortured by guilt, and coming to Larkmore was never going to drive it out. Because when she asks herself those questions, the answers that she hopes for – the things she yearns to be true – fill her with dread.

Suppose Julianne did tell Kyle she wanted to bring the baby up with Emma? Suppose she told him that Emma was the first person to know, and that Emma had gone with her to the doctor and the hospital and to look at the baby things in Mothercare? Suppose she told him she'd held Emma's hand while she looked at the picture of the baby flickering on the ultrasound screen, and afterwards in the cinema?

Suppose Julianne said all those things that Emma longed to imagine her saying, and they triggered that mad, murderous fury neither of them had ever suspected Kyle had inside him?

Suppose it was her fault, all of it? Suppose Julianne would still be alive if she'd never met Emma?

She grips the edge of the dresser as her heart races and thumps. *I didn't will it,* she tells herself. *I didn't know. I would never ...*

And then she pushes her mind on along the paths it carved out after Julianne's death, because at least now she feels alive. Because the pain running through her veins is better, after all, than the numbness she's tried so hard to embrace.

Perhaps, she used to think, Julianne had lost the baby by the time Kyle killed her. Perhaps that was why it was never mentioned in the news reports. Had Kyle wanted her to get rid of it? Had they argued about that? Perhaps Julianne had said no, and he'd hurt her, made her miscarry, and then he'd realised he had to kill her – or perhaps he couldn't stop himself by then?

Sometimes she imagined Kyle attacking Julianne as though she was one of the enemies he killed by the thousand on his screen, hardly noticing that she was a real person at all. She thinks again, now, about those silent evenings when she sat beside him, watching him exterminating people, waiting for him to say something. Maybe she should have asked him how he was feeling? Maybe if he'd talked to her, and she'd explained to Julianne how upset he was about them breaking up ...

Was that her chance to save Julianne? she asks herself now, as she's done a thousand times before. Did she pass it up because she didn't want Julianne to get back together with Kyle? Because she liked it better when there were just the two of them?

Oh, she can't bear it. She feels breathless; beyond despair. There's that terrifying sense of spinning round and round the edge of an abyss, knowing that any moment she could tip over and plunge down into the depths. Where Julianne has gone; where Rose has gone. Wouldn't it be easier to let herself fall: to give up the terrible effort of clinging on?

And then there's a sharp shock: a cup of tea she doesn't remember making has spilled, tipping boiling water across the table and into her lap. Emma gasps, rushing to the sink to sluice cold water over herself. And the jolt of it, the hot and then the cold, pulls her back into herself, and it's as if the part of her that's been watching her these past few weeks is there, waiting. Expectant.

But waiting for what?

Another door should open now, Emma thinks. There should be a cue, an insight, but there's nothing. Just her, standing in the kitchen all alone, with her dressing gown soaking wet and a red streak down her front which is starting to sting. She feels foolish now, as though all the emotion of the last hour has meant nothing – as though it's some cosmic joke to remind her of her own insignificance. But she's too sad, too wrung out, to laugh, or even to weep. She has no idea what to do, what to think, where to turn.

And then it occurs to her that she's ravenously hungry.

It feels suddenly as though her body has woken from a long sleep and taken charge, shushing her poor exhausted mind, telling it to sit quietly now and rest while she ransacks the cupboards and the fridge. She finds cold pasta and peanut butter, cheese and chocolate and bread. She swigs milk straight from the carton, breaks off chunks of bread and cheese, shovels up flabby strands of spaghetti. And doesn't think: doesn't think about anything except filling the great hole there seems to be in her belly. She boils the kettle again, carefully, and makes herself another cup of tea, searches the larder for biscuits, the freezer for ice cream. People will notice, she thinks, but she doesn't care. She can't hide herself, her grief, any longer.

When at last she's finished, she puts everything away, and then she stands for a moment looking out of the window at the pale flame of dawn lighting the sky. She feels like going back to bed, but it's almost time for the day to start now, and although part of her is exhausted, another part is fizzing with energy. She climbs the stairs to the attic as quietly as she can, finds some clothes and pulls them on, and then she goes back down to the kitchen. The house is silent still: not even the babies are stirring. She fetches the cleaning stuff from the pantry behind the kitchen and gets to work. However often this kitchen gets cleaned, there's always a layer of dirt over the floor, a layer of grime over the surfaces. There are cobwebs in the high corners, mould on the windowsills, ingrained grease on the stove. She'll do what she can, Emma tells herself, before the babies wake. And she'll think. She'll keep going along that convoluted path that brought her to Larkmore.

During those endless days after Julianne died, when she sat alone in her room with questions and pictures and memories churning in her head, she thought several times about visiting Julianne's parents. Part of her longed to be in that house just once more, to touch the pink puffy hearts over the bed and the duvet where they'd sat with the pregnancy test – to meet Julianne's family, step into the space she'd left behind – but she couldn't do it. Julianne's parents knew her name, but they'd never met her, probably never heard of her before Julianne died. They didn't know what she and Julianne had meant to each other, and why would they want to know now? What difference could it make?

She went to the funeral, of course; her parents came with her, and sat on either side of her, but there was no one else there that Emma recognised. She'd never imagined Julianne had so many other friends – all the other kids who'd grown up in her road, all the people she'd been at school and college with – but the church was full to bursting. Afterwards, her parents steered her swiftly away. There were photographers lurking, and there was no way they were going to let Emma's face be in the papers.

It was on the way home from her last interview at the police station that something fell into place in Emma's mind. The police had been in reassuring mode, keen to play down the risk to Emma, to emphasise that Julianne had been the primary target all along, and most of all to stress that none of this was in any way Emma's fault.

But Emma knew that wasn't the whole truth. Julianne and Kyle had been fine until she came along. The more she thought about it, the more it seemed to her that she'd been the trigger for everything that had happened: that Kyle had been jealous of Julianne's friendship with her, and when Julianne had told him, maybe only as a fuck-off throwaway line, that she was going to get a flat with Emma, bring up the baby with her, it had tipped him over the edge. Maybe, until then, it had just been a game, the photographs and all that – something he would never have acted on. Most likely, if he'd had a plan at all, it was to kill Emma, not Julianne. Wouldn't he have preferred to see her dead, after all? To keep Julianne for himself?

And then, as she sat huddled in the back of her dad's car, another penny dropped.

This wasn't the first time someone else had died instead of her. This wasn't the first time someone else had died *because* of her: because she'd been too close to them; because of what she'd taken. It must be built into her, a fatal, congenital greed.

That was when it began, the deepest darkness. The place beyond consolation. After that day, she knew she couldn't go on living the life Rose might have lived; the life Julianne might have lived. The cosy, ordinary life her parents wanted her to have. A great burning rage took hold of her. She couldn't stand the sight of herself, or the thoughts in her head; couldn't bear the comforts her parents kept offering. They thought they understood, believed they could help, but they couldn't. There were things no one could ever understand. Things no one could ever forgive.

For a while, life carried her along. She went to school most days, and on the days she didn't she walked around the outskirts of Fulford, the places she and Julianne had been together. At home, she shut herself in her bedroom, out of reach of her parents. *You've been through so much,* they said, whenever she lingered long enough for them to speak to her. *Things will get better. You mustn't blame yourself.* The gap between them and Emma got wider and wider; the gap between what they thought they knew and what they actually did. And then it was Kyle's trial, and the three of them went to court every day, except that it felt as though only the husk of Emma was there any more. The rest of her had shrivelled into a tiny kernel, a black hole deep inside her.

When Kyle was convicted, her parents' relief was obvious. *Thank God that's behind us at last,* they said. They began to talk about a holiday, about celebrating Emma's eighteenth birthday. Behind closed doors, she heard them wondering whether they should be firmer with her now, whether they'd let her mope for too long. As if Julianne's death was something she'd got caught up in by chance and had been allowed to wallow in; as if prurience and a kind of morbid teenage self-indulgence had taken her over.

'It's gone on long enough,' she heard her father say one evening. 'It's almost a year now. We have a responsibility.'

Her mother's voice was harder to make out, her tone less certain.

'What do you suggest?' she asked.

'Can't we insist…' Her father's footsteps came towards the door then, and Emma scuttled away. Up in her room, she wept tears of despair. The world would be better without her: she had nothing to give it, and she dreaded taking any more from it.

And so she started planning. The internet was her friend, full of information and suggestions. But it was easier to read than to act. Squeamishness and cowardice held her back, and an occasional gasping, startled moment of reality, like a drowning reflex, when it felt as if something inside her was fighting for survival. On one of those days she stumbled through the doors of the crisis centre in Fulford.

It wasn't what she expected: a smell of stale coffee; A4 posters advertising user groups and helplines; fading pictures of children holding hands, like a primary school classroom. There was a sense of things moving very slowly, as though any crises that unfolded here would do so in slow motion. In the depths of her anguish and self-loathing, Emma was almost indignant. Was this the best they could do? It seemed the world really didn't care whether she stayed in it or not.

She was on the point of slipping back out into the street when a tall woman with shoulder-length greying hair came through the door, spoke to one of the women in the glass-walled office, then sat down opposite Emma with a muffled sigh of frustration. It was that sigh that caught Emma's attention. She looked up, and the woman looked at her.

'Hello,' she said. 'I'm Penelope.'

The kitchen smells of bleach and lemons. Every surface is clear and scrubbed, and the morning light is flooding in now. Emma feels very tired, and a little numb – but not numb in the same way she has been. Numb in the way you feel when you've run a long way, or stayed up all night to finish a book.

Has she, after all that, got back to where she started, she wonders – or to a different place entirely? For the moment she can't tell. But one thing seems clear: one tiny, vital thing. She wants to survive. She has pulled back, each time, from the brink, and even if it feels as though sheer chance has saved her, she's glad of it.

Somewhere above her, she hears a baby crying. She puts all the cleaning stuff back in the pantry. The crying has stopped by then, but she starts up the stairs anyway, and on the first landing she meets Penelope, with Jonas in one arm and Daisy in the other.

'Morning,' she says. 'You're up early.'

'I've been up for a while,' Emma says.

'I thought perhaps I heard someone.' Penelope looks at her for a moment. 'Do you need to go back to bed?'

'No.' Emma smiles. 'I'll fetch Lukas and Addy.'

They part then, Penelope heading down the stairs and Emma heading up, and Emma imagines Penelope coming into the kitchen and seeing what she's done. She imagines her wondering what it means: whether it's a penance, or some kind of therapy, or merely a gesture of gratitude.

JUNE

Emma sleeps a lot in the weeks after her night of feasting and cleaning. Dreamless sleep, as deep as Jeanie's, that leaves her dazed and bleary. It feels as if she's got a lot of sleep to catch up on, many months' worth, and she can't do anything much until the debt is paid off.

But gradually, she begins to feel as though she's coming back into her body – the strangest feeling, as if the different elements of her have been taken apart, and now that they are being reunited she can hardly believe the vitality, the energy, the fluency of herself. She moves carefully, as though she doesn't know her own strength. She speaks carefully, because she hardly knows who she is any more. Everyday things fill her with wonder: the sunlight in the garden, the smell of toast in the kitchen. She can't explain it. She's known they were there all this time, but even so they seem like marvels.

She's grateful, meanwhile, that her mind is content with the present for now, and doesn't insist on picking at the raw scab of the past. One day, shelling beans on the terrace at the back of the house, she looks around at the other women. Jeanie's sitting beside her, her face intent as she splits the pods and thumbs out the waxy beans. The babies' mothers are on a rug on the lawn, toys scattered around them. Kadisha and Mila are peeling potatoes at the other table, and further down the garden some of the others are kicking a ball with the older children.

'Such a beautiful day,' she says.

'You keep saying things like that,' Jeanie says.

'Yeah, well . . .' Emma hesitates. 'I like the summer.'

'Me too.'

'Well then.' Emma grins, and Jeanie shrugs. She's wearing another of her home-made dresses, with a cardigan that looks too hot for a warm day. She's so skinny, though, Emma thinks: she must feel the cold. Her fingers, her wrists, look almost translucent, moving nimbly through the pile of beans and dropping the husks into the bucket beside her.

It occurs to her that Jeanie has been a bit subdued lately. They've hardly talked, these past few weeks: at night, Jeanie turns away as soon as she gets into bed, and during the day, her stream of questions has dwindled. Since Naomi left, Emma thinks. And then she remembers what it felt like when Naomi was here, and after she left: how it affected everyone.

Emma pauses, the bowl of shelled beans half full in front of her. Is Jeanie still missing Naomi? she wonders. Or is there more to it than that? Has she been too preoccupied to notice that something's bothering Jeanie – or is Emma herself the thing that's bothering her? Emma's anguish and self-absorption, and then her blithe contentment. *You keep saying things like that.*

She wants to push the thought away and reclaim the blameless pleasure of the morning, but she can't. At the end of the garden there's a cry, and she looks up to see Danny, accident-prone Danny, sitting on the grass hugging his ankle. Emma leaps up to fetch the first-aid kit from the house, but by the time she gets there Danny is back on his feet.

'Yeah, thanks, Emma,' says his mother. 'He'll be all right, won't you, Dan?'

Danny doesn't answer, tackling one of the other boys for the ball.

Abigail grins. 'Ungrateful little sod,' she says.

'I'm glad he's OK,' Emma says. 'It looked as though he was hurt.'

She feels sheepish walking away again, for reasons she can't quite fathom. When she gets back to the terrace Jeanie's scooping the last empty pods into the bucket.

'Done,' she says.

'Sorry.' Emma picks up the bowl of shucked beans. There are never as many as you imagine there'll be, she thinks. 'Danny was fine.'

'Of course.' Jeanie looks scornful: she doesn't have much time for boys, even eight-year-old ones. Emma remembers her saying how much she wanted a little brother – *I dunno why* – and she wonders what that was about, whether Jeanie really meant it. She follows Jeanie into the kitchen now, watches her tipping the discarded bean pods into the compost bin, flicking on the tap to rinse the bowl, and she has a sudden wish to be closer to her. No: not that, not exactly. To be not the thing that's unsettled Jeanie.

Emma's never thought much about herself in relation to the other women here. She's accepted what Larkmore offers, she thinks, in return for throwing in her lot with the community. Like everyone else. But it occurs to her now that she's not like everyone else; not really. That she's taken her place here for granted, and hasn't given anything except what she's wanted to give. Just like Naomi, she thinks. Is she like Naomi? *I see someone who's been loved,* Penelope said once. Has that marked Emma out all along? Someone whose mind flies to first-aid kits when a child falls over; who doesn't want people to know she's got parents who've never harmed her?

As she reaches in the cupboard for a pan to put the beans in, it occurs to her that she's resisted asking questions, and being asked them in return, because she was ashamed. Because the other women here have really suffered, but what brought Emma to Larkmore was the suffering of other people, and her part in it. Larkmore has saved her life – but all along she's taken what she wanted and not thought to ask whether it was fair on anyone else. Just as she's done before.

June

It's too early to start cooking: they won't eat for another two hours. Emma leaves the beans in a pan of water and slips away upstairs while Jeanie is still drying up the big bowl. She hasn't been near the computer room for a while, but the knot of pain inside her drives her there now. She slips into the chair, flicks the switch and waits for the ancient desktop to boot up. And while she waits she remembers some more of Penelope's words from those conversations months ago. She remembers what Penelope said about finding the way out of Larkmore, about finding the right moment.

Has she reached that moment? Emma wonders. Has all the thinking she's done, these last few months, brought her finally to the realisation that she's never really going to belong at Larkmore? Perhaps it's not just that she doesn't deserve her place here: perhaps, like Naomi, she's doing more harm than good by staying. Perhaps what she has, what she is, makes everyone else feel a little less secure; a little less valuable.

The computer's ready now: she signs into her Facebook account and clicks on the first few posts in her feed, and the lives of her one-time friends are displayed in all their colourful, carefree glory. There they are dancing on a beach, partying in a club, queuing for a gig. Is that really where she should be? She can't imagine it. Can't imagine ever going back to that life. Maybe she doesn't belong anywhere any more.

She doesn't hear Jeanie coming up behind her.

'They your mates?' Jeanie asks.

'Kind of.'

'Look like they're having fun.'

Emma looks at the screen, seeing the images through Jeanie's eyes: the laughing faces, the make-up, the parties.

'Yeah,' she says.

'Do you wish you were with them?' Jeanie asks.

'No.'

Emma clicks a switch and the computer powers down, and instead of the technicolour party scenes she can see Jeanie's face reflected in the screen now, her small features tightened by distress. Emma stares at her, but she doesn't turn round. Part of her wants Jeanie to go away and leave her alone, and part of her badly wants her to stay. She thinks of the things Jeanie could ask her – the questions she's asked before – and the things she could ask Jeanie. *Are you OK? Is there anything wrong?* What kind of person is she that she can't manage that?

A person who hurts everyone, she thinks. A person no one should get too close to.

Jeanie hesitates, shifting from foot to foot.

'D'you want anything?' she asks, and Emma has to bite her lip to keep the tears back.

She shakes her head. 'I'll be down later,' she manages to say.

Jeanie nods. Her silhouette looks slumped and strange in the shadowy reflection of the computer screen. Can she see Emma's face too? Can she see her watching her?

After another minute Jeanie turns away, and Emma listens to her footsteps crossing the landing. And then she turns her gaze on herself, on her own face reflected back from the blank screen, and she tries, really tries, to look at herself honestly.

She's been deceiving herself, she realises – yet again she's been deceiving herself, these last few weeks, thinking that remembering what happened with Julianne, and with Rose, was somehow the end of the road. Imagining that understanding herself and her past a little better was the answer to something. Because this isn't just about her – and it's not just the other women at Larkmore she's failed to think about. There's one more instance of her taking and taking and offering nothing in return, isn't there?

She hears Jeanie's voice, that time when they were cooking: *Have you got a mum and dad, then? Do they know you're here?*

There's a reason she doesn't think about them – doesn't let herself. Self-protection, she's called it, but she understands now that all she's been protecting herself from is the truth. Because guilt and shame are all very well, but guilt and shame towards people who are dead aren't any use, are they? She can't hurt Rose or Julianne any more, but her parents ...

Her parents didn't understand anything, and she couldn't tell them. They didn't understand *because* she couldn't tell them. She told herself she couldn't stay with them, that it was right for her to give up everything they offered her: that it was her punishment, her sacrifice, as well as her salvation, to come and live in a sort of vacuum, away from everything she'd ever known. But all the time she's been here, *they* haven't been existing in a vacuum, have they? They haven't been conveniently left in suspended animation. And the thing is, Emma thinks – the thing is, it wasn't just her taking things from them: it was letting them give. She knows now that that matters; that giving is important. The most important thing, perhaps. And her parents don't have anyone else to give things to. All this time they've had no one else.

Emma's hardly surprised when Penelope catches her at the end of supper and takes her into the study. She's beginning to think that Penelope has known everything about her all along; that she's been watching Emma's thoughts unfolding, like the flowers coming out in the garden, waiting until they reached just the right moment.

'You haven't been quite yourself, Emma,' Penelope says, when they're sitting down. 'I've been worried about you.'

It seems a long, long time since those conversations earlier in the year, Emma thinks. She remembers the Milk Tray, the early sweet peas. There are no props this evening.

'I've been wondering how I can help,' Penelope says.

'I don't think you can,' Emma says – but that sounds churlish, so then she says, 'I mean, I don't know how.'

Penelope sighs. 'I don't know what happened before you came to Larkmore, Emma, and you don't have to tell me, but ... Some women who come here – most women who come here – have nothing left for them outside. No one to look after them. I think things are different for you. I have a feeling that you were running away from happiness as much as from misery. I know' – Emma makes a small noise of protest, and Penelope acknowledges it, lifting her hand – 'I know it's more complicated than that; I don't doubt for a moment that terrible things have happened to you. Things you feel can never be put right, perhaps. Things you'll have to live with all your life.'

Emma shuts her eyes for a moment to keep her emotions under control.

'Yes,' she says.

Penelope sits in silence for a few moments, looking at her.

'Sometimes, Emma,' she says at last, 'the most painful things aren't those you can't put right, but those you can.' She waits, and when Emma doesn't speak she says: 'But if there are things you can put right, there's always a way to do it. And you won't regret it.'

Emma is trembling now. She sees her father behind the wheel of his car on Fulford High Street, the fraction of a second when she imagined he might have seen her, too. She sees herself in the kitchen with her mother, hears her mother's voice: *Bouquet garni*, she says. *It's what the French call mixed herbs.* Holding out a thing like a teabag for Emma to sniff, and laughing when she screws up her face at the smell of it, like a garden crumbled to dust.

In the days that follow, Emma's parents are on her mind so much that she can hardly believe she managed to think about them so little for so long. It feels like not eating some basic food – apples, or cheese, or bread – for more than a year, and then wondering not so much how you'd done it, but why. Because she had no choice: that's the only answer she can come up with. Because she couldn't have gone on any longer with her old life, and Larkmore offered her a way to survive. Somewhere the past didn't exist and the present was completely absorbing: a new life so insulated from the outside world that when someone went shopping, or to a doctor's appointment, it was as strange as a moonwalk.

But that argument just begs more questions now – questions about what she refused to look at, to think about. About what she's left behind.

It's too painful to think of her mother and father in the present, so she occupies her mind with the past: the time when Rose was alive, and the time after that when the three of them felt incomplete, but they all tried to pretend they weren't. Going to the seaside, the cinema, the zoo, without Rose's wheelchair or the anxiety of leaving her behind, and feeling weightless. Forgetting, slowly, what life had been like with Rose. That feeling was alarming, certainly to Emma, and perhaps to her parents too.

They tried, she realises now, to make up for the child-hood they felt she'd missed out on, and she tried to make up for her lost sister. All of them watching each other anxiously, constantly aware of a shadow, a ghost; never quite able to count on anything, and guilty, guilty, every time they enjoyed something.

Did all that make things worse when Julianne died? Emma wonders one night, lying awake in her little attic room. Certainly they'd always been more anxious, more protective, than other parents. And no doubt when the police came to tell them that Kyle had pictures of Emma on his computer – photoshopped pictures of her tied up, stabbed, raped – the idea that she'd been so close to harm had been even more painful to them because they'd lost one daughter already.

She'd seen that and not seen it, Emma realises. She saw her own side of it – the double guilt because she'd been the one to survive again – but she didn't think very hard about how it was for her parents: that they'd felt twice the responsibility for her after Rose died, and twice the anguish when they discovered she'd been in danger.

Twice the loss when she left.

The thought slips into her mind before she can stop it. She stares into the darkness, her heart thumping in her chest as though it's still pumping all that extra blood she syphoned off from Rose when they were attached to the same placenta.

It could easily have been her who came off worse: she read up about it, when she was old enough. The twin

343

that gets more blood doesn't always do better. And it could easily have been her in Kyle's flat that evening, too. But it wasn't. In both cases, it wasn't. And she was so busy feeling sorry for herself, resenting the burdens her good luck placed on her, that she allowed herself to ignore what she was doing to her parents when she walked out on her life.

She gets out of bed now and tiptoes across to the window. It's a hot night, and the sash has been left open. She tweaks the curtain aside and leans on the sill, gazing out at the shadowy garden, the dazzling half-circle of moon above the trees. There's an owl in the woods, screeching intermittently, oblivious to the fact that the world is asleep. Oblivious to Jeanie's snoring, louder now as she stirs and settles again. Both sounds make Emma sad: sadder than she can remember being for a long time. She thinks about the modest garden at home with a swing, a dog, a wooden den – the father who photographed village fêtes and the mother who made elaborate birthday cakes – and she feels a wash of grief flooding through her. She can't stop herself, now, thinking of the present. Their present. She's filled with an urgent need to know how her parents are, what they're doing.

She stares up at the sharp pattern of stars above her. If it *was* her father she saw that day in Fulford, she thinks, he looked older. Might he be ill? Or her mother? She imagines, with a shock of dismay, her mother lying in a hospital somewhere and her father doing his best to look after her, furious with Emma for the harm she's done.

Or might they have moved house, filled their lives with other things to help them forget her? It's months since that day in Fulford: they could have emigrated, even. They could be dead.

She needs to know. Before she can think, plan, she needs to know where they are, how they are. She turns abruptly and slips out of the room, avoiding the creak in the middle of the floor, then across the narrow landing and down two sets of stairs. She doesn't turn on the light in the computer room: the brightness of the screen will be enough.

She googles their address first, and up comes a Rightmove link – sold house prices. Her heart thuds, but when she clicks on it there's relief: the last sale was years ago, when they bought the house. Then she tries the *Surrey Gazette*, and within moments she finds her father's name, and a photoshoot he did a few weeks ago. Prettiest Surrey villages. She almost smiles, but somehow the pathos of it is unbearable. St Mary's Primary School's website doesn't list their staff, but she spots her mother in a photo from sports day last summer. The photo is small and blurred, but it's definitely her mother, standing with a group of children in blue T-shirts.

Emma sits back, taking stock. Knowing that her parents are alive, and continuing along the same familiar paths, is an intense relief. But the internet can't tell her what she really needs to know: how they are, what they talk about. What they think about when they wake up in the morning. She can't bear the idea that their first thought is of her – but the idea that it might not be is even worse.

And then she tries to imagine what it might be like if she went home. Her parents on the doorstep, joy and disbelief on their faces? No. It couldn't be that simple, not after all this time. Perhaps she could write to them – send another card, maybe suggest a meeting, so that they had time to prepare. But she can't give them the address here to write back; that's against the rules. And what if they didn't come? What if they don't want anything to do with her, after the way she's treated them? Her brain spins wildly, searching for a way to meet her parents without arranging it; a way to assure herself they want to see her again. But she can't think any more. She can't see any way forward, and it's all her own fault.

She drops her head into her hands, suddenly conscious of how tired she is, and how stupid, how cruel, how blind she's been. But she's still got the primary school's website up on the screen, and just as she's about to close it something in the News section catches her eye. *Come and support Mrs McCluskey at Grove Park this Sunday, when she'll be raising money for cancer research …* It's the fun run on Sunday, Emma realises, with a leap of excitement. The Midsummer Fun Run. The whole of Fulford will be at Grove Park: might her parents be there too? Her father at least, taking photographs for the *Gazette*?

*

Penelope's pleased when Emma tells her she wants to go to the event in Grove Park. She offers her a lift, and when they arrive she hands over a twenty-pound note – more than Emma could possibly spend on food and drink in one day, so that Emma knows she's guessed there's more to this outing than a couple of hours wandering around the park. She'd asked Emma, that morning, whether she'd mind taking Jeanie with her, and Emma's reaction must have told her all she needed to know. Penelope nodded, then smiled in a way that allowed Emma not to feel selfish, and after breakfast the two of them slipped out quietly, climbing into the battered car and pulling off down the drive as though it was the most normal thing in the world.

'Take this too,' she says now, when Emma's mumbled her thanks for the money, and she passes her a mobile phone – an old-fashioned one, not even a smartphone, but Emma stares at it, the audacity of what she's doing suddenly hitting her. 'So you can ring me if you want a lift home,' Penelope says. 'My number's on there.' Emma nods and opens the car door. 'Have fun,' Penelope calls as she walks away, but Emma's mind is already dazzled by the echo of the loudspeakers, the bright buzz of people filling the park.

It's a strange day. Emma had forgotten how easy it is to be anonymous in the middle of a crowd: it's as though her presence makes no difference at all. She passes among the throngs of runners in their numbered vests, the groups of teenagers who look both years younger than her and aeons older. Her eye is drawn to babies in buggies, to a family pushing a wheelchair, to couples the same age as her parents. She doesn't recognise anyone and she doesn't catch anyone's eye, except a beautiful toddler who looks like a slightly older Jonas, who stares back at her and then shoves his dripping ice cream defiantly, defensively into his mouth. She watches some of the heats finishing, looks at some of the stalls, buys herself a bacon sandwich and a bottle of Coke.

By three o'clock she's ready to go home, but she suspects Penelope won't be expecting to be called back so soon, and she doesn't want to disappoint her. Instead, she climbs the hill on the far side of the park and finds a tree to sit under. There are a few other people up here – a giggling couple sprawled in the long grass, and a little further off a mother reading while her baby sleeps – but it's a relief to escape the hordes down below, to look down on them from a distance that blends them all into a single straggling mass. The noise of the crowd sounds like the whisper and hum of the sea, the compère's voice echoey and distorted so that it's impossible to tell what he's saying.

This feels better. It's more like the place she's occupied for the last year, at the edge of the world. She wonders, as she sits gazing out over the scene, whether she'll ever be back in the middle of things – not an anonymous observer, but a participant. Someone with a proper life. Is that what she wants, even? Maybe it's enough to come and look at what a proper life looks like. *Dip your toe in*

the water, she remembers Penelope saying. *Remind your-self that there are people out in the world who are happy.*
Well, she's done that. She's done that, and now she's
retreated to the edge again, climbed up here out of the
way of them all. She feels a little bubble of relief, as
though she's proved something.

She's almost forgotten the real reason for coming
today – but then something catches her eye. There, barely
thirty metres away, is a man with a camera around his
neck. A middle-aged man, tall and skinny, wearing jeans
and a faded blue shirt. She tells herself it could be anyone, but she knows instantly that it's not. That it's her
father – and that it was her father all those weeks ago in
Fulford, too. He's facing away from her, walking up the
hill on the far side of the clump of trees, but she can feel
his presence like an electric field.

Her body doesn't respond at first when she tries to
move, but she forces herself to slide across the ground,
closer to the trunk of the tree, so that she's hidden from
view. She doesn't dare to peer round it to see what he's
doing: she has to trust her imagination, believe that he's
looking out over the park, taking some photographs. She
can't tell how long she sits like that, pressed against the
rough bark, but eventually she sees him again, walking
back down the hill. After a few more moments she clam-
bers to her feet, fighting off pins and needles, and follows
him down the hill.

For the next couple of hours she trails him around the
park, watching from the closest distance she dares as he

crosses between the start line and the finish line, wanders off to watch a children's dance display or to buy a
drink. It requires constant alertness to keep him in sight
without being seen herself. She veers between feeling
blurry, dizzy, disbelieving, and breathless with terror
and anticipation. The crowd sometimes surges between
them, threatening to conceal him, and at other times
thins without warning so that she's terrified that he
might turn suddenly and see her. Sometimes she has the
feeling he's looking for someone – at first she wondered
whether her mother was there too, somewhere in the
park, but after a while she's pretty sure that her father
has come alone. He's working, after all. He used to take
Emma with him occasionally on photoshoots, but she
doesn't ever remember her mother going. No, she tells
herself, he's just looking for images to capture. For a
photogenic face, a striking scene. Perhaps he's not so different from her, looking at all this from the outside. An
observer.

But if she hoped to get an insight into her father's
thoughts, his life, she's disappointed. His face reveals
very little – why should it, when he's working? – and he
hardly talks to anyone except to ask for their names and
permission to print their photos in the *Gazette*. She
strains her ears at those moments to catch the sound of
his voice: the voice that used to tell her the story of her
parents' first meeting. She imagines that now – her father
thirty years younger, with his camera around his neck
just like today, leaning out of a window to get the best

angle and catching sight of her mother's face on that float – and her eyes fill with tears. Sorrow sweeps through her, and then anger. How can her father be carrying on as though nothing's happened? How can he wander among the crowds here and not wonder whether his daughter might be among them, and where she might have been all this time?

By the time the MC announces that the races are over and the crowd starts to disperse, Emma's exhausted. She's no closer to understanding what's going on in her father's head; no closer to judging how she might be received if she turned up on her parents' doorstep. She feels miserable, lost, hopeless.

She takes out the phone and calls Penelope.

'Ready to be picked up?' Penelope asks. 'I'll come to the main gate. I'll be there in half an hour.'

No questions, thank goodness, but no doubt there'll be some in the car. Emma has no idea what she'll tell Penelope; whether she'll mention her father. She wanders slowly towards the gate, caught up by the press of people heading home. She kills ten minutes in a queue for a Mr Whippy, an extra-large cone with two flakes, but it doesn't make her feel any better.

Just as she reaches the gate, the phone buzzes in her pocket.

'The traffic's terrible,' Penelope says. 'Can you come to the other side of the park? I've parked behind the cricket pavilion. Do you know where that is?'

'I think so,' Emma says. 'I'll find it.'

She can see a low white building with a few tables still standing around it, a few cars and people milling among them. She walks quickly, impatient to be gone now. Penelope's car isn't one of the ones on the grass, but she can see a small car park by the road, and she's almost there, almost back in the safety of Penelope's old Golf, when something stops her in her tracks.

It's her father. Her father in the arms of a woman who is definitely not her mother.

'Dad!' she shouts, before she can stop herself. Her father leaps back as though he's been stung. His face, seen full on for the first time, is frozen with shock.

'What the fuck ...?'

Emma stares at him. All those hours of imagining, hoping, dreading, and this scenario never once occurred to her.

PART 3

JUNE

Jim

The world slows as Jim turns to face Emma. She's standing just a few feet away, looking straight at him.

'What the fuck are you doing, Dad?' she says.

'Oh, God,' he says. 'Oh, God—'

'This is my fault,' Dido says. 'I'm so sorry. I'm going, right now. Emma, your father ...'

'Who are you?' Emma demands. 'Where's Mum?'

'Mum's fine,' Jim says. 'At least – Mum's at home.' He takes a step towards her, but she backs away. 'Please, Emma, don't ... It's so good to see you.'

It's taking everything he has to keep him upright, keep his voice saying things. Probably the wrong things – but what could possibly be the right thing to say? Emma's staring at him, and he can hear questions clamouring in her head. And in his, too. Where has she been? Is she all right?

Dido's in her van now, reversing away. Jim doesn't dare look towards her. He remembers her words: *Emma, your father* ... Giving away more than she meant.

'Emma,' he says. 'I understand – I know what this must look like. I can't tell you how sorry I am that you ...' He swallows. 'But – your mother would so love to see you. Will you come home with me? Or can I call her? Just – let her see you?'

Emma doesn't move, doesn't react, and for a moment he wonders whether she's heard anything he's said.

'We've missed you so much,' he says, watching her face. Emma's staring at the ground, twisting the toe of her trainers in the scrubby grass. 'It's not – I won't pretend that what you saw ... But please, Emma, don't make my behaviour into an excuse to punish your mother.'

The word *punish* makes her flinch. A misstep.

'Does Mum know?' she asks.

'Mum doesn't know where you've been for the last year and a half,' Jim says, before he can stop himself. Emma's head jerks up. 'I shouldn't have said that,' he says. 'I'm sorry. I shouldn't – God, Emma, I can't believe this is really happening. That you're here.'

He can't take his eyes off her face, and he tells himself to absorb every detail, in case she vanishes again. Ordinary clothes – jeans and trainers, a stripy T-shirt. Shorter hair, like the girl he saw in Fulford. Was that her? Has she been that close, all this time?

Emma doesn't speak again, and Jim feels desperation rising inside him. There must be something he can say, some magic formula. If she hasn't run off yet, she must be weighing things up. Or is that wishful thinking?

'We both love you so much,' he says. 'It would mean so much to your mother to see you. To know you're safe and well. Would you come home with me, just for a bit? Just for ...'

He hears a car door opening a few yards away, and Emma's head turns sharply.

'I've got to go,' she says. 'Someone's waiting for me.'

'Please,' he says. He's trying to see the car, but he doesn't want to take his eyes off her. 'You could bring whoever's ... Bring them too.'

Emma swallows, and he can sense her hesitation. Then she shakes her head. 'Please just go,' she says, her voice suddenly fierce. A voice he recognises.

'Emma,' he says, imploring now, 'please think about it. Please ...'

And then at last Jim feels as though he's thinking clearly. Perhaps if he does what she asks, he won't jinx things any more. If she's getting into a car, someone must be looking after her, surely? That's something; more than something. Perhaps once the shock of seeing him passes, she'll get in touch. She knows where they are.

He turns, and starts walking away across the flattened grass. Behind him, he hears a car door open and shut, an engine starting – and then he wheels round, cursing himself. Idiot: he should have got the registration number. He should have – Christ, how can he have been so stupid? He didn't ask her anything. *Where are you living? Do you have a phone?* Not even *Is everything OK?* It's as though he forfeited the right to ask questions when she caught him with Dido – but he's her father, for Christ's sake. He should have stuck his ground, insisted on having a phone number, at least. The person in the car might be keeping her prisoner. They might – but she looked well, healthy. She'd been here, in the park, on her own, hadn't she? She wanted to go back to them.

All the way home the argument rages in his head. He drives without seeing anything, his mind filled with Emma's face, Emma's voice. It's more than he's dared hope for: to see her, speak to her, find her not just alive, but flourishing. Her clothes were clean, and her hair. She's not sleeping rough, he's sure. All his worst fears tumble through his head – drugs, accidents, self-harm – and he dismisses them one by one, gratitude and relief swelling in his chest.

But then the flip side hits him.

What that means, he thinks, is that there's still no explanation. No reason for her to disappear: no problem they can help to solve. Could she have hated them so much? Could that really be all there is?

He racks his brain for the millionth time for the things they did wrong, the seismic mistake they've missed each time they've searched their souls. Emma knew they loved her, surely? Couldn't she see they were doing their best?

But perhaps the reason she wouldn't come today isn't the same reason she left, he thinks. If Dido hadn't been here – if Emma had turned up five minutes earlier – how differently might the encounter have gone?

It would mean so much to your mother to see you, he hears himself saying. The right words, surely? But should he have suggested a meeting, another time, not tried to drag her home at once? When he replays the conversation in his head he sounds craven, contemptible.

God, what a mess. What a bloody mess. He'd never imagined things could be worse than they've been – but then he thought he could get away with having an affair, didn't he? That it wouldn't change anything, wouldn't do any harm. He's an idiot. He's been a total fucking idiot. And the worst of it is that if he'd stuck to his resolution, if he'd resisted that last kiss, Emma would have come round the corner and seen him helping a friend load boxes into a van, not locked in the arms of his mistress.

He's got a pounding headache now, but he needs to think. He needs to decide what he's going to say to Cath, whether he should tell her that he's seen Emma. After all the agony of the last fifteen months, how can he not share the news that she's alive and well? But then Cath will wonder why Emma wouldn't come home, he thinks, and he'll have to tell her about Dido, about what Emma saw. And how could Cath live with the double blow that Jim's infidelity has driven Emma away again, perhaps forever?

No: he needs to keep quiet, he decides, although it makes his heart ache. He needs to add this secret burden to the ones he's already carrying. Because if Emma vanishes again, it would be better if Cath never knew about today. Never knew about Dido. And if Emma does come home, and Cath finds out about his affair – well, then she'd have Emma. She could blame him, hate him, all she liked; it would be no more than he deserves.

The house is very quiet when he comes in.

'Cath?' he calls. 'I'm back.'

His voice echoes up the stairs, deceptively ordinary.

He goes through to the living room and puts his bag down on the desk in the corner, and then he stands for a moment looking out at the garden. It's a beautiful evening, and there are lots of things in flower, gaudily colourful in the late sunshine. An evening to sit outside with a drink. The idea makes his heart swell with hope, then shrink with shame.

'Cath?' he calls again. He looks into the kitchen, then heads up the stairs. Perhaps she's gone out?

But she's asleep. Lying on the bed, curled up like a small child, fast asleep. He's about to creep away again when she stirs.

'You're home.'

He smiles. 'Just.'

'What time is it?'

'Nearly seven. Sorry. Long day.'

'You must be tired.'

'A bit. What about you? Are you OK?'

She pushes herself up, tugs a pillow under her head. 'I've been better.'

'I'm sorry. Anything I can help with?' Listen to him, he thinks. The thoughtful husband. He can almost hear Emma sneering. 'Can I get you a drink?' he asks. 'A cup of tea?'

'I had some, I think. Hours ago.'

'Do you want more?'

'Maybe.' She shuts her eyes. 'Jim – sit down a moment. Sit with me.'

He feels a shot of ice through his chest.

'What is it?' he asks, as she shifts to make room for him. 'What's wrong?'

'I wish I'd come with you,' she says.

I wish you'd come, too, he thinks. What a difference that would have made.

'What's been happening?' he asks.

'Nothing,' Cath says. 'Nothing today. It was last night, after you'd gone to bed.'

'Last night?' His mind's turning, refocusing. Nothing to do with him. Nothing to do with today.

'Lara came round,' she says. 'She was – There was something she'd talked to me about before, something important that she'd never told Nick. She wasn't sure whether she should. But she did tell him, yesterday, and it was … He didn't take it well.'

'So she came to see you,' Jim says. *Something important that she'd never told Nick,* he thinks. Cath holding other people's secrets, not knowing about secrets closer to home, things being kept from her.

'It was about half past ten,' Cath says. 'You were already in bed. I made her a cup of tea and let her talk, told her things would work out, everything would be OK. But then Nick appeared on the doorstep, and he was angry. Really furious. Not just with Lara, but with me.'

'With you?'

Cath nods. Her lip's trembling, and Jim puts his hand over hers. He still feels like a fraud, but she gives him a quick, grateful smile.

'He said some horrible things,' she says. 'He said he knew I was behind it all, that he'd always thought it was too good to be true.'

'What was?'

'Our being friendly to them. The rent being low. He said we – I – just wanted to interfere. To come between them.'

Jim frowns. 'Did he threaten you?'

'No – he scared me a bit, being so angry, but then Lara took him away. It's just …' She's weeping now, and Jim pulls her closer. 'You were right,' she says. 'You were worried about me getting involved with them, and you were right.'

'No,' Jim says. 'I didn't—'

'He said I couldn't bear to see them happy,' Cath says, 'but it was completely the opposite. I *loved* seeing them happy. I loved imagining – remembering us happy like that.'

June

Jim sits very still beside her. *We're still happy,* he ought to say, but he can't. Certainly not today. He feels the warmth of Cath's body against his, the rise and fall of her ribcage. He wants to offer her something – dinner, candles, reassurance – but there's a spiteful voice in his head telling him he's a hypocrite, that he'll get caught out. Cath deserves the truth, the whole truth, but how can he give her that now? She deserves to see Emma, but he's denied her that. He has no more idea how to find Emma now than he ever did.

'Shall I cook something?' he asks. 'What do you fancy? I could bring it up.'

'No, I'll come down.'

'Sure?'

She nods. 'We can cook together; that would be nice.' She smiles then: another quick, wan smile. 'I'm glad you're back,' she says.

It's not until the middle of the night, as he lies tossing and turning, torturing himself on one count and then another, that Jim realises he does have a way to contact Emma. He can send her a message on Facebook, can't he? She might ignore it, but he can try. He can explain. He can throw himself on her mercy. Beg her to come home.

Lara

It's been a horrible weekend. Saturday was terrible – the argument on the London Eye, and then Nick turning up at Cath's house late at night and behaving like a thug – but Sunday has been almost worse. Lara has been on her own all day, with no idea where Nick is.

Last night, as she bundled Nick into the taxi outside Cath's house, she felt a brief glimmer of competence and of hope. But they drove home in silence, opened the door of the house in silence, and then – in silence – Nick collected sheets and pillows and dumped them on the sofa. So Lara took herself upstairs, stood under the shower for as long as she could manage, then fell miserably into bed and into the deep, blessed sleep of pregnancy.

When she woke this morning, the house was empty. There was no note, no cup of tea left beside her bed. Lara made herself a cup of tea and a bowl of porridge and took it back to bed – and she's been there for most of the day.

At first she thought Nick might have gone for a run or a cycle ride, and that he'd be back by late morning, ready to talk. But lunchtime came and went, and there was no sign of him. No texts, no voicemails, nothing on social media. In the middle of the afternoon, despondent and hungry, she ordered a pizza from Deliveroo and ate it at the kitchen table. Afterwards, she thought about going for a walk, but she couldn't muster the energy. Instead, she fell asleep again, and woke feeling groggy and frowsty. Still no Nick; no messages. She dragged herself out of bed for a shower, and brought a plate of toast and honey back upstairs with her.

She's not used to spending so much of the weekend apart from Nick, and it feels scary and strange. Especially being in this house on her own: this precious house where they've been so happy. She can't let all that slip through her fingers, she tells herself. Their marriage, their baby. She's been feeling too numb to think clearly, but she needs to try: she needs to remember exactly what happened yesterday; what they both said.

What upset Nick the most, she thinks, is that she kept things from him. Lied to him. *I don't understand why you didn't tell me,* she hears him saying. Would she feel the same if things were reversed? If there was some dark secret from Nick's childhood he hadn't told her, would that upset her? Honestly, she thinks, reaching for the glass of water beside her bed, she can't imagine she'd mind. Their pasts are their own business, surely. Of course she knew all along that keeping the abortion secret, pretending her parents were dead, wasn't a good thing to have done. But can it really be so treacherous when nothing depended on it? Would Nick have decided not to marry her if he'd known about those things? Surely not. *So who are you?* she remembers him asking. *Do I know who you are?* But she hasn't been pretending, all this time, to be someone different. Nick married Lara, not Ruth: the grown-up she's become, not the unhappy child she left behind.

Lara feels a bit better for winning that argument with herself. Perhaps after all it's a storm in a teacup, she thinks. Perhaps at this very moment Nick is feeling sheepish, wondering how to break the ice when he comes home: perhaps he's buying flowers, even, as a peace offering. But just as she's starting to allow herself to hope, the argument sneaks up on her from the other side. The point is – Nick's point is – that she didn't trust him with her secrets. He was hurt by that – and more hurt by her running off to find Cath last night, instead of following him home. And that's understandable, she thinks reluctantly. She can see why it upset Nick. And she let slip that she'd already talked to Cath about the abortion, didn't she? That she'd asked Cath's advice about whether to tell him?

He wants so badly to be the perfect husband, she thinks; to be everything she needs. Poor Nick: she can see his desperation, sometimes, through the smiles, the frowns, the little acts of kindness.

But something about that catches her attention now. The effort to be a particular kind of husband, to behave in a certain way: isn't that pretending, too? Masquerading as someone he's not? All Lara revealed yesterday was the misery of her childhood, and the fact that she'd turned her back on it more deliberately, more thoroughly, than Nick had known. Perhaps, after all, Nick revealed something more significant. He wasn't just hurt and upset, Lara thinks: he was angry, self-righteous, overbearing. He behaved abominably to Cath. He reminded her, she thinks now, of her father. The certainty that he's in the right; the violent temper hidden below a mild and virtuous exterior. Has this episode revealed something fundamentally, fatally flawed in their marriage?

But then fear clutches at her. The baby, she thinks. The baby. All this time that she's been worrying about the past, about Ruth's untold story, the baby has been in the background – a fact, a circumstance, a responsibility. Something unknown, waiting around the corner. But what she feels now, quite suddenly, is like a dawning of divine grace. That's probably a sacrilegious thought, but the imagery of her childhood is at hand, and what it offers her is the Virgin Mary receiving the news that she's going to have a child. For the first time Lara feels the immensity of that joy, the fierceness of maternal desire. And it's more powerful, she thinks, because of that other child – the baby conceived in a field – whose existence was impossible. Inconceivable. She's never felt the grief of that loss. She was too much occupied, at the time, with trying to survive in a world she hardly knew. But she feels it now: the tragedy of that tiny life torn from her womb, and the desperate need to protect the child she's carrying now.

So should she throw herself on Nick's mercy, beg for his forgiveness at all costs, because he's the father of her child? No: the lessons of her childhood tell her that *at all costs* can sometimes be too high a price even when the cause is just; that having parents who are present, dutiful, even loving, is sometimes not enough. The answer is more complicated, and it will take both of them to find it.

Just at that moment she hears the door slam. Her heart races – a bolt of fear, and then of anticipation. She glances at her phone: it's nine fifteen, later than she thought. She waits, listening for the sound of Nick's feet on the stairs. For a few moments she allows herself to hope that for all the hurt feelings and all the raw edges yesterday revealed, the solution might after all be simple: a hug, a few tears, a long evening of talking and everything back to normal by the morning.

But Nick doesn't come upstairs. Lara can hear him clattering around in the kitchen: maybe he's going to bring up some tea, she thinks, or a cold beer. They've laid in some non-alcoholic Stella for her, and he makes the same joke about it every time – *Probably the least alcoholic beer in the world.* Based on an old advertising slogan, apparently. A very Nick joke.

It's gone quiet again downstairs, and still Lara waits, wondering whether Nick's looking for some crisps, or a packet of biscuits. She checks her phone again. Nine thirty. Surely it can't take him fifteen minutes to make a cup of tea, or pour a drink? So maybe he thinks she's asleep – or out, even.

Lara gets out of bed, slips on the flip flops she wears around the house, goes downstairs. Nick's not in the kitchen, but she can see him through the back door, standing on the terrace with a can of beer. It's still light, although the sun's very low now, the sky a modest pink. She stands for a moment watching him, grasping again at the idea of a swift reconciliation: her mind skips on to the supper they might cook together, the evening curled up on the sofa.

But even though Nick hasn't even seen her yet, even though neither of them has said or done anything to set the course of the encounter to come, she can feel the image of that happy resolution slipping away. Is it his stance, feet apart as though he's braced for combat? Or the knowledge that on any other day he'd have called up the stairs when he came in? Or simply the clarity that comes from gazing at the back of his head and knowing, somehow just knowing what expression he has on his face?

Nick turns, sees her standing in the kitchen, turns away again. Lara's heart races, but she clings on to the common sense she talked to herself earlier. She's not going to run away this time; she's not going to ask for help elsewhere. She opens the door and steps outside to join him.

'Hello,' she says.

She can feel him tensing beside her; hear him taking a deep breath.

'Have you had a nice day?' she asks – aiming for neutrality, for civility, but might he hear passive aggression in that phrase? *Have you had a nice day while I've been here feeling sorry for myself?* Better, perhaps, to suggest that she's been worried about him. To admit to vulnerability. 'I didn't know where you'd gone,' she says.

Nick crumples the empty beer can in his hand. Just like he always does, Lara tells herself, but even so the gesture feels hostile, his silence ominous. What has he been thinking about all day? she wonders. Doesn't he want to mend things? Doesn't he have anything to say?

She takes a deep breath. 'Do you want to talk, Nick?' she asks.

'Not tonight,' he says.

Lara is shivering now. Is *Not tonight* grounds for hope? she wonders. It's better than *No*, surely, but it feels like a blow. Is this really the man she married: kind, joyful, earnest Nick? Did that man ever exist?

She goes back inside, retreats to her bed, and bursts into tears.

Emma

The day after the fun run, Emma wakes up late. It feels as though she's hardly slept, but she realises almost at once that the morning is already half gone, the sun high in the sky and Jeanie's bed neatly made.

The room is stifling, but despite the heat she pulls the covers up over her head and curls into a foetal shape, knees tucked against her chest. She'd like to vanish, she thinks: not in the way she vanished before, slipping from one life into another, but completely. To be up there somewhere among the birds, the clouds, the stars, looking down on the world from a place where there's nothing but emptiness.

When she got into Penelope's car at Grove Park yesterday afternoon she was trembling with shock. Penelope drove in silence at first, and the absence of small talk, of casual questions, made it obvious that she knew something had happened. She waited a few minutes, and then she glanced across at Emma.

'Are you OK?'

Emma made a small movement, not quite a shrug or a nod. She could hear her voice, her furious tone – *Please just go* – and her father pleading. The knot of dismay and disgust in her stomach tightened. Her father, her reliable, familiar father, kissing a stranger in plain view. The world turned upside down.

'Do you want to talk?' Penelope asked. 'Do you want to tell me what happened?'

Emma had no idea whether she wanted to or not, but she heard herself answering.

'I saw my dad.'

Penelope kept her eyes on the road. 'Did you expect to?' she asked.

'Maybe.'

There was another silence, carefully judged, and then Penelope said: 'It upset you?'

Emma nodded.

'I'm sorry.'

Emma couldn't stop thinking about the fantasy she'd had of that meeting on the doorstep, or in the street, or even at Grove Park – the joy and surprise; the last fifteen months wiped away in an instant. Instead there'd been her father's anguished expression, her own angry words, and that woman. That woman who knew Emma's name: who knew what she was doing to her family. What her father was doing to his family. The fantasy had been such a delicate, tentative thing, too. It had only needed a gust of ill wind to blow it away, not a tornado. Its destruction had left Emma winded.

Emma didn't look at Penelope, but she knew she was speculating, weighing up, and Emma couldn't bear the effort of it.

'Thanks for picking me up,' she said. 'Thanks for the money. I've got some change.'

Penelope nodded then, pursed her lips, smiled. They drove the rest of the way home without speaking again, and Emma wasn't sure whether to be glad or sorry.

At some point during the morning Jeanie knocks timidly on the door, bringing a plate of avocado on toast: the most special of special treats at Larkmore. Emma's touched. Against the blankness in her mind the green of the avocado, the kindness of the gesture, are bright and sharp.

'Shove over,' Jeanie says, settling on the end of Emma's bed so she can watch her eat.

The avocado's delicious, and Emma's hungry. Too hungry to resist.

'Want some?' she asks. Jeanie shakes her head, but when Emma holds out a piece of toast she takes it. She's always hungry, Emma thinks. She's like a stray dog that can never get enough food.

'What happened to you?' Jeanie asks, after a bit.

'What d'you mean?'

Jeanie screws up her face. 'You were all upset when you came back yesterday. Something must have happened.'

Emma's ready with her usual rebuff – *None of your business* – but she looks at Jeanie's anxious face and instead she says, 'I saw someone. It was a shock.'

'Someone you used to know?'

Emma nods.

Jeanie doesn't say anything for a bit, and then she asks, 'So you're not leaving, then?'

'What made you think I was?'

'Dunno. I just thought …' Jeanie hesitates again. 'I don't want you to go,' she says. 'You're the best thing about being here.'

The best thing since Naomi left, Emma thinks, but she knows that's not fair. She tries to find a smile, but even Jeanie's eager, lopsided grin can't conjure one. Jeanie looks down at the empty plate.

'I can stay here, if you like,' she says hopefully, but Emma shakes her head.

When she's gone, Emma pushes back the covers. She'd be better off outside, she thinks. Those few minutes with Jeanie were enough to tell her she needs to be away from everyone today. She pulls on her clothes and slips down the stairs and out of the house.

When she reaches the woods, she takes an unfamiliar path, one you can't manage with a buggy. It's a beautiful day: the sun's directly above, and shafts of dust-filled light fall between the trees like stalactites. There are birds singing, green growth everywhere, a thick carpet of leaf mould to make her steps bounce. It's hard not to feel the magic of it, but it seems to Emma like a magic made for someone else.

As she walks – slightly breathless now, sweat dampening her T-shirt – she forces herself to peel back the layers of memory behind yesterday's encounter.

She was always closer to her father than most little girls because, from very early on, he paid special attention to her to make up for her mother's absorption in Rose. There were the bedtime stories, the little outings, the pictures she drew for him. She realises now that in her mind he's always been a kind of totem: the ideal man, unchanging and utterly dependable. The antithesis of Kyle Jenkins, or the men who've damaged the lives of the women at Larkmore. Thinking of her father pressed against that other woman, whoever the hell she is, makes Emma's heart thump and the blood flood furiously through her head.

But if she hadn't left home, it would never have happened. She's certain of that. Every storyline she can imagine starts in the same way, with her departure, and leads inexorably to the same place: her father kissing that woman in Grove Park. And for all that she's imagined illness, death, emigration, this feels like the worst possible outcome. Her parents' marriage, launched on that carnival day with a glimpse of dark eyes beneath a green headdress, and enduring steadfast through Rose's birth and death, has been undone at last by Emma's selfishness. Her father's peace of mind, her mother's security, all ruined.

There's nothing more to think, really, so instead she just walks. She imagines walking until she's left Larkmore behind her like a stop on the railway, with everything else, everything before, getting further and further away until it's lost in the distance. Now and then she looks up through the branches, cowed for a moment by all the space above her, but then she pulls her gaze back to the path, twisting onwards between the trees, and forces herself to walk a little faster. She has no idea how far she's come, or how long she's been out. No idea which path leads back to Larkmore, either, but she doesn't care about that.

If she wants to vanish, she thinks, this is the place to do it. Walk until she's finally worked off the anger and disappointment, the guilt and shame, then curl up under a tree and let the night birds lull her to sleep. Bury her face in the dead leaves and the bracken, or tangle herself in ropes of ivy; fill her head with the bittersweet smells of the wood.

And let her body be found by a dog walker, like Julianne's?

No: she can't allow herself that easy escape. Can't let other people suffer the anguish of it. Her parents. Penelope. In the quiet of the woods, she hears Penelope's voice. *If there are things you can put right, there's always a way to do it*. But is that true? It feels as if things have gone too far for that. She's been gone too long, done more damage than she could have imagined. Not that she ever stopped to imagine the damage she might do: she was too busy regretting the devastation behind her to see the next wave coming. Her mind was consumed by Rose, by Julianne.

But she's more to blame this time; that fact seems blindingly obvious now. She wasn't even born when the damage was done to poor Rose, and when Julianne was killed, she was an unsuspecting onlooker. All she did was to escape unscathed: it's difficult to remember, now, why that felt so hard to bear. But walking out on her parents was a deliberate act, and any reasonable person would have seen that it was cruel. Was she really so caught up in her own self-pitying narrative that she couldn't see that? Did she imagine her parents propping her card on the mantelpiece and getting on with their lives, or did she not even think that far?

She stops now, finding herself in a glade where the trees are laced with honeysuckle and the air is filled with its sweetness. The sun has dropped; golden light slants through the trees. She can't guess at the time, but it must be getting towards evening. In her mind she's halfway to dissolving, like one of those wood nymphs in Greek legends. There's a hollow tree she could crawl into, a mossy log she could lie down on.

But Fate seems to have intervened, one way or another. As she stands among the honeysuckle, she hears the roar of a car, not far off, and then she recognises the path at the edge of the clearing. It seems she hasn't walked in a straight line, further and further from civilisation, but in a circle, with Larkmore at its centre.

Cath

Jim is tender and solicitous in the days after Lara's late-night visit, and Cath allows him to look after her. He takes Monday off work and brings her breakfast in bed.

'What do you want to do today?' he asks, as she toys with a plate of toast and jam. 'We could go out somewhere, if you like?'

And it's a beautiful day, a proper summer day, so she suggests the seaside. A walk on the beach with the dog, who's so lame now that he can't go very far, but who has always loved the sea.

For most people the beach conjures family holidays, Cath thinks, but not so much for them. It's not an easy place to take a wheelchair. Even so, as they get out of the car she's seized by something which is perhaps a kind of folk memory: a yearning ache evoked by seagulls swooping low over damp sand and the smell of fish and chips.

For a moment she glimpses Emma holding an ice cream, her hair whipped back by the wind, and then she takes Jim's hand and they follow the short path down to the shore.

There's no escaping memory, Cath knows that now. There's no balm to blank out the pain of recollection, except for Jim's company and Jim's kindness. That's all they've got: the marriage they started out with. But that was enough at the beginning, and maybe – despite the damage done by grief and guilt and loss – maybe there's still enough left to sustain them. She has to hope so.

Like two old people, they walk slowly up the beach with their old dog. Despite the sunshine, the sea is a greyish green today, whispering restlessly. The tide is high, and waves fling themselves towards them.

And Cath is almost happy. She hardly recognises the feeling now, but she used to be finely attuned to happiness, once upon a time. Joy surged at the least thing, and she felt it sharply, sweetly – even after Rose was born. Even, sometimes, after Rose died. She can't blame herself if the years have eroded it. They have eroded her capacity to feel pain, too, and that's been a blessing. But today, now, walking on the beach with Jim and Hector, there's a hum, a quiver, in her chest that feels – real. Like something pushing up through the ground. She squeezes Jim's hand and he turns towards her.

'OK?' he asks.

'Yes. This is nice.'

'Good.'

Cath shuts her eyes and tips her head back, feeling the sun on her face. 'We should do this sort of thing more often,' she says.

'Yes.' Something in his tone of voice makes her open her eyes again. He sees her looking at him and attempts a smile, but it's not entirely convincing.

'Are you OK?' Cath asks.

'Yes, of course.' He smiles again, squeezes her hand back, but doubt has lodged in her mind now; the hum of contentment is fading.

'If there's something on your mind, Jim, you can talk to me about it. I realise – I know you try to protect me, but—'

He shakes his head, but he looks strained now; definitely not OK.

'Please, Jim,' Cath says. 'Whatever it is ... Are you ill? Is there something—'

'No,' he says. 'No, no. I'm absolutely fine, I promise.'

'Something else, then. Your job?'

'No – work's fine. Really, Cath, there's nothing – It's lovely to be here. To be with you. Let's enjoy it.'

Cath looks at him for a few moments, and then she nods. He's right; it's too easy to let things be spoiled. There's plenty of material to do it with: not just Rose, and Emma, and the horrible business of that poor girl Julianne. There's Lara and Nick, the way things have turned so sour, and the fool she's made of herself, letting herself believe they were all part of some feel-good movie where amends would be made, gaps filled, consolations found from unexpected quarters. It's a relief to put all that behind her and to fall back on Jim. As they walk she leans into him, her head resting against his shoulder.

'I love you, Jim,' she says. 'I hope you know that. I'll always love you.'

There are tears in his eyes as he bends to kiss the top of her head. 'I love you too, Cath.'

The day at the beach ends happily, very happily, with a lovely meal in a fish restaurant above the beach. Sea bass and samphire and a bottle of Sancerre, which they first drank on their honeymoon. By the time they've finished eating, the shadow of the previous evening has been banished.

While they're waiting for their coffee, Jim cocks his head.

'Fancy staying the night?' he asks. 'They've got a room free.'

'Here?'

Jim nods. 'I asked, when we came in. We could go for another stroll on the beach, have a nightcap ...'

Cath looks at him, her gut twisting with a curious mixture of pleasure and pain. It's only an hour's drive to get home, and ...

'What about Hector?' she asks.

'They don't mind dogs.' He grins at her. 'Go on, let's be devils. What's to stop us?'

There's no one waiting at home for us, Cath thinks, but doesn't say. Is that why she's hesitating? Because it feels wrong to take advantage of that?

June

Because they've hardly spent a night away since Emma left.

'All right,' she says. 'Why not?'

Jim leans across the table and kisses her.

'We could stay a couple of nights, if you like,' he says. 'I've got plenty of leave owing.'

JULY

Nick

The aftermath of Lara's birthday weekend reminds Nick of the time after his father left: the weeks and months when he and his mother kept pretending life could continue along the same tracks – breakfast and school and tea and bedtime, one day after another – never acknowledging the calamity that had befallen them. It's not quite the same with Lara, but there's the same yawning hole in the middle of his life; the same dismaying sense that he's powerless to put things right.

That first day, that Sunday, after a sleepless night on the sofa, he took himself off to an event he'd found on the local Facebook page – a sort of fair in Grove Park, in the middle of Fulford. He thought it would be a good distraction, but all day he felt the absence of Lara beside him. And he couldn't stop thinking about Ruth: he kept imagining her as a shadowy presence in their marriage, someone he'd never known about but who'd been there all the time, like a ghost.

When he finally went home that evening, weary and sunburned and full of beer, she came to find him in the garden, and he couldn't get it out of his head that he didn't know whether it was Lara speaking or Ruth, whether they'd been the same person all along or whether Ruth had come back now to steal away the Lara he knew. And she seemed so calm, as though they'd had a tiff that could be brushed away by a few casual words, but his head was full of fire: all he could imagine was another blazing row, and he couldn't bear that. So nothing happened, nothing was said, and that night they went to bed separately, miserably again.

The next morning, Monday, he met her in the kitchen at six thirty, dressed for work. She looked awful, but she didn't say anything, just poured herself a cup of tea and pushed the pot towards him, and a few minutes later they set off for the station. Being with her, walking beside her, was both a comfort and a torment, fixing him in a state of tongue-tied agitation – and by the end of that day, after the brief respite of work and another journey on which they walked, sat, stood side by side like strangers, the pattern seemed to have been set.

Neither of them, since that night when they rode home in dead silence in the taxi, has referred to the row, or to Lara's revelations. But Nick can't stop thinking about it all: about Lara's parents being alive; about her being pregnant before. Is there more, he wonders, that she hasn't told him? At night he dreams that Lara's in court and the police won't believe he knew nothing about her crimes. And by day, they've fallen into a kind of stalemate. They travel up and down to work, not in silence but with a minimum of interaction. At home they're polite but distant, like flatmates who hardly know each other.

One morning, sitting on the train among the blank faces of their fellow commuters, he wonders whether things are going to be like this forever, and whether it's not so different to how they are for most people. This sense of disillusion; of life being colourless, joyless. For most of history, human beings haven't been able to think much beyond survival, so maybe they're not really designed for happiness. Maybe the joy he and Lara have glimpsed is something people rarely achieve. Or maybe it's a trick of biology: a magic that dazzles you when you're young, designed to get you – well, to the point of procreation, which is, after all, the biological purpose of existence, isn't it?

Thinking like this brings him a painful sort of comfort. He stares through the train window at the outskirts of London gathering them in, the sudden density of houses crowding along the railway tracks. Hundreds of them; thousands of people who think there's a point to their lives. That they matter. And he feels, for a moment, a sense of superiority, as if he's looked up at the sky and seen that the stars are made of burning dust.

But there's a sneaking thought, deep inside, that he can't quite silence. There's a little voice asking what might have happened if he'd reacted differently when Lara finally steeled herself to tell him the truth. If he'd been gentler – if he'd asked questions instead of blurting out his dismay and disappointment – might Lara have said more, and might he have understood better? Might they have avoided this misery?

For a moment, seeing life as a long slide down towards nothingness feels faintly ridiculous, and the freezing well of self-pity he's lowered himself into feels like a bad choice. But they're almost at Waterloo, and he's held out against this voice, held on to the tough comfort of that other certainty – and then the train jolts roughly over the points, and before he can stop it his hand flies out towards Lara, to hold her steady as the carriage wobbles, and there's a flash of electricity through him that not even the sturdiest rationality can neutralise. And he knows she's felt it too, because he can see a flush rising up her neck – and then he notices that her hand, with its plain gold wedding ring, is resting gently, protectively, on the growing mound of her belly. On the swelling form of their baby.

The loudspeaker clicks into life above their heads and the guard announces their imminent arrival at Waterloo, and Nick's hand is still on Lara's arm, and he can't meet her eye.

For another second they sit, connected in that accidental, inevitable, devastating way, and then Nick gets up and reaches for their bags in the rack above them, and the train judders to a stop.

And in the last seconds of the journey there is another view of the situation: that he has always seen himself as a clear thinker, armed with precepts and principles that will keep him from mistakes, tragedy, unhappiness. And that now that blueprint has been found wanting, he has absolutely no idea what to do.

Emma

As July advances at Larkmore, a kind of listlessness takes hold of Emma. The days get steadily hotter and more languorous, and after weeks of waking at dawn, Emma finds herself sleeping later and later.

All that thinking and remembering over the past few months has brought her not to a safe shore of understanding and calm, but to a quagmire where nothing makes sense any more. In the days after the encounter with her father at Grove Park, and the fresh bout of torturous self-blame that followed, she pushed the knowledge of her father's affair as far away as she could, and the messy, painful bundle of the past with it. The constancy of Larkmore life is more of a balm than ever, like an imaginary world she can escape into, and she finds herself feeling grateful for Jeanie, too: ever-present Jeanie whom she catches looking at her from time to time in a way she would have found annoying a few months ago. *I don't want you to go,* she hears Jeanie's voice saying. *You're the best thing about being here.* Although Emma can't bring herself to believe that, she likes to hear the words in her head.

One particularly sultry afternoon, when it's their turn to cook again, Emma comes into the kitchen to find Jeanie already halfway through grating cheese for macaroni.

'It's too hot for mac and cheese today,' Emma says.

Jeanie looks at her, surprised. 'I love mac and cheese,' she says.

'I do too, but I like it more in the winter.'

Emma picks up the other block of cheese, but Jeanie's put hers down now.

'They eat hot things in hot countries, don't they?' she asks.

'I suppose so.'

'Curry,' Jeanie says.

'True.'

'So, then.' Jeanie glares at her triumphantly.

She takes things so seriously sometimes, Emma thinks. 'Did you have mac and cheese when you were little?' she asks, by way of diversion.

'Yeah.' Jeanie pulls a face. 'But the food was horrible in the children's home. We once had this guy who made fajitas and stuff like that, but he didn't stay long. Prob'ly got a job in a restaurant or something.'

Normally Emma would let the conversation slide at this point, or steer it back to the cooking, but today she doesn't. 'When did you go there?' she asks. 'To the children's home?'

'When I was five,' Jeanie says. 'I was in foster care 'til then. After my mum died.'

Emma feels a squeeze of discomfort. Too close, she thinks, to all that stuff she's shoved back out of sight. But Jeanie doesn't notice anything.

'I like it much better here,' she says. 'I like grown-ups better than kids. Being treated like one, too.' She cocks her head on one side. 'Do you think I'm more grown up since I got here?'

Emma laughs, then stops when she sees the expression on Jeanie's face. Jeanie looks so much like a child, she thinks, with her little pointed face and her thin arms. But that's not the same thing as being grown up. Jeanie's melting butter for the white sauce now, and she's got the flour measured out in a little bowl, like they do on cookery programmes, with salt and pepper already added, and a dusting of paprika. They should have let her do the cooking in the children's home, Emma thinks.

'Definitely,' she says, 'you're definitely a grown up,' and Jeanie grins as broadly as if the compliment was unsolicited.

'Where do you go when you go for your walks?' she asks now, in one of those startling changes of direction she specialises in.

'What do you mean?'

'When you take the babies out, or go on your own.'

'Just into the woods,' Emma says. Jeanie's been for walks with her, she thinks, but maybe not recently. 'Where do you think I go?'

'I dunno. To meet someone, maybe.'

'Who would I meet?'

Jeanie shrugs. 'You said you met someone the other day. When you were gone all day.'

'Oh.' Emma bangs the grater to get off the last bits of cheese, then chucks it into the sink.

'Shall I add the cheese to the pan?' she asks.

'Yeah, go on.' Jeanie catches her eye briefly, then looks away, but not before Emma has spotted the anxiety in her face, and the effort she's making to conceal it.

'So you're not meeting anyone?' Jeanie persists.

'No. I'm really not.'

Is Jeanie jealous, Emma wonders, or just curious? Or has she sensed that there are things on Emma's mind, however hard she tries not to think about them? Her stomach turns again at the reminder that she's living in a kind of suspense; that all this chat, all this stuff with Jeanie, is just pretending.

Except who's to say what's real and what's not? she asks herself. Who's to say making mac and cheese for everyone, being nice to Jeanie, doesn't matter?

'I like it in the woods,' she says. 'I found this little clearing once, not very far from the road, but hidden by the trees so it feels secret. There's a big hollow tree, and a log you can sit on, and honeysuckle everywhere. It's like a place in a fairy tale.'

Jeanie frowns. Maybe no one ever read her fairy stories, Emma thinks. 'Like Hansel and Gretel,' she says. 'Or Red Riding Hood.'

'I never liked them stories,' Jeanie says. 'There's always something bad in the woods.'

Emma nods. 'Wolves,' she says. 'Or witches.'

'Not in them woods, though. Not in our woods.'

'No,' Emma says. 'No.' She thinks of that moment when she wanted to lie down in the undergrowth and wait for the leaf mould to bury her. *Not in them woods.*

'You're OK, then?' Jeanie asks. She's standing a little oddly, a little awkwardly, holding on to the edge of the table with the stiff, creased cotton of her dress like a sort of giant seedpod around her. Her legs are bare, her feet planted wide apart as though she might blow away. Has she only got one dress pattern? Emma wonders. This one's blue, but exactly the same as the others, and they're a peculiar shape on her. For a moment questions, thoughts, gather in Emma's mind, and then—

'Fuck, I can smell burning. Quick, grab that cheese sauce.'

Cath

The trip to the seaside buoys Cath up for the rest of that week and well into the next. She misses Jim when he goes back to work, misses the intimacy they recovered in those couple of days, but she fills the time while he's gone with long walks and cooking and an attempt to sort out the garden shed, which they've promised themselves they're going to replace.

And then a day comes when Cath has a migraine. She goes back to bed at lunchtime and lies in the dark, waiting for the medication to work. She doesn't feel much better by the time Jim comes home, but she lets him make a fuss of her, bringing her hot soup, trying to tempt her to eat. The waves of pain continue for most of the night, and she curls up against Jim, wondering whether she's got something worse than a migraine. In the deep dark of the night, she imagines a stopclock being started on the rest of her life, the days ticking steadily by.

In the morning the headache has gone, but it feels as though it's taken part of her with it. She feels exhausted, emptied out.

Jim brings her a cup of tea and a plate of toast before he leaves.

'Sure you'll be OK?' he asks. 'I can take a day off if you'd like me to.'

What Cath would really like is to have the seaside trip all over again. The migraine has undone the peace of mind those few days left her with, she thinks. Couldn't she say, *Yes, please, stay with me*? But she doesn't.

'I'll be fine,' she says.

'I'll see you tonight, then.' But he hesitates, looking at her. 'We could go out, if you like. If you're feeling better.'

A few minutes later he's gone, and Cath lies back against the pillows and wonders how she's going to get through the hours ahead. She managed it until yesterday, she reminds herself – but perhaps the trick of it depended on her keeping going. Now she's stopped, she can't think how to get started again. The fear she felt in the night has stayed with her.

But she tells herself she's being melodramatic; that she always feels like this after a migraine. She just needs to take it easy today. So she stays in bed, eats her toast. Hector heaves himself up the stairs to keep her company, and Cath lifts him on to the bed, as she used to when he was a puppy. He wheezes and sighs as she strokes his head, and she feels a pang of anguish for him, poor old dog, and a sudden plangent wish that he could start over again as a little bundle of dark fur, smelling of sawdust and newness.

Starting over, she thinks. That thought has been lurking in her mind, these last few months, hasn't it? Wishing they could go back to the beginning: to those earliest days, before Leytonstone even, when she woke up in Jim's flat in Clerkenwell, scrambled into the same clothes she'd worn the day before and went into work on an unfamiliar Tube line, feeling twice as alive as everyone else in the carriage. Imagining they could see the glow of sex and love and happiness around her.

But if she could turn the clock back – if she could start over – would she choose again the life she's had, or pick a different one?

The question unnerves her. Surely she wouldn't choose not to have Rose – or Emma? Not even knowing she was going to lose them? But she's not sure she could live through it all again: the hope and the heartache; the happiness that proved so precarious and the long, long months of suspense. She's not sure she could bear it.

That thought makes her sad – more than sad. But admitting it is a relief. It's as if she's making peace with something; facing the worst. As if she's reached, at last, the end of the tunnel. And with it comes something else, countering the regret and the guilt and the anguish, and it feels like a sort of grace. It's as though she *is* starting again: starting from this place, this moment, with what she has now; with what has endured through the years of turbulence. She doesn't have to go back, only forwards, and she knows better, now, than to hope for too much.

She climbs out of bed, borne on a current of energy, and Hector pushes himself up on his haunches and watches her get dressed. Outside, the sun is shining. A walk, she thinks. A sandwich in the garden. Simple pleasures. No mad schemes. She pauses in front of the chest of drawers to select a pair of earrings, and then she notices Jim's phone lying there in the little dish where he leaves his watch and change overnight. Oh dear, she thinks: won't he need it? Should she take it to the office, or will he be out on the road already?

As she hesitates, a message flashes up on the screen. *Sorry I haven't picked up your calls. The Grove Park encounter threw me. I'm in all day if you're free. Dx*

For a long minute Cath stares at the phone. There's an obvious conclusion, but she pushes it aside. So often in life the obvious conclusion is wrong, she tells herself. And it's as if her body refuses to go any further than this: her racing heart slows again, the fuzzy tingle of adrenaline in her limbs subsides. Grove Park: could that mean the fun run? Jim must have bumped into someone that day. The message has disappeared now and she can't get it back without Jim's passcode, but there was no name at the top, just a number, so it's not someone who's saved in his contacts. An old friend, perhaps. An old colleague.

She puts the phone back in the dish and helps Hector off the bed, and together they go downstairs to the kitchen. Cath puts on the kettle, opens the cupboards. She'll make something nice for supper, she thinks. Spag bol, their old favourite. They can sit together with a bottle of wine and she can ask Jim about the fun run, and the person he met there. Or perhaps not. Perhaps ...

Belatedly, a shudder runs through her. Surely not, she thinks. Of course there would be every reason – but surely not.

Jim

Jim doesn't notice at first that his phone is missing.

He's started the day in the *Gazette* office, catching up on admin and gossip. There are rumours about redundancies again, and a running gag about Bob the sports editor's new trousers. Jim joins in, but while he's laughing along with a joke about creating a Facebook page for the trousers, he remembers his message to Emma: remembers that he hasn't checked for a reply for a day or two. What if she's screwed herself up to answer him, and been met with silence?

His pulse quickens as he types in his password – but there's nothing there. For a second he's relieved he hasn't kept Emma waiting, and then his heart contracts in disappointment. It was a long shot, but still ... For a few moments he stares at the screen. Should he try again? He can't tell whether Emma's read the message, or even whether it's reached her account – and he can hardly ask Nick Smith for more technical advice just now. He goes back to his *Gazette* email, deals with a request for some photos which have gone astray, looks up and grins when someone includes him in a Bob's-trousers joke.

It's almost ten when he logs off, picks up his bag and keys, pats his pocket to check for his phone. Damn: it must have fallen out. He scans the floor beneath his chair, shuffles the papers on the desk in case it's got buried. Then he picks up the office phone and calls his mobile number. No. The car, then. He stops at Karen the office manager's desk.

'I've lost my phone,' he says. 'It's probably in the car, but just in case. I've got my schedule: cathedral, Leeming Ponds. Anything else?'

Karen flicks through her big black book – no paperless office for her, and just as well when the IT system crashes, as she delights in saying – and shakes her head.

'I'll call the Wildlife Trust if there's a message,' she says. 'Have a chat with them about their hedgerow project while you're there, will you? Kill two birds with one stone.'

Jim grins: the metaphor's not accidental, he's sure. He's going to Leeming Ponds to photograph a rare wader someone's spotted.

'Will do,' he says.

Back in the car park, he scours the Citroën's footwell, the door pockets, the glove compartments, without success. The loss of the phone makes him feel twitchy, and that annoys him. It's mad how dependent everyone is on the sodding things these days, he thinks. It's like going back twenty years to the days of phone boxes and map books. At least he knows the way to the cathedral and the wildlife reserve. But he's thinking of Cath, too – it occurs to him too late that he should have rung her from the office to let her know he's not contactable today. Not that she usually rings him, but she could have had a look for the phone, too, let him know if it's at home.

But he baulks at the idea of going back inside. Baulks at the idea of drawing Cath's attention to his phone, too: she might suggest she checks for messages, and he could hardly say no, and – yes, definitely better to leave it. He hasn't heard from Dido since the day of the fun run, but he's tried her a couple of times. Things were left unresolved; she must feel that too, and she might ... The twitchiness edges towards panic, but he fights it down. The phone'll be on silent from the night, so it won't ring anyway. His edginess is the work of a guilty conscience, he tells himself as he pulls up at the cathedral, and he deserves it.

He's greeted by the young canon who's set up an exhibition of contemporary religious art from Guatemala. The paintings are huge: they remind him of medieval frescoes. Full of the drama of God, Canon Julie tells him. Full of colour too, and vivid contrasts – a dream to photograph in the cathedral's light-filled interior. Jim lingers for a while, taking photos of the building. The place is so peaceful: it makes him think of medieval monks, a daily round of chanting and calligraphy and digging up turnips. Before he sets off for Leeming Ponds, Canon Julie gives him a leaflet about the next exhibition she's planning, and he promises to come back for it.

The twitcher who reported the green sandpiper has all the hallmarks of eccentricity. As he relates the story of his long wait and lucky break, Jim feels increasingly doubtful that he'll see the wretched bird, let alone get a printable photograph. But he accepts a pair of binoculars, and follows the man to his preferred viewing point.

'He's a winter visitor, see,' the man explains, 'although he does occasionally arrive as early as July.' He beams, and Jim nods. 'We might spot him at the edge of the lake, looking for insects on the surface. He doesn't dig in the mud like other waders, see. I'll show you a picture, shall I, so you know what we're looking for?'

He pulls an iPad from his bag and opens it to reveal a photograph of a disappointingly nondescript-looking bird with a grey-green back and a white underbelly.

'Quite a big boy, he is,' the twitcher continues fondly. 'You won't miss him.'

He beams again, and Jim feels more certain than ever that he will. But his cynicism proves misplaced: after a few minutes his companion emits a muffled shriek, and Jim swings round towards where he's pointing. And sure enough, there's the exact replica of the iPad bird, standing at the edge of the water and bobbing up and down in an engaging sort of way.

'See that?' his companion says. 'That's his little dance. Very characteristic, that is.'

Jim whips out his camera, the long lens already in place, and starts snapping. A minute or two later the bird lifts off over the lake, zigzagging up into the air, and the twitcher coos with delight.

'He's showing you all his tricks!' he says. 'Ooh, he knows he's got an audience, doesn't he?'

It's all over in a few minutes: the bird disappears from view, and Jim's guide grins and sighs. Jim clicks the view button on the camera and scrolls through his photos: the twitcher, looking over his shoulder, makes admiring noises.

'You can see why they pay you for this,' he says, and Jim smiles benignly.

'Beginner's luck,' he says. 'I couldn't have got them without you.'

The man's delighted blush is almost more of a reward than the shots of the sandpiper.

Before he leaves, Jim calls in at the Wildlife Trust office to set up a photoshoot for the hedgerow project. The press officer's new: bright and competent, fiftyish, surprisingly glamorous for this place. She reminds him, just a little, of Dido.

And that thought catches him off guard.

He's on his way back to the car now, crossing the rutted parking area. There's no one around, but even so he feels strangely exposed, as though someone's watching, monitoring his reactions. He checks his watch: it's only three o'clock. There's nothing more on his schedule. He could go back to the office, but they're not expecting him: the sandpiper photos could easily have taken all afternoon. He could go home, then: Cath would be pleased to see him so early, especially after the migraine.

But he doesn't do either.

Instead, he turns north when he reaches the dual carriageway, towards Dido's house. To finish things off properly, he tells himself; and certainly that must be all there is to it. Certainly now, after the Grove Park fiasco – after what he's told Emma – he knows what has to happen. But even so the prospect of seeing Dido fills him with pleasure. Clutching the steering wheel more tightly, he keeps his eyes on the road and pushes everything else to the back of his mind.

When Dido opens the door, Jim has the impression that she's expecting him. The smell of gingerbread fills the house, just as it did the first time he came here.

'Come in,' she says. She's wearing a thin cheesecloth blouse with a string of beads he hasn't seen before. Jim thinks of complimenting them, but doesn't.

In the kitchen, Dido fills the kettle, gets out a teapot. Neither of them says anything more until the tea is poured, slices of cake cut, and Jim has followed Dido through to a little sitting room he's never been in before. Dido gestures at the clutter in the kitchen by way of explanation, but Jim can't help feeling the choice is deliberate. Making him into a different kind of visitor.

Fleetingly, he thinks of his mother, who kept the front room of their tiny house for best; for the kind of callers who never came.

'I'm sorry I didn't answer your messages,' Dido says, when they're both sitting. 'But you got my text, anyway?'

Jim looks at her for a moment before the penny drops.

'Today?' he says. 'Did you text me today?' She nods. 'I left my phone at home. I didn't – I just finished early today. I thought ...'

'Synchronicity, then.' Dido smiles, but carefully.

Jim is thinking about that text, about his phone sitting at home – but he's been through all that, he reminds himself.

'How have you been?' he asks.

'OK,' Dido says. 'Fine.'

He hesitates. 'Dido, I—'

'I know,' she says. 'I know.' She takes a sip of tea: a punctuation mark. 'We've been on borrowed time; I've always known that. I'm just sorry it had to happen like this. That Emma—'

To his horror, tears are rising in her eyes. He didn't expect such generosity, nor such sadness. His own heart feels swollen and painful.

'Have you heard from her?' Dido asks.

'No.'

'I'm sorry. I'm truly sorry.'

'Dido,' he says again, and he reaches towards her, takes her hand. 'It's my fault, all of it, not yours.'

She doesn't reply.

'I haven't deserved – this,' he says. 'You. But it's been ...'

He looks at her. She meets his eyes for a moment, then gently withdraws her hand from his.

'Are you going to tell your wife?' she asks.

'I should,' Jim says. 'Don't you think?'

Dido shakes her head gently, as though it's not her problem, but then she stops, looks down.

'Maybe,' she says. 'A bit of breast-beating, throwing yourself on her mercy. Hoping to be forgiven, in time. Feeling better about it because you've come clean.'

There's something in her voice that makes Jim uneasy.

'Of course you may not have the choice,' Dido says. 'Emma might spill the beans. But otherwise ...' She shrugs. 'You know what, Jim, I don't think you get to have that. The satisfaction of confession. The relief. I don't know your wife—'

'Cath,' Jim says. He clears his throat. 'Her name's Cath.'

'I know her name.' Dido looks up at him briefly, her face full of compassion. 'I know what she's been through, too. Two terrible losses.'

Jim thinks of Rose's little coffin, gleaming white, a wreath of pink roses on top. Of the first night after Emma left, when he and Cath sat waiting, hour after hour. My losses too, he wants to say.

'I'm glad we've had – this time,' Dido says. 'I'm glad *you* have. I'm glad if it's helped. But there's a cost, isn't there? There has to be.' She takes a deep breath then, and Jim thinks: There's a cost for her too. Those things he let himself believe – imagining that this was nothing to her, one dalliance among many – maybe none of that was true. And even if it was, she cares. Clearly she cares. He wants to take her in his arms, but he can't move, can't touch her again.

'Maybe,' she says, 'your punishment is living with it. Living with a secret, knowing there'll never be a moment when you're forgiven.'

'But if Emma ...'

'Then you won't have a choice. But Cath gets her daughter back.'

Jim nods: that's how he reckoned it too.

'But if Emma doesn't come back – especially if she doesn't come back because she saw us together – and you tell Cath about us because you're needing resolution, absolution: aren't you just offloading your suffering on to her? And I don't think that's fair.'

Dido allows her eyes to meet his now, and Jim feels a swell of love and sorrow and admiration. It would be easy, he thinks, to mistrust her motives: to think she simply wants to avoid being implicated in a messy marital row. But he knows that's not what Dido's thinking. And he knows her wisdom and her thoughtfulness are more than he deserves.

'You're right,' he says. 'Of course you're right.'

Her head dips again, but not before he sees her lip tremble.

'I love you, Dido,' he says. 'I love Cath, of course, but I—' For a moment he thinks he might cry too, but he pulls himself tight. 'If things were different ...'

'I know,' she says. She doesn't look up again. 'I know that. But I think you'd better go now.'

Emma

Emma keeps hoping that Penelope will whisk her off to the study again for another dose of wisdom and advice, but the days pass and it doesn't happen. Penelope has had a lot on her mind lately, though. The two oldest boys have taken to fighting each other whenever they get the chance, and it's caused tension between their mothers which has rippled out to affect the whole household.

There's always so much for Penelope to worry about, Emma thinks one evening, when Penelope once again slips away on her own after supper – the bills, the legal problems women bring with them, the never-ending repairs on the house. How do some people get to be like Penelope, she wonders, carrying all that on their shoulders, and others end up like the rest of them, depending on her? Can you ever cross that divide? But then she thinks: didn't Penelope come through her own bad times and out the other side stronger and braver and more competent? That thought lights a flicker of hope, but it's an uncomfortable sort of hope, and she doesn't know what to do with it. She can't imagine ever being as competent or as wise as Penelope.

Abigail and Courtney are washing up tonight; the children are all in bed. Emma watches *Strictly* with some of the others, but when they start channel-hopping afterwards she slips away. The more she wants to cling on to Larkmore, she thinks, the more the niggling sense of not fitting in bothers her. The longer she spends hanging out with the other women, the more she feels like the odd one out.

She hasn't been up to the computer room since the day of the fun run, but as she climbs the stairs to her bedroom she sees the door standing open and finds herself being drawn in. Maybe she should try to write some stuff down, she thinks. She's never kept a diary, never done anything like that, but perhaps it would help. She gazes at the screen for a while, trying out phrases in her head, different ways to begin, but they all sound terrible. And there's so much to say: she could never get through it all, so what's the point, really? Almost without thinking, she opens Facebook – and there, at the top of the page, is a new message alert.

For a moment she stares, and then she clicks on it: a message request from someone she's not connected to. No photo, but a name she knows only too well.

And sure enough, it's him. It's her father.

My darling Emma – I can't imagine what you must think of me. I don't have any excuses, and I don't expect you to take pity on me. If you want to punish me, that's fair enough. If you never want to see me again, I'll have to live with that. But if you can find it in your heart to let your mother know you're OK, even to see her, it would mean more than you can imagine.

I won't say any more now, except that what you saw is in the past. It was a comfort I had no right to, but it was never a threat to your mother in the way you might think, and it'll never happen again.

You probably won't read this anyway – I know it's a long shot. But I love you, we both love you, and it was wonderful to see you alive and well.

Dad

Emma's not sure how long she's been staring at the screen when the door opens. She's conscious of it, the click of the handle and footsteps approaching, as though they're happening a long way away.

'Emma?' Penelope's voice. 'Emma, have you seen Jeanie?'

'Jeanie?' Emma's mind spirals out again from the tiny space it's been curled into.

'She disappeared after supper. She was supposed to come and talk to me, but I can't find her anywhere.'

Emma has turned to face Penelope now, and she's surprised by her expression.

'I wouldn't usually worry, but she's ...' Penelope stops. 'You know her better than anyone here. Do you have any idea where she might be? Where she might have gone?'

'Gone – somewhere outside, you mean?'

'Did she ever mention anywhere? Anyone?'

'No. A bit about her family, once, but – she said her mum and dad were dead.'

Penelope looks at her for a moment, and Emma can't tell what she's thinking, what she suspects. She looks more distressed than you'd expect when someone's only been gone for a couple of hours.

'Would you come upstairs with me, Emma?' she asks. 'You might be able to tell whether anything's missing.'

The little attic room feels cold and bare. It only takes a few minutes to look through Jeanie's belongings: the strange baggy dresses and oversized sweaters; the little box of cheap jewellery and knick-knacks.

'I don't think anything's gone,' Emma says. 'Her bag's here, and her jacket.'

'It's not cold out,' Penelope says. They glance, both of them, towards the window, where the summer dusk is just colouring the sky.

'But she feels the cold,' Emma says. 'She likes ...' She stops, conscious suddenly of how much she doesn't know about Jeanie. All the things she's never asked.

'Have you seen her today?' Penelope asks. 'Spoken to her?'

'Yes.'

'How was she?'

'She was fine, I think,' Emma says. 'I didn't notice anything unusual.'

Apart from the faint noise of the television, the house feels deserted. No one else has been asked to help find Jeanie, Emma guesses, and that makes her feel both important and afraid. She thinks of Jeanie bringing her a plate of toast, not quite daring to look at her; Jeanie hanging on to the kitchen table as though a gust of wind might carry her off at any moment. Has she missed something important – something Jeanie wanted to tell her? She remembers Jeanie's questions about whether Emma was planning to leave, and her grin when Emma agreed that she was a grown-up.

'Is something the matter with her?' she asks. 'Has something been going on?'

'Yes,' says Penelope. She doesn't say any more, and for a moment Emma thinks angrily that Penelope should have told her, should have warned her – but that's not how things work here. 'It's not ...' Penelope stops. 'I'm probably overreacting. Perhaps she forgot our chat. I expect she's just gone for a walk.' She forces a smile. 'Let me know if you see her, will you?'

After Penelope has left, Emma stands for a moment looking at the tiny collection of clothes and possessions on Jeanie's bed. She's suddenly furious – with Penelope, for not taking her into her confidence, but mainly with herself. Jeanie would have told her anything, everything, if she'd asked. If she'd shown any interest. She racks her brain, searching for hints in the conversations they've had – but what she hears is herself. *I found this little clearing, like a place in a fairy tale.* She sees the honey-suckle glade, and Jeanie's face wide with fear and curiosity.

Could Jeanie have gone to find Emma's magic place? It's a long shot, she thinks, not worth telling Penelope about. But she could go, couldn't she? She imagines herself finding Jeanie, and Jeanie confiding in her, and her heart swells.

Lara

The baby is both a consolation and a source of dread. Lara's sixteen weeks pregnant now, and she keeps thinking she can feel it move: little flutters that could almost be nerves. She can certainly feel the bulge, and she loves the idea of carrying the baby around with her all day. She thinks of it as her secret friend – she talks to it, sometimes, when she's on her own. *Time for a cup of tea, I think,* she says, or *What about this green dress today, then?*

But she doesn't tell it what she's thinking about Nick. She doesn't want to worry it. And the fact that it's there, growing steadily, makes their predicament ten times worse. They really can't go on like this forever, she keeps telling herself. She'd never have believed they could hold out for so long, hardly speaking to each other. But it doesn't feel like stubbornness. It feels as though they're both lost; as though neither of them has a clue what to do.

Sometimes she thinks it would only take a little thing, a missed step or a joke or a tiny shock, to tip them back into normality. They were so happy, she thinks, and surely what's gone wrong, what there is to settle between them, can't be enough to destroy all that? Surely the hurt, and the bad things they've thought about each other, would evaporate as soon as the sun came out? But then she thinks how young they are – how they've only known each other a few years – and the solid base she thought they'd built feels too flimsy to support them through this nightmare.

She takes to working from home more often, taking advantage of Mordant's flexible policy, mainly because it spares her the train journeys with Nick, but also because even though she's supposed to be in the blooming phase now, the second trimester, she still doesn't have much energy. This Friday she feels more tired than usual, and the baby must be tired too, because there've been no flutters this morning. She takes her laptop to bed with her and works on her latest project there, fighting off waves of sleepiness and of guilt.

It's late afternoon when she gets up to go to the loo and finds blood in her knickers. Not just a few spots, but lots of blood, clots of it.

Her heart clangs, and she cries out: 'Nick!'

But Nick's in London.

For several long moments she feels frozen, hopeless. Nick's in London and she's here, bleeding. Why's she bleeding? Why is there no one to help her? But then something inside her kicks into action, a little voice telling her what to do. She blots the blood as best she can, pulls her knickers back up, staggers to the bedroom to find her phone. The row, the anger and sorrow between them, flies out of her head as she taps Nick's name and waits for him to pick up. But his phone goes to voicemail, and when the beep sounds she finds she can hardly speak.

'Call me, Nick,' she manages to say. 'Please call me.'

She tries again, but still he doesn't pick up. His extension at Mordant is saved on her phone and she tries that too, but he's not at his desk. Could he have left already? Could he be on his way home?

She can feel more blood now, and panic overtakes her again. She calls Nick again.

'I'm bleeding, Nick,' she says, when the voicemail kicks in. 'I need to go to the hospital. Will you come and find me?'

And then she dials 999.

Nick

It's as though he's been plunged into a sequence of alternative realities these past few weeks, Nick thinks. Surely it's not him but his fictional alter ego who ran for the train, leapt into a taxi to the hospital; who's watching the screen, now, on which black and white shadows shift and blur as a woman in surgical scrubs looks for a heartbeat inside Lara's belly.

He can't bear the thought that he wasn't there, that Lara had to call an ambulance for herself. He holds her hand tightly, his eyes flitting from the ultrasound screen to her face. Her eyes are shut; she looks deathly pale.

The nurse beside him seems to notice Lara's pallor, the drowsy expression on her face, at the same time Nick does. She grasps Lara's wrist, speaks loudly to her, and before Nick can work out what's happening, other people have come into the room and crowded around Lara, and someone's putting a hand on Nick's shoulder and explaining that they're taking her to theatre.

'Is she OK?' he asks stupidly. 'Is the baby OK?'

'I'm afraid we couldn't find the baby's heartbeat.' The woman gives him a practised look of sympathy. 'I'm so sorry, Mr Smith,' she says. 'Your wife will be fine, but she's bleeding quite heavily and we need to clear things out to stop the blood loss. They're taking her to theatre now so we can get straight on with that.'

'The baby's dead?' Nick asks. 'Why did it die? What happened?'

'I'm afraid I can't tell you that,' the woman says. 'I'm so sorry.'

'But it was fine.' Nick thinks of Lara's maternity dresses in the wardrobe, the scan photo on the fridge. The baby's life seems too real, too certain to be undone like this. 'Everything was fine this morning.'

The woman's shepherding him down the corridor now, taking him to a room with yellow curtains and plastic flowers that looks like the place they bring people to break bad news.

'Have a seat, Mr Smith,' she says. 'If you wait here, they'll come and find you as soon as they're done in theatre. Can I get you a cup of tea?'

'Is it because she had an abortion?' The words seem to come out on their own, as though Nick's subconscious has bypassed the bit of his brain that usually gets to decide what he says.

The woman looks surprised. 'Excuse me?'

Nick's almost as shocked as she is, but he can't take the words back now. 'My wife had an abortion a few years ago,' he says. 'I just wondered ...'

'I'm sure that has nothing to do with it.' She gives him a tight little smile. 'It often turns out that there was something wrong with the baby, with the way it was developing.'

Nick nods. 'I see,' he says, but he doesn't really. How could there have been anything wrong with the baby? Wouldn't they have known by now?

But of course it wasn't the abortion that caused this. How could he even think that? No, it's obvious what's behind this disaster, isn't it? It's staring him in the face. How stupid he is: how despicable he's been. All that moralising about not doing what his father did, and he's done something a hundred times worse. How will Lara ever forgive him?

It's almost an hour before they let him see her. She's in a side room off the gynae ward with drips and monitors attached to her. Her eyes are shut, and for a few moments Nick stands just inside the room and looks at her, so full of emotion that it's all he can do to stay upright. His darling Lara. His precious love.

Despite the reassuring tone of the medical staff, he knows she's had a close shave. And he knows, too, that there's heartache and sorrow ahead – for both of them, but particularly for Lara. His own part, he promises himself, he'll bear without a whimper. The recrimination and regret; the knowledge of what he's done. He can't bear to think of the nonsense that's been filling his head, the adolescent crap about the pointlessness of existence. The fact that he thought even for a second that what they had, he and Lara, meant nothing any more.

When Lara opens her eyes he's still standing beside the door, and for a moment he thinks she hasn't seen him, but then her mouth moves and he's across the room and picking up her hand, bending down to kiss her.

'My love,' he says. 'I'm so sorry.'

'I lost the baby,' she says.

Nick can feel tears welling in his eyes now, but he fights them down.

'I know,' he says. 'I know. My poor Lara. But you're all right. You're safe. That's all that matters.'

'I'm sorry,' she says.

'Why are you sorry?'

He can't stop the tears now, but Lara's eyes have shut again, as though some great weight is pulling them down. Or perhaps because she can't bear to look at him, Nick thinks, with a stab of pain.

'There's nothing to be sorry for, my love. It's me who's sorry. I've been ...' But he stops. Too many words, he thinks. There's time enough for all that. 'What can I do?' he asks. 'Do you want anything?'

'I want my mum,' she whispers, and he squeezes her hand tight.

'Do you want me to call her?'

'No.' She attempts a smile, her eyes still shut. 'No. I just ...'

'I'll look after you,' he says.

'I know.'

'I'll always look after you, Lara. I promise.'

There's a chair in the corner of the room; he brings it over to the bed and sits down beside her.

'Just rest now,' he says. 'I'll be here.'

'Thank you.'

For a while after that she's so quiet and still that he thinks she must be sleeping, and he shuts his eyes too, exhausted by all the emotion of the last few weeks. But then he feels her stir, and when he opens his eyes she's gazing up at his face.

'Are you sure there's nothing I can get you?' he asks again. 'Are you hungry? Thirsty?'

'I'd like ...' A tear runs down her cheek now, but she shakes her head.

'What?' he asks. 'Anything at all. Tell me, Lara.'

'I'd like Cath,' she says. 'I know you—'

'Of course.' Despite himself, he feels a stab of pain. *Anything at all. Anything but this.* But of course, of course: not her mother, but Cath. And there could hardly be a more fitting penance for him. He gets to his feet, his phone already in his hand. 'I'll call her now.'

Emma

The rolling of day into night has turned the woods inside out, the pale skin of the silver birches lighter now than the sky between them. There's still a bird singing here and there, far above her, and the occasional distant door-squeak of an owl. Emma's not sure she can retrace her route, and even less sure whether Jeanie could have found the place from her brief description. She could be any-where in the woods – or nowhere. Emma picks her way along a path that's hardly a path, tripping now and then on a root, bracken catching at her legs.

But then, as she hesitates beside a tree she thinks she recognises, something reaches her: the smell of honey-suckle. There could be honeysuckle anywhere in the woods, but it feels like a sign – a fairy-tale clue, like a trail of breadcrumbs or a robin calling from a branch. And surely she remembers that stump? The one that's hunched like a bear in the shadows now, watching her pass ...

And then she hears something that makes her stop dead. There's the owl again, maybe two of them calling across the wood, but there's something else, too. A cry, or a moan: something animal-like and visceral that Emma knows is not an animal. She starts to run.

'Jeanie!' she calls. 'Jeanie, I'm coming!'

Jeanie is curled up on the forest floor a few feet from the hollow tree, almost exactly where Emma stood a few weeks before. She's writhing in agony; the sounds coming from her mouth are horrible, but even so they seem too muted for the painful contortion of her body.

Emma crouches down, one hand cradling Jeanie's sharp forehead and the other reaching for her hand as it thrashes in the dead leaves. 'What's the matter, Jeanie? What's happened to you?'

And then Jeanie's body goes slack. Emma's heart leaps in horror – but she's not dead, she's alive, awake. She rolls her head towards Emma, her eyes wide and terrified.

'Emma,' she whispers.

'I'm here,' Emma says. 'I've come to find you.'

'Emma ...' Jeanie says again. She licks her lips, shakes her head, panting a little. Has she had a fit? Emma wonders. Has she hit her head, or been poisoned, or ...

'What's happened, Jeanie?' she asks. 'Did you fall? Are you ill?

Jeanie's mouth seems to be forming words; Emma bends over her, leaning in close, but then Jeanie groans and twists, clutches Emma's hand, and the writhing and wailing start again. Emma lets her hand be squeezed tight, murmuring reassurances she has no faith in – *Everything's OK, you're going to be fine* – and with the other hand she strokes Jeanie's poor tangled body. And then she stops. Jeanie's belly is swollen, tight, as though she's swallowed a rock. A tumour? Emma thinks. Some horrible illness like you see ...?

No. The light dawns, miraculous and extraordinary.

'Oh my God, Jeanie,' she says, 'are you having a baby?'

The clues flash through her head now: the baggy dresses, and Jeanie changing in the bathroom; asking whether Emma's ever been pregnant. How could she have shared a room with Jeanie every night and not noticed anything? She counts back – it was almost Christmas when Jeanie arrived at Larkmore. Seven months ago. Was that why she came?

The contraction has reached a peak now and Jeanie lets out an agonised howl, bracing her whole body as if she's trying to fight it off. Emma's heart is racing, but her mind is moving slowly: too slowly. She hasn't got a phone. She couldn't carry Jeanie, and Jeanie couldn't make it back through the woods now, even with Emma supporting her. She could run back to Larkmore, ring for an ambulance, but that would mean leaving Jeanie, leaving her for fifteen minutes at least, and some intuition tells her she can't do that. There's hardly any gap between her contractions, and Emma knows that means the baby's nearly here. She can't leave Jeanie lying in the woods to have her baby alone. But she needs help: more help than Emma can give. Oh, why didn't she bring Penelope? Why did she think it would be brave and clever to come on her own in search of Jeanie?

'Emma ...' Jeanie's body has relaxed again, and when she looks at Emma now her face seems clearer. 'I should have told you,' she says.

'You tried to,' Emma says, but Jeanie shakes her head. 'Don't worry now,' Emma says. 'We need to – I think the baby's nearly here.'

Her mind feels sharper now. When Julianne was pregnant, she watched lots of videos about childbirth – secretly, a little guiltily, preparing herself for what lay ahead. She needs to remember everything she can now. At the end of that last contraction Jeanie was wanting to push, she thinks. That might mean she's reached the second stage – but if she pushes too early she might tear badly.

'Jeanie,' she says, 'I need to have a look at what's happening, quickly, before the next contraction. I need you to roll on to your back, and ...'

This feels like a shot in the dark – she has no idea how to check for dilation, or whatever it is you need to know – but as soon as Jeanie's in position everything becomes clear. When the next contraction starts, Emma can clearly see the baby's head. A little circle of damp hair, just like in the videos.

'It's right there,' she says. 'The baby's ready to come out. You can push, Jeanie: push as hard as you like now.'

There's no time for doubt now; no time to think about complications. Emma's tried to spread Jeanie's dress over the ground between her legs so the baby won't spill out on to the earth. One hand is holding Jeanie's hand while she rages and gurns, bracing her body to push, and the other is cupping the top of the baby's head – so it doesn't come out too fast, she remembers from somewhere. But in the rush and fury of the next few minutes Emma can't tell what she's remembering and what comes from some kind of instinct. There's a sense of urgency and purpose now that's thrilling – and after two more contractions, there, suddenly, is the baby's head, sticking out of Jeanie. It looks purple, hardly human: more like an alien that's got inside Jeanie somehow and is bursting its way out than a baby in the middle of being born. Emma fees a clutch of fear: it can't breathe, can't get any blood like that. It can't stay there.

'Push,' she says urgently. 'The contraction's still there: keep pushing, Jeanie.'

And then there's a slither and a rush, and the baby is in Emma's arms, wet and slippery and still purple. For an agonising second she's afraid it's dead, but then it curls up its tiny face in a grimace of disgust and yells so loudly that Emma laughs in delight.

'She's fine!' she says. 'Oh Jeanie, she's beautiful!'

She lifts the baby over Jeanie's belly and lays her in her arms. The expression on Jeanie's face, the elation and relief that floods through them both, is too much for

Emma. She feels herself dissolving, tears streaking down her cheeks.

'Oh, Emma,' Jeanie says. 'Oh, look at her!'

'You did so well,' Emma says. 'You were brilliant. I'm so proud of you.'

'I couldn't have done it without you,' Jeanie says. 'I couldn't.'

Emma doesn't want to think about that – what might have happened if she hadn't been there – although she's pretty sure Jeanie would have been OK. Her body, her tiny childlike body, did most of it without any help. A miracle, she thinks. A proper miracle. She can't stop looking at Jeanie, her face radiant with pleasure as she wraps the baby in the cardigan she must have thrown off earlier, and the baby's perfect little face gazing up at her. Thank God, Emma thinks, there were no complications, no delays. It was all so quick there was hardly time to worry about things going wrong, but that doesn't mean they couldn't have done.

And then, sitting back on her heels, Emma looks around at the clearing, the honeysuckle and the log and the towering trees, and other things begin to creep in on the moment of triumph. They haven't finished, she thinks. The baby's born, the baby seems to be fine, but there's the placenta, there's the umbilical cord. And there's still just the two of them, out here in the woods. How quickly do you have to do all that other stuff? she wonders.

The baby squawks then, a fractious little cry. 'Should I feed her?' Jeanie asks. 'Is she hungry?'

'I don't know. Do you want to try?' Emma leans in closer and helps Jeanie to sit up, and then to unbutton her dress. It makes her smile a little to think how careful Jeanie has been, all these months they've shared a room, to keep her body hidden, and she feels deeply touched to be here with her now: to watch the tiny mouth questing for the nipple and to hear the wonder and pride in Jeanie's voice as she murmurs to her baby. Another miracle: that the child seems to know how to suckle, and the child-mother manages it all so calmly.

But those other things are pressing more urgently on Emma now. There's a lot of blood, and the cord still looping from inside Jeanie to the baby's belly. All that makes her feel panicky.

'Jeanie,' she says, 'I need to get help now. Will you be OK here for a few minutes?'

Jeanie lifts her wide eyes to her. 'I don't want you to go,' she says.

'I know.' Emma smiles, puts a hand on her shoulder. 'But you'll be OK. I'll be as quick as I can.'

Jeanie leans against Emma, resting her face on Emma's hand for a moment, and Emma feels the touch of her dry skin with a fierce rush of affection. All those months with such a big secret inside her, Emma thinks. All those months when Emma never asked the right question; never took enough of an interest to notice what was going on.

Jim

Jim's back home before six. As he walks through the door he's conscious of something in the air: not quite a smell or a sound, but a sense of anticipation. His imagination, maybe. But in his imagination it reminds him of coming home to Leytonstone. He drops his bag in the hall and goes through to the kitchen, where the table is laid, a salad waiting in a bowl, a loaf of bread on a board. Despite himself, he smiles. Not so much like Leytonstone with its disastrous culinary experiments, botched food left behind in the kitchen while they fled to the curry house down the road.

He's still looking at the table, remembering that grotty little house, when Cath appears.

'I didn't hear you come in,' she says, and he turns and smiles.

'I've only been back two minutes.'

She looks at him now, an open, unguarded look he remembers – oh, remembers very well – but hasn't seen for a long time. A slightly quizzical look, too.

'Nice and early,' she says.

'I got through everything in double-quick time,' he says. 'I'm glad to see you're feeling better.' There's a voice inside him screaming deceit, reminding him that half an hour ago he told another woman he loved her, but he ignores it. *Offloading your suffering on to Cath isn't fair,* he reminds himself. So here he is, making everything smooth and cheerful and comfortable. Keeping his guilt invisible.

'Supper's all ready,' Cath says. 'Spag bol. I just need to cook the pasta.'

Leytonstone food, after all.

While Cath puts the water on to boil, Jim finds a bottle of wine and pours them each a glass. For a moment he feels dizzy: this feels too easy, too good to be true. He can almost hear Cath humming. But this is how they started off, he thinks. Just the two of them. Shouldn't it be possible for things to be like this again?

He hands Cath her glass of wine and slips a hand around her shoulder, leaning over to smell the ragu bubbling in the pan. Perhaps he should feel like an impostor, but he doesn't. Because he's not, he tells himself. He's been here all these years. They've been together through everything life has thrown at them.

While they eat, Jim tells Cath about the green sandpiper, and she smiles at his account of the twitcher. He describes the Guatemalan paintings, and she asks how long the exhibition's on. As the minutes pass, though, his sense of ease begins to fade. It feels as though something's missing, something's not quite aligned. His imagination again, he tells himself. His guilty conscience. But the suspicion that there's something on Cath's mind won't go away.

After a bit Cath puts down her fork. 'I found your phone, by the way,' she says. 'You left it in the bedroom.'

Jim suppresses a lurch of panic. He smiles, hesitates; he doesn't want to make too much of this, nor too little. 'Thanks,' he says. 'I thought it must be here. I should have rung to let you know I didn't have it.'

'I found it first thing,' Cath says, and then there's a pause, a twisting of her face towards a smile or a question, and Jim's stomach drops.

Maybe this is it, he thinks. Maybe this is the moment where, after all, he should tell her the truth.

But the silence extends, and no words come. Cath's gone back to her supper now, winding spaghetti on her fork. Not waiting for him to speak, and not saying anything herself either. He imagines the words she might use: *Someone called you, earlier.* He knows Dido didn't ring – but would Cath have picked up if she had? Might she have thought it was him, trying to get hold of her? And if she had – if, God forbid, she'd heard Dido's voice on the other end – would Dido have had the presence of mind to produce a convincing story?

A wild thought rises in his mind now: that Dido *did* ring, did speak to Cath, told her everything. That Dido cast him as the villain, maybe even told Cath he pretended not to have a wife. That between them they've cooked up a punishment for him. The plausibility of it drains the blood from his heart. He thinks back to this afternoon – Dido being gentle, generous, feeding him gingerbread. Advising him not to tell Cath anything; letting him walk away without recrimination. And then Cath making supper, having it all ready when he got back, even though she couldn't have expected him for another hour at least.

He watches Cath chasing the last bits of spaghetti around her plate, lifting it to her mouth. Could he possibly believe the woman – the women – he loves could hatch such a conspiracy?

This is what Dido meant about his penance, he thinks; about living with a guilty secret: that it would torment him, make him paranoid, undermine every ordinary moment of pleasure. His heart's racing, his skin prickling with sweat. It'll kill him, he thinks. He can't stand it: he'll have to tell Cath, get it out in the open. But if Dido's right, if that's more than she can bear ... The argument circles in his head, chasing its own tail. *There has to be a cost,* he hears Dido saying.

And then a phone rings: not his, Cath's, sitting on the side behind her. She looks round in surprise. People rarely ring her, Jim knows, even though she keeps it with her all the time, just in case. She hesitates, and Jim gets up and fetches it for her.

'Hello?' she says, and he watches her face transmit shock, dismay, sorrow.

'What?' he says, even though he knows she's listening to whoever's on the other end.

'I'm so sorry,' Cath says. 'How awful for you both.' And then, after another pause, 'Of course I will. Of course. I'll come now.'

She clicks the phone off and looks at Jim.

'That was Nick,' she says. 'Lara's lost the baby. She's asked for me.'

Beneath the consternation, Jim can see something else in Cath's face: the delight of being needed. Summoned. Especially by Nick. But other things flare in his own mind in those few seconds. He thinks that he doesn't know where the conversation about his phone might have gone if Nick hadn't rung, and that he doesn't know whether – or when – it will be picked up again.

'I'll drive you,' he says.

Cath's already on her feet, gathering up her bag, a cardigan.

'You don't have to,' she says.

'Of course I will,' he says. 'It's the least I can do.'

Lara

Lara has done a bit of sleeping and a lot of crying. The sleep is fitful, only a few minutes at a time, but each time she wakes she's forgotten what's happened and has to remember it all over again – and then sorrow overwhelms her and weeping empties her, and the exhausting cycle continues. Her body is filled with dull pain, and she can feel blood still leaking between her legs as though there's a wound inside her that will never heal.

She badly needs to sleep properly, deeply, but grief and humiliation press at her subconscious, and the ward is too busy. Too noisy. Nick has been sitting beside her all the time, and the nurses have been so kind, but she longs for silence and peace, for oblivion. And then Nick touches her hand and whispers that he's going to get a cup of coffee, that he'll be back in ten minutes, and when he's gone she feels utterly desolate. How stupid she is; how feeble.

This baby wasn't even a baby yet, just the hope of one. How can she feel that the world is ending?

When she opens her eyes once more and Cath is there, Lara's first thought is that she's a mirage. Did she ask ...? Did Nick ...?

Cath leans forward and takes her hand.

'You poor girl,' she says. 'You poor, poor girl.'

Lara shuts her eyes and grasps Cath's hand, and it's as if a draught of something cool and calm trickles into her body. Cath understands, Lara thinks. Cath of all people knows what it means to lose a child.

'I'm so sad,' she whispers. 'It wasn't even a proper baby, and I'm so sad.'

Cath squeezes her fingers. 'Of course it was a baby,' she says. 'Of course it was. A baby you'd loved for months.'

'How can I bear it?' Lara asks. 'I don't think I can. I don't ...'

Cath doesn't say anything, not *You're still young* or *You can try again* or any of the other supposedly comforting things people have already said. Cath just holds her hand in both of hers, and for a long moment they stay like that, Cath holding her and Lara's breath catching, settling, and the pain throbbing again so that she moans a little, then relaxes into a shuddering sigh. And then she opens her eyes and looks at Cath, kind Cath.

'Is it my fault?' she asks.

'How could it be?'

'Because of the argument,' Lara says. 'Because I made Nick so angry, and myself so upset. Because ...'

'Of course not,' Cath says. 'Goodness, babies survive wars. Mothers can almost starve and their babies still live.'

'But not mine,' Lara says. 'Maybe it knew we'd fought.'

'No,' says Cath.

'Maybe it thought I didn't want it any more.'

Cath shakes her head. 'You can't get rid of a baby by not wanting it.' She flinches, almost imperceptibly, and Lara knows what she's thinking.

'Because of the abortion, then,' she says, although it hurts to speak the words; to think how different, how horribly different this feels, even though it's the same thing. Another baby that was growing inside her and then gone.

'No,' says Cath more firmly. 'And in any case, you *did* want it. And so did Nick.' She pats the back of Lara's hand, a gesture that reminds Lara of her mother. She feels tears surging again.

'Everyone argues,' Cath says. 'Especially when they're pregnant. It's normal.'

Then why? Lara wants to ask. *Why me? Why now?*

Maybe Cath can hear her, because she says, 'Life's not fair, that's all. Things happen for no reason, all the time. It's a savage truth, and there's no easy way to learn it. The only way to survive is not to blame yourself.'

Lara nods. Cath's words echo in her head; she's too tired to think now, too tired for anything, but the sound of Cath's voice is comforting. The sound of someone wise and calm.

'Thank you for coming,' she whispers. 'I wanted you to come.'

'You're welcome,' Cath says.

'Don't go,' Lara says. 'Please don't go. I think I need to ...'

Cath doesn't say anything more, but she sits, holding Lara's hand, as sleep starts to flow at last through her bruised body.

Emma

Jeanie looks incredibly small in the hospital bed. She's lying still and straight, her arms resting on top of the sheet, like a girl on her deathbed in a Victorian painting. But when she sees Emma, her face fills with a smile so wide and so joyous that Emma can't stop herself rushing forwards and gathering Jeanie in her arms. Jeanie's hands grip her hard.

'Everything's OK,' she says. 'Everything's fine.'

'Thank God, eh?'

Only a couple of hours have passed since she left Jeanie in the wood, but it feels like forever. What's happened since then is a blur: running to Larkmore, finding Penelope, running back to Jeanie and waiting for the ambulance, the paramedics. And then Jeanie and the baby being taken off to hospital, and Penelope and Emma following in the car. Having to wait what seemed an impossible length of time for the doctors and the midwives to sort everything out before she was allowed to come and see Jeanie.

'I was so worried,' she says. 'I thought I'd done something wrong.'

Jeanie grins again. 'I just needed a few stitches,' she says, 'but they said I'd probably have needed them anyway. They couldn't believe we did it between us.'

'You did it,' Emma says. 'I did nothing.'

'Course you did. You did all the things people usually do. Told me to push and all that.'

'Well ...' Emma smiles, blushes. There's a little silence then. Emma looks at Jeanie's face: her bones are as sharp and delicate as a cat's, she thinks. A little lost cat that people have hardly looked at. 'I'm so sorry,' she says.

'What for?'

'Not noticing. Not thinking.'

Jeanie screws her face up. 'You had your own stuff to think about,' she says. 'It's my fault too. I could have just come out and said it.'

'Well.' There's nothing more to say about that, Emma thinks, and it doesn't matter any more. Everything's OK.

'How's the baby?' she asks.

And then it seems to Emma that Jeanie's face changes completely: as though it's suffused, suddenly, with mother's milk. 'She's so pretty,' Jeanie whispers. 'She's like a little tiny doll. I can't believe it: I can't believe she came from me.'

'Where is she?' Emma asks.

'They took her away to put her under a light,' Jeanie says. 'They'll bring her back soon.' She fixes her eyes on Emma then, and her expression is familiar: beseeching, Emma thinks. Nervous. 'Will you help me?' she asks. 'With the baby? I keep thinking – Emma loves babies.'

'I do.' Emma looks back, her gaze steady. 'Of course I'll help you, Jeanie. I promise. I won't let you down.'

And she means it. She vows it to herself, more solemnly than any promise she's ever made. This is her chance, she sees. Her remedy. She thinks about Jeanie's big eyes watching her, gazing at her, while she fed one of the babies at Larkmore, or waited for the answer to a question. The same way she used to look at Julianne, Emma thinks, and something shifts in her head: something hot and confusing is released inside her. Maybe she could – little Jeanie, so different from ... But couldn't it be? Couldn't she make it be?

She smiles at Jeanie as things swirl and settle in her mind. Jeanie needs her, that's the main thing. Jeanie needs her, and that feels good.

The baby has neat little features and soft, soft skin, faintly yellowish around the eyes, and the beginnings of a sharp chin.

'She looks exactly like you,' Emma says, leaning over the plastic cot.

'Yeah, well, I don't want her to look like her dad,' says Jeanie – and then she pulls a face. 'It wasn't rape, but it was – I didn't like it. I didn't like *him*. I wanted ...' She bites her lip, and then she looks at her baby, sleeping peacefully in her hospital shawl. 'I wanted someone to look after me.'

'Well, you found that. A place to look after you, anyway.'

'Yeah.' Jeanie strokes the baby's head. 'I didn't know I was pregnant when I first came. I didn't realise for a long time.' She screws up her face. 'My periods had stopped before, and it was nothing. So I convinced myself ...'

'But you must have had a bump,' Emma says. 'I mean – I can't believe I didn't notice.'

'I was very neat,' Jeanie says, with a prick of pride. 'And those dresses, you know ...' Emma laughs. 'That should have given it away, eh? You just thought I was bad at dressmaking. Which I was. Terrible.' Jeanie pulls a face. 'But in the end I couldn't pretend any more, so I told Penelope. I should've told her sooner, but – anyway.'

Emma nods. Neither of them says anything more for a while, but then the baby's eyes flicker open and she makes a little noise, a sort of squeal. Emma leans forward and lifts her out of the cot, then lays her in Jeanie's arms. She badly wants to hold her herself, but it's important that Jeanie does, she knows that.

'What are you going to call her?' she asks.

Jeanie hesitates. 'I dunno,' she says, looking down at the baby. 'I thought – I need to think about it.'

Emma remembers the names she dreamed up for Julianne's baby. She liked old-fashioned names: Abigail, Stephanie, Marigold. She never mentioned them to Julianne. Never asked what names Julianne liked. She waits for the stab of pain, but when it comes it's softer, fainter, than usual.

'What's on your list, then?' she asks.

'I was thinking maybe ... Rose.'

Emma looks up sharply, and Jeanie's gazing straight at her, her face tight and anxious.

'Not if you don't want,' she says. 'I just thought – I thought you missed her so much. I thought maybe ...'

Before she can work out why, Emma is weeping. Because she *does* miss Rose, and maybe she's never really said it properly. Because of Jeanie's kindness, thinking about Emma's losses and not her own. And because this baby feels like an answer to everything, and although she knows that's not what she deserves, she can't help the great balloon of joy swelling inside her.

'That would be lovely,' she says. 'That would be really lovely.'

She smiles at the baby, and just at that moment she opens her mouth and yells with such sudden, surprising force that they both laugh.

'I need to feed her.' Jeanie says. 'Can you take her, while I get ready?'

'Of course.'

The child feels astonishing in Emma's arms. So small, so soft, so *real*. Her weight settles against Emma's body as though it was always meant to be there. She's never held a baby so tiny and new: she thinks of it growing, this perfect creature, in Jeanie's belly, night after night, only a few feet away from her.

And then she thinks of the photograph in the album at home which shows two newborn girls curled against each other in an incubator. Two babies so alike, except that one is a fraction larger, stronger, than the other. Two lives beginning, and their mother standing over them, her hand just visible in the corner of the photograph. If Emma shuts her eyes she can almost imagine she remembers it: that first day of her life, and her sister as close as she'd been for nine months in the womb. How can she not miss her? Life of my life, she thinks. The part of me that is lost. Tears blur her vision again, one or two escaping to run down her cheek, fall to her hand, slide gently down to christen the head of the tiny child lying against her chest.

'Hello, Rose,' she murmurs. 'Hello, beautiful girl.'

Cath

Sitting beside Lara's bed while she sleeps, Cath feels herself slipping into the familiar patterns of nurture: selflessness, competence, love. It's been a long time since she was needed like this, and it makes her heart swell. She feels terrible, sorrowful, about the circumstances – but who could see anything unseemly now in the daughterless mother looking after the motherless daughter? Who could blame Cath for letting everything else that has been on her mind slip away, just for a little while, and giving herself up to the raw emotions of this night?

She's forgotten, though, about Nick. Barely ten minutes have passed when he appears – coming up behind Cath, his abrupt halt catching her attention. She makes to stand, but he gestures at her to stay where she is. He has a paper cup of coffee in his hand, and he offers it to Cath – a token of truce, she thinks – but she shakes her head with a smile. His eyes drop to Lara now, giving Cath a chance to study his face. He's been crying too, she can see. He looks exhausted, defenceless; a little boy trying to be a man, shouldering a crisis. Poor Nick: shouldering guilt too, no doubt, unless she's reading him all wrong.

When he speaks, it's in a hoarse whisper.

'She looks peaceful now.'

Cath nods, ventures a cautious smile.

'Thank you for coming.'

'My pleasure.' Does she sound brusque? Cath wonders. She doesn't mean to.

Nick sighs, lifting Lara's hand gently from the bed and enclosing it in both of his.

'I've been such a fucking idiot,' he says. 'I wanted to ...' He stops, wiping tears crossly from his face. 'I just wanted to be everything to her.'

'I understand,' Cath says.

She thinks he's going to say something sharp – *I doubt it* – but instead he sighs again, and shakes his head in bewilderment.

'I'm sorry,' he says. 'About the other night.'

'Don't worry,' Cath says. 'I've got broad shoulders.'

She wants to laugh then: not broad enough to bear her own troubles, she thinks, not for a long time. And not broad enough to bear Nick's furious outburst without two days by the sea to recover. But it's true now, here.

'I thought I should be all she needed,' he says. 'I was jealous, I suppose. That she came to you. That I couldn't ...'

'I could go now,' Cath says. 'I told Lara I'd stay, but now you're back ...'

'No,' he says. 'Stay.'

'You don't mind?'

'She wanted you. She needs – you know she doesn't see her parents?'

'Yes.'

He nods. 'It's good,' he says. 'It's good she's got some-one else. With the baby—'

He stops suddenly, his face stricken, and Cath feels a stab of pain. For him, but for herself too. For the way memory catches you out. She waits, gathering herself, and then she says, 'There will be a baby, you know. I wouldn't say that to Lara, but it's true. And ...' Should she go on? Should she risk more? 'You won't ever forget this baby, this loss, but you'll love the next one, and that'll be ...'

She can't finish the sentence. What will it be? What can she possibly say? That'll be wonderful; that'll be enough? It'll be as agonising as this, one way or another. Perhaps Nick understands. He doesn't answer, but he holds her eyes for a moment before they both let the con-versation slide into silence again.

Cath's mind stays with Lara for a while, tracing the outline of her face, the drip running into her wrist, and then it slips back in time, lulled by the murmur of voices and the bustle of uniforms, all so familiar. So many hours, she thinks, sitting beside Rose – in the hospital where she was born, and at Great Ormond Street, and once, scariest of all, in a hospital in Devon when they'd risked a holiday two hundred miles from home and she went down with an infection. So many hours without speaking, holding her little hand. And Emma's too, the time she fell off her bike and broke her arm; when Emma whimpered in pain as they waited half the night for an X-ray. And before that – before that, in the Women's Unit at the Royal Free, the antenatal appointments, the endless scans. The delivery: the hope and fear and anguish of that.

She feels, suddenly, profoundly tired. So much emotion these past few weeks, and these past two decades. How strange to think that they have brought her to this point: sitting beside a stranger's bed, mourning the loss of a stranger's child. There's never a moment when life resolves, she thinks – not until the very end, and then who knows whether everything will tie up satisfactorily – but there are moments when it seems to linger over a cadence, a still point, and wills you to see its symmetries; to imagine a shape for it.

Her mind hovers, drifts, looking down on herself – and then she must have slept, because she wakes to find Nick's hand on her shoulder, shaking her gently.

'They're going to wash her,' he says. 'D'you want to ...'

There are two nurses standing beside Lara's bed.

'Sorry,' Cath says. 'I must have dropped off.'

'I'd do the same myself if I sat down for long enough,' says the younger nurse, with a smile. Cath gets to her feet. Lara's awake, still very pale but more alert, more herself.

'I'll come back,' Cath says. 'I'll go and get a coffee.'

She makes her way to the area by outpatients where the Friends operate a café during the day and vending machines take over at five. She doesn't usually drink coffee in the evenings; it keeps her awake. But she selects the latte button and waits while the pale liquid trickles out into a flimsy cup. There are chairs here, but she's been sitting for a while, so instead she walks on down the corridor, towards the stairs. The walls are bare, except for the occasional noticeboard carrying information about clinic times and complaints procedures, the occasional bland painting, all of it deeply familiar. Even the wards are generic, numbered rather than named, and the scuffed flooring and off-white paintwork could be anywhere, any hospital in the country. It feels like a time warp to Cath. It reeks of memory.

There aren't many people in the corridors at this time of day, but Cath thinks of all the other visitors scattered around the hospital, sitting beside the beds of women who've given birth, people who've had operations or accidents: people whose lives have been turned upside down for better or worse. So many stories; so many variations on the same themes. It's odd to think that for these walls and corridors, and for the staff who work within them, all the crises and tragedies people experience here are normal, workaday. No individual story lingers long, she thinks. Each one is written over, day by day, with new layers of pain and joy. But perhaps at this hour of night you can feel the echo of them: of other people's stories and of your own, suspended in time like a specimen in a glass jar.

And then she comes round a corner and sees two people coming towards her: perhaps real people, or perhaps ghosts conjured up from the collective memory of the hospital. One of them – older, taller – she doesn't recognise, but as they come closer she feels more and more certain that the other one, the younger one, is not a stranger, nor a ghost. The younger one is part of her own story, and she's truly real. Truly here.

Emma

It's late when Penelope comes back. Emma's been so immersed in Jeanie and the baby that she's hardly noticed the time passing. She's watched Jeanie breastfeeding, helped her change Rose's nappy; she's held the little bundle in her arms and breathed in the miraculous smell of her head, then rested her on her shoulder and rocked her to sleep. It's been blissful, every moment of it. She's glad now that she finished the child development course: as this baby grows, day by day and week by week, she can be useful. The thought of that fills her with joy.

She wants to tell Penelope to go away again – she begs to be allowed to stay all night, to sleep in the chair beside Jeanie's bed so she can be there when the baby wakes. So she won't miss a second of Rose's life, the tiniest gesture or sound: so Jeanie knows she means it, that she'll stay with her.

But Penelope is firm. The ward staff won't allow it, she says. Emma might have taken on the nurses, but disagreeing with Penelope is harder. And she *is* tired. It's been a long day; a long night. She kisses the baby, kisses Jeanie, and follows Penelope out of the ward.

The hospital is very quiet. Penelope doesn't rush, and Emma's glad. She'd like to stop time, she thinks, pause it right now when there's so much to look forward to and everything else can be pushed aside for a bit. Even if it means roaming these dingy corridors for ever, she'd like to prolong the magic of this night.

'She's doing well,' Penelope says, as they pass the lifts.

'Jeanie?'

'Both of them.' Penelope glances at her. 'Another baby for you to look after.'

'Yes.' Emma wants to say more, to explain that this baby is different, but she can't find the right words for that. And it's all too new, too tender, to be spoken aloud.

Penelope looks at her again, and Emma senses just before she speaks that Penelope is going to do something unusual.

'I can't help blaming myself,' she says. 'I should have realised.'

'That she was pregnant?' Emma hesitates. 'When did you find out?'

'Just a few days ago. Jeanie came to tell me she thought she was having a baby, and at first I wasn't sure it could be true – she'd been at Larkmore for nearly seven months, and she hadn't been out during that time. Not without me, at least.' Penelope swallows. 'And then I realised that if it *was* true, she must be a long way gone. I wanted to take her to a doctor straight away, but she was frightened – it was a big enough deal to tell me, I think. She said if she'd managed all this time another few days couldn't hurt, and I agreed, like an idiot. I made an appointment – we were supposed to be going on Monday.'

'Lucky she told you when she did,' Emma says, 'so you knew to be worried when she disappeared. I wouldn't have gone looking for her otherwise.'

Penelope smiles briefly. 'Perhaps I should insist on medical checks when people arrive at Larkmore,' she says.

'You couldn't make people,' Emma says. 'They might not stay, if you insisted on things. And everything's turned out all right, hasn't it? Jeanie's fine, and the baby. Sometimes there's good luck instead of bad.'

'And you can't punish yourself for both,' Penelope says. 'That's very wise.'

That wasn't what Emma meant, not quite, but ... She stops. Is that what she's done? Is that what Penelope means?

All of a sudden her head is swirling with things she wants to say, things she's trying to grasp. She needs to tell Penelope about Rose and Julianne and her parents; about why she ran away; about what she saw in Grove Park. About how much she's blamed herself, hated herself, tried to make amends and got things wrong all over again.

And about the things she needs to put right. The things she can't push aside forever, that she needs to ...

They come round a corner then, and there's someone coming towards them. Someone Emma couldn't mistake even at this distance, in the half-dark. She stops again, and for a second, an infinite second, the world stops too. And then she's running, shouting, throwing herself into the arms of her mother.

Jim

It's after midnight when Jim hears the front door open. He's been on the verge of going to bed for an hour or more, lingering in front of the television, but he's glad now that he's waited up. He can't take any chances, he thinks. He still doesn't know whether, or what, Cath suspects. He needs to be alert, attentive, if he wants to keep his balance.

He flicks off the television – and then he freezes. He can hear Cath whispering, and another voice, someone with her. A woman. Could it be Lara? Who else could Cath be bringing home so late at night?

He's still standing there, in the middle of the floor, when Cath pushes open the living-room door. He registers her radiance, the extraordinary change in her, in the tiny sliver of time before she speaks.

'Jim! Oh, Jim, look who I found!'

And then she steps aside, and Emma is standing there, looking straight at him.

'My darling girl.' He opens his arms, and she comes towards him and lets him hold her.

'Can you believe it?' Cath is saying. 'Alive and well and ...' Her voice chokes, and Jim can't speak either. He lifts one arm from Emma's shoulder and holds it out to enclose Cath, and for a long time the three of them stand there, he and Cath clinging to Emma as though they daren't let go.

'She hasn't been far away,' Cath says, through the tangle of arms and faces. 'She's been perfectly safe.'

Where? Jim wants to ask, and *Why?* and *Who with?* But there's time enough for all that. All there is to do just now is hug his wife and his daughter, and give thanks for this moment, which he has imagined for so long but had almost given up hope of seeing.

At last Cath's grip loosens and they pull back a little, looking at each other. Emma's eyes meet Jim's for the briefest moment, and his heart drops a beat and skips through the next. *It's going to be all right,* he thinks. There might be – but they understand each other. They know that Cath ...

'What do you want?' Cath is asking now. 'Something to eat? Something to drink? We could open – We should celebrate. We've got a bottle of champagne somewhere.'

Emma smiles at her, and the look on Cath's face is almost more than Jim can bear. She reaches out a hand to touch Emma again, as if she needs to check she's really there, and then she turns to Jim.

'Emma's friend's has a baby,' she says. 'Isn't that exciting? She was there visiting, and I – We met in the corridor.' She brushes away more tears. 'Maybe hot chocolate would be better, at this time of night?'

Emma nods. 'Hot chocolate would be great.'

'I'll make it,' Jim says.

'We can all come through,' Cath says, but Jim shakes his head.

'You both look shattered,' he says. 'Sit here: I won't be long.'

In the kitchen the lights buzz in the way they do sometimes at night, and Jim's head buzzes too. While the milk's heating in the microwave he has to resist the urge to go back to the living room, to assure himself he hasn't fallen asleep and dreamed all this – but he can hear their voices, Cath's and Emma's, and he forces himself to trust in the truth of it. In the possibility of a happy ending.

In the cupboard he finds a packet of Bourbons, Emma's favourites when she was a little girl, and he wonders whether Cath has kept them here all the time Emma's been gone. Kept them ready, like the bottle of champagne. She's kept faith, he thinks – and for a few moments shame and remorse rise through him and he can taste a bitterness that taints everything, the joy of the reunion and the pleasure of the imagined future ahead.

How could he have let them down so badly, his beloved Cath and Emma? How could he have spoiled things for himself? But he has. He did. That was the way he found to get through it, and there's nothing he can do to erase it. Nothing he can do now but bear his guilt. *Your punishment is living with a secret,* he hears Dido saying, *knowing there'll never be a moment when you're forgiven.* He can do that, he thinks. For Cath. For Emma.

When he comes back into the living room, the two of them are sitting together on the sofa, and he sees for the first time how alike they are. Emma has changed; grown up. And Cath has shed, almost miraculously, the shadows that sorrow had painted on her face this last year or so. In the soft light of the table lamp, they both look uncannily like the girl he first saw so long ago on a float on Cheapside. They could almost be sisters.

Cath

It happens quite naturally that Emma sleeps in her old room that first night. Cath hasn't allowed herself to imagine anything beyond that, still less to ask, and as she lies in bed in the silent house that holds her daughter safe and sound again at long last, she tells herself that this is enough. This night is what she has longed for, and she must savour it, revel in it, and not let her hopes fly forward.

Relief and rejoicing have exhausted her, but she's determined not to miss a minute of the time Emma's here, and so she holds herself awake and replays in her mind that extraordinary moment in the hospital corridor. The words are hazy, somehow, but Emma's face is sharp and clear – the shock of mutual recognition, turning unmistakably to joy rather than dismay.

She sifts the few details she managed to grasp: the sanctuary where Emma has been living; the strange, tall woman who runs it; the friend who'd given birth. How odd, Cath thinks, that the loss of one baby and the birth of another should be what brought them together. How odd and how apt. And all this time Emma has been in a place safer than they could have imagined, hidden away from danger.

The woman – Penelope – managed everything very skilfully, getting Emma into the car Jim had left for Cath, smiling at them both as she waved them off. Cath tried not to ask too many questions on the way home, and she drove very slowly, very carefully, as though the world was in danger of turning over, tipping them clean off, because this was too much good fortune for anyone to get away with. And then there was Jim, so happy, talking for all of them, and Cath unable to take her eyes off Emma as she sipped hot chocolate, dunked Bourbon biscuits, measured out brief, shy smiles.

She remembers, now, how she didn't dare go to sleep on the first night after the twins were born, in case that might sever the lifeline holding them both so tenuously to the world – although it wasn't her love and care that kept them alive, that night or for many nights afterwards, but the skill of the neonatal intensive care staff. Nor is it, she thinks, her love and care that has preserved Emma safely through these long months of absence: not the daily remembrance, keeping her bed made and her room dusted, wondering and worrying and hoping. Not even the despair and remorse, the terrible see-sawing of self-blame and self-pity. None of that has made any difference, she knows. But now that Emma has been restored to her – brought home from the hospital, as she was all those years ago – it's impossible not to feel that something vital is required of Cath. A tithe of gratitude and responsibility; a tight thread of concentration which she must never let go, never lose sight of, never allow to slacken ...

When she wakes, there is a vision: Emma, standing beside her bed with a cup of tea. Cath gazes at her for a few seconds in agonised yearning, and then she remembers. Not a vision. Emma is here. Emma has come home.

'Morning,' Emma says. 'Did I wake you? Dad thought—'

'What time is it?' Cath heaves herself upright.

'It's only eight,' Emma says. 'I'm always awake early at ...'

Her eyes drop; she puts the cup of tea down on the bedside table. Cath wants to reach out and touch her, but she doesn't risk it.

'Thank you,' she says instead. 'How kind of you.'

Emma gives her a darting smile, and Cath fears she's going to go straight back downstairs. Belatedly, she hears Emma saying *Dad thought*, and she thinks: Jim saw Emma first this morning. Jim spoke to her, gave her a cup of tea to bring upstairs. What has she missed? Why did she fall asleep, when she meant to keep a vigil all night?

But then Emma sits down on the edge of the bed.

'I need to go back to the hospital,' she says. 'I need to see Jeanie. Could you take me?'

'Of course.' Cath thinks of all the things she should have said, the openings she's missed. 'Have you had breakfast?' she asks instead.

'Dad's making it,' Emma says. There's a tiny hesitation before she veers back to the point. 'Could you maybe take me to the hospital after breakfast?'

'Of course,' Cath says again. This time the question feels more worrying: not so much asking for a lift, a normal thing, but perhaps – leaving them again.

'Thanks.' Emma hesitates a moment longer, then she stands up. 'I'll see you downstairs,' she says.

Cath watches her go with a convulsion of pain. Will this be it? she wonders. One night, and then the rest of their life without her? Nothing more than a few banal exchanges, a cup of tea brought to her bedside?

She climbs out of bed and throws on the clothes she wore yesterday, then follows Emma down to the kitchen. Jim looks as wary as she feels, behind his broad welcoming-dad grin.

'I've made bacon and eggs,' he says. 'Hope that suits.'

The table is laid, toast sitting in a rack Cath doesn't remember them having. Like a hotel, she thinks. But Emma's smiling, and they are all here. For this meal, at least, they will all sit round the table together in a way she feared they never would again.

It's not until they're on the way to the hospital that Cath remembers she has someone to visit there too, and she feels a dart of guilt – towards Lara, but also towards Emma. The attention she's paid to Lara these last few months feels now like disloyalty. But she left last night without going back to Lara, and Lara had asked for her, wanted her there.

She must have revealed some sign of disquiet, because Emma turns to look at her. Cath smiles quickly, reassuringly.

'I could visit Lara – our tenant – while you're ...' She stops. Did she mention Lara's name to Emma? 'She had a miscarriage,' she says. 'Did I tell you? That's why I was at the hospital last night.'

Emma nods, says nothing, and Cath keeps her eyes on the road. Of course it's nothing to Emma what she does: why should it be?

But then Emma says: 'I was thinking you could meet Jeanie. My friend Jeanie, who's had the baby.'

'Oh, I'd love to!' Astonishment fills Cath again, almost as powerful as it was last night. 'Would she like that, do you think? Should we – We could stop and buy the baby a present, if you like?' She's babbling now, saying too much, but Emma smiles.

'Maybe we could do that later,' she says.

And that *later* is full of significance too. It echoes in Cath's head as they pull into the hospital car park, gives a lightness to her step as she and Emma walk together through the main entrance. When they part, close to the point where they met last night, she risks a quick hug, and it feels very good. Perhaps, she thinks – but hubris is waiting and watching. She holds the hug to her, and turns towards the gynae ward.

Lara is sitting up in bed, looking better than Cath expected. Nick isn't there, and Cath is relieved. Simpler, she thinks.

'I'm so sorry,' Cath begins. 'Something happened.'

'Sorry for what?' Lara asks.

'For not coming back last night. I said I would.'

Lara shakes her head. 'I fell asleep,' she says. 'I slept for hours. It's sweet of you to come back this morning. I wasn't expecting it.'

'How are you feeling?' Cath asks.

'Not too bad.'

Lara's face tells a different story, but somehow Cath can't find the right words for her.

'You look better,' she says. 'Rested, at least.'

And then she can't hold her news in any longer.

'I've found Emma,' she says. 'Last night, in the hospital. Just after I left you.'

'Oh!'

'She …' Cath hesitates. This isn't fair, she thinks, but it's too late to take the words back. 'She was visiting someone. We ran into each other in the corridor and we – she came home with me.' There are tears in her eyes now; she can't stop them. Lara has lost her child and she has found hers, and she can't help weeping for joy.

'That's wonderful,' Lara says. 'Is she – Has she been all right?'

'Yes.' They've been sworn to silence about the sanctuary, Cath remembers. 'She's been staying with someone. Quite safe.'

Lara looks at her, and Cath reads the questions, the trains of thought. She thinks of Lara's mother, who doesn't know where she is, whether she's safe. There are tears in Lara's eyes too now, and Cath takes her hand.

'I'm sorry, I shouldn't ...'

Lara shakes her head, her lips clamped tight shut, and then a tear spills on to her cheek, and another.

'I'm so sorry,' Cath says. 'I'm so sorry, Lara.'

Lara shakes her head again, wiping away tears with her free hand.

'I'll have to hope for my happy ending,' she manages to say. 'At least – at least I've got Nick. Got him back.'

'I'm very glad about that,' Cath says. 'I really am.'

And then they are both crying, their hands clasped together on the hospital blanket, and it seems to Cath that she has rarely felt a greater sense of understanding with anyone; and that, despite these tears which won't stop falling, her heart has never been more full of love – for Emma, and for Lara, and for the other child, the other baby, she will meet very soon.

Emma

The plan Emma has in her mind seems so perfect she can almost believe it must be meant to happen. Jeanie and baby Rose coming to live with her, with Jim and Cath, would answer so many needs, fill so many gaps. Like fitting the pieces of a jigsaw together and realising that the picture is exactly right, even if it isn't quite what you expected when you started out.

But she knows it isn't, it can't be, as simple as that.

How can she expect her parents to welcome her back as though nothing has happened, let alone take in a stranger and her baby? And how can she expect Jeanie to fill the place of Rose, of Julianne – to restore, somehow, the version of Emma's life that has been lost?

How can she expect herself to bear the happiness, and the hope?

But hope is what she has to rely on. Hope that some-how all the error and wrongdoing can be forgotten, all the scars healed. That between them they can make a whole life again.

And meanwhile, she thinks, as she sits beside her mother in the car on the way to the hospital – mean-while, she needs to be patient, not to rush in. She remembers the care that went into asking her mother, years ago, if a friend could stay the night: measuring her mother's mood, judging the time and the auguries, tak-ing a deep breath before risking the question. She needs that small child's wisdom, she thinks. She needs to remember the time when she and her mother understood each other implicitly.

She arrives on the ward just as Jeanie is about to bath baby Rose. She looks even smaller unclothed, her skin reddish against the white hospital towel: her fragility catches in Emma's chest like a stab of fear. But Jeanie is beaming.

'I was scared you weren't coming,' she says.

'Why?'

'No reason.'

Jeanie grins, but Emma feels suddenly wobbly. Jeanie doesn't know what's happened, she reminds herself. Doesn't know anything about her parents. Unless ...

'Has Penelope been this morning?' she asks.

'No. She phoned, though. They said she phoned and she'd come later.'

'That water's just about right now,' says the midwife. 'Have a feel, so you'll know what temperature she needs.'

'Emma knows,' says Jeanie. 'She knows all about babies.'

'Not babies this small,' Emma says. 'Not newborns.'

She looks curiously at the midwife for a moment: at her dark skin, her high cheekbones. She looks a bit like that photo ... but she can't be. They moved away. She knows that. After the trial, they moved away. The midwife notices Emma's eyes on her, and she smiles.

'They used to say test the water with your elbow,' she says. 'But don't try that with baby in your arms.'

Emma's mind lingers for a moment on Julianne, on her beautiful mother in that wedding photo, but then Jeanie lifts baby Rose towards the bath and it's as if a blanket, a soft shroud, has been laid over her memory. A new life has such power to heal, she thinks: to claim your attention – gently, insistently – for itself.

When they lower Rose into the bath her arms and legs jerk outwards like flailing tentacles, and her dark eyes open wide. She looks like an anemone opening in the water, Emma thinks, a creature being returned to the habitat she's just been taken from. She blinks, frowns, then fixes her gaze on Jeanie, a tiny imperious being so full of expectation and vulnerability that Emma wants to gather her up in her arms and squeeze her tight. It seems impossible that she was in Jeanie's belly until yesterday; more impossible still that in a few months she'll grow into a solid, pudgy, smiling thing like Jonas.

Thinking of Jonas causes Emma another stab of pain. Jonas belongs to a world that doesn't feel quite real any more. But is that world the fairy tale, or this one?

'Hold her hand,' Jeanie says. 'Give her your finger, Em.'

Emma slides her finger into the baby's fist, feels it grasped tight.

'She's strong, isn't she?' Jeanie says. 'She doesn't look it but she is.'

'She's a beauty,' says the midwife, cupping her hand to sluice water over Rose's head, which makes her crinkle up her little face and wail.

Emma's finger, released, traces a wondering arc down the tiny soft cheek.

'Sweet Rose,' she says. 'Sweet baby.'

'Let's get her dry now,' says the midwife. 'She'll want feeding any moment. Are you ready for her, Mum?'

The midwives are kind, patient, cheerful. They smile at Emma as she rocks Rose in her arms after Jeanie has fed her, and when the tea trolley comes round Emma gets a cup too. They must be used to all sorts of families here, Emma thinks, and that thought gives her courage.

'I need to tell you something, Jeanie,' she says, when Rose is sleeping peacefully and the two of them are sitting watching her, lulled by the noises of babies and mothers all around them, the soft tread of the midwives walking tirelessly to and fro. 'Something happened last night, after I left you.'

'Oh yeah?' Jeanie's sleepy, Emma thinks; perhaps this isn't the right moment. But Jeanie's looking at her – and Cath must surely have finished visiting her tenant by now, she realises. How long has it been? Could she have left already? Surely she wouldn't have ... She feels the tug of those two opposing things again, the possibility and impossibility of what she wants, and the rush of adrenaline galvanises her.

'I met someone, in the hospital,' she says. 'On our way out last night. I met my mum.'

'Your real mum?'

Jeanie's wide awake now, her eyes startled like Rose's.

Emma grins. 'I've only got one,' she says, before she remembers that Jeanie probably had several, foster mums or whatever, and that she's never asked. 'Yes, my real mum,' she says.

'Did you say hello?'

Emma nods. 'I went home with her,' she says. 'I stayed the night at home.'

Jeanie looks stricken. 'So are you ...?' she begins. To Emma's horror, tears start sliding down her cheeks. 'You're going to leave, aren't you?' she says. 'You're not going to come back to Larkmore.'

Emma takes her hand. 'I said I'd help you, Jeanie, and I meant it. I don't know ...'

'You'll come and visit, then? Come every day?'

'Sshh,' Emma says. 'I don't know what's going to happen. Please don't worry.'

'But you won't be living at Larkmore. It won't be the two of us in our little room any more.' Jeanie looks at Emma, her face crumpled with sorrow, and Emma can't bear it.

'I was going to ask my parents ...' she begins. 'I don't know what they'll say, but – I was going to ask if you could come home with us too.'

'To stay for a bit?' Jeanie looks astonished, disbelieving. 'Do you think I could? And Rose?'

The excitement in her voice is almost more poignant, more pathetic, than the sadness, Emma thinks. It reminds her ... but she won't think of that. She smiles, and takes Jeanie's hand.

'I hope so,' she says. 'I really hope so.'

And then, like a little piece of miracle, an aftershock from last night's grand miracle, there is Cath coming towards them across the ward. And when Emma sees her face, the gladness in it as she looks down at Emma and Jeanie and baby Rose, the question doesn't seem so hard to ask after all. There's so much that needs to be said, and asked, and understood, but this question she'd imagined would need to come after all that seems instead like the right place to start.

AUGUST

Cath

The sun should be shining today, for this August beach outing, but instead it's grey and blowy, with a damp sting in the wind, reminding them that autumn is almost here. It doesn't matter, Cath thinks. Perhaps it's better like this: a day for trudging slowly along the sand, not for sitting still. And they have the beach to themselves. Seagulls flit, grey against grey, but there's not another human soul to be seen.

She's glad they've got this day, this whole day when Jeanie and Rose are at Larkmore with Penelope; she's glad Emma wanted to come to the beach. It's the first time the two of them have been alone for any length of time. She'd thought they might talk in the car, but Emma had found a CD she must have burned six or seven years ago, and she played it all the way down the A3, exclaiming as each song came up – and Cath smiled at her pleasure, laughed at the way she sang along in horror and delight at her childish taste. That was fun, and important in the way everything has seemed important these last few weeks. But there's something she's still waiting for, hoping for. Something they've swerved away from, or been interrupted on the way to, several times since that fateful night in the hospital corridor: a kind of intimacy that might dissolve, at last, the uncertainty that still overshadows her happiness.

Cath finds it hard to map the order in which things have happened since the night she found Emma. Time has seemed oddly capricious, looping back on itself to revisit the distant past or simply the day before, reprising familiar pleasures and pains. There's been the retrieving of clothes and equipment from the attic, and Jeanie's fierce delight in setting up Emma's old cot in the spare bedroom. There've been the broken nights, the tears, the hugs. There've been visits from midwives to check on the baby, so tiny and perfect, that seems to be at the centre of everything: that seems to have pulled the threads tight, drawing them all together again.

Except that the them is different now; the relationships have shifted and multiplied. And despite the happy absorption of the baby's routine, there is a ravel of loose ends that catch Cath's eye every time her mind drifts; every time the veil is twitched back from the lost months when Emma was gone. Cath longs to give herself up to the reassurance of the house being full again, but there's a part of her that can't settle. Everything has been both simpler and stranger than she expected, and she can't quite hold it in her grasp.

They've only been walking for a few minutes when Emma bends to pick up a cockle shell – a pair of them, rather, flecked with gold, still attached at the hinge.

'Do you remember I used to collect shells for Rose?' she says.

'Yes.' It's been strange hearing Rose's name around the house again, but Cath realises now that it's the new Rose her mind jumps to first, and she feels a flash of guilt and grief which she washes away with a smile.

'Twin shells,' she says, and Emma nods.

'I thought it was my fault,' she says.

'What was?'

'Rose. The way she was. I thought I'd stolen her life away.'

'Oh, my love ...'

Cath stops, turns. Emma's holding the shells on the palm of her hand: two perfect, identical halves. Then she speaks again.

'I thought Julianne was my fault, too. I thought maybe he'd have preferred to kill me.'

Emma's eyes lift to her mother's face, and suddenly Cath is full of trepidation. So this is it, then: the conversation she's been waiting for not just for the last few weeks, but the last two and a half years. The explanation she's longed for. But now it's here she's terrified. She has no idea what will be asked of her: whether she'll have the right words; whether she'll understand. Whether it's still in her power to make things better.

She takes a deep breath.

'Why?' she asks. 'Why on earth would he have preferred to kill you?' She can't bring herself to speak Kyle's name; maybe Emma can't either.

'Because I took Julianne away,' Emma says. 'Because maybe she wouldn't have broken up with him if she hadn't met me.'

'If you told her he was no good for her, you couldn't have been more right,' Cath says. 'But you couldn't have guessed what he'd do, my love.'

Emma's shaking her head. 'That's not what I meant,' she says. 'I didn't persuade her to leave him. I ...' She sighs, staring down at the damp sand. 'I loved her,' she says. 'I was in love with her. Julianne. I wanted us to bring up her baby together.'

'Her baby?'

Emma nods. Cath's heart is beating furiously. It isn't the baby she should have picked up on first, she thinks. *I was in love with her.* She thinks of Emma hiding in her room after Julianne's death, of the broken heart they never suspected. Never even thought of.

And if they had ...?

'My darling,' she begins.

Emma bites her lip, sniffs furiously. 'I don't know if she knew,' she says. 'I don't know ...'

She's crying now, and Cath folds her into her arms, holds her so tight that she can feel Emma's hard fist against her chest, the cockle shell still clutched inside it. Poor, poor Emma, who lost the other half of herself not once, but twice.

'I'm so sorry,' she says. 'I'm so sorry, Emma.'

'It's not your fault,' Emma says, her voice curdled with tears. 'None of it's your fault. It's all been my fault.'

'That's not true,' Cath says. 'That's not true.'

Emma gives a little moan, and Cath squeezes her harder. For a long time they stand there, clasped in each other's arms, above the incoming tide. Mother and daughter, solacing each other at last. Beginning to understand each other again.

And Cath does know what to say, after all.

'Tell me,' she says. 'Tell me about Julianne.'

Just then a wave washes over their feet, and Emma jumps back with a little exclamation. And then Cath takes her hand and they fall into step, tracking onwards above the tideline among the jumble of seaweed and flotsam.

Cath waits a little, and then she says: 'What was she like? Julianne?'

'She wasn't like anyone else.'

There's a long pause, and Cath is beginning to think there won't be any more, but then Emma gives a little shake of her head and says: 'She was fearless. She could dive perfectly, and – she was the wheelie queen, when she was little. Better than all the boys.'

Cath makes a little noise of encouragement, but now she's started Emma doesn't seem to need it.

'She was so – alive,' she says. 'So loud and mad and funny. She didn't care what anyone thought, but she ... she wanted to be my friend. And with the baby ...' There's another choking sigh, and the blinking back of more tears. 'I don't know if she knew what I – that I loved her. I don't think I really knew either. We kind of – joked about it. She said we could pretend to be lezzies and get a flat together.'

Emma kicks a stone, and Cath watches it curve away down the beach.

'I thought there'd be time,' Emma says. 'Plenty of time to sort everything out. But then she was dead. I'd been with her for her scan that afternoon, and to the cinema, and then she was gone.'

She lifts both her hands to scrub at her eyes, bringing Cath's hand with her, and Cath puts her other arm around her again and murmurs comforts into her hair.

If they'd been more persistent, she thinks, might Emma have talked to them, told them all this? Should they have insisted, or would that just have made things worse?

'Did anyone else know she was pregnant?' she asks. She doesn't remember it being mentioned in the press reports.

'She was going to tell Kyle that evening,' Emma says. 'That's why she went to see him. I don't know ... Maybe she never got that far. But I thought – We'd talked about bringing the baby up, her and me. I was going to get a job. I imagined Julianne telling him that, and him losing his temper.'

'But it wasn't a spur-of-the moment thing,' Cath says. For a moment she imagines Emma moving out, leaving school, and what they'd have said. 'All those pictures on his computer. He'd been making those for a long time.'

'I suppose so.' Emma draws back, looks at her. 'But there were pictures of me, too. He hated me.' She swallows. 'Maybe he was getting up the courage to kill one of us,' she says. 'Maybe he would have done it eventually, whatever happened.'

'Maybe.' Cath holds Emma's hand tight. 'And if Julianne had stayed with him, all those photos would still have been there, on his computer. In his head. Or if she'd moved in with you, and he'd insisted on seeing her, seeing the baby ...'

'Yes.' Emma looks very pale; her voice is barely more than a whisper. 'Yes.'

All this time, Cath thinks, she and Jim have struggled with not knowing, trying to make sense of things, and Emma has been doing the same. Having no idea what Julianne said to Kyle, how things unfolded that night. She can hardly imagine what Emma's been through – except that she can. She understands only too well. She wants to say that, but it's too much, too dangerous, to put into words.

'Will you tell Dad?' Emma asks.

'Of course. Of course I will.'

And then for a moment Cath can't speak for the pressure of tears, and it's Emma's turn to squeeze her hand. Her grip is so tight that her fingernails dig into Cath's palm, a line of sharp pain impressing itself on her mother's flesh.

'I wasn't myself,' she says. 'At Larkmore. I needed to be someone else, because being me was ...'

Cath nods.

'You don't need to explain,' she says. 'I'm just so very glad to have you back. We both are.'

'I'm sorry,' Emma says. 'I know that's not enough, but I am. So sorry for what I've done to you.'

'I know,' Cath says. 'It's all right. It's over now.' But then she can't help plunging on. 'I wish we'd understood about Julianne. I wish we could have helped you.'

There must be a tremor in her voice, an intimation of suffering, because Emma's face changes. She looks at Cath, eyes wide.

'Have you and Dad ...' she begins.

Her gaze is too much; Cath lets her eyes drop. She thinks of Jim, and the different shades of his patience – thinks of the night of the storm, the full moon, the forgotten phone – and then she pushes it all away. They've come through, she thinks. That's all that matters.

'We've survived,' she says. 'Haven't we? It's a happy ending.'

But those words are too much for her. For the Cath who has endured every day of Emma's absence and gone nearly mad with the grief of it; who still can't quite believe in her return. Emma puts her arms around her mother, and Cath lets herself cry. Lets herself feel the exquisite pain of this moment – a necessary pain, purging and healing, like dipping her fingers into a well that contains all the joy and sorrow of the world. All the emotion of the last two years, the last twenty, and those still to come.

They walk a long way in the end; almost as far as the beach will take them. When they turn at last, the light has changed, as it does so often, so rapidly, over the sea. The sky is still grey, but it's a shimmering silver grey, foreshadowing a spectacular sunset: the whole horizon, sand and sea and sky, looks like a giant oyster laid open before them.

Halfway back along the beach, they turn up into the dunes, and the little tea shop Cath remembers is still there. They order a pot of Earl Grey and a large slab of Victoria sponge. Nothing like tea and cake, Cath thinks, to anchor you to life. To the thread of it, running on.

As she pours them each a cup, it occurs to her that there are still things to ask, and she wonders whether this is the moment for it, or whether they've talked enough for one day. She thinks of sweet, strange, spiky Jeanie, who isn't Julianne, isn't anything like the Julianne Emma has described, but ...

'We mustn't be late for Jeanie and Rose,' she says.

'What time is it?'

'Only five. Don't worry. Penelope said after supper.'

Emma looks sideways at her, a forkful of cake in her hand.

'Are you happy about her staying with us?' she asks.

'Of course I am,' Cath says. 'Are you?'

'Yes.'

Cath waits.

'Is there a but?' she asks.

'I don't—' Emma begins. 'No. Only ...'

There's a silence then, while Cath musters her courage. The tea shop has shut its door now, and there's no one else here. No one else to hear them.

'Do you love her?'

Emma shakes her head. 'Not like Julianne,' she says. 'But sometimes – sometimes Jeanie looks at me the way I used to look at Julianne, and I ...' She shakes her head. 'Maybe I could. Maybe I should.'

'My love,' Cath says.

She looks at Emma's worried face, and leans across to kiss her forehead as she used to when she was a little girl. *Keep that kiss with you all day,* she'd say, when Emma was five and didn't want to let go of her hand in the playground. When her worries seemed so small, but already so heartbreaking.

'Jeanie adores you, but I don't know ...' Cath hesitates. This is hardly her area of expertise, she thinks, but ... 'There are lots of ways to love,' she says, 'and maybe sometimes one kind merges into another, but I don't think you can make that happen.' She smiles at Emma. 'Jeanie's got a baby, and a home, and a big sister, and she's never had any of those things before. You're a very good sister. You always have been. And you're wonderful with the baby. I should enjoy all that for now, and let things take their course.'

'I promised to look after her.'

'And you are. You're doing everything you can. You don't need to – pretend.'

'No.'

Emma smiles – the first smile Cath has seen since they arrived at the beach.

'Thank you,' she says. And then, to Cath's surprise: 'How's your friend? Your – tenant?'

'Lara?' Cath says. 'That's kind of you. She's OK. She's had a hard time, but she'll be fine.'

'I'd like to meet her,' Emma says, and Cath's eyes fill with tears.

'I'm sure she'd like to meet you too,' she says.

In the car on the way home, Emma sleeps. Cath is exhausted too, but her nerve-endings are buzzing still with salt and revelation.

The Emma they've got back is not the Emma they lost, she thinks – and the Emma they lost wasn't quite the Emma they thought they had. They understood, back then, that they didn't know her as they used to, that she was slipping out of sight before their eyes, but the last year and a half has changed her again. Changed them all.

This Emma is someone she admires, Cath thinks. Someone who has thought and loved and suffered deeply. Not a child any more, but still – her child.

EPILOGUE: DECEMBER

Nick

They stop at Leigh Delamere services, just before the motorway exit. While Lara's in the loo, Nick buys two cups of coffee and a tin of boiled sweets that remind him of holidays as a child, before his dad left. Barley sugar was his mum's favourite, but he and his dad preferred blackcurrant. He buys mixed fruit today; more choice, he thinks.

It's funny he should think of his parents when it's Lara's they're on their way to see. Or perhaps not so funny. Parents are on both their minds. Lara's been good about his mum: she's coming for Christmas, even. She and Robert, driving up for the day. They've ordered a turkey from the butcher round the corner.

'Should I call you Ruth?' he asks, when they're back in the car. 'When we're with your parents, I mean?'

'No.' Lara doesn't look at him, her eyes firmly on the road as though she has to will herself along each mile of the journey. 'I'm not Ruth any more. They know that.'

Hard for them, though, Nick thinks. Hard to think of your child as a different person, with a different name. But he doesn't say that to Lara.

They're not going to the house. Nick's not sure whether that was Lara's choice or theirs. They're meeting at a garden centre near Chipping Sodbury which is supposed to have a nice café. Lunch, and perhaps a wander round the garden centre if all goes well – although that last bit is Nick's invention.

'Nervous?' he asks.

'Yes.'

He puts a hand on her knee. 'It'll be OK,' he says. 'I'll be there with you.'

Since the summer – what he's come to think of as the time of calamity – they have been careful, gentle with each other. More deliberate, perhaps; but you could call it thoughtful rather than deliberate, and it would sound better.

This trip is a deliberate act too, Nick thinks. He's encouraged it, though not too eagerly: he doesn't want Lara to think he doubts her account of things, or that he's especially curious to meet her parents. Although he is, of course. It feels like the missing piece of the jigsaw. The Ruth-shaped piece he can't stop wondering about.

Lara

They're already there when Nick and Lara arrive. Lara wasn't sure she'd recognise them – but that's ridiculous, of course. It's only been nine years, even if it feels like much longer. Her father upright and angular, and her mother smaller, rounder, softer, sitting with their backs to the door. Lara's grateful for the few moments that gives her to take in the fact that they've come; they're here. They're wearing the same brown woollen coats, and her mother's hair – greyer now – is wound up in the same bun. They look like an island, she thinks, among the pink Lycra and dyed hair, the garishness of modern life. She feels, then, a stab of raw pain, not for herself but for them, and at the same time something even less expected. Envy. For the simplicity of their world view, she thinks, the cohesion of their lives. But it's gone in an instant.

'That's them,' she says. 'Over by the window.'

'OK.' Nick looks at her. 'Ready?'

'No,' she says. 'But we're here now.'

They look up just before Nick and Lara reach the table.

'Hello,' Lara says.

'Ruth.' Her father stands up. There's no hug, no handshake. Her mother hasn't met her eyes yet: waiting for permission, Lara thinks.

'Hello, Mum,' she says. She'd like to touch her, but it's as if there's a force field keeping them apart. Two chairs have been placed for her and Nick on the opposite side of the table. Panic courses through Lara: this isn't going to work, she thinks. They might as well leave now.

'Sit down,' her father says, as though he's read her mind. Lara glances at her mother, and Nick holds out a hand. He's wearing a tie, and a new jacket.

'Hello, sir,' he says. 'I'm Nick. I'm Lara's husband. It's good to meet you.'

Her father nods. 'It's good of you to come,' he says.

And then Lara has to choke back tears, because she knows what that has cost him – what this whole trip has cost him – but also because she knows that it's not a bridge across the divide. Not the start of a thaw. It's more like a brief truce: a moment when they can acknowledge each other's existence, perhaps each other's humanity, despite the fact that they live in different worlds.

How much of this Nick has picked up she's not sure, but she's grateful that he's acting as though he hasn't. He picks up a menu now, and smiles across the table.

'Have you ordered?' he asks.

Might things have been different if the baby had survived? Lara wonders, as they set off for home. Might that have been too much for her mother to resist? She casts her mind back over the conversation – the stilted questions about her job, and about where they live – sifting it for signs of hope. No questions about church, about God, but she didn't expect that: the wrong God would be almost worse than none. No mention, either, of whether they planned to have children. Lara hasn't told them about the baby – the miscarriage. Perhaps they assume she can't have them after the abortion. Children are a gift from God, and why should He bless her with any after what she's done?

'Are you OK?' Nick asks.

'Ish.'

He raises his eyebrows. 'They weren't what I expected.'

Lara wonders what he did expect – whether he thought she'd exaggerated, or whether he'd imagined complete monsters – but she can't bring herself to ask. She doesn't want to hear Nick criticising them any more than she wants to hear him defending them. She stares out of the window at the cars slipping past, the houses and the garages and the shops, and for a moment she sees them all through different eyes. She feels the strangeness of this world they live in, the presumption and the waste and the flailing for meaning.

'I'm glad we did it, anyway,' she says. 'I'm glad you've met them.'

'I really can't see how you came from them,' Nick says.

Lara turns to him. She can see he wants to say more, that he's struggling to work out what, and how, and she feels a great wash of love. *If I have a faith that can move mountains, but do not have love,* she thinks, *I am nothing.*

'The point is,' she says, 'that I've found you. That's what matters now.'

Cath

'Careful,' Cath says. 'Don't lean over too far.'

She grips the ladder more tightly as Emma reaches across to hook the fairy lights over the top of the door.

'Done,' Emma says. She grins down at her mother. 'Shall we turn them on? Check they work?'

Penelope comes through from the kitchen just as the hall lights up.

'Goodness!' she says. 'I can't think when we last had fairy lights. What a sight!'

'I bought far too many,' Cath says, but Penelope shakes her head.

'It looks wonderful,' she says. 'All that greenery too. What a party we're going to have!'

Cath smiles, surveying her handiwork. There's holly and ivy, tinsel and baubles. Through the sitting-room door, she can see the enormous tree that was decorated last week with an eclectic collection of ornaments – some from Penelope's attic, others made by the residents and their children. It's such a beautiful house, Cath thinks: it's nice to see it in its party clothes.

Cath has been helping out at Larkmore for a couple of months now. At first she was shy about it: she was reluctant to intrude on Emma's territory, and perhaps more to the point on Penelope's. Was she afraid of being judged by Penelope for letting Emma down, she wonders now, or did she blame Penelope a little for keeping Emma here all that time? Perhaps a bit of both, in truth. But it's impossible to feel judged by Penelope, and almost as hard to blame her for anything. She's admirable, Cath thinks. And a friend, now. There are even moments when Cath feels that Penelope is more than passingly grateful to have her around; when she feels that she, too, might have admirable qualities.

'What next?' asks Emma, folding away the stepladder. 'Should we see if Jeanie needs any help?'

Jeanie is in charge of the party food. She's got Rose in a sling, tied to her front, while she arranges sausage rolls and samosas on baking trays. She's wearing a dress Cath gave her, a cornflower blue that suits her beautifully, with streaks of flour down the sides now where she's wiped her hands.

'We've got the lights up,' Emma says. 'Come and see.'

But Jeanie scowls at her. 'I haven't got time for lights,' she says. 'Look at all this!'

'I'll help,' Emma says. 'Give me a job.'

Jeanie jerks her head towards the vegetables on the table, waiting to be cut into sticks. She's already got a touch of Gordon Ramsay about her, Cath thinks, and she hasn't even started her catering course yet. But it gives Cath pleasure to think of Jeanie's enthusiasm for that, and of the days when she'll be in charge of baby Rose while Jeanie's at college. She'll have to fight Emma off, she thinks – but Emma seems to be serious about getting some A levels next summer. She's thinking about midwifery training after that, which gives Cath even greater pleasure, but she and Jim aren't getting their hopes up too high. Slowly, slowly, they keep telling each other. It's still a novelty to have Emma home; there's still a heart-in-mouth moment each morning when they listen for her footsteps on the stairs. A daily miracle, Jim said last week. And it is.

Jim isn't coming to the Larkmore Christmas party. It's nothing personal, Penelope said with an apologetic smile, just the rules. No men. But secretly, guiltily, Cath likes having Larkmore to herself. And she loves having an insight into the life Emma led during those lost months. Someone else has her attic bedroom now – hers and Jeanie's – but Cath has seen it. She's seen the nursery where the babies sleep, the little computer room where Emma did her childcare course, the garden and the woods and the falling-down greenhouse.

Some mornings, when she wakes up early, she likes to imagine herself floating back in time, visiting the Cath who was so sad and lost, and reassuring her. *Emma's fine,* she'd like to tell her. *You should see the house she's living in, the view from her little window.* And she'd like to float back further, too, to meet Julianne – to watch her dive, and see Emma laughing with her – and then back, back, to before Emma was born, when she and Rose were just smudges on a scan. When anything could have happened.

But what has happened is more than good enough, she thinks. Much, much more than she could have hoped for. There are things to look forward to again: she can't wait for the party this evening, and for Christmas next week; for Nick and Lara to come for a drink, for Jeanie to hang up Rose's stocking, for more strings of fairy lights to fill their little house. The first Christmas for nearly twenty years with a baby in the house.

Suddenly there are tears in her eyes. Tears for their precious Rose and her tiny namesake; for Julianne and her baby, who played such a profound part in Emma's life; and for Lara and her baby who became so entangled in Cath's. The shadows of so many lost children, she thinks.

But mostly tears for Emma, the only one to have been lost and found again.

Acknowledgements

Fondest thanks, as always, to Richard, for his infinite love, wisdom and wit, and to my children and my parents for their enthusiasm and encouragement.

I'm grateful to the many friends who have taken an interest in the progress of this novel, especially Chiara Harker – and to Meera, Sabrina, Nigella and Marcella, our constant companions in the kitchen and the chief source of our sanity during lockdown.

Patrick Walsh and the team at PEW Literary did a wonderful job of finding *The Shadow Child* a happy home, and Selina Walker has been an inspirational editor and a pleasure to work with. Thank you to all of them, and to everyone at Penguin Random House, for bringing this book to life.

Credit list

Publishing a book is a team effort and Penguin Random House would like to thank the following people at Century for their work on *The Shadow Child*.

PUBLISHER
Selina Walker

EDITORIAL
Sophie Whitehead
Rose Waddilove
Joanna Taylor

PRODUCTION
Helen Wynn-Smith
Linda Hodgson
Nicky Nevin

UK SALES
Mat Watterson
Claire Simmonds
Olivia Allen
Jade Unwin
Evie Kettlewell

INTERNATIONAL SALES
Richard Rowlands
Erica Conway

PUBLICITY
Najma Finlay
Charlotte Bush

DESIGN
Ceara Elliot

AUDIO
Meredith Benson

MARKETING
Claire Bush
Rebecca Ikin

Rachel Hancox read Medicine and Social and Political Science at Cambridge, qualified as a doctor three months after getting married, and has juggled her family, her career and a passion for writing ever since.

She worked in Paediatrics and Public Health for twenty years, writing short stories alongside NHS policy reports, and drafting novels during successive bouts of maternity leave.

She loves singing, cooking, gardening and pottery, and has five children, three dogs and a cat. As someone once said, she thrives on chaos. She lives in Oxford with her husband and youngest children.